A.J. SCUDIERE

NIGHTSHADE

FORENSIC FBI FILES ✦ BOOK 8

DEAD
TIDE

"There are really just 2 types of readers—those who are fans of AJ Scudiere, and those who will be."
-Bill Salina, Reviewer, Amazon

For *The Shadow Constant*:
"The Shadow Constant by A.J. Scudiere was one of those novels I got wrapped up in quickly and had a hard time putting down."
-Thomas Duff, Reviewer, Amazon

For *Phoenix*:
"It's not a book you read and forget; this is a book you read and think about, again and again . . . everything that has happened in this book could be true. That's why it sticks in your mind and keeps coming back for rethought."
-Jo Ann Hakola, The Book Faerie

For *God's Eye*:
"I highly recommend it to anyone who enjoys reading - it's well-written and brilliantly characterized. I've read all of A.J.'s books and they just keep getting better."
-Katy Sozaeva, Reviewer, Amazon

For *Vengeance*:
"Vengeance is an attention-grabbing story that lovers of action-driven novels will fall hard for. I hightly recommend it."
-Melissa Levine, Professional Reviewer

For *Resonance*:
"Resonance is an action-packed thriller, highly recommended. 5 stars."
-Midwest Book Review

CHAPTER 1

Donovan stood with his feet in the sand, looking out over the vast, open ocean. With each wave that licked at his feet and ankles, his anxiety ratcheted up a notch.

They shouldn't be on this case.

Beside him, Eleri stood whispering a prayer. It was one he'd heard from her before. Something old from her grandmother, or maybe a wish to one of the Voodoo gods a branch of her complicated family worshiped.

The words were foreign to him and, right now, he couldn't hear the sound of her voice. The rush of his own blood in his veins was louder than whatever his partner whispered. The roaring in his head was louder than the gentle, relentless waves.

"Eleri?" he asked, but the wind snatched his voice away and she didn't answer.

There were so many things wrong with this case, the first of which was the ocean lapping at his feet. He *hated* the water.

Eleri, on the other hand, often joked about being a mermaid. Even now, she looked as though she might run three steps forward and gracefully disappear under the waves, heading toward the home of her heart. The thought petrified Donovan.

He'd seen her do it before and was confident he couldn't stop her. He prayed she didn't try.

They should never have been put on this case. The death of a marine biologist—a strange death, at that—should not have been assigned to an FBI agent who could not handle the sea. A case that involved a friend should not have been assigned to Eleri Eames. And Donovan should not have been pulled away from finding the man he believed was his brother, even though he believed that having a brother was impossible.

Yet, here he was, fighting the overwhelming urge to run away and leave Allison Caldeira's death in the hands of some other agent. The waves reaching for him and the sand pulling him under gave him a distinct, sinking sensation, surely a harbinger of how this case would go.

Donovan had to keep telling himself the riptide couldn't grab him and pull him under, not when only the biggest waves even managed to touch his ankles. But he was unable to step away from Eleri, unable to step away from the one person who had ever loved him unconditionally.

"Eleri?" he asked again, and this time she looked up at him. "Do we have to do this?"

"You don't." She shook her head. "But I do. I have to do it for Allison."

Eleri wasn't his only friend anymore. He had others to lean on now, but the difference was that she needed nothing from him. Nothing but his time and support. So he stood there as the sand slowly sucked him under and the sinking feeling in his heart convinced him there could be no good ending on this one.

CHAPTER 2

E leri had almost run directly from the parked car—leaving the open door and everything else behind her—down to see the water that she hadn't quite realized she missed so much.

It had been more than a decade since her mermaid days, yet she felt she could still dive right into the water and swim away.

She wasn't ready to face Hannah. Wasn't ready to learn just how Allison had died, nor to tell Hannah the truth about it. She didn't even know the truth for herself yet. She would have known the details by now had they gone straight to the medical examiner's office, but she'd come here instead. She needed this stolen time with the ocean, time to reset in a way she clearly wasn't going to get enough of.

Her head snapped around at the sound of Donovan's voice. "Eleri, I can't do this."

She blinked back her surprise. He didn't have to get into the ocean for the case. "Why do you say that?"

"I don't swim."

Bingo. "You don't have to," she replied. "We'll be in boats. You know, vessels for people who don't swim."

"I don't do boats," he protested, jamming his hands into his pockets and immediately pulling them back out, as though worried he might suddenly need them.

Eleri frowned at him. "What do you mean you don't *do* boats? They're easy. Once you get inside them, they're just like land."

He threw his head back and laughed. But what should have been a rich, hearty sound came out thready and missing beats. "It's not at all like land, Eleri. That you think it is shows just how much you don't understand about how much I don't do the water." He paused before changing the subject, maybe so she couldn't protest. "I can't believe Westerfield didn't recuse us."

Eleri shrugged. Donovan was right. Westerfield was wrong.

She should not be on this case. But she couldn't leave Allison's death in hands that might not be as dedicated as her own or as competent as Donovan's.

Maybe it was deliberate on her boss's part. Maybe he'd put her here for a reason—not that Westerfield would ever tell them. She'd placed her trust in her new boss when she'd first joined the division. Recently, however, she'd begun to wonder if the "blind" part of that trust had been a mistake.

There was no time to question him now. She had a job to do, and she couldn't shake the rough feeling she had about Allison's death. Was it because she'd known the woman? Or was something deeper at play?

She and Donovan should have been able to handle a case like this easily—murder was their bread and butter. But this one sat uneasy in her chest. Sucking in another breath, she held the heavy air in her lungs, waiting for the fear to seep out of her system. It didn't.

Turning to Donovan, she pushed a smile onto her face. "You're are going to be okay on this. Westerfield is sending us two more agents. I'm scuba certified, and one of the other agents will be, too. You can stay in the boat and you'll have somebody else with you."

Donovan nodded at her. She crossed her fingers that whoever stayed in the boat would help make Donovan comfortable. Despite her burning drive to dive into this one— metaphorically and literally—she was trying to be supportive.

Eleri looked up into the sky as though the answers might be in the clouds instead of in the water. The afternoon sun rode high and hot above her and she fought the urge to look and let it burn tiny spots into her retinas.

This case was already digging up old memories and throwing them at her. She was chucked backward to her college days, back to defying her parents and attending the tiny liberal arts school on the bay. Back to getting the job as a mermaid where she'd met Allison and where Hannah and Allison had first fallen in love. Somehow, they'd managed to stay together all these years.

Just the thought of the loss of something so strong made Eleri's heart sink lower. Turning to Donovan, she said, "We should go. We need to see the body."

CHAPTER 3

"Excuse me, *what?*" Eleri felt the words falling out of her mouth. She almost apologized for saying it, but the agent's statement was so backward that she held her tongue lest something worse tumble out.

The agent who had been showing them Allison Caldeira's case merely shrugged. Apparently, he didn't take much offense at Eleri's outburst. Behind her, Donovan said nothing.

"I understand," the agent offered without much feeling behind his words. "We should still be in possession of the body. However, the family put up a stink, and the wife came and reclaimed the remains quickly. She did so with her lawyer in tow." He paused a moment, his calm demeanor not adequate to soothe Eleri's outrage. "To the best of my knowledge, the body has already been cremated."

Just when Eleri thought it couldn't get any worse, there it was. Allison's body was no longer in the local morgue. Allison's body was simply *not* anymore. Furthermore, it appeared the issue rested at Hannah's feet.

Had it been anyone else, Eleri would have questioned their sanity. Trying to keep her anger in check, she forced a "thank you" and didn't push harder. She did this simply because she had known Hannah forever and had never known her to be anything other than forward-thinking and rational.

Still, she felt her eyes blink several times in shock. Even Hannah should know that having the remains on hand would dramatically improve the odds of finding her wife's killer.

Eleri had expected—as she and Donovan often did—to arrive on scene and examine the body in question. Instead, she silently fumed all the way to the Miami FBI branch office where the attending agent looked at her as though to ask *now what?*

Shit, she thought as she tried to remain professional, tried to think of the proper order of information she would need. What would she do if the case wasn't personal?

"First, we'll need to see what evidence has been retained, et cetera. Secondly, our SAC is sending additional agents to assist on this case. I'm curious if you've received word—"

"Ah." The agent in front of her almost smiled as though he knew the answers to these things. That, in turn, made Eleri feel better. . . until he spoke.

He waved his hand, leading them down the hallway. "We have photos and access to all the tests and evidence the ME's office gathered, and we'll gladly share any of it. I'm assuming your SAC is Agent Derek Westerfield?"

So Westerfield had called ahead? Had he known the body was already gone? Eleri only nodded in response to the agent, her lips pressed tight as she wondered how many more surprises today held for her. Why would this man know Westerfield, when he didn't seem to know much about the case? Was there some information he was withholding?

"I'm one of the other agents assigned to the case. Your SAC wanted someone local involved. The fourth agent assigned will be. . ." He paused for a moment. *"Janson?"*

He said it with a question mark at the end, and Eleri felt her head swiveling to look behind her at Donovan. His eyebrows were already up but she couldn't read how he felt about this. GJ Janson would likely be an excellent resource and was someone they already knew. Despite their personal history, she was an agent with the NightShade division, which would make working the case much easier. That was all good.

However, it now appeared this agent in front of her—an agent whose name she'd already forgotten—was also going to be their new partner.

Three NightShade division agents and one agent from Miami. That would make things incredibly difficult.

Eleri bit down on her tongue to stop herself from making any comments she might not be able to take back. Docilely, and fighting her growing anger at Westerfield for doing this to them, she followed the tall blond man down the hallway.

The agent led them into his office and Eleri flicked her eyes to the cards on the desk which read "Noah Preston" and "Federal Bureau of Investigation" and "Miami/Dade." He handed a file folder to each of them. "These are paper copies you can keep. We'll give you access to all the data, as well. . . as limited as it is."

Nodding, Eleri took the far seat, leaving the one near the door for Donovan, as Noah Preston settled behind his desk. She flipped through the eight-and-a-half by eleven glossy photos of Allison's corpse.

It was hard to fight back the tears, to appear professional and detached. Eleri was not able to look at her old friend quite as clinically as she should have. Again, she thought she should have been recused from the case, but Westerfield had heard her objection and dismissed it. So here she was, looking at a body with huge pieces missing.

The jagged edges and the rounded shape of the wounds said, *teeth marks*. As she noted the size, she realized the agent was already speaking.

"—appears to be a Great White. We have a few every several

years. And this year has seen an increase in encounters and outright attacks." He sighed, as though this was a personal problem for him. "We're not confident that Allison Caldeira was in US waters when the attack occurred. And I have no idea why a shark attack has not only been handed to the FBI, but another division has been brought in, as well."

He left the sentence hanging in midair, as though Eleri and Donovan could answer it. *There!* Eleri thought. That was why he'd seemed so nonchalant. It appeared that Westerfield hadn't given the Miami office even as much as she and Donovan had. This agent wasn't even confident there was a murder. No wonder their folders contained only a few pictures, tox screens, maps, and reports.

Donovan had stayed quiet since they entered the building and Eleri wished she knew what he was thinking. She was still trying to process the information of the case and also determine why Westerfield had assigned Noah Kimball to the case. Her boss had been giving them strange directives more often lately. She needed to stay alert.

Still, she tried her best to answer the local agent's question. "Allison's wife called the FBI specifically requesting that we look into this case. She managed to get put through to our SAC." Eleri held back mentioning that her own name might have been tossed around to get a seemingly random citizen an audience with the Bureau. "Whatever she said, she convinced him an investigation is needed."

Dark eyebrows rose beneath surfer-like, sun-bleached blond bangs. This guy looked far too young to be an FBI agent. She couldn't help thinking it, even though Eleri knew she had no right making such judgments. She hated when others suggested she was too young, too small, or too female to do her job.

Noah Kimball wore a suit and spoke like an agent, but he looked like someone had pulled a surfer from the beach, dressed him up, and given him an office. Eleri wondered just what Kimball would bring to the table and why Westerfield had allowed it. But as usual, her boss hadn't told her.

Adding to the surfer image, Kimball was good-looking in the clean-shaven way of boy band members. But his expression now was serious. "What did this woman's wife tell your SAC that convinced him it was a murder?"

"That's just it," Eleri replied. "I don't know."

CHAPTER 4

D onovan could practically hear the cogs clicking in Eleri's brain and he didn't want to jump into that mess. Though this was *their* case, he was thinking of it as *hers*.

Eleri spoke to the new agent as though she did not know the victim and the wife personally. Still, her incredulity shone through. "How did the wife just take the body? Did the FBI not oppose that?"

Noah Kimball shook his head. "Not really. The wife has that right."

Donovan's head turned, watching as Eleri's brow pulled together, fighting the hair she'd scraped back into a semi-neat knot. She'd changed clothes and her entire look since standing on the beach, unwilling to walk into the Miami branch in a wet skirt. Now, as she began tugging at strings that she disliked, he understood why.

"The FBI should have fought harder," Eleri demanded, though the deed was already done. "We have that legal right—"

But the agent cut her off. "We're discussing a same-sex couple. The wife was threatened with a lawsuit by the victim's family members."

"Still," Eleri protested, though her force was weaker this time.

"No." Suddenly, the very young agent was standing his ground. "Florida may have removed its ban on same-sex marriage, but we didn't get rid of all the bigotry. Understandably, the wife needed to be given control of her spouse's body—and quickly—before anything could be brought up in court. An interstate case could have questioned her rights as the spouse and held everything up."

"But the laws—" Eleri protested. Donovan understood. Nationally, the marriage should be recognized, but Agent Kimball was pushing back.

"Honestly, I don't need to be lectured on how this system still fails LGBTQ couples." He let the statement hang for a moment.

Eleri seemed to not be getting the hint—one that Donovan began to recognize in the vehement defense the agent offered.

Opening her mouth one more time, Eleri tried again to establish an order that would give her something to be angry about. But Kimball adequately held her back.

"No, please." He said the words politely but firmly. "I fully understand the damage a family can do to a gay couple."

Eleri's jaw snapped shut, and she nodded quickly. Either she realized she agreed or she'd decided this was not the hill she wished to die on—not when this agent clearly had a stake in it himself.

The silence hung between them for a moment, so Donovan jumped in figuring a change of topic would be welcome. He'd been examining the photos—instead of arguing the lost body— and he found this case landed right between their two areas of expertise.

He often dealt with fresh corpses; Eleri usually saw highly decomposed or skeletonized ones. This body—ravaged by the ocean and apparently bitten by several sharks along the way—fell somewhere in between.

"I think I found why this might be an FBI case. What might make it a murder."

Both faces turned to look at him, one new and curious, the other familiar and trusting.

"We—Eleri and I—" He pointed between them, "were told this was a murder. So that's our starting point. I'm looking specifically for something the preliminary investigation missed that makes this killing deliberate. I don't know what Hannah said to convince our SAC that was the case, but 'murder' was what we were told. Looking through these pictures, I see a few small marks that might offer an explanation."

Eleri flipped her folder back to the pictures. As he watched, Agent Noah Kimball also picked up a folder from the desktop. He pulled out one picture and held it up to ask if this was the one, but Donovan shook his head and pointed to another.

Once all three of them were on the same image, he spoke again. "Here." Donovan put his finger on his own photo. "I think this is a knife wound, though it's hard to tell from the photo alone."

Beside him, he heard Eleri mutter under her breath, "I hate pictures," and he almost smiled. He understood, but only asked Agent Kimball, "Do you see? Nothing seemed to have taken a bite out of this portion of the body. This is a small wound, narrow and likely deep, and appears to have been made by a sharp object. I can't be more certain without better photographs."

Pulling a third photo out, Donovan rotated it around to show the others. "There's a similar mark here, as well. Very similar—which makes both wounds even more suspicious."

"Fish bites aren't this consistent?" Kimball asked as the side of his mouth curled up.

Donovan shook his head. "Sadly, no." But he pointed again to the upper right quadrant of the victim's chest, where the second mark that also might be a knife wound appeared.

The sea and the creatures in it had gotten to Allison's body. Any marks it might have borne beforehand would be hard to distinguish from what the fish did later. Making those distinctions was difficult, even when he had the body on a table in front of him. Marks were "consistent with" things. Marks were "consistent with" a baseball bat upside the head. But even if the bloody baseball bat was nearby, the exact cause of the injury wasn't something the medical examiner could fully determine.

From the photographs, it appeared easy to determine that the large marks on her legs and the missing pieces of flesh were consistent with bites by sharks, but Donovan couldn't say what species.

Agent Kimball had already told them Great Whites had been indicted in the incident. But maybe it wasn't an accident.

"Hold on," Kimball said, tapping on his keyboard. Turning his monitor toward the two visiting agents, he pulled up of more pictures, making Donovan very happy. He'd been afraid that these few photos and the short, written notes were all the Miami office had to offer regarding Allison's body. He knew there should be more—even for a shark attack. Scant evidence would have amounted to a serious breach of protocol.

While Eleri seemed more than willing to tell this branch they weren't doing their job, Donovan wasn't ready to call them out within minutes of walking into the building.

The building itself was all glass and angles, reaching up into the sky. Donovan's emotional impression—the way they'd been checked in and greeted by name—led him to believe that the Miami office had their shit together. But this folder had concerned him. Agent Kimball was now making him feel better as he showed Donovan a file with possibly thousands of photos of the body.

"Find me those two spots in close up." Donovan motioned to the screen. He would have asked nicely, but this was important. This was the heart of whether or not they even had a case.

It took a few moments of Donovan rejecting various photos before he said, "Wait. There. Zoom."

Kimball gladly obliged, and the three of them leaned in closer, peering at what was almost clearly a knife wound.

A knife wound.

"Why is this not in the notes from the ME's office?" Donovan demanded. Maybe it was now his turn to be irate. They hadn't been here thirty minutes and they'd already discovered the case was being radically mishandled.

This time it was Kimball who was frowning as he looked at the screen, tapping back and forth, pulling up the records. "I don't know. It appears someone photographed the body and filed the photos and lab work and not much more. The local ME concluded it was a shark attack and left it at that."

Donovan found his patience this time. It seemed they would all do it in turn. Maybe if the examiners had believed this was just a shark attack, and that all they needed to do was confirm it, this evidence might be passably adequate.

Still, any body that came across *his* table would have been more thoroughly examined—suspicion of murder or not.

"I've been told they're very busy. I don't think they have time for cases that are already written off as accidents." Though Kimball spoke in clear defense of the local office, he didn't put any force behind it.

He'd stopped tapping on the keys to look up at his new partners, his green-eyed gaze hopping between Eleri and Donovan. "So you're suggesting that she was murdered via stabbing and then left to the sharks."

"It would be underwater," Donovan added. "Assumedly, she was in a wet suit, or a suit of some kind, when this occurred."

The wetsuit would be valuable evidence, if it hadn't been destroyed or lost.

Kimball nodded. "The death did occur during a dive. However, the water around here is plenty warm at this time of year, and she might very well have been in just a swim suit."

"Let's see what we can locate," Donovan pushed. As the local agent, Kimball would have an established relationship with the ME's office. As Not-Eleri-or-Donovan, he was already in a better position and wasn't pissy about the way things had been handled.

Donovan tried to put on a happier attitude. "Well, it's not good, but we have somewhere to start."

CHAPTER 5

"No," Donovan replied. "I'm not suggesting that she was killed by the knife wounds. I do believe the sharks were the actual agent of death. However, if she was knifed underwater, then the blood would have made the sharks see her as bait and kill her. So it is still a murder." He looked to Eleri and Kimball.

It was the Miami agent who asked, "Do you dive?"

Donovan almost laughed. He not only didn't dive, he didn't enter his whole body into water at any point that could be avoided. But he merely shook his head.

Kimball picked up the thread of his theory, apparently to yank at it and pull it all apart. "She should have headed for the surface."

"Wouldn't that have given her nitrogen toxicity?" Donovan asked. "If she was down deep enough. . ."

"Absolutely," Kimball replied, nodding. "But decompression sickness is far preferable to death by great white shark. At least decompression can be treated."

After thinking it through for a moment, Donovan came back around to where he started. "All right. Let's say the knife wounds aren't fatal. If they hit internally where I think they did, and where the pictures indicate. . . Again, I'd be able to tell if I had the body."

Kimball interrupted him with a frown, as if to say, *Don't go there.*

Honestly, Donovan understood. He wanted the case to go the way the case should go. He wanted clear evidence. He wanted to get his hands on the body himself. He didn't like relying on other people's conclusions, especially when the case had already been brushed off as "not a case" and most all the evidence disposed of. Maybe the case was fucked from the start. He hadn't had a good feeling about it, but he'd dismissed the churn in his gut—after all, he was no Eleri.

"These knife wounds," Donovan continued, "don't appear fatal. But they do appear to hit places that would cause the victim to steadily lose blood. If sharks are in the area, and if they're as sensitive as I've heard, blood should be enough to draw them in for an attack. Right?" He was learning to ask, as he clearly hadn't learned much about diving from simply watching National Geographic specials.

Kimball was still shaking his head. "Shouldn't she have been close enough to the boat?" he asked, losing Donovan once again. He didn't know how it worked. How close should she have been to the boat? How far away did divers swim once they were down?

Eleri was nodding along though. "Maybe not. Maybe they got her before she got to the surface. Maybe she was far enough away that she couldn't get back."

"She still should have broken the surface and alerted the divemaster," Kimball threw back. "And what about her dive buddy?"

Another new piece of information for Donovan. Though he didn't dive at all, it made sense. Divers were going into unknown places—in a section of earth where humans didn't belong—and where great white sharks were encountered more and more frequently. Being in pairs made sense, much as it did for walking in the woods at night.

"Have we interviewed the dive buddy?" Donovan asked, catching up to the ideas.

"That," Kimball replied, "is a very good question." He tapped a few of the keys and pulled up another screen. "It looks like we haven't. Again, this was brushed off as a shark attack. The FBI was merely emailed all of these pictures this morning from the local medical examiner's. That same email said that you were arriving and that this would be opened as a case."

The news made sense of the Bureau's appearance of having only scattered information. Apparently, Kimball was almost as out of the loop as the rest of them.

Sighing, Noah Kimball leaned back in his chair. "If it was a shark attack, then the local Marine Services Bureau at Port Miami would have looked into it. Maybe they interviewed her dive buddy and the driver. It should have been done. That means either they did it or they handed it off to someone else."

Mentally, Donovan noted the Port Miami Marine Services as another place to start.

"I'd like to have a better theory before we interview these people, since Marine Management must also have declared it an accident. I still don't think the stabbing idea is a very efficient murder method," Kimball sighed his remark into the air.

Donovan shrugged. "Seems highly efficient to me. You don't have to actually kill the victim. You just wait and let something else do it. Also, a lot of the evidence gets destroyed. The death was almost brushed off as a mere accident—if Hannah hadn't called and worked her way up the FBI chain, this would have been completely ignored beyond your Marine services marking the date, location, and severity of the attack." Donovan felt what he'd gleaned from his TV shows allowed him to say that much with confidence.

"True," Kimball conceded, "but the dive buddy should have been there. And you can't guarantee the sharks will get to the body. . . unless you can already see them in the vicinity. If that's the case, you run the risk of becoming a victim yourself—especially if you introduce fresh blood into the water. Sharks are much faster than humans, even ones with fins. And if you're swimming away, you're a moving target, which they seem to prefer. Orchestrating up a 'murder by shark' is a good way to get killed along with your victim."

"What if our killer *did* get killed?" Donovan thought it through. "I mean, Allison's body was found in the water several days later. Maybe the killer was attacked, too, but never found."

"I understand the idea, but in practicality. . ." Agent Kimball was still frowning at him, poking holes in what had seemed a nice clean theory to his lay-person mind. "I still think it would be very difficult to pull off. Let's talk to the dive buddy and whoever else was on that boat before we go further with this theory."

Their back-and-forth was interrupted by a knock at the door. Kimball hollered out, "Come in."

Slowly, the door creaked open and a smiling face peeked in. The expression was wholly wrong for the mood in the room, which just further confirmed that this was GJ Janson.

GJ was, in turns, both brilliant and obnoxious. When they'd first met her, she was working on her PhD in Forensic science. Westerfield had put an end to that, though, bursting her research bubble and eventually making her arrest her own grandfather. He'd seen fit to send the young scientist through Quantico, and she had passed with relatively flying colors probably, in large part, due to the fact that Westerfield had paired GJ with Donovan's girlfriend, the kick-ass Walter Reed.

Though he was glad to see the familiar face, Donovan wished Walter was here instead. Still, Walter was even more water-averse than he was. When he told her about the case and asked if she was coming, she'd merely laughed at him and offered up, "No, I have no desire to get rusty."

Walter's prosthetic devices had not been designed for water or diving. Donovan had begun to wonder if she could, in fact, rust.

Walter had grown up outside of Los Angeles—as Lucy Fisher —and entered the military at a young age. She'd not grown up like Eleri, rich to her eyeteeth, or even like GJ, whose family was very well-off. Thus, like Donovan, Walter had not been exposed to very many water sports. Her family had not owned boats nor had leisure time on the water.

"Eleri. Donovan," GJ offered up as greeting in a tone that sounded much more professional than he was used to hearing from her. His mind flooded with a memory of when Eleri had handcuffed the young and overly exuberant forensic scientist to the safe in their hotel room—just to keep her from ruining the case she'd illegally stalked them through. But from those inauspicious beginnings, GJ had grown into a talented agent.

"You must be agent Kimball." She now stepped firmly into the office and offered her hand across the agent's desk. Donovan watched as Kimball stood in a most polite manner, leaning forward and shaking Janson's hand. "So you're the fourth agent on this case?"

GJ nodded. "I'm Arabella Janson. I go by GJ."

A tip of his head and a frown preceded Kimball's, "Doesn't Arabella become A.J.? Or is it something wholly different?"

The joyful laugh was pure GJ, though it tapered off into something sadder, something Donovan only had a hint at. "GJ is for *Grandpa's Joy*. I'm the only grandchild and. . . it stuck."

Kimball accepted the odd explanation of a seeming adult with a child's nickname and jumped in with both feet. "Do you dive?"

"No."

She shocked Donovan with that. Surely, GJ should be scuba-certified and own three or four jet skis. But apparently, that had not been on her docket growing up. He did know she'd been dragged all over the world, acting as a junior intern on her grandfather's famous archeological digs.

"I'm here to crunch the data," she explained. She looked around the room, realizing the announcement had startled even Eleri and Donovan. "Our victim was a marine researcher. Westerfield already sent me reams of her research. I have to tell you, the numbers are not pretty."

CHAPTER 6

GJ felt the overwhelming urge to growl at the four walls around her. White and plain, set with square windows that looked out over the Miami landscape, they held her back from what she really wanted: to be out and about, not stuck inside with the paperwork.

The large conference table was a stark reminder that she was here alone. Empty seats stared back at her and told her that if she wanted to get out, she would first have to finish the work.

As low man on the totem pole by every possible measure— age, status, and possibly even education—she had been relegated to the conference room and the data sets. Though she had agreed that this was where she belonged, she had clearly not been the deciding force.

Donovan and Eleri had headed off to interview Hannah, the dead woman's widow. It was the obvious place to start. GJ understood what a feat it was that Hannah had convinced Westerfield to open a case. He had probably acquiesced because of Hannah's connection to Eleri. Otherwise, how could she have gotten a direct line with SAC Westerfield in the first place?

It was GJ's understanding that Westerfield prowled each

week's new cases and hand-picked the ones he wanted for his agents. From what she'd heard, he had the power to pluck any case he chose, no questions asked. He operated as though NightShade was some sort of elite group—and they were, if only by virtue of the necessity of keeping their secrets.

No one seemed to know the criteria by which Westerfield chose cases. Maybe that was his special talent. But GJ wasn't going to solve that mystery in this conference room. Instead, she sat at the table pondering how she'd wound up alone in Miami.

She'd been of the belief that she and Lucy Fisher, a/k/a Walter Reed, would be partners all the way. Maybe not for their entire FBI careers, but constantly assigned together, the way Donovan and Eleri were. Right now, it seemed Westerfield was playing an intricate game of chess with his agents. Walter had been sent off in entirely the opposite direction to find a psychic named Christina Pines, who'd gone AWOL recently. Apparently, Westerfield did not consider running down missing agents one of GJ's strong suits.

But why was it Walter's? Ironically, Westerfield had sent one of his only non-psychic agents after the most powerful psychic GJ had ever met. Then she rescinded her thoughts a little bit: *Really, how many psychics had she even met?* Given what Christina could do, GJ had to consider the possibility that she'd actually met many psychics, but they'd all made her think she hadn't.

She forced her attention back to the pages in front of her. Examining the probability of a Men-in-Black style mind wipe was not her job today. She was supposed to write up her findings on the sketchy data she'd mined from Allison Caldeira's reports.

The problem, GJ thought, was that she would prefer to tell her findings to her fellow agents, answer questions as they came up, and never write *any* of this up. But one of the things she had learned at Quantico was that she had to produce a document trail. One of the things she'd learned in NightShade was that the trail had to look perfectly normal, when it *never ever* was.

She pulled out several of the pages that had first caught her attention.

For starters, the research she'd been given had been conducted by Allison, Hannah, and several other investigators and interns they'd been working with. Some had come from universities in the Florida area, and others from overseas. Some had been funded by organizations that cleaned up the water; and while their goals appeared to be purely scientific, GJ couldn't discount that they were funded by groups with agendas.

The second problem was that the research was all over the place. Literally. When GJ researched, she preferred to focus on a very specific topic. She looked at femurs across various cultures and eras—just femurs, and sometimes just a certain knob on the femur. By contrast, these marine biologists were looking *everywhere*.

They were counting lionfish populations. They were testing chemical intake in oysters. Apparently, at one point, Allison had been checking barnacles, counting species varieties and mapping their locations.

They had data from Miami, Naples, Tampa, and several other cities in between. They had data from the open Gulf near oil rigs and more in the Bahamas. Now GJ was wracking her brain, trying to make sense of all of it.

Hannah had given them documentation for every project they had been working on when Allison was killed. Some of the projects went back as far as five years.

Digging further, GJ found oyster data supported by the US government, and even some funded by NASA. Then she found notes from port cities in the Bahamas—though those were a different species—and her brain was about to freaking explode. *So*, GJ thought snarkily, *no problem sorting that shit out.*

And that was just about the damn oysters. She next tackled data on Lionfish. As GJ sorted it, she saw the populations went up and down in cycles, though she got the impression they wanted this one to go down. *Not very conservation-y*, she thought as she felt her brows pulling together and set that page aside.

She also discovered that Allison, Hannah, and several of the other researchers kept a *kill chart*—which was not what she'd been expecting at all. It was growing more apparent that lionfish were no one's friend. The divers proudly went full zombie-killer on them! Allison was apparently a lionfish marksman, or spearperson. GJ did not know.

A sharp knock brought her head up. She'd spread all the data across the table, batching the pages and looking through everything, but she'd written nothing. She forced a smile as agent Noah Kimball came into the room.

At least he, too, was one of the junior agents on this case. They weren't called that, of course, but Noah clearly looked it. She hoped he would become her buddy.

"How far are you?" he asked. She merely shrugged and pointed at the array of papers. Though no one else sat at the table with her, she had enough data and copies for everyone. "You didn't put that on a tablet?"

"Yes. I did," she replied, trying to not snap back after being called out for her methods. "But I wanted to spread it out and organize it, piece by piece."

He nodded at her, though something in the movement accused her of deforestation. "Need a hand?"

She didn't, but she played nice and said, "A second pair of eyes is always helpful." Then she shifted topics. He, too, had an assignment he'd been sent for. "Did you find the dive buddy?"

Noah nodded. "The report from the interview is on the way, along with the pertinent information of everybody who was on the boat the day Allison was reported missing. Once we get through that, I'm figuring we'll conduct our own interviews."

GJ agreed, though she wondered if *conducting our own interviews* occurred the same way today's interviews did. Namely, that only Eleri and Donovan got to do them. Only they would talk to Hannah.

Though GJ desperately wanted to go along, she understood that meeting four FBI agents was too much for a grieving widow and likely to not get them what they needed. So she'd stayed behind. Now she figured she'd get left behind on the next interview as well.

"So what was the sketchy thing you found?" Kimball motioned with his chin to all the pages. At least he had been listening.

Walking around the table to where she'd spread out as many pieces as she could, GJ looked up at him and set her finger on the first thing she found that had alerted her something was up with Allison Caldeira.

CHAPTER 7

Eleri sat awkwardly in the overstuffed chair, though it should have been comfortable. There was no way to relax. Not with the situation that she was in.

Hannah was openly crying, and no wonder. Eleri couldn't imagine what she would feel in the same circumstance. How would she would handle it if she lost Avery? And Hannah and Allison had been together for a decade not just a handful of months.

Hannah had seemed to settle her nerves, as so many grieving people did, by offering seats, drinks, and generally fidgeting around once she had completed all the basic tasks of welcoming someone into her home.

Eleri held her tongue, and Donovan did the same, until Hannah eventually sat in one of the big chairs. Though Eleri sat across a glass coffee table from Donovan, she tried to be more open, less demanding in her body language. But Hannah still didn't relax. Now she responded by sitting stoically, staring straight ahead, and answering questions directly as they were asked.

The only thing that betrayed her emotions were the tears

silently running down her cheeks, leaving not inconsequential tracks. Eleri hated that she had to ask the questions that were bringing such rough emotions to the surface, but she needed to get Hannah talking more. So far, she'd only said, *yes, no,* and *I don't think so.*

With a glance, asking her if he could take over, Donovan leaned forward and laced his fingers together. He'd come a long way from sitting back and letting her drive the interviews. Maybe they'd get more expanded answers if he handled the questions.

Eleri thought again that she was far too tangled in this case to be working it, let alone asking the questions. But she was balancing that against being a friendly face and a trusted source for the person they most needed answers from.

"How did you manage to speak to our Special Agent in Charge?"

Donovan opened with a question Hannah couldn't answer in yes or no terms. Eleri appreciated that he didn't even use the shorthand of "SAC," which often confused lay people.

"It was about three days after we found Allison, and I just had a feeling it wasn't an accident. So, I called." Hannah's eyes flitted around the room as the words finally came out, but at least she was talking. "Actually, I was just looking for Eleri. I wanted to talk to her, get advice." Her gaze landed on Eleri, as though her old friend would obviously understand the need to reach out.

They hadn't really stayed in touch. Eleri wasn't active on social media. A job with the FBI didn't lend itself to cute puppy pictures or exercise and diet updates.

"I knew you worked for the Bureau," Hannah explained, shrugging her shoulders slightly. "And I didn't have any other number for you. I knew you would know what to do, but you weren't in." She paused, licked her lips, and turned once again to face Eleri. "I heard about your sister. I'm so sorry."

Eleri only nodded. Here was Hannah, neck deep in her own grief—grief that was fresh when Eleri's was old—and yet she was offering Eleri consolation. It took a moment to realize she should offer a simple *thank you*. Because maybe Hannah was looking for connection when she picked up the phone and called the *FBI*.

"I got a little crazy. I demanded to speak to someone. I really was just trying to find you. Then agent Westerfield—I figured out he's your boss—said that a murder wasn't his jurisdiction. I guess I just reacted. I told him it happened in international water and he said that made it even *less* his jurisdiction, but it also made it not a local police matter, either."

She sucked in a breath. Now that she was talking, the words didn't seem to stop. "So I had a case, but no one to solve it."

Eleri didn't say it, but as of yet, Hannah hadn't even said what the case was. Eleri herself still wasn't sure, beyond the fact that Westerfield had seen something that made him send three agents down here and pull a fourth from the local Bureau.

"He asked why I thought it was an FBI issue. Honestly, I hadn't thought it was. I was just looking for my friend." She waved a hand toward Eleri as though to explain it to Donovan, beseeching him to somehow understand her grief and her demands. "I thought Eleri might know how I could hire a private investigator, that kind of thing. But when he asked why I thought it was an FBI issue, I told him Allison and I had several fights right before she died. She was hiding something from me, and that was unusual. She said, if she could put the pieces together, it would blow everything open."

A sniffle and a pause. "I guess he was being nice because I'm your friend." Hannah pushed the words out with a watery sniff.

Eleri appreciated that Donovan only had to ask the one question to get her rolling.

"But he said I should send Allison's information, make copies and all," Hannah continued. "At one point, I gave up and sent originals. I couldn't deal with it. It was a mistake." Her gaze bounced back and forth again. Then Eleri watched it ping from Donovan to her, then back to Donovan again and—for whatever reason—her eyes came to rest on her partner.

"I can get that back. Right?" Hannah pressed, finally realizing she needed a tissue and reaching for one. She was scattered, grief-stricken, and trying to explain. Eleri was trying to follow a story that was as tangled as the person telling it. Her heart broke for Hannah. Eleri missed Allison, too, but she couldn't feel her own grief while Hannah's permeated everything in the house.

"I believe so," Donovan replied, offering up an answer that didn't make any promises, but certainly sounded soothing.

He was right, Eleri thought, *the answer was 'maybe.'* If this truly was a case, then that data might never get back into Hannah's hands.

"When I went to gather and copy everything, I found a few things I hadn't seen before. In Allie's files. That was when I realized I probably *did* have a real case for the FBI."

Hannah stopped, staring straight ahead again. She was wringing her hands, and each time she seemed to notice that she was doing it, she would stop, lay her hands back on the overstuffed arms of the chair, where she perched awkwardly. "Let me show you what I found."

CHAPTER 8

Donovan looked to Eleri, silently wishing that she could hear his unspoken question and answer it just as silently.

Hannah had gotten up to retrieve the papers. Apparently, she hadn't been prepared for the FBI to show up on her doorstep and ask specifically *What did she know?* She hadn't been ready to share the evidence that had gotten the attention of their FBI director.

Across from him, Eleri tried fake relaxing in the big chair while Donovan had the couch to himself. His senior partner offered the slightest shrug of her shoulders, letting him know they were both flying blind here. It seemed her friendship with the widow was only enough to confuse the issue, not enough to help.

Hannah came back with a sheaf of papers in her hands. Askew and disorganized, they made Donovan wonder if this was her usual MO or if the messiness was merely an outward sign of her grief.

Jerking her hand sharply, she aimed the papers toward Eleri. Then, just before Eleri could lift her hand to take them, Hannah turned and thrust them at Donovan, as though she had no idea who should have them.

Donovan made a decision then: This must be grief. He had a hard time imagining that Eleri would be friends with someone so scattered and disorganized. Nodding a quick thank you, he took the papers before Hannah could change her mind and set them on the coffee table.

Standing up from her chair, Eleri moved to sit next to him on the couch. It was something that they had decided long ago *not* to do—sit together in a friendly situation. Sitting side by side presented a united front. It allowed the two of them to stare down whomever they were interviewing. If intimidation was the goal, this was great. But they wanted Hannah to feel comfortable.

Donovan wasn't sure if Eleri had come over to sit next to him simply because there was no way Hannah was ever going to become comfortable, or because it was more important to get close to the papers.

"I copied these," Hannah volunteered, pointing to some of the papers, though Donovan couldn't tell which from the mess she'd handed to him. "I sent the copies to your Agent Westerfield. The others, I just sent the originals. Those are the ones I want back. I sent seven full data notebooks that were too hard to copy."

The ones Westerfield handed to GJ, Donovan wondered. It was bad enough to come into the case without the knowledge of why Westerfield thought it was worth an FBI investigation, but this strange sorting of evidence. . . What was his SAC up to?

There wasn't time to figure that out now. Hannah was still talking. Once she'd gotten going, she seemed unable to stay silent. "When I got to these last two, I just kind of stopped dead."

Eleri's eyes flicked up to take in her friend. Every page, it seemed, was different from the one next to it. What connected them was scribbled writing—small, neat, and round—that appeared anywhere on the page it seemed to feel like. One page was an electric bill in Allison Caldeira's name, but numbers deemed important enough to keep were pushed into the margins. The rest was pages filled with columns of numbers, bills, letters on letterhead, invoices, contracts, and more.

What might make any one piece important escaped Donovan.

The page Hannah pointed to was an offer on a letterhead from Miranda Industries, a name Donovan had never heard before and now made a mental note to look up.

He flicked a quick, questioning glance to Eleri, but she missed his look. Instead, she turned to Hannah. "What was it about these pages that grabbed you?"

Donovan moved the short stack side to side, revealing a series of letters, offers, and more from the same company.

"It's *Miranda*." Hannah stated it as though they should know what the problem was.

Since Eleri was Hannah's friend, and she obviously didn't understand any better than he did, Donovan volunteered himself as the fool. "What's Miranda?"

Watching Hannah closely as he asked, he found no obvious answer in her expression. He was trained to catch eye movement, to find the tells of a liar, to determine exaggeration. Hannah's expression revealed nothing but the belief that Eleri should understand.

Directing his attention back to the paper, he saw the logo was a series of wavy lines with rectangles dispersed intermittently between them, some horizontal and some vertical. If it was a code, he wasn't following it. If it was an abstract picture, he had no idea what it was about.

"You don't remember?" Hannah was beseeching Eleri now, though it was clear Eleri didn't.

"I'm sorry." His partner almost stuttered over the words, as though she was sad to make her friend have to explain.

"Blake," Hannah said. "Blake Langley."

As Donovan watched, Eleri shook her head one more time. Then the bloom of memory washed over her features. "From Weeki Wachee?"

In that moment, everything clicked in his head. *Weeki Wachee.* He almost threw his head back and laughed, but he held it in because of the somber situation.

Eleri had always said she was a *mermaid!* He'd thought it was a joke, because she liked to call him a *werewolf.* He'd only just now caught on that it was far more literal than that. Hannah and Allison-the-marine-biologist and Eleri must have been swimmers at Weeki Wachee Springs. His partner had been in the famous mermaid show. If he was right, it wasn't very far from where they had gone to college.

Son of a bitch, he thought. *All this time.* He'd thought she was joking about being an actual mystical sea creature, but was merely referring to a job she'd held in college.

He fought the laugh. The situation was wholly inappropriate for it. Pressing his lips together to keep it from escaping, he turned to the two women and listened to Hannah, who was still explaining. She offered a few extras for Donovan's benefit. "Blake was a grad student. He was finishing his thesis, research on the manatees in the Weeki Wachee Springs area. And he was working at the park."

Donovan waited, as that still didn't explain anything.

"So it was—*what?*—two summers that we overlapped?" Hannah turned again to Eleri, who nodded in reply. "The last summer that you and Allison and I all worked there, Blake got a job offer."

"Was it from Miranda?" Eleri asked, clearly not remembering as well as Hannah did.

"Yes!" Her emphatic reply made it clear that everyone should have known this. "And Blake accepted."

"I remember he was excited, and he took the job. They

wanted him to start right away, even though it meant dropping his thesis."

"Exactly," Hannah replied, triumphantly. "Allison stayed in touch with him, or she *tried*. She was considering picking up the research where he'd left off. But then he just quit replying. Don't you remember?"

"Shit," Eleri sighed out the word, leaning back into the chair. Donovan watched as a memory hit her. She turned to him to explain. "Blake went missing." She aimed her next statement at Hannah. "But eventually they found him, right?"

Apparently, Eleri hadn't followed up on Blake at the time. Maybe she hadn't known the man very well.

"*No*." Hannah shook her head for emphasis. "He went to his parents' for a few weeks before starting the job. He and Allison stayed in touch then, but there was no contact after leaving his parents' home. No one has heard from Blake since the day he started his new job. At *Miranda*."

But Donovan wasn't listening. He was looking down at the papers again. They held short missives, first inviting Allison to join Miranda for an interview. In the letter from the subsequent date, the tone changed to a more demanding request for her presence. A third piece of mail offered her a contract doing research for the company and following letters upped the price.

Donovan held the last Miranda letter. "Is this a reasonable salary for a marine biologist like Allison?"

Hannah shook her head, her eyes wide. Though she'd been triumphant at getting Eleri to remember grad-student Blake, her whole demeanor changed as Donovan held up the letter. "No. That's *exorbitant*. It's hush-money big."

CHAPTER 9

Three hours later, GJ had discovered that she actually liked Noah Kimball much better than she'd originally thought she would.

He was kind, quick to smile, and sharp. He'd already found three different issues in the mess of papers, things that she hadn't spotted on the first round.

"So, if I line them up by date," he told her, "we see that Hannah—and the remainder of the research team—are examining oysters for several months earlier this year. And you can see a trail where they traveled. If we follow them on a map, we can see they started in Mississippi, hit the Alabama coast, and then Pensacola. Next they go to Tampa Bay, Sarasota, Naples, and Miami. Then there are several stops in the middle of the ocean, all the way to Nassau and several other ports in the Bahamas."

GJ had stood up and come around the table to where he was pointing at the papers he'd moved. Normally, she got pissy at other people touching her work. But he hadn't moved them too far, and he had lined up specific pieces in order.

The whole thing was a mess, but he didn't complain. Some

of Allison's papers were receipts. Some were reports. Some were invoices, but GJ could see that Noah had lined up dates— even though the type of information was all different—and traced the path where Allison and Hannah had gone.

"But look here," Noah said, just as GJ was putting the path of the journey together for herself. "Right here, there's a change. I can't tell if it's a side trip or what, but Allison scraped barnacles at this location. She collected them as specimens, saved them, and made note of the species. . . and that's it."

"How is that weird?"

He tapped at the page. "Everything else they did, they were prepared for. They did instantaneous research on the water and the fish. They used chemical kits or took consistent, specific sets of notes. They knew what they were doing. But the barnacles weren't tested at all—just scraped and put away for later." He took a deep breath in. "And it appears that it was Allison, and only Allison, who took this barnacle scraping."

"Interesting," GJ replied, though last week she would have bet anyone a hundred dollars that she never would have said that about barnacles. "So, we don't know what's odd about these barnacles, only that they are odd."

"Well, we don't know anything about the barnacles themselves. We know it appears odd that Allison collected them without any further work. And here. Look, she did it again. And again." Noah pointed to other spots on the pages, then turned to his tablet.

"Those are in the middle of the ocean," GJ frowned as his finger tapped the map he'd pulled up.

Each time he touched, he left a tiny dot behind, marking the research trail as he went.

Then GJ had a thought. "Don't barnacles form, or grow, on the bottoms of boats?" She paused, trying to let her mind work out the details of a research program she didn't understand at all. "Was Allison hitting up boats out in the middle of the ocean by herself?" Another pause, another thought. "And there's no other documentation on these barnacles?"

"Exactly. I mean, it might exist in here somewhere." Noah waved his hands at the reams of information spread across the table. "But her work is very organized, and the barnacle results and even the tests run aren't here with the collection data. So that's why I think it's strange."

They paused a moment, both looking at pages, flipping things over and checking for clues. Then Noah spoke again. "Honestly, I don't think these stops are boats. . . Let's pull up another map."

He didn't say what he thought it was, just grabbed the tablet, taking away the visual of the ocean. This was exactly why she often still preferred paper.

"It's what I thought." He turned the small screen around to face her. GJ saw then that of the three dots, two appeared to be oil rigs.

The empty ocean space on the new map showed far more dots than she'd ever imagined there would be. "We have that many oil drilling rigs?" She wanted to vomit.

Noah nodded, seeing her distress. Maybe when you lived on the coast here, it was part of life. She'd known there were many, but the screen showed thousands of dots. "What about the third?"

That location had seemed too far into the gulf to be a rig or a platform. Noah seemed to be as uncertain as she was on this. "Don't know. I mean, it could be an oil rig. Maybe one that's not on the map?"

"There are *more*?" The stress in her voice must have been harsher than she planned. He offered a conciliatory shrug.

"It could have been a boat passing through. We could check the date and see what was in the area at that time."

She almost asked, "You can do that?" but she didn't doubt they could. There was far more going on off the coast than she'd ever thought about before. Surely shipping licenses and planned routes were recorded somewhere.

Noah turned the map back to the original one with the dots he'd colored for Allison's collection points and set it on the table. They'd grown quiet as each began combing through the papers again. As they searched, they would go through periods of intense discussion about weird things they found. Then Noah would drop back into silence, letting her work on whatever trail she was following while he did something else. GJ found she rather liked it.

At one point, his phone rang, interrupting her thoughts. Even as her head came up, he got up, left the room, and headed into the hallway. But the big square windows did nothing to mask the conversation. Though she couldn't hear it, GJ had stopped looking at the research pages and began watching the man in the hallway. As his face reddened in anger, he waved his hands into the air and eventually jabbed his finger at the phone, harshly jamming it off. Whoever it was had gotten hung up on.

He turned then, trying to get himself back together before he came into the room. But GJ was too late turning her gaze back to the work, and it was clear she'd been watching. Rather than trying to cover it, she went for being open. She was a crappy liar anyway. "Are you okay?"

He didn't say *yes*. What he did say was, "That was my husband, soon to be *ex* husband. Let's just say he's not handling the divorce proceedings in a polite and kind manner."

GJ nodded her sympathy, and that should have been the end of it, but then the words fell out of her mouth. "You know, I was really hoping that gay marriages would be the ones to get it all right. Like it was fought for, so it meant more."

As soon as the words were out, she realized she shouldn't have said it. Fighting the urge to slap her hands across her face, as though she could put the sounds back in, she froze and waited for whatever harsh reaction she deserved. Luckily, Noah didn't take offense. *Thank God.*

"We're no better or worse at it than anyone else. We just deserve the right to be as shitty at marriage as straight America." Then he aimed his thumb at himself. "Case in point."

GJ grinned, partly from relief and partly from his answer. "That's a good way of putting it." Then she added, "I'm sorry you're getting divorced."

This time he looked up at the ceiling and then down at the table, before finally letting his eyes come back to GJ. "Honestly, the divorce is a good thing. A bad marriage is a life sentence if you don't get out of it. It's not the divorce. It's *him.*"

She found she was laughing again at Noah's "It's not me, it's *him*" take on things. But even so, she'd managed to turn at least some of her attention back to the scattered notes and put her fingers on something else concerning.

That was when the door to the conference room opened. No knock, no polite fanfare. Of course not. These were the *senior agents* coming into the room.

Stopping just inside the door, Eleri and Donovan looked at the papers all over the table. It was Eleri who first moved forward and asked, "Did you find anything?"

"Oh, yes," GJ replied. She was nothing if not useful. "I have this." And she laid out copies of five letters written to Allison Caldeira from Miranda industries.

Eleri and Donovan looked at them. "Yes," Eleri said as she touched one of them, seeming to need the contact with the content the same as GJ. "Hannah just showed us the same thing. She also thought they were concerning."

"Oh, they are," GJ quipped easily. This was ground she could stand firm on. Not like the oil rigs or barnacle data. "I checked Allison's tax returns. This offer is about four to five times as high as it should be." Then she picked up another piece. "I finally got a chance to start flipping through the lab notebooks, trying to match up some of the dates and some of the paperwork. And I found this."

She pulled out a note that Allison had stuck in between the pages of her research notes and watched as Eleri and Donovan's eyes went wide.

CHAPTER 10

E leri took a seat at the conference room table. This was worse than what they'd already suspected. The Miranda Industries offer was suspicious as hell, but this?

She would have put her hands flat on the surface but for the papers laid out everywhere. Though she couldn't tell exactly what the pattern was, she could see that one existed and didn't want to mess it up. Reaching out, she asked. "Can I read that?"

GJ held the paper by the corners as she handed it across the long conference table. "Sorry, I touched it before I realized what it was. We've been touching everything." She motioned between herself and Noah Kimball.

It was Donovan who let it slide. "I can't imagine there's much fingerprint or DNA data left on any of this. So I guess it's already gone and we can touch things as we need."

Despite Donovan's assessment, Eleri held the page by the corners. When she'd read it carefully, she didn't find anything she hadn't seen from across the room. It merely said, "If you don't stop, there will be consequences."

"Kind of dull, as threats go," Eleri offered up to the room. No one disagreed. She held it out as though one of them would take

43

it from her or need to look closer. "Can we get any evidence from the paper? The ink?"

It was Noah who answered. "We can send it in for testing. But I think that looks like notebook paper. The loose-leaf kind you buy anywhere, really. And the ink looks like regular permanent marker. Again, there'll be no tracing that, even if we get a batch number. I'm sure it was distributed to forty thousand different stores all across the US." He took the note from her and set it carefully aside. "But we can check. We might get lucky."

"Handwriting?" Eleri grasped at straws, but even as she asked it, she thought about the letters. They were all capitals, mostly block-style. Analyzing it was likely pointless. "Never mind."

She spoke the word just as Noah was opening his mouth. At least he held back the shut-down he probably had ready to tell her. Going for another tactic, Eleri tried again. "So, this was just tucked into the lab notebook, GJ?"

GJ nodded, not quite looking up, still flipping through pages. There were seven lab notebooks.

"Did Westerfield send you these?" Donovan asked, and Eleri understood the connection he'd made. Hannah had sent them in, and Westerfield had handed them off to GJ, but hadn't told the rest of them what he'd done.

GJ nodded absently to the table, but when she looked up, she only asked, "Did Hannah Raisman provide anything to support or contradict any of this? It's my understanding that she was the source for this material."

"We saw most of these papers," Donovan supplied. He explained Hannah's issues, how she'd gotten tired of photocopying once she had found the Miranda letters. He didn't tell her that Westerfield hadn't informed them of the notebooks' existence. "I think it was the grief, and that she was stunned by the offer."

Eleri piggybacked on that. She and Donovan had only gotten to rehash the interview a little while in the car. "We both agreed that Hannah's reaction seemed genuine. She said she'd not seen the letters while Allison was still alive. She only found them while trying to cobble enough information together to convince Westerfield she had a case."

"You saw these same letters?" GJ pointed to where she'd pulled out the Miranda Industries notices.

Eleri nodded. "We saw the originals." She was turning to Donovan when she stopped cold. "Wait. We saw four. Right, Donovan?" When he frowned and nodded, she went on. "There are five here. Did Hannah pull one out? Lose one?"

"Clearly, she copied it," Noah volunteered, popping into the conversation again. Eleri was getting the impression that he was hanging back until he had a better feel for the way they worked. She understood, but she wished he'd just dive in. At least he asked another question. "Was it an honest mistake, or something more?"

There were no answers for that, and Eleri could only tuck the thought away for later. Her brain didn't want to let it go. Hannah was too smart to think she could hide something she'd already photocopied and sent into the FBI. *Wasn't she?* But Eleri's thoughts were quickly derailed by GJ and Noah.

"Look!"

"I found one."

The words came simultaneously from the other agents. Both had returned to flipping through lab notebooks, simply trying to shake loose whatever might fall out. And both now held new papers toward Eleri and Donovan, who had hopped to their feet.

The four agents moved like a fluid around the table, coming together at one spot. Eleri tried to look over GJ's shoulder, but even the younger woman was too tall for that. She inserted herself where she could see, letting Donovan hover easily in the back.

"What dates were they tucked into?" Donovan asked.

Looking up from where she was already making notes on exactly that, GJ replied. "The first one was from April. This one that I just found was from early May. What do you have?" She leaned toward Noah as all three strained to see his note.

"Three weeks ago?" he replied in a somber tone. "This one would have been sent just before Allison died."

Eleri didn't say it—no one did—but they knew Allison must have received the message because she had tucked it into *her* lab notebook. "By how many days?" Eleri asked softly. "Does the lab notebook continue after that threat?"

Noah took a moment and then looked up. "She got this three days before she died."

So the last threat—the one that Noah held—arrived just before Allison's fatal dive.

Did they all say the same thing? She hadn't looked. She'd only noted that each of the other agents held up a scrap of notebook paper with the same black sharpie and same block lettering.

Looking at the one Noah held, she read it carefully. But it had only two words: LAST CHANCE.

"Well, that's not suspicious at all," Donovan snarked to the room at large.

Despite the seemingly accidental nature of Allison's death, there was now clear evidence that Hannah had been right. This was almost definitively a murder. And it was starting to look like it was a little bigger than just personal revenge.

"This one says 'You've been warned,'" GJ read from her paper. She gingerly handed it off to Eleri and turned to make another note. She also pulled a sticky note and added a tab into the lab notebook where the threat had been found. Then, she recorded in her own notes dates that Allison appeared to have filed the threats, the current date—the date they'd found it—and more.

Eleri tried to wait patiently, but she wound up picking up all three notes and placing them side by side in the center of the conference table. It was the only place clear of paper, letters, contracts and notebooks.

So as not to disturb GJ, Eleri spoke softly to Donovan. "It's the same paper. Same marker. Same handwriting. It looks like one source."

Donovan nodded. "We should get at least one of them tested."

"It wouldn't hurt." Eleri thought of Westerfield possibly pushing back on the budget, given that they were testing for something they suspected would not play out at all. Eleri didn't think they would find anything, either, but if there was something to be learned, leaving it on the table was a fool's mistake.

If whoever was threatening Allison was halfway smart, they would have made sure to use paper that, no matter how traceable, was too widely used to indicate anything specific about the sender. They would use generic markers. It was obvious they'd disguised their own handwriting to some degree. *No*, Eleri thought, *they wouldn't find anything*.

GJ's voice then pulled her out of her side discussion with Donovan.

"Oh shit."

All three of them turned to look at the youngest and newest agent in the room.

"What did you find?" Eleri asked.

"That warning. . ." GJ let the words trail off as she picked up the lab notebook to show them something. "Look, look at this. See how it was wet at one point?"

She held the notebook up facing them and turned several pages. They were wrinkly and blurred in places. "This writing was done before the lab notebook was wet." GJ waved a gesture at the page. "But it looks like Allison continued using it after it dried out." GJ now pointed to a specific note: dates Allison had entered. "You can see a several-day gap here. But look at the words."

They all leaned forward, but GJ kept talking. "I just thought the lab notebook got wet because. . . well, because she's an oceanic researcher and. . . *water*. But now the notes on the first page after the notebook dried out say that they were outside of Nassau on that date. And they were boarded by some kind of *pirates*. . . and their ship was *blown up*."

GJ took a deep breath to steady herself, and Eleri found she needed one, too.

"The researchers were all okay?"

GJ nodded, now having turned the book back to her own view and reading from it. "She says they were thrown overboard, but all the data was lost. All the samples were gone. She somehow managed to save this lab notebook."

CHAPTER 11

E leri woke to the feeling of air being dragged into her lungs, wet and heavy. The feeling made it immediately clear that she was in Florida again. Even the smell that lingered in this state's oxygen was different from most other places she'd been.

While many locations had a sense memory that took her back to some past visit, Florida was like no other. It wasn't just a scent or a familiar landmark. It was the way the light fell, the constant hum of ocean in the distance, and a pressure to the air that made life feel slower. It was more than a little drugging.

All of that might be her own personal reaction, she figured, because she'd spent her formative college years here, defying her parents, leaving home, and attending an elite, private school rather than one of the grand "ivies" her parents had chosen for her. They'd refused to pay for any of this, but she'd broken from their expectations for the first time at eighteen.

In a unique position, Eleri had simply stepped out. Her trust fund had made it all possible. As she hit legal age, the money converted to her own management, and she managed her way through an education that she—not her parents—had chosen.

It had been shocking to Thomas and Nathalie that the child they'd raised one way suddenly had a voice and a will of her own. Sure, Eleri had warned them all along, but she could tell from their reaction, it simply hadn't occurred to either of her parents that she would actually *do* the things she'd said. Though they never threatened to disown her, they made it clear they disapproved wholeheartedly. Eleri went anyway.

She lay in bed now, staring at the hotel room ceiling. So much of the past came flooding back as the air pooled in the bottom of her lungs. Memories came rushing in with each inhale, swamping her as surely as the humid air did.

The school had just over five hundred students when she attended. And it was easy to believe, even still, that she had been the wealthiest person on campus, even without her parents' money. When she left Patton Hall in Kentucky, she'd told her parents to stay behind, that she would get herself to college. It had been easy to do; her mother didn't like to leave the grand home, because *What if Emmaline came back?*

Emmaline wasn't coming back. Eleri headed straight into her future, no longer having to pretend she agreed with her parents' plans. She'd been driving a BMW they'd given her on her sixteenth birthday. They didn't suspect she would stop in Georgia and trade it for a less splashy Toyota.

She'd made it through all four years without disclosing to the other students that she had a trust fund and that her family owned several homes—the grand kind, with their own names— in cities and on beaches throughout the country.

When she talked tuition and fees with her friends, she said that her grandparents were paying for it. It wasn't untrue. She went home for holidays and breaks. And—aside from the one Thanksgiving she spent with college friends, where she was surprised with a vegan Tofurky—she mostly stayed out of other people's celebrations. She was dutiful in that way, because she wasn't able to do it in other ways. Studying French, traveling abroad, and becoming someone's wife simply weren't in her DNA.

When she returned home the first time, her mother was appalled by the Toyota—not because it was a Toyota, but because it was a little bit dinged up and because she'd sent her daughter to school in a nice BMW. Eleri weathered that storm, and didn't tell her mother that she'd not be coming home to stay next summer. She planned to get a job.

She was a bit of an odd duck at the small, tight-knit, very *liberal* liberal arts school. She wore button-down shirts and never took her scissors to her jeans. She always showed up on time and with her work done, and she took advantage of the availability of the professors.

Most of the other students were taking history classes, creative writing, art, and math. Many were doing their own deep dives into science, like Hannah had.

Eleri had always known what she wanted to be: not even just a law enforcement officer, but specifically an FBI agent.

Her mix of poly sci, history, law, and culture seemed to be relatively unique among the student body. She did individual projects on law enforcement and defended a thesis on DNA testing, errors, and a calculated percentage of convicted innocents.

And in the spring of her second year, she followed her roommate Hannah to interview at Weeki Wachee Springs. The park featured sea life and was known for hiring young marine biologists, ecologists, and zoologists for a summer job that gave them access to information and research in their chosen fields. That's why Hannah had gone. Eleri had hoped to get into security.

But as she filled out the application, intending to merely get social credit for holding a real job and learn a little about entry-level security, she was pulled aside and asked if she wanted to be a mermaid. She didn't need the paycheck. What she needed was a work history and a reason to stay away from home. At that point, her past with the swim team and a junior water ballet program suggested she might be better suited for the show than the entry gate.

Eleri made the cut. She spent her summer getting into and out of a mermaid tail and performing several times a day for audiences that came to see the underwater theater. Her job became something she loved. The hot air and the cool water, her friends, and the mentorship she found there gave her a first profound sense of belonging. She didn't regret not getting her credits as a junior security guard. Suddenly, she'd joined a sisterhood of other mermaids, including Allison.

Pulling her thoughts back to the present and away from her summers past, Eleri turned her head and looked at the glowing red numbers on the hotel clock. It was almost time to get up.

Hitting the buttons on her phone, Eleri turned off the alarm and then dialed Donovan.

"Yes?" he answered, the question hanging in the thick air. It was earlier than they had decided to get going.

"I knew you were awake," she offered by way of greeting.

"Of course you did. What are we doing?" He didn't even yawn. She felt no guilt. That simple "What are we doing?" let her know that, if she was calling him earlier than intended, he would assume there was a reason. There was.

Eleri liked that he trusted her. "I think we should go up to Weeki Wachee Springs today."

"Where is that? . . . And why?"

"Near Tampa. We'll puddle jump it. Driving would be a nightmare. And we need to go—because of the connection to the guy who was doing his thesis there. The one who got the letters from Miranda Industries and then disappeared."

"Blake Langley," Donovan filled in, his memory solid.

Eleri nodded at the phone. "I don't remember him well, but I remember enough. His studies were performed in conjunction with the park. They do a lot of research themselves, and the visitors help fund it. So I want to go back and see if we can talk to any scientists who remember him or find any information on what he was studying. I'm sure they had grants, so some kind of records must exist. And I'm confident we'll get more information in person."

"You want to go flash some badges?" he clarified.

"In a sense."

He agreed readily. "Then let's find a flight. But Eleri, first I need something."

She paused, his words stopping her movement as the air pressed in from all sides. This was not a phrase Donovan was prone to utter. It didn't sound case-related, either. The cautious tone grabbed her, and it was so un-Donovan-like, she couldn't refuse. "Anything."

This was her partner. He'd gone to New Orleans with her and risked his own job to help find her sister. She owed him big time, but she would have done anything, even if she hadn't. When the empty space was met with only silence, she grew more concerned and pushed back. "What is it?"

"Before we left, I got a box in the mail. And it was addressed to only 'brother'."

CHAPTER 12

Donovan had tried to open the box on three different occasions. But each time, he hadn't been able to do much more than stare at it.

The call from Westerfield—and this subsequent assignment—had given him permission to ignore the box. He'd simply stuffed it into his bag and brought it along, not quite able to leave it behind, but clearly still unable to open it.

In New Orleans, when he'd caught that scent—one he hadn't smelled before but recognized immediately—he'd experienced some kind of innate familial tracking. Though he tried to reason how this other young man could be something other than a brother—perhaps a cousin, or some half-sibling—the box had made that speculation pointless.

A half-sibling on his father's side made the most sense. His father had likely spent most of his days cheating on Donovan's mother. So it was no shock to Donovan that he might have half-siblings out there. Aiden Heath had been an asshole of epic proportions. Honestly, he knew his father might still be out there, giving Donovan even more poor, abused half-brothers and sisters.

Donovan thought he'd left Aiden Heath in his rear view mirror a long, long time ago. He certainly didn't have it in him to hunt up random children based on a tenuous genetic connection, but this box had thrown him.

He'd reasoned it through eight different ways, each one working, but his senses, especially his sense of smell, said this man wasn't a half-sibling. Every alert told Donovan the two of them shared both mother and father. Still, he couldn't fathom a scenario in which that could happen.

This man smelled like family. He looked *Indian*. He *looked* like Donovan's mother. The day he'd seen him, Donovan had almost been stabbed, failing to jump out of the way because he'd been so stunned to discover that shocking relationship in the middle of a brawl in a back alley in New Orleans.

Apparently, it didn't matter what Donovan had talked himself into—or out of. The box had arrived. The label said *Brother*. So whatever Donovan suspected, this other man already knew.

Putting his hands on the lid, he took a deep breath, knowing that he was about to discover something big. By asking Eleri or help, he'd forced his own hand, creating a scenario where he not only had backup in the case of something strange, but also someone who would make sure he opened the damn box.

He was filled with both trepidation and relief.

Though he stared at it as if the box likely held a snake, Donovan told himself he knew it didn't. Eleri had been right. He had been awake and dressed already by the time his phone had rung. He was sitting in the same position when the knock sounded at the door.

"Come in." He didn't get up. He'd heard her footsteps from down the hall. He knew them as well as he'd known his father's as a kid. Only the sound of her approach didn't make him tense.

Letting herself in, Eleri found him as he'd been for a while, with the box waiting him out. His ass was still planted in the modern-shaped, rounded chair that looked far more comfortable than it was. His gaze was likely still bleak.

She didn't ask, merely came over and sat down across from him. For a moment she, too, stared at the box. At last she opened her mouth. *"Brother?"*

He nodded. "He *looked* Indian. That was the kicker. I mean, if I smell a *brother*, then surely the answer is that my father cheated on my mother. I mean, I must have half-siblings, both older and younger than me, all over the United States."

Eleri nodded along as though this were both obvious and no affront at all to her Main Line, blueblood upbringing. Although she held the clout to do it, he'd never seen her judge anyone on their genetics or even hold anyone to the sins of their father. "So he found you, and he sent this. . . and you think he's actually a full-blooded brother because it was your *mother* who was Indian. Not your father."

"My father's a Brit."

"Then how would that work?" she asked, brows furrowing as she arrived at the same conclusion he had.

Had he not been staring at the box, it would have made him smile.

Eleri continued, "I mean, your mother died when you were —*what?*—six or seven?"

He nodded.

"And you had no siblings?"

He shook his head. "So, either I had an older brother that they never told me about, or a younger brother. . . that they hid from me. I don't remember my mother being pregnant."

"Would you?" Her head tilted as she grabbed onto this possibility. "I mean, young kids often miss things like that. Especially if you didn't have a baby around afterwards. Did they give him away?"

"I can't promise that didn't happen. But I cannot imagine my father giving up a male child—something that *belongs* to him. I also can't imagine my mother sneaking something of that magnitude past him. My father was a controlling bastard. I don't know how she would have accomplished it. So I've been trying to work my way through to anything that makes sense. I'm hoping the box holds some answers."

Eleri didn't seem excited. Truly, he'd not expected her to; this was bizarre, and nobody knew how to feel about it. "The last time he saw you, this man tried to stick a knife in your side. And he was hanging out with the Dauphine sisters, which is no ringing endorsement."

Donovan only nodded. The Dauphine sisters were bad news every way they measured it. The quartet ran all kinds of powerful Voodoo, drugs, and trafficked children through New Orleans. They had *Lobomau* working with them—a faction of wolves that used their unique talents in gang warfare and illegal activities.

It appeared that Donovan's brother was one of them.

"But if I have a brother. . ." he let the words trail off. He looked away, shrugged his shoulders, and shook his head as though he could shake off reality. It didn't work. "I think I need to open the box."

He reached for a pocket knife, but Eleri's hand shot out to stay him. "Have you checked it? You're sure it's not a bomb or anything?"

"Yes," he said, the side of his lip quirking upward. She had clearly forgotten. "I sniffed it myself."

Eleri's laugh lightened the mood. She would keep him sane, no matter what was in the box. "Good point. I guess you don't really need the bomb-sniffing dogs."

He shook his head and, as her hand pulled away, he flipped open the knife and slit the seam down the top. Surely she could hear how his breath sucked in as he slowly peeled the flaps back and looked inside.

The box had been lightweight, so Donovan wasn't sure what

could possibly be inside. He reached down in, finding a wadded newspaper for stuffing. Without lifting his eyes, he pulled it out and passed it to El, who opened it and examined it. Always the FBI agent.

But Donovan was looking at what was inside: three photographs.

He was frowning even as Eleri held up the date on the paper and said, "New Orleans. From just a few weeks ago." But he let the information slide away as he stared at the photos in his hand.

One picture was of his mother, one of his father. The third one was of his mother with a teenager.

Eleri was leaning over to get a better look. "Is that him?"

Slowly, stunned, Donovan nodded. He remembered what the man looked like. He'd been so startled, his eyes had gone wide and the face had imprinted in his brain. "That's him. And that's my mom. . . And he's a teenager. . ." his brain still wasn't putting together everything it meant.

The man was a *teenager*. . .

"Wait!" Eleri cried, startling him. "There's something else in the box."

CHAPTER 13

Eleri stepped from the tiny plane and onto the hot tarmac, her emotions already in a jumble. She'd tried again to talk to Westerfield, to talk him into removing them from the case. There were so many reasons now that neither she nor Donovan should be working this.

"Sir," she'd rebuffed his first answer, mid-flight, the phone tucked between her shoulder and her ear, indicating she was just old enough to have not been born into the cell-phone era. "I'm too attached to this case." She could feel it. Even just being in Florida was stirring her up. It was a heady return to a time in her life when things had been fresh and new. Only now, two of the friends that she'd made then had been murdered.

She so desperately wanted to solve the case that she knew she couldn't handle everything as rationally as she should. So, before Westerfield could say anything else, Eleri added, "Donovan needs to be removed as well." Another pause hung between them, so she tacked on the phrase, "Family issues."

If Donovan wanted to tell more, he could do that on his own. But a single word came back from her boss. *"Family?"* And tucked inside the question was all the reasoning he needed. They both knew Donovan didn't have any family.

"Exactly, sir. There may now be family to have issues with." She'd said more than she intended, but let it fall.

Ignoring the new problem with Donovan, Westerfield had asked her, "Will you be giving the case your best?"

"Of course, sir. I was invested before it even began." *That's exactly why I shouldn't be on it.* Even though her heart desperately wanted to be here, she was growing more aware of her own bias every minute.

"You'll both stay on it," he said. And then, almost too abruptly, he ended the call as though he'd either been interrupted or he was desperate to get off the line and have her stop recommending recusals.

Eleri wasn't going to get her wish. She fought the irritation that washed over her along with the hot air. She trudged toward a building as small as the plane and the tarmac. People thought large airports were better, but Eleri had learned smaller meant faster, and time sometimes meant saving lives for them.

Behind her, both GJ and Noah Kimball followed along. Eleri had considered bringing only Noah, but she'd known the man less than twenty-four hours. Though he seemed solid and dependable, those traits weren't enough to make him into her only backup system. Though Westerfield had recommended him, her boss wasn't the most reliable source these days.

Who would have thought that GJ Janson would become the stable *one?* Clinging to that thought, Eleri tried to push away the memory of how Donovan had practically shoved her out of his hotel room, asked her to cover for him today, and not told her what was going on.

She only knew that she'd pulled a slip of fabric from the bottom of the box and then everything had gone to hell. The patterned piece had acted as additional padding in the box, but it seemed to be some kind of emotional time bomb going off in front of Donovan's face.

He'd first stopped dead and stared at it. She could have sworn he'd whispered, *No*. But she hadn't seen his lips move and she couldn't be sure she'd even heard it. His eyes had gone from wide and petrified to blank in a heartbeat. Then he'd stood up quickly enough that—had it been any lighter—the chair would have toppled. But he quickly told her that he would figure it out.

At least he didn't lie and say everything was fine.

Despite the drama of the contents of the box, they still had a job to do. And they knew it. If they both went AWOL to cover whatever Donovan needed, Westerfield would have their asses. Since Donovan wasn't telling her exactly what he did need, she'd come here.

As it was, Eleri had already tipped her hand a little by asking Westerfield if Donovan could be excused from the case. Hopefully, her SAC wouldn't notice that Donovan had gone rogue today. Hopefully, he'd be back on the case tomorrow, but Eleri didn't really know.

She watched as Noah Kimball carefully sidestepped in front of her and made a motion to follow him. Maybe he was impatient at the way she had paused or maybe he thought she didn't know where she was going. Truthfully, she was playing it by ear. When she had come to Weeki Wachee as an employee, she had traveled into town via the roads, from Sarasota through Tampa.

The tourist attraction had been far enough from school that four of them had rented a tiny apartment for the summers. She'd gone along with the cheap little stucco house with the gravel "flower bed" out front rather than admit that she had the money for something much nicer.

Shaking the memories away, she followed Agent Kimball to the rental cars. She hadn't ever flown into this tiny airport before. Clearly, Noah knew his way around, and he walked confidently toward the small patch of cars and flashed his badge at the guy sitting in the tiny booth. Eleri prayed the rental employee had air conditioning, but Noah was already turning away. Apparently, they'd quickly assigned a car and Noah was hitting the button, blinking the lights, and popping the locks.

He held out the keys then toward Eleri. "Do you want to drive?"

Though he asked the question, it was clear to Eleri that he was also offering to do it if she wanted. But she said, "I will. You should give me directions until we get there. I think I'll remember my way around the park and the employee entrances."

She'd said it to be clear that she wasn't driving because of ego, or that she simply felt she should, as the senior agent. She was willing to hand responsibilities to the person best suited for them. That's why she'd brought GJ Janson along today.

Noah was her local eyes and ears, though none of them was actually local to the Weeki Wachee area. Eleri was closest to that, but her last contact with the park had been well over a decade ago. Things often changed. In fact, she might not even know where the employee parking lot was anymore. But she was going to try.

GJ was her analyst—at least, that's what Eleri was counting on. Having never been here before, GJ would look at everything with fresh eyes. She would not judge by Florida standards. She would count, she would catalog, and she would conclude. Eleri was praying for anything solid.

The drive was much the way Eleri remembered once she turned onto the familiar roads. She bypassed the main park entrance and took her passengers around to the back. They headed toward the hidden gate, which was taller and more aggressive than she remembered, but still in the same place.

Once they were parked, she hopped out into the oppressive heat, grateful that she knew how to pack for this weather. She looked to GJ, who clearly didn't.

At the entry gate, the guard stopped them. Gone were her days of waving an employee ID or simply being recognized as one of the mermaids. This time, she whipped out her Bureau ID. The guard's reaction told her that, behind her, both Noah and GJ did the same.

When she was a kid, Eleri had played games of "agent" and she'd loved flashing her pretend badges. Her mother had always dismissed her, but Eleri dreamed of being able to walk up to someone and say, "FBI," and flip that wallet open, commanding instant respect. She'd not been fully prepared for the rigors of Quantico, but the badge was everything she'd always hoped. She'd certainly become accustomed to it.

It felt good as the guard simply slid the gate open, ushering them inside. Still, he stopped them and asked politely, though it was clearly a demand, "How can I help you?"

They were next directed into a small room in a low office building that did a reasonable job of blending into the wild Florida landscape. They were offered sodas and snacks, and Eleri waited as patiently as she could. The fizz of a coke sliding down her throat helped to pass the time.

Next to her, GJ ate chips as though she were in a college lunch hall, waiting for her friends to show. Noah relentlessly tapped his fingers on the table. Eleri didn't comment. Fifteen minutes later, the director made it into their room, having had to be fetched from the other side of the park.

"Genevieve?" The name fell from Eleri's lips before she could stop them. She recognized that face and was shocked that the memory surfaced so clearly.

The woman frowned at her, as though trying to make the same connection.

"Eleri Eames," she continued. "I was a mermaid here." She rattled off the year and which section of the park Genevieve had managed at the time. Genevieve, too, had once been a mermaid, though she'd been promoted to management before Eleri had come through. This time, her eyes lit up.

"Eleri! You're an FBI agent now. Are you just visiting?"

"I wish I could say so. Unfortunately, I have a case and it leads back here."

Genevieve tried to stop her head from visibly snapping back but didn't quite succeed.

Eleri kept her voice soft and soothing, because the information she needed to share wouldn't be. "We actually don't know if it's serious, but we're following a tip, and we'd like your help looking into it."

"I don't understand." Genevieve seemed more confused than frightened, as good a response as could be hoped for. "We run a clean system. We're a state park."

Eleri knew all of that, and during the time she'd worked here, she'd never seen anything that hinted of illegal activity. Conservation efforts, arguments, and letter-writing campaigns to a Congress that didn't understand the importance of saving the Everglades were all par for the course— but never anything under the table. She tried to offer a smile. "It's an old issue. From before you were park director." Eleri hoped that would make the other woman more open and let her know that she wasn't being investigated. "When I was here, there was another student doing marine research on the waterways. His name was Blake Langley."

Once again, Genevieve was unable to disguise her reaction. "You're investigating Blake Langley?"

Eleri nodded, having noticed that beside her, Noah was paying rapt attention, and even GJ had set aside her chips and soda for a more professional demeanor. They were simply taking all of this in, filing what they saw and heard, and waiting.

"Yes."

This time Genevieve let out a breath and sat back harshly into the metal chair. "Well, thank God someone finally is."

CHAPTER 14

Donovan stared at the fabric in the box for some unknown amount of time. It could have been two seconds, two minutes, or two hours. He couldn't really tell.

He knew that pattern. He knew the lightness of the linen. It was his mother's scarf, the one he had kept after she died, the one he had hidden from his father. It was the first thing he grabbed each time his father picked him up in the middle of the school day, or woke him in the dark of night, demanding that they suddenly move.

For a while, Donovan had tucked the fabric down into his backpack, carrying it to school with him every day, just in case his father pulled him from classes and pushed him directly into the car. Once had been all it took for Donovan to learn that nothing was sacred to the man. He'd scooped their things into trash bags, and it was sheer luck the scarf had been bagged with Donovan's belongings. Many of his toys and clothes hadn't made it that time. Or other times.

Now, the scarf somehow sat in the bottom of this box that had been mailed to him. When he was younger, Donovan had taken it out and touched it every day, using it as an emotional anchor. But somewhere during college and med school, he'd grown more confident about his things. His home was his own. Since he no longer worried about his father ferreting him off into the night, he'd let the practice slide. It had been enough to see it at the bottom of his t-shirt drawer every once in a while.

When had he last laid his hands on it? He didn't know.

That was when he reached into the box and snatched it out as though it were on fire.

Maybe this was a duplicate. Somebody had figured out which scarf his mother owned and bought another one like it. But, before he even got it to his nose, he knew that theory was dead wrong. *It smelled like her.*

Fuck. The only way this worked was if someone had broken into his home, stolen it, stuffed it into this box and mailed it from— he didn't know. Grabbing the box, he flipped it over, examining it. He'd looked before. He already knew it was missing a return address, but maybe there was other information. This time, he used his laptop to open systems he had access to as an FBI agent and keyed in the red-inked postage marks. It took only a handful of tries to determine that the box had originated in New Orleans.

Fuck, he thought again, wondering whether it would have been worse if it had been mailed from his own hometown. Or if it was worse that the scarf was stolen, taken back to New Orleans, and *then* mailed to him. None of those options was good.

Once again, as if to reassure himself that his initial assessment had been correct, Donovan lifted the scarf to his nose and inhaled deeply. It was definitely his mother's scent, and it catapulted him back into a mix of clearly defined and fuzzy memories of her. One was the classic scenario of his mother making him cookies. Another memory hit—the non-classic scenario of curry wafting down the road from his kitchen. He had memories as well of his father raising his hand to the woman Donovan loved most. Donovan's memory cut off abruptly at the threat of a fist. To this day, he remained unsure of what had happened next.

He did have faint memories of applying Band-aids to his mother. But in the memory, he was so young that he couldn't tell if he was actually helping or simply playing along. Some of the memories were far fuzzier, just feelings of warmth and being held. Feelings of safety, or at least what he had taken for safety at the time.

It was almost too much, and he set the scarf onto the tabletop, unwilling to put it back into the box. He immediately picked up the phone and called Walter.

Luckily, she answered. "Hey, Donovan."

"Hey, babe." The affectionate term had begun rolling off his tongue a few weeks ago, and he found he liked it. "Not a pleasant call, I'm afraid."

"Is everything okay?" He could practically hear the expression on her face through the line.

"Everyone is physically fine." Not a great start but. . . "I got a box. In the mail. That was addressed to me. . . as 'brother.' It came from New Orleans."

"Holy shit," she replied.

"Yeah, and it gets worse. Inside is a scarf—it's one of the few things I have from my mother. There are also several pictures of this man with her." He clarified, making sure Walter understood that the scarf was the pressing issue. "The scarf was in my T-shirt drawer. I need someone to go to my house and see if they can figure out how this person got into my home."

"So when would they have been in your home? When did you get the box?" She asked questions he should have been ready for, but it left him having to admit that he had hadn't told her about the box, despite having it in his possession for a while.

"Minimum timeframe is probably two or so weeks ago. Maybe longer. I don't know when I last saw the scarf in my drawer. It might have been missing for as much as several months. I don't know."

Even as he said the words though, that timeframe didn't make sense. He'd only seen the startling face for the first time just over a month ago. The other man appeared to have been as shocked as he was. He couldn't have even known to break into Donovan's home, steal the scarf—and who knew what else?—at any time before that. It simply didn't make sense. So he told Walter his idea and the amended timeframe.

"I can't help." She sounded sorry about it, thought. "I'm in Colorado. Westerfield's got me chasing down Pines. Let me tell you, this is the biggest suck-ass assignment ever. How do I trace a psychic who can make anyone believe she wasn't ever there?"

Donovan didn't have an answer, and he let the silence hang between them. Because while he appreciated her dilemma, his own felt far more pressing. "All right, I'll see if I can find someone else. Good luck catching up to Pines. And good luck remembering that you did it the next day."

She chuckled and they chatted briefly for a few more minutes, but there wasn't too much to catch up on. Donovan hung up and called Wade.

"I'm in Atlanta," the other agent told him. "At a conference. I can maybe get there in three or four days. But if someone broke into your home, wouldn't you have smelled it?"

Donovan stopped dead. Wade was right. He *should* have. The two men lived secure-feeling lives in part because they could smell most everything that would happen, often even before the threat arrived. They only used smoke detectors because they left their homes to travel for long stretches of time.

Sometimes, when someone managed to be very, very quiet, or when Donovan was asleep, he smelled the person before he had any other sensory information of them. Had someone rifled through his clothing, surely Donovan would have at least known that another person had been in his home. He would have sensed this even if he hadn't found any windows or locks tampered with.

"I didn't notice anything," he confessed to Wade. "I mean, I guess I might have not been paying attention—"

"I don't know," Wade interrupted. "I've been in hotel rooms where someone went in when I wasn't there. I can smell that the maid has been in the room, and I'm not ever paying attention for that. One time, the room wasn't made up and I could smell that the maid who had come the day before had been in there anyway. So I would imagine you wouldn't miss it if someone broke into your home—far enough to get into your bedroom?"

He asked the last word with a question. And Donovan replied, "Yes. It was in my bedroom dresser, in my T-shirt drawer, under the shirts." He was thinking it before Wade said it.

"You wouldn't have missed it. You would have smelled that."

"My brother. . ." the words felt strange coming from his own voice, "he's running with the Dauphine sisters. He's *Lobomau*. I mean, do you think they've discovered a way to completely disguise their scent?"

He waited while Wade worked out what he could. "It's plausible. But the things I think are most likely to occlude a scent include coffee beans and peanut butter and covering yourself with mud. Even that only works partially against someone as sensitive as *us*. I mean, if you've been in wolf form in your own home in the last week"—which Donovan had— "then you would have had a *more* open nose. You would have noticed it, even if it wasn't a human scent. They would have had to make *all scent* disappear for you to not notice."

"Shit," Donovan replied. Wade was right. Then how had his brother gotten the scarf? And why did he send it to Donovan? What specifically did the message mean?

"I'll still go and check," his friend volunteered. "I'm several days out on the end of this conference. Let me know if you find someone else who can get there sooner." Donovan agreed before letting Wade go. But, as of right now, there was no one else he could think of. He knew of Wade's relatives, who also had their skills. But he'd not yet met anyone else in NightShade, besides the two of them, who had this particular skill set. Certainly no one he trusted to go into his home and rifle through his personal belongings.

Though he'd hung up with his friend—knowing that it was impossible for Wade to call back in a few hours with an answer, as he had hoped—he wasn't ready to take the next step. Sitting back down, he again stared at the three pictures laid out across the surface.

Something was nagging at him about the middle photo.

So he mentally listed everything he could about them. . . until it hit him.

In the middle picture, this *brother* was younger, much younger but still definitely in his teenage years. And he was standing with his arm around Donovan's mother.

CHAPTER 15

GJ sat in the hard metal chair, attempting to look comfortable. It was incredibly difficult, as she was sweating like a stuck pig.

She'd been bulking up her professional wardrobe since officially joining the FBI as an agent a short while ago. There had been information on the dress code, and GJ was following it almost to the letter. However, she had not learned what Eleri had clearly figured out some time ago. Or maybe her senior agent had not only been born into serious money, but also the knowledge that *professional* in Florida in the summer looked a hell of a lot different than *professional* anywhere else.

Not that her senior agent didn't look neat and as though she could easily be the CEO of a major corporation, but Eleri wasn't acting as though she had sweat running down her spine. Neither was Noah. Fucker looked as cool as a cucumber. *Probably a native Floridian.* GJ was supposed to be paying attention to the director, and not to her colleagues' wardrobes. At least the case was interesting enough that she was still staying tuned into the conversation, despite her discomfort.

Slowly, she shifted her position, not liking the way the metal seat trapped her body heat. Tonight, she would need leave time. She had to buy a new wardrobe. She needed some fucking advice. For now, she pushed it aside and kept her gaze on the director, watching as the woman who ran the entirety of the Weeki Wachee State Park spoke directly to Eleri.

Genevieve LeBlanc was red-headed, bright-eyed, slim, and curvy. In other words, she was born to be a mermaid. But as GJ listened, she realized that this woman was no simpering Ariel. She was more a siren bringing the sailors to their deaths, all while laughing and smiling. GJ could easily imagine the woman hoarding the skeletons of her victims in an underwater cave. But she liked Genevieve.

The director had a firm, fair, but take-no-prisoners attitude, and she had said she was relieved that someone was finally looking into the case of Blake Langley. "There was only a short time where I was managing the section of the park where Blake worked. We had just been declared a state park and I had just started managing a full section. So he was there doing his research for at least a year before I became part of it."

The woman was telling them everything she could remember. GJ sensed that Eleri was holding back on questions. So GJ did too, though mentally, she was listing them for when she got an opening.

"He was so gung ho, so dedicated to his research," Genevieve went on. "Then, one day, he hands in his two-week notice, says he's leaving his research behind. He left us his specimens, collection containers, nets, everything. Even *his notebooks.* Then it's his last day and he hugs everyone and we all say good-bye."

Though the story was bittersweet, it wasn't bad. Blake hadn't been fired, and there weren't any angry feelings—at least not in this story. But Genevieve was waving her hands as she spoke, gesturing as though she were angry about this. "I couldn't figure out what would make him abandon the work. And he *didn't* leave the data."

GJ felt her own eyebrows perk up at that, the need to jump in welling up in her chest. She couldn't wait any longer for Eleri to take the lead. "Did the notebooks belong with the park?" She waited a beat, and then explained. "I mean, the research was conducted here. This was a state park at the time, right? So does the state own or have access to the data that Langley collected?"

GJ knew all about this. In many cases, federal grants were given with strings. With corporate grants, the research and data often belonged to the parent corporation that paid for it. There were always special provisions so the researchers could publish under their own names, but they seldom fully owned the work they had done. State grants tended to have fewer strings, but GJ struggled to believe that a grad student had done fully autonomous work at a state-supported park.

"Blake Langley's numbers should have stayed here, yes." Genevieve looked at her. "They were supposed to. Between the fact that he was a student at a state university and that his grant money was federal and specific to this park, we should have retained all of it for our own research. Honestly, we have most of the data, but he didn't hand in the last of it." Genevieve shifted her glance to the other agents. "That's mostly why I stayed in touch with him. I'd love to say I was just a good friend or a friendly boss, but he ran off with data that was ours. We at least deserved to keep a copy of it."

Interesting, GJ thought. According to Eleri and Donovan's reports, Allison had supposedly stayed in touch with Langley as well. GJ waited for Genevieve to give the magic number. She didn't have to wait long.

"He corresponded with me for about two weeks—"

There it was. The same timeframe Allison Caldeira had given.

"—and he said that the new job wanted to look at his data. That he'd been hired to continue the work but in a corporate-funded setting. He was going to have more money and free reign. It's the only reason I could imagine that he would have abandoned a PhD. His project was already so close to completion, and he was passionate about conservation."

Eleri didn't seem to mind that GJ had taken over the questioning, and maybe it was better that she did. Eleri had admitted she was too close to the case, though GJ was surprised her senior agent had said so in front of the new guy. NightShade agents weren't keen on making close friends wherever they went. Hell, GJ was only in the NightShade division because she'd figured them out. She had no special skills of her own—unless you counted the ability to read data like text.

She watched Noah now as he sat back in the awful chair, his eyes watching Genevieve, his expression kind but neutral. GJ had the impression he was taking in everything.

"And after two weeks?" GJ pressed.

"Radio silence." Genevieve shrugged as though she had nothing. Then she suddenly paused, frowned, looked over her shoulder for a moment, and turned back to the agents.

When GJ tilted her head as though to ask what had happened, Genevieve merely said, "I thought someone tapped me on the shoulder. Oh, well. Blake, while he was here, was talkative, open, and friendly. He left quickly, though, and then once he was gone, he kept in touch briefly, and then just stopped."

Genevieve's hands were flat on the table. She was leaning forward, offering an information dump, simply because she was excited that someone was finally investigating. At least that's how she appeared: calm but angry, informed but understanding that she was missing pieces as she dug up the past.

"So the radio silence wasn't something you would have expected from Blake?"

Then those bright eyes honed in on GJ, and for a moment, GJ could imagine a smile and a singing voice to match.

"Absolutely not. I would never have expected Blake to ignore us. I expected him to write back with data and conclusions from his new job. I expected him to share with us. We deal in conservation. Every bit of information helps us get grants, keep the park open, and fight legislation that harms the habitat. We are prime wetlands. We are a karst aquifer, and our park is necessary for the continuation of at least fifteen different species."

The director took a breath. She might not be preaching to the choir per se, but she'd sidelined herself into an impassioned speech. "Anyway, Blake knew all that and was a champion of the land. So when he wouldn't even respond to simple requests, I thought it was odd. I tried to find him a couple of times over the years and I got nothing. Just a few years ago, I tried again. I wanted to let him know we had moved one of the offices and found his files. They're ours, but he also would still have access to all of it. His silence didn't make sense."

After a moment, presumably to let the director unwind, Eleri finally leaned forward. "What exactly was he researching?"

Genevieve looked at the three of them as though she were making a decision. GJ could tell when the woman made it. "I don't remember exactly. But I can show you."

CHAPTER 16

Eleri stood to the corner of the room, tapping on her phone, as GJ and Noah sat at the small table. Silently, they flipped through the work left behind by Blake Langley.

Genevieve had been called away. As director of the park, she was needed to put out fires all over the place. Eleri remembered rarely seeing the director when she'd been employed here. Weeki Wachee Springs seemed even bigger now, and she wasn't surprised that the FBI agents had temporarily lost the director. In fact, Eleri was grateful for the amount of time Genevieve had been able to give them.

She was also glad the woman seemed to have no problems leaving them alone in a room with all this information at their fingertips. Though Genevieve had pulled Blake Langley's work and laid it out for them, other notebooks, thumb drives, specimen containers and more waited for prying eyes to check them out. Genevieve seemed to offer a blanket trust. Whether it was the FBI badges, or her own personal history with Eleri, none of them questioned it.

Now, Eleri felt the hate boiling up for the tiny screen in front of her as she tapped on it with her thumbs. In case sending text messages wasn't difficult enough, trying to look up scientific papers on the tiny keyboard was positively maddening.

She'd found and saved several papers with Blake Langley's name on them. So far, he didn't turn up as the primary researcher on any. So Eleri hadn't looked too carefully. She would put them together later, with GJ's help—and maybe also with Noah's—and see if they could get a picture of what Blake's work was, by looking at what other researchers' works he had chosen to take part in.

The FBI maintained online databases that allowed access to paid, peer-reviewed works for Donovan and her. She was searching in JAMA, NCBI, NOAA, and more. Though she hadn't expected to use her scientific background in the FBI, it seemed the majority of her work now relied on it in some way or another.

Across the room, GJ made a huffing noise. She'd been sitting but then stood sharply, as though suddenly irritated, walked around a little bit, and eventually gave in and took off the lightweight sport jacket she'd been wearing. Eleri had been waiting for that. Clearly, the young woman was too hot, but she was working to stay professional, and Eleri gave her credit for that. "What is it?"

"It looks like he was studying. . . water of various levels of. . . *clarity*. . . and the effects on fish." GJ spoke the words haltingly, as though trying to figure out how to string them together to make scientific sense.

Eleri frowned, and GJ answered without making her ask. "He was studying whether or not dirty or polluted water had an effect on fish." This time, the words came out exasperated. "Why is that a study that got a federal grant? Isn't that too obvious for funding?"

Eleri nodded, but it was Noah who answered. "Maybe it wasn't already done for these particular pollutants. So it's important to do that research, even if it seems basic. When science used to support legislation—like the work here—the research is often just done to have data to back up what's considered an obvious claim. Whereas you and I would easily say, *Polluted water is bad for fish,*' who's done that research?"

It was a good question, Eleri thought. "Hold on."

She tapped on the phone again, no longer looking for Blake Langley's name, but looking for something to tie to the research he was doing at the park. It took a few minutes while Noah and GJ continued to flip through the lab notebooks.

They were examining individual entries, columns of data points, photos, sketches, and more. Eleri didn't envy them the job. In fact, what she envied most was GJ's love for the work. Whether Noah liked it or not, she couldn't tell, but he wasn't complaining.

"I'm not finding much of anything," she said. "Granted, there may be other studies out there that aren't showing up in my databases, but this is pretty extensive and I'm not finding it."

"So," GJ concluded, her finger holding her place in the lab notebook. "No one really studies whether these particular pollutants harm fish. So Blake does it and he makes a PhD out of it."

Noah closed the notebook he was examining and said, "That seems to be the case."

"So what here would make Miranda Industries want to woo him away?" GJ asked.

Eleri admired the euphemism of *wooing* Blake away. Though there was every possibility the information she had was benign and coincidental, what Eleri had strung together in her head was not. In her scenario, Blake had been seduced by Miranda. Miranda had offered him multiple times his expected salary, just as they had done to Allison. The problem was that Eleri didn't *know* any of this yet—it was all conjecture. She tapped herself out a note to follow up.

She continued working through her scenario. Next, Blake goes home, visits his family, and two weeks later he shows up for work at Miranda. After which he's never heard from again.

Eleri added to her list of people to interview, because like assumptions about whether these pollutants harmed fish, her assumptions about Blake couldn't be stood on. She needed data to back this up or prove her theory wrong.

"Well," Noah hopped in with a new topic, his voice quiet. "What about Genevieve? Do you like her? Did she seem solid and honest when you worked here? And what do you think now?"

"Can I ask you the same question first?" Eleri posed to both of them. "I'd like your unvarnished and unbiased opinions about her before I give you mine."

Easily acquiescing, Noah looked between them. "I thought she seemed solid. She believes somebody should have investigated Blake's disappearance long before now. And she didn't startle easily—so I would conclude she wasn't hiding much of anything."

Eleri agreed and turned to GJ, who added her own two cents. "She didn't seem to know enough about the research. Is that because of the position she held at the time? Or is it because she was holding back?"

Great question, Eleri thought. "I can't say for sure, but I suspect it's because of her position. Still, we should look into it." She tapped her fingers on the phone again, leaving herself yet another note. "But if I remember correctly, she had a combination of economics and conservation degrees. Her conservation degrees seemed more the way public health looks at medicine. So I don't think she was doing the same kind of research or work that Blake was. I think she held a master's in it —it might be a PhD by now. But I don't think that she had the kind of research background that he had, either. So I didn't find it odd that she wasn't able to read his notebooks the way you or I can."

GJ nodded, seeming to accept that. But Eleri continued, "What that means is, we need to get a good bead on Genevieve's background and make sure that my memory from over a decade ago is correct. And if it's not, we need to figure out what it means."

The conversation stalled out for a little bit then, and they all buried their noses back into their work.

"This may be something. . . Look." Noah held up a page of photos that ranged from Blake collecting oysters, to clear bins full of sea water and oysters, to open and dissected oysters.

Just like Allison's notes.

CHAPTER 17

Donovan didn't know how long it would take to get his heavy breathing under control. His chest was still heaving. With the emotions roiling through his system, he could feel the bones in his face start to shift beneath his skin. It was happening, whether he willed it or not.

That terrified him.

When his father was angry, Aidan's face would push forward, his gums would draw back, the teeth seeming longer and sharper. His eyebrows would slam down, his face becoming the wolf, though he wouldn't quite fully change. Donovan had known that his father was a monster before he'd known anything else in life.

He asked himself now, *Had his mother known?* Or had she married the man before she found out what he really was?

Donovan couldn't answer that; he might never be able to answer it. And there were too many other questions right now. Like the one that was making his breath draw heavy.

Quickly, he made a decision. Though he wasn't giving up on examining the truth of it, he was going to think of this man who had sent him the box as his brother for now. At least, until he found evidence to the contrary. Everything suggested that the man was actually his full-blooded relation, despite Donovan's continued belief that it was nearly impossible.

Donovan had no doubt the man was Aiden Heath's son. His assailant had smelled like his father, something only genetics could produce. It had felt shocking when Donovan first encountered the idea, but now he was accepting it. If the man was also his mother's son, there were too many options to consider...

Donovan didn't have time to dwell on the exact genetic nature of their relationship. What he needed was to figure out how this man had made it to his teenage years with Donovan's mother at his side.

Maybe she wasn't with him. It was the first option that passed through Donovan's mind. Maybe it was someone else. That was the first lie he told himself as he picked up the photo and examined it again and again and again.

He compared it to the one he carried with him from when he was small. Pulling up the image on his phone, then scrapping that and going for his laptop to get a bigger image, he compared the pictures piece by piece. His memory of his mother matched the woman in the photo. But Eleri always stood firm that human memory was faulty at best, and Donovan had learned to compare by fact.

First, he checked the scarf, but it was the same. More than that, her face, her smile, and the crinkle at the edges of her eyes were all identical. Though Donovan didn't want to admit it, there was something in the way she stood in this picture that was more relaxed and happy than in any picture he'd seen of her before. Regardless, this picture was definitely his mother.

Next, he told himself it had to be photo-shopped. Though he was no expert, he'd been through a few short tech courses at Quantico, and one of them had covered the rudimentary skills necessary to ID pictures that had been altered.

Donovan checked first for changes on the woman herself, wondering how this man could have stuck Donovan's mother into the picture. When that failed to produce any obvious signs, he checked the man's face. Perhaps it was a picture of his mother with someone else, and the face had been altered to look like the teenaged version of this other man. It might even just be a very good cut-and-paste job.

But after thorough examination, Donovan found nothing.

Twenty minutes later, Donovan declared his skills depleted. He couldn't find anything in this photo to indicate that any work had been done to it. It wasn't even digital, it was a print— high gloss, without tampering. That didn't mean it was a film print, though it looked like it might be. Photos could be altered and then printed. Still, Donovan could only say he hadn't found what he was hoping for.

Son of a bitch.

His next thought was that this brother was older than him, rather than younger. That meant this picture could have been taken while Donovan was young, or even before he was born. By that calculation, this guy would be at least ten years older than Donovan, if not more.

Donovan wasn't buying that. He'd seen the other man's face and, more than that, he'd smelled him. Donovan was in his thirties; the man he'd encountered was not in his forties. Trying to reason his way through it, he pulled out his computer, typing information into the search bar, and coming up with what he'd been looking for: The Dunedin Study.

The famous study had followed a group of high school graduates through their class reunions. At each reunion, the returning students had photos taken, gave blood, and had ultraviolet tests of their skin. All to test for aging.

What the study concluded was that people of the same chronological age could vary by large amounts in their biological age. But even after having perused the results,

Donovan could see the data didn't allow for someone ten years older than him to be ten years younger biologically. It was too much of a stretch. And ten was the minimum number of years older that Donovan thought this brother could be. Fifteen or even twenty was more likely, but none of that math worked. Even the smaller options defied the family history he knew.

Donovan could feel his heart pounding harder as he came to conclusions he didn't like. Had this picture been taken after Donovan was born?

To make this work meant Donovan had had an older brother that he didn't know about for seven years. It would have meant that his parents had successfully hid another child from him the entire time he was growing up.

While his mother might have done it, his father never could have pulled it off. Some night, in a fit of anger, Aidan would have yelled at Donovan for not being as good as this older brother, or for being just as worthless. There was no telling what would come out of Aidan Heath's mouth, only that everything eventually would.

The fly-by-night family moves had been happening even before his mother died. *Where would the brother have been?* There had been no brother in the car. There couldn't have been. Donovan had clear memories of sitting next to piles of their family crap.

At the time, he'd thought of it as treasures. But looking back, he was in the backseat buckled in—by his own choice, not his father's—sitting next to garbage bags, swollen with whatever the family could shove in at the last moment. There had been no brother in his small life.

Donovan did not like the only logical conclusions this line of thought was leading him to, and he began to shut it down. There were other things he could do. Besides, he knew he wouldn't hear back from Wade about who might have been in his house, not for several days.

Taking a deep breath and attempting to find some physical—if not mental—calm, he made himself a short checklist of things he could do *now*.

The first, most pressing, thing was to find out exactly who this *brother* was.

And that meant using his FBI data access for his personal use. He could only hope it didn't get him fired.

CHAPTER 18

"**D**onovan, look at this."

He pulled his eyes from his plate and checked out the notebook GJ was sliding toward him.

They all sat in their designated conference room at the FBI branch office in Miami. Eleri had orchestrated a fantastic food delivery, claiming it had been a long day and they needed to eat well. It was still going to be a long haul.

She brought in steaks, stuffed baked potatoes, green vegetables, and even chocolate cake for dessert. Everything but wine.

When it was only himself and Eleri, they could often grab a table in the back of a restaurant and work quietly without worrying about letting the details of the case into the public. But the four of them would be far too conspicuous. Besides, Eleri wanted the papers out, and that meant they were back in the conference room.

So he sat there, not joining the conversation nearly as much as he should, and picked at his steak while Eleri frowned at him. He knew she expected him to make his food disappear before she had her third bite, but he didn't have it in him tonight.

Though his mouth salivated, his stomach turned. Instead of eating, he worked to aim his attention to the talk around him.

He was grateful to Eleri for letting him have the day to himself. Even so, it had not been enough time and—while he had no solid conclusions—what he'd learned was earth-shattering.

Still, his job was here in front of him now and he couldn't afford to lose it. It was no longer about the money, but rather about his identity. He was an FBI agent, and he wasn't sure he remembered how to be anything else. He needed the people at this table—okay, maybe not Kimball, but definitely Eleri and even GJ. It was also about his access to FBI databases, which he knew would find him what he needed faster than anything else.

So he tried to be useful. "I understand that Blake Langley was studying oysters and so was Allison Caldeira. . . but don't lots of people study oysters?"

Around the table, GJ, Eleri, and Noah Kimball all looked at each other. "I guess so," Noah replied. "Maybe we need to find out."

Donovan added, "I remember something from early bio classes about oysters being studied because they're an indicator species, like frogs. So if you want to find if something's wrong with the water, the oysters will be the first ones to show it. They'll have alterations from even low levels of change in the water composition."

"What else?" Eleri asked.

For the first time all day, he laughed. "I don't know. We've just exhausted all of my knowledge about oysters."

"Well," Noah said with a grin, "except that they're delicious."

Donovan shook his head. *They were not.* He didn't say it out loud. This was no time to get into his odd eating proclivities. He wasn't about to tell how he favored red meat, nearly raw. Not in front of Noah Kimball.

GJ had figured out what he was on her own. Donovan was

not going to have that happen again. Westerfield would never let him hear the end of it. So, while he had one job to solve the case, he had a second job now to find his brother. And he also maintained the job he'd had ever since he'd learned what he could do: He could never let them see what he could become.

"So," Eleri replied, tapping out notes on her keyboard and seemingly unconcerned about spilling dinner on it, "one of us needs to learn everything we can about oyster research." She looked around the table like an expectant teacher until her gaze landed on GJ.

GJ nodded reluctantly. "Of course, it's me. I'll do it."

It was nice, Donovan thought, having underlings. He hadn't had any for several years, not since he'd been a medical examiner. And what he was learning from Eleri was that he'd not been good at utilizing subordinates.

"Then again," GJ interrupted, "It's plausible that—even though oysters are an indicator species and might be highly studied—there's still a connection between Allison Caldeira and Blake Langley. Because in a short period of time, during their oyster studies, both of them received letters with exorbitant offers by Miranda industries." GJ paused. "I'll still look into the research. I'm just suggesting there's a likelihood of connection."

Eleri was nodding along. Even Donovan was following GJ's reasoning.

Then Eleri took another bite of her own steak and Donovan realized she might have gotten it for him. *Shit.* He took another bite, chewing slowly as Eleri switched topics.

She looked to Noah Kimball. "How are we coming on Blake Langley?"

"Not good," the young agent replied. Donovan knew now that Noah was not as young as he looked. So far, he seemed solid, but Donovan was still trying to figure out how to leverage that cute baby face in their favor.

"Not good *how?*" Donovan asked, wanting to stay in the conversation.

"I can't find anything. There's no death certificate, but there's no follow-up information, either. No proof of life or even recorded presence. Blake Langley disappears from all records. No social media. After he leaves for the Miranda job, he has no listing on any publications, no articles, no *banking records.* Nothing after that, except for one thing: His driver's license was renewed in his home state of Massachusetts three years later."

Donovan frowned and watched a similar expression grow on Eleri and GJ's faces. "Was he in Massachusetts?" Donovan pushed.

"There's no indication that he was," Noah replied, lifting the edge of a page as though he was checking for info, but Donovan suspected Noah didn't need the notes. "But there's no indication that he was anywhere else, either. Not even internationally."

"Could the driver's license have been renewed by letter?" GJ asked. "Perhaps a family member signed for it, wanting to keep it current."

This time, Noah nodded. "That happens a lot here in Florida. Dead people get their driver's licenses renewed because the spouse returns the paperwork. It's plausible." He made a note. Then Noah took a deep, telling breath—and Donovan became worried.

The Miami agent looked to the three of them for a moment, his eyes landing on Donovan's still partially full plate. "I was waiting until you all finished your dinners. But I have more bad news."

Well, shit, Donovan thought and pushed his plate away. That seemed to be an indicator to Noah to go ahead with his bad information.

"The dive buddy for Allison Caldeira on her last dive was one *Neriah Jones.* Neriah made it back to the boat and reported that she and Allison had become separated, but she said she was unworried. According to the initial report, and Neriah's and Hannah's claims, she and Allison were excellent dive buddies, because they didn't panic. And while they were generally good about staying together, they had become separated before and would simply surface and reconnect at the boat."

Noah stopped for a moment like a teacher assessing his class. He still wasn't looking at any notes. "So it was some period of time before Neriah and the others on the boat developed any real concern for Allison. Hannah, too, had apparently been trying not to worry. But then they mounted an all-out search, and eventually it got dark. And then they reported Allison missing."

Aside from the addition of the name, Donovan couldn't tell where anything was different now. Then Noah dropped his bomb. "During her initial interview, the Marine Services Bureau reports that Neriah Jones seemed nervous and jumpy. And as of five days ago, no one has heard from her."

CHAPTER 19

E leri ended her day as she began it, knocking on Donovan's hotel room door.

When he let her in this time, he appeared less tense but more bedraggled. Pushing past him, she headed into the room, waiting until he closed the door behind her before she asked, "What did you find?"

She didn't ask what was going on. She knew. She would have checked earlier, but she wasn't about to air his strange familial laundry in front of GJ and Noah. God forbid Noah asked how Donovan knew this was his long-lost brother. That would get dicey. So she'd held her tongue.

While Donovan was used to being stoic, today he hadn't hidden any of his emotions well. Eleri only hoped that Noah didn't pick up on much, including Donovan's half-eaten steak during dinner.

Looking at him now, it was clear that whatever Donovan had found, it hadn't been butterflies and rainbows. In answer to her question, he waved his hand at the tiny table, which was buried under whatever he'd been searching through. Half the bed, too, was covered in papers, documents he'd produced from their little portable printer. The thing was handy, but obnoxious. By the sheer volume of paperwork he'd produced, she knew he'd been dedicated.

"This is him." Donovan handed Eleri the picture she'd seen that morning, the one he'd snatched back from her.

This time she was allowed to examine it thoroughly. "Who is she? Is this your mother?"

On Donovan's nod, she launched into a barrage of other questions. "But he's got to be at least fifteen—maybe twelve or thirteen, if he was big for his age—in this picture. And if that's your mother. . . He'd have to be much older than you."

"Exactly." Donovan let the word out on a rough sigh. Apparently, she'd asked all the same questions he did.

"Any conclusions?"

"No. I mean, I smelled him. He didn't smell like a forty-year-old. He has to be younger." Jamming his hands into his pockets, Donovan paced a tight circle in the tiny space. "I examined the photo as best I could, to see if it was photoshopped or altered in any way. Will you look?" He faced her now, his expression imploring her for help, or at least confirmation.

Eleri nodded. It was the least she could do. Going over to the small table, she held the photo under the light and ran her fingers across the surface, though she certainly did not expect any physical alterations to it. In the end, she said, "This looks pretty authentic, but we need to send it to someone much better at this than either of us."

She noticed the expression that flitted across Donovan's face and decided to ask first. "Are you okay with letting the photo go so we can get it to a specialist? I'm sure there's someone here in the Miami branch office. It doesn't have to go far."

His nod was short and terse, as though the motion hurt.

"If that's your mother, and if that's him and he's younger than you—then your mother must have lived another decade or so beyond when you thought she died. That doesn't make any sense." She, too, was shaking her head. She knew enough of Donovan's personal history to know that math didn't work. Then Eleri snapped her fingers and she could feel her face light up. "Did your mother have an identical twin?"

That seemed to give Donovan pause, and Eleri was grateful she had the ability to introduce something new into the conversation, rather than simply running him over the same rough tracks he'd been dragging himself across all day. "A twin could have posed for this picture. Hell, a twin could have birthed him—"

"With my father?"

Eleri only paused and let the "maybe" show on her face. What she'd heard about Aidan Heath made it plausible. The glimpses she'd gotten of Donovan's past made her think that, if his mother had an identical twin, Aidan would have tried to bed both of them. Donovan didn't dispute her, so she added, "That would explain the genetic scent identifiers. And even the scarf. Maybe they both had one?"

"I don't know. She's from Calcutta. She always had the scarf, but I don't know where it's from. If she had a twin, the twin would be here in the US. . . right?"

"I don't know. We need to find out where this picture was taken."

When Donovan only nodded, she continued.

"Okay," Eleri replied, trying to keep a positive note in her voice. "Let's add that to our list of things to find out."

She had no idea how they might find birth information on a woman older than fifty and from a poor area in India. If she wasn't born in a hospital—and there was a good chance she wasn't—Eleri had no clue how to trace that information at all. But for now, she nodded as though it was something she could do.

Pocketing the picture, she tilted her head slightly, feeling out the situation. When Donovan seemed to have no protests to her suggestion, she asked about the scarf. "That fabric in the box—are you certain that was her scarf?"

"It's the same one she's wearing in that picture."

The scarf sat on the tabletop at an odd angle, almost as though Donovan had dropped it and didn't want to touch it again. So Eleri respected whatever he was doing, and didn't touch it herself, but held the picture down close. "It does look like a good match."

He shook his head. "It's not a good match, it's the same scarf. It smells like her."

"What?" Eleri stood up sharply, picture still in her hand. "Your mother actually wore this scarf? Where would your brother have gotten it?" Then she stopped herself. "I guess he would get it from her, since she was wearing it around him."

But Donovan was shaking his head. He explained his entire thought process and his subsequent request for Wade to check his home. Eleri found herself joining his frustration. It would take several days to get an answer.

She wanted to ask him to drop this for now, to focus on the case they shared, and to pick this back up when they were done. But cases ran crazy. It might be three months before he could come back to this. And Eleri's estimation was that this brother, whoever he was, was batshit crazy.

"He's already sent you mail, which means he knows your name and address and your relationship. What do you know about him?"

She watched as her partner almost crumbled. "That's just it. I can't find *anything*. I've looked through the FBI databases of everybody who got processed after the take-down at Darcelle's store in New Orleans."

Eleri almost hesitated to ask, but she prompted him to finish, though she knew the answer wasn't good.

"Nothing! None of the mug shots matched him. I've pulled

old shots from the New Orleans district. It looks as if he's never been arrested."

Donovan paused and Eleri entertained a new thought. "Or maybe one of the Dauphine sisters erased the records."

Donovan's eyes widened. His head nodded, as though the information physically hit him and made him move a little. "I hadn't considered that possibility."

"But if that's the case," Eleri said, "then the information may very well have vanished, no matter where we look for it."

"I don't even know where to check next." His hands went back into his pockets, as he had been periodically waving them around and then shoving them back down as though to stop himself. "I spent a good portion of my afternoon combing through mug shots by hand. I tried facial recognition programs, too. But I've got nothing. I tried the surrounding areas; I looked in Baton Rouge. Same, nothing."

Eleri's heart hurt for her partner. Even if he found the brother, he wouldn't likely find family there. She knew she was his family now, and she needed to act more like it. It was hard, being both FBI partner and family member, but she was trying. Wanting to be helpful, she wracked her brain. "Maybe I can ask Darcelle."

Donovan's eyes flew wide, and he stilled for the first time. "You know how to get in contact with her?"

"Not really," Eleri replied. "But I have a feeling I could conjure her."

"Jesus. Darcelle Dauphine is the *last* person we should be conjuring. Besides, if you do it, she'll be pissed."

"Sure," Eleri offered, sounding far more confident than she was, "but she might be willing to trade information on your brother for me to let her go."

Eleri thought she heard him mutter, *assuming you can do that,* which was solid. She *wasn't* certain she could do it. She was nowhere near as practiced a witch as Darcelle or any of the sisters were. But she was determined to remain hopeful, so she indicated that she could. "I have blood that we know for a fact can summon a Dauphine."

She left it at that for the night. "Donovan, we have to get up early and hunt down Neriah Jones. But I want you to know—this is an option."

Donovan nodded at her. They had a path, something they could do.

It was nothing she *wanted* to do, certainly not with Miami agent Noah Kimball watching over her shoulder. Honestly, she wasn't even willing to tell GJ about this. It would have to remain strictly between her and Donovan. They would show this to no one who hadn't already been exposed to it in New Orleans, which meant. . . no one.

She wished Donovan a good night, hoping that he slept well. It was the best she could offer right now. But as she pulled the door closed behind her, she clicked her jaw shut on an idea she almost put voice to.

Donovan had been looking for his brother by his *face*. But it wasn't working. It occurred to her to look by *name*.

She wasn't confident she would find anything. But if he was Donovan's full brother, then they should definitely check for anyone in New Orleans with the last name *Heath*.

CHAPTER 20

G J ran her hand along the surface of the old sideboard pushed against the wall. It was definitely an antique and it was gathering dust like one. She would have counted it as part of an estate collection, except for the fact that it didn't match any of the other furniture in the apartment.

Neriah Jones had not been wealthy by any measure, but her small apartment was on the second floor, and the wide windows let in plenty of morning light. GJ wondered now if prying eyes had come in along with the sunbeams. With a purposefully vague gesture, she checked out the window, but saw no other units with a direct line of sight to this one.

Turning her eyes back to the apartment itself, she tried to make sense of the mishmash of belongings. It seemed Neriah spent all her money on dive equipment, swimsuits, and an extensive superhero DVD collection. The place did have a haphazard charm to it.

GJ kept that thought to herself. To Noah, she said, "Dust. It's everywhere. Looks like no one's been here for a while. I'd guess it's about the same timeframe as the report of Neriah going missing."

They'd pulled the official paperwork, though it didn't carry much weight, having been filed by her next-door neighbor. The Miami Dade Police Department had done their due diligence and contacted Neriah's parents. They turned out to be absolute pieces of crap.

Though they'd agreed to try to get in touch with their daughter, they hadn't returned any other MDPD phone calls.

Noah agreed with GJ's dust statement, and she asked, "What do you think is the possibility that her parents did get in touch with her and simply haven't informed Miami Dade because they know she's found?"

She watched as one of his blond eyebrows slowly rose, exhibiting a control she didn't know was possible. "You lost me at the *possibility that her parents called her.* The notes alone make them seem unlikely to be any help." He sighed, clearly not wanting to deal with the elder Joneses. "But I say we call them today. Maybe they'll answer if the call comes from the phone here." He held up a handset that he'd found. "It was next to the laptop. And it's dead."

GJ glanced at the table top he was examining. It looked like Neriah used the small dining space as a desk, and that she ate at the bar that bracketed the even smaller kitchen.

He held up the handset with two gloved fingers. "Do you want to check anything? I'm going to need to put it on the charger for a bit before we can make that call."

Shaking her head, GJ sent him off to search for the charger. The place wasn't messy, but it was cluttered. Too many things in too little space. Shiny oxygen tanks sat next to the antique sideboard, and together, they took up the entire wall. Instead of having a curved, wood mirror, the antique hosted a smallish, flatscreen TV above it.

Noah called out that he'd found the charger. He motioned to the corner and a tall, triangular shelf that reached almost to the ceiling and held far more things than it was intended to. GJ watched as he gingerly set the phone into its cradle, probably afraid this would be the last straw and the whole shelving unit would come tumbling down.

When it held, she turned away, skirted the edge of the bar, and hit the kitchen. The oven was empty, the dishwasher non-existent. The stovetop held no heat, though she hadn't expected any. She knew she would have been remiss if she didn't check. Finally, she opened the fridge.

Turning to Noah, she called out, "No one's opened this in a while. There are a few food items here going out of date, and they're not shoved to the back." These were things she'd been taught to look for at Quantico, and she was still fresh enough to remember to check each one.

When she turned back, she found Noah had seated himself at the makeshift desk. Gingerly, he flipped open the laptop, but then he looked to her. "How are you with computers?"

"Passable," she replied. She could do what she needed for her research. She could plug her data into several programs and calculate standard deviations, chi squares, things like that. But forensic computing? Nope. Accounting and computing were well beyond her forensic limits.

"Is it password protected?" she asked, even as he laid his fingers almost gleefully across the keys. Turning back to the fridge, GJ hoped to glean more clues.

"Looks like," came the reply, and she figured he'd be a while trying to crack it.

With her head down in the smaller-than-usual fridge, she discovered Neriah was a vegetarian, or at least her refrigerator was. The milk was about to turn—just about right if she'd bought it in the week before she disappeared. The woman drank too many sodas, but not much beer. . . and there was nothing of real value here.

"I'm going to go check the bedroom," she called over her shoulder.

"Uh huh." He didn't look up.

But as she watched for a moment, GJ saw him hold his fingers just over the keyboard, almost as though doing some kind of psychic healing. Even though he didn't appear to type like everyone else—with fingers bouncing around the keys—she saw that, on the computer screen, dots entered the password box and the screen opened.

Damn, she thought, *he was good.*

She opened the bedroom closet and thumbed through swimsuits neatly hung on hangers, as though this were a store rather than a closet. *It must be a Florida thing, or a diver thing,* GJ thought. Half the closet was swimsuits and the other half held more conventional clothing. A few outfits appeared relatively professional-looking, but the remainder were sloppier than anything GJ had probably ever owned, even when she used to go on archaeological digs.

With a sigh and some irritation that she'd not yet found a good smoking gun, she'd headed for the bathroom. First, she checked shampoo, toothpaste, and toothbrush.

Yes! This was what she'd been looking for. Just a few, small white stains marred an empty spot in the drawer. So GJ began to scrounge. There was no hairbrush, either.

Once she'd identified missing pieces in the bathroom, she began examining the mix of items more carefully. She was looking for the kinds of things someone wouldn't leave behind if they planned to be gone for a while.

She found a pack of birth control pills, but the date indicated they were more than a year old. There was no current set, but that didn't mean anything.

There was also no suitcase—not that GJ could find—and she certainly couldn't tell if anything was missing from the closet. Giving up, she headed back to the dresser in the bedroom where she'd seen a few framed pictures on display.

She pulled one of Neriah and a friend, obviously taken in the apartment's living room. Heading back out, she held it up to compare and quickly noticed something. "Noah. This picture has five oxygen tanks, but there are only three here." As he came over to join her, she pointed and kept talking. "There are two separate pieces that go on the top of them—the spider things. . ."

"First stage," he filled in for her. "And there are two BCDs in the picture, as well."

When she clearly didn't understand, he pointed to two black vests that sat upright near the tanks in the photo. The wall was now empty where they'd sat. It sounded like Noah at least knew *something* about diving.

"And look at this," he said. He stepped to the small table and turned the computer around, revealing what appeared to be online bank statements. "There's no activity on any of her cards since two days after the interview. However, the last thing she did was withdraw a very large amount of cash."

"Shit," GJ said out loud. Neriah hadn't just left. She'd ghosted.

CHAPTER 21

E leri kept her gaze on Donovan while she spoke to GJ on the phone. "No, that sounds right. What did they say?"

Aiming the phone outward, she put it on speaker, letting Donovan listen in. Even though his attention seemed directed elsewhere, she kept going on as though he were fully present.

"We dialed the parents from the charged home phone," GJ told her. "A woman answered, presumably the mother, who chidingly told *Neriah—*" Eleri could hear the air quotes in GJ's tone, "—'It's about time you called. You fucked it up again, and made your friends worried. The police called us.'"

"Wow. Oh," Eleri responded. She knew bad parents existed. Hell, she'd seen glimpses of Donovan's childhood, and that was beyond bad. But every time she encountered people who treated their children this way, it took her aback. Apparently, even when the contact was only second hand, it had the same effect. "So, I guess they're not going to be part of the search efforts then, are they?"

"They seemed to have no interest in it," GJ replied.

"All right. Can you and Noah follow up on that? See what you can do today to find Neriah Jones. . ." Eleri adjusted her tone so she seemed to ask rather than order. "Donovan and I are going to take Blake Langley's information and compare it to Allison's to see if we can find any connections."

There was a pause, and it took Eleri a moment to catch on. "Would you rather check through the data yourself? After all, you are the best at this."

"Actually. . ." GJ's tone made Eleri wonder. "I'd rather *not* do it. I'm already good at that, and I'm not an analyst. I'm an agent now. I'd like to do more. . . agent-y things."

Eleri laughed at the pause and stutter as GJ searched for and failed to find the correct word. "Sounds good. So, unless you have objections, you and Noah Kimball are hunting down Neriah today."

"Well, the good news is that she took out cash," GJ continued. "A large sum, in person, from the bank. We're going to check the footage there first—" there was a pause and Eleri imagined GJ was getting an agreement from Noah. "—and if that matches, we're going on the assumption that she left of her own volition."

"Good plan. I hope she's safe."

After hanging up with GJ, Eleri turned back to Donovan. "Let's get into the Bureau databases and do what we can to locate anything on Neriah, and also anything on Allison Caldeira or Blake Langley. While we're at it, if we happen to check on any males with the last name *Heath* located in New Orleans, so be it."

He didn't say anything in response, but his gaze caught hers, and she saw the thanks there.

Ensconced in the conference room with a soda and a bag of chips, Eleri buckled down. It did not escape her attention that, despite her offer, Donovan remained foodless. He was going to start losing weight at the rate he was going. If she hadn't already noticed how much this issue with his brother was bothering him, this would have done it.

Pulling out one of Blake Langley's lab notebooks, she began reading it simply to get a feel for what he was studying. The document, though handwritten in only passable penmanship, was a beautiful thing. He'd recorded *everything*, starting with hypothesis and null hypothesis. He'd added references on the second page. The notes, which were not in any style that Eleri could identify, made it easy to locate articles that he was using to back his theory. She found she still liked Blake Langley.

In the oldest lab notebook, his hypothesis was that the pollutants in the water could be detected in oysters upon dissection. He later posited that specific pollutants could be tested and verified, and that perhaps even the quantity of pollutant could be measured by correspondent numbers in the deceased oysters.

As a secondary hypothesis, he then suggested the wild oyster population would decline as a result. Next, depending on level of pollutant, he suggested this might have an exponential effect on the ecology as the oysters declined in numbers, and thus the pollutants increased—because the oysters weren't able to filter them all out—and the oyster numbers would again decrease.

Eleri felt herself shrugging at the paper's conclusions which, of course, made perfect sense. But she remembered their discussion about how research had to be done, even when things seemed obvious.

Flipping through the notebook, she noticed pages filled with pictures of tanks of oysters. The photos were color printed on mid-quality paper, with just enough clarity for her to see the project, but no more. Blake apparently cultivated the creatures and kept them in the tanks for several months prior to beginning the experiment—to prove that these individual oysters were stable and thriving in this environment prior to the introduction of pollutants. *Nice*, she thought. He'd already countered possible arguments against his conclusion.

She continued flipping through the information, mostly

ignoring the data and trusting that Langley had done it correctly. As she got toward the end of this first set of experiments, she found that he had concluded what he set out to prove. Whether that was experimenter bias—that Langley had introduced a series of small tweaks, either on purpose or unconsciously, to arrive at the conclusion he wanted—or if it was merely that the conclusion was so obvious that he couldn't be wrong, Eleri didn't know.

Next to her, Donovan tapped away on his keyboard. So far, it seemed he hadn't found much. He wasn't commenting on anything. But as she was opening the second notebook, he called out, "Shit, El. You were right. I found him. Bodi Heath. I hadn't even tried looking for *Heath* yet." He shook his head. "It didn't occur to me. I mean, I understand he's my father's child, but it never occurred to me that he would be using my dad's the last name. . . I don't think my father even knew—knows—about him."

Eleri nodded, trying to be supportive. There was nothing she could say. Though her sister Emmaline had gone missing, she'd never doubted who her family was.

"So here's the kicker—"

That got her attention.

"His last name used to be Bannerjee. But about five years ago, he changed it to Heath."

CHAPTER 22

E leri jumped up and leaned over Donovan, peering past his shoulder at the screen.

"That's him?" She pointed to the picture that appeared alongside the other Louisiana Drivers License information. When they'd run into each other in New Orleans, the man had not made much of an impression on her—not enough to remember his face. In fact, what she remembered about that night was the woman with the dark hair in tight braids, who showed up out of nowhere and saved their asses. Their individual assailants did not stick in her mind.

She remembered Carson and Cabot. She remembered the faces she had worked to memorize from mugshots, but this Bodhi Bannerjee/Bodi Heath guy hadn't been among them. She would have remembered a "Heath." It wasn't until later that she had spoken to Donovan and understood what had startled him so much that day.

"That's definitely him," Donovan replied. "He was a little harder to find, because there's no birth certificate under the name Heath."

"But now that you do know his name, his Social Security

number, and even his previous name, you should be able to find his birth certificate."

"I'm already on it." Donovan wasn't looking at her, just speaking straight ahead, tapping on the keys. He had already pulled up several sites before she'd managed to pop out of her chair. "It will all depend on whether Bannerjee was his birth name or another name change."

Eleri nodded, thinking that people who changed their names once often changed them more than once. Women who divorced and remarried, or retook their maiden names, accounted for most of the names changes they encountered. Men who changed their names often did so for various other reasons—sometimes to go into hiding, or to throw creditors off the scent. And if they did it once, they would likely do it again.

Beside her, Donovan suddenly went still.

"It looks like it's here."

Eleri stopped, almost holding her breath, to see what Donovan would find.

The FBI had access to all kinds of data, so they could pull up a birth certificate as fast as they could find a driver's license. She paused for a moment, wondering if Westerfield, or anyone in Miami, was going to ding them for doing personal research.

She should care. But she didn't. "The good news," she was saying as Donovan typed, "is that it's not a common name in the US. At least, it's not one that I'm familiar with."

"Me either." He was still looking at the screen and not her. There were some international names, like Singh and Li, that were other countries' equivalents of Smith and Jones. And even in the US, there would be too many Garcias to count. But probably not Bannerjees.

"Here," he said. "California. San Diego."

"How will you know if it's the right birth certificate?" she asked. But Donovan tapped a few more keys, seeming not to have the answer to that until the digital copy appeared on the screen.

"Holy fuck! Eleri? That's my mother's name."

Leaning over to read specifically where he pointed, she saw that yes, indeed, Amisha Bannerjee was listed as the mother of Bodi Bannerjee. She also saw the birth date was about eight years after Donovan's. She was opening her mouth to say so when Donovan seemed to catch that as well.

Turning, he finally looked at her, his neck craning up to where she was standing over him. The bleakness in his eyes made her heart stutter.

"That date—it's after she died, Eleri. My mother gave birth to another son. *After she died.*" He punctuated each word.

Eleri could only shake her head at him. It didn't make any sense. She didn't even know where to find answers to something like this. She spoke the first thing that came into her brain. "How common is her name?"

"Not common," he said. "But not uncommon either. And we didn't get here by finding *her*; we got here by tracing *him*. That was his face on the New Orleans register. Under *Heath.* And why would this kid become *Heath*? If his father was unlisted and his mother was a Bannerjee?"

"Because his mother was actually a Heath, and so was his father," Eleri supplied with a sigh, acknowledging that this new information was more than a coincidence.

"There's no other way for this to have happened. Though we found him under Heath in New Orleans, that was his *face*, El. That was him. And so is this."

At that point, she was forced to concede. There was no workaround, no error in their reasoning that had led to somebody else with a similar name. "Okay. Our next order of business is to look for a death certificate on your mother. Because if she died, then some other woman used her name and

Social Security number and produced a child. And that child later posed for a picture with a woman with your mother's face."

"I don't know how that would happen. Stealing her identity, sure. But her face? That was *her* in the pictures," Donovan replied, seemingly at a loss.

"I still have the identical twin theory," she offered. "But honestly, it's not holding much water."

With a nod and a quick glance away, he went back to tapping on the keys.

Doing the only thing she could, Eleri stayed beside him when she should have been doing research on their assigned case. It definitely warranted their attention, but so did Donovan's personal matters, and she was unable to turn away.

Fifteen minutes later, they gave up.

"There's no death certificate, Eleri." His expression was even bleaker than when they started. "I looked all through the years before and after she died. Now that I'm thinking on it, how do I know that my mother actually died?"

"Did you see her body at the funeral?"

"No." He stood up and threw his hands in the air, as though trying to physically let off some of his agitation. "There was no funeral. My father was such a piece of shit. He told me she died, and we left. Or if there was a funeral, I didn't go to it."

"Oh fuck, Donovan." The pressure in her chest was almost too much to bear and she couldn't imagine how he felt. "So all this time you believed your mother was dead just because your father told you."

Whirling in a tight, angry circle, he planted his hands on his hips, his gaze not catching hers. "I don't know why I never questioned the source before. But now, looking at it, it seems so obvious. Why would he tell the truth about that? He never told the truth about anything else."

"So what happened to her? Any ideas?"

"I don't know." It was a whisper, stark and cold.

Eleri wanted to say, *I can't imagine how you feel.* But unfortunately, she could come close, and it had taken her twenty-plus years to put her own demons to rest. She didn't wish that on Donovan.

"I need to go. I need to just take a walk. I'll. . . stay in the building," he told her, but he was already to the door before she called out.

"Donovan. Do me a favor. Walk downstairs to the vending machine. Get yourself a soda. Drink it and come back. Okay? I know you need time. And I know you need to process—but you also need to eat something."

He was out the door before he said yes. Eleri could only hope he would heed her words.

Her breath still coming heavily, she tried to sit back down and look at the evidence of the case. She had to do this. Westerfield would jump all over them if this case didn't progress quickly enough, and now it seemed she needed to pull Donovan's weight as well as her own. She was barely able to think straight.

Trying to do the easiest task first meant opening Blake Langley's notebooks again. The second book was a continuation of the first, and she flipped through it as quickly as she could, knowing she wouldn't process anything anyway.

But the fourth notebook yielded new information. He had begun a new study. This time, instead of studying standard pollutants, he was looking for the effects of *cocaine and heroin* on the oysters.

That information gave Eleri pause. It was possibly the only thing that could have pulled her brain away from the scramble with Donovan, his brother, and now his mother.

Oysters with cocaine and heroin?

She flipped back through previous notebooks, finding where he noted anomalies in oysters that he had found. But how had

Schedule One drugs gotten into oysters in Weeki Wachee Springs? That didn't make any sense.

She began scrambling through the pages backward, looking for whatever might have triggered this research. She checked where Blake had referenced previous research and hopped online to look up individual papers. But though the research referenced cocaine and heroin, none of them mentioned the area or his method of oyster collection.

She was horribly confused until she remembered some sage advice from her first senior partner when she was new to the FBI. J. Raymer Binkley was the kind of man who wore cowboy boots and spoke in cute phrases. He'd also been full of great advice. He'd told her, *When you're walking on a path that's not yielding anything, turn around and go the other way.*

So she did that now. Ignoring the research prior to Langley's change of direction, she decided to check what he'd written after it. But the notebook he'd started with the new hypothesis turned out to be his last one. It was barely three quarters full.

And it ended right when he got the offer from Miranda Industries.

Eleri was starting to smell something.

CHAPTER 23

G J leaned forward in the chair, looking at the monitor that the bank manager had swung around to face her and Noah.

"She matched our photo," the manager offered to explain why he had handed several thousand dollars cash to the young woman in question. "We had no reason to believe it wasn't her."

"That's her," GJ replied, hoping to set the man's nerves at ease. Surely the FBI showing up in your branch and demanding to see your footage from the previous week wasn't comfortable. Though she and Noah had tried to wait politely at the back of the snaking line when they walked in, they must have clearly looked like Feds. They'd been immediately swept into an office, as if they were making the customers nervous.

Once their ID's had been verified through the Miami FBI Branch Office, the manager was all help, immediately pulling up footage from almost a week earlier. He had no trouble finding Neriah withdrawing her money.

Though GJ didn't say so, this was exactly what she had expected to see. Neriah appeared somewhat nervous, occasionally glancing over her shoulder, but wasn't quite twitchy enough to alert the bank staff.

"Is there anything else we can get for you?" the manager asked, interrupting her perusal of the video. He appeared a little nervous, too, like the young woman in the video, but he was probably just worried about making missteps. GJ didn't get the impression he was trying to hide anything.

"Can we have a copy of this section of the footage, please?"

In a few moments, she'd watched him hit send on an email with the video clip attached, and they were out the door. Someone at the Bureau could analyze the hours of footage before and after Neriah's visit to determine if there was anything else of importance. GJ was not up for that.

Noah waited until GJ climbed in the passenger side, starting the engine before he asked, "What did you think of her on the video?"

"She looked a little bit rattled, but not enough that it made me think someone was outside and threatening her." Though she didn't say it out loud, GJ thought that what she'd seen of Neriah so far indicated the young woman was highly adventurous. She had framed photos of herself and friends riding roller coasters and bungee jumping. She also was a certified scuba diver and a martial artist.

When she included the smiling faces in the pictures and the messenger chains that had popped up on Neriah's computer screen, GJ had to conclude that *that woman* would have leaned over the counter at the bank and said, "I've been forced to come in here and withdraw all my money."

No one else was in the bank at the same time she was—which may have been the plan, since she was leaving with so much cash. Or maybe she simply didn't want to be found. GJ was also putting the facts together to conclude that Neriah was smart.

The bank could have locked down, had she said something

that alerted them. So GJ concluded that Neriah had gone there of her own accord, afraid, and leading anyone following her to this point. Once she left the bank, she practically disappeared. Her phone was already off, her car hadn't returned home, and she wasn't even leaving a credit card trail.

"That's my impression, too," Noah piggybacked onto her thoughts.

They had combed through Neriah's phone records for exactly this reason, first checking through her email to get her monthly billing, then pulling up any statements and contacting the company. Her monthly billing hadn't revealed much beyond her plan type, but it did get GJ the provider so she could request further information.

They had anticipated this outcome. The interesting thing, GJ thought, had been watching Noah hack all the emails and records. In the FBI, she'd been taught what to look for. But until now, she hadn't really thought about how much more security there was on an electronic document. Sure, a good hacker could get to them from across the country. But someone in your home actively looking for them—like, say, an FBI agent—could no longer simply rifle through the stack of bills on your desk or pick the lock on your file cabinet.

"Where are we going next?" Noah asked her as he sat at the edge of the bank lot, waiting to make a turn one way or the other.

"Back to her apartment is my guess. I'm thinking we start with interviewing the neighbors to see if any of them know anything." She sucked in a breath, wishing she had a better lead than just flashing a picture and hoping someone had been nosy enough to remember the young woman coming and going. "At least, until we get a better lead."

He turned the car and headed out through stoplights until he hit the on ramp for the freeway. They were halfway there when GJ's phone pinged.

Yes, she pushed the button. She liked being an FBI agent. If a random citizen requested the phone records, they would be put in the queue to get that information. But for an FBI agent, the phone companies tended to hustle a little better.

"I just got her phone records," she told Noah. "I also got the records of the people she chatted with. It's a long list." Chances were most of them were unimportant. "Give me a minute. Maybe we'll head to one of these first."

She'd expected that the phone hadn't been on since Neriah left the bank, which was exactly what GJ now saw. It looked as though she'd had the phone turned on until the bank withdrawal, and then turned it off before she left the parking lot.

"She left a trail right up to where she got the money out of the bank," GJ told Noah as she scrolled through the information. "Then she disappeared."

"Smart enough to turn the phone off," he said. "Good for her."

"So, you don't think she's the culprit. You don't think she's hiding information?" GJ didn't suspect Neriah, but she wanted his take. He'd been at this gig longer than she had. Hell, everyone had been at it longer than her—everyone except Walter, but she'd been special forces in the Marines. GJ almost sighed. So basically everyone.

"No, I don't. It took her a week to pack up and leave. If she killed Allison, she would have been gone sooner. Nothing happened a week ago to make her think they were onto her."

"Not that we know of," GJ mused. Turning in her seat, she faced him. "So what *did* happen a week ago? Because Neriah was going about her business and then, boom, she grabs all her money and a handful of clothes, and disappears."

"Don't forget the dive equipment," Noah added casually as he took the turn hand over hand.

Don't forget the dive equipment. . . The words rang through

GJ's head, though she didn't really know what to do with them. She wasn't a diver, but Noah was. "So let's start at the beginning. If she saw something happen to Allison, wouldn't she have gotten back into the boat and said so?"

"Or Eleri and Donovan would have reported that Hannah said Neriah was acting oddly that day."

"Unless Neriah is simply a stellar actress."

Noah seemed to think about if for a few seconds. "I have a hard time imagining acting at that level under that kind of duress. Plus they all went back out the next day, looking for Allison."

That must have sucked, GJ thought. "Was there any chance that Allison was still alive?"

"Sure. She had a buoyancy device. She would have run out of O-two, but she should have been able to float, and she had an orange or yellow inflatable signal to alert passing boats that she was there and in distress."

GJ hadn't known any of that. "So they went out the next day, worried but hopeful."

"That would be my take. But Eleri and Donovan report that they didn't catch any idea from Hannah about Neriah being more than simply worried for Allison."

"So something happened to Neriah—the last person who saw Allison—about one week after Allison disappeared, and about four days after Allison turned up dead. If Neriah had killed her, it would make sense that she'd disappear when the body turned up—when it might reveal some evidence. But she didn't." GJ was following where the logic led. "Instead, something made Neriah pack up and disappear *three days* after that. So Allison's disappearance was almost definitely involuntary, but Neriah's was voluntary."

GJ thought on it for a moment. When her thought process hit a dead end, she scrolled through her phone again. "Here, head to this address." She tipped her phone toward Noah enlarging the tiny print until he could see.

"I know where that is." He switched lanes, pulled up to the next light, and made a left.

Turning back to the listings the phone company had sent her, GJ scrolled through the information to see who Neriah had talked to most before she bailed.

"Well, shit, Noah," GJ said, causing the new agent to turn his head and look at her. "She copied and pasted the same message to three different people. It's her last message, probably sent from the bank because it's from right before she turned the phone off. It says,

Going dark. If anyone asks about me, you don't know anything. If anyone threatens you, or asks where I might be, tell them anything you can think of. I won't be there. I'll be safe. Will tell you more later. Don't worry.

CHAPTER 24

D onovan was back in front of his computer screen, and he was once again *not* following up on the case of Allison Caldeira's disappearance—murder.

He'd taken Eleri's advice. He'd walked the stairs several stories down, unable to wait for an elevator and not wanting to get packed in with anyone else in his agitated state. He'd bought a soda and a bag of chips, exactly as Eleri had requested. And he'd eaten them, not tasting any of it.

When his fingers had hit the bottom of the bag and the soda can had turned up empty, he tossed them before pacing the building for probably half an hour more. Then he realized he needed to get back to the conference room. Back to the one person keeping him sane. Back to the job he was supposed to be doing.

When he slipped through the doorway without saying anything, Eleri seemed relieved to see him but didn't comment. She was still going through the notebooks, and Donovan let her work. He would ask for an update later. He'd returned because he had an idea.

He knew Bodi's name now and his face. So Donovan popped

online again, checked all the current social media he could think of, and grew more frustrated when it yielded nothing. He'd hoped this might be a window into his strange new brother, but it was a dry well. When the last site turned up with nothing, he smacked his hand on the table, clearly startling Eleri.

"What's wrong?"

He almost barked out, *Everything!* But instead, he steadied himself with a deep breath and he explained the problem.

"It makes sense," she offered kindly. "Think about what the Dauphine sisters were doing with the *Lobo*mau in their area. They don't need social media to communicate. And if you're running any kind of drugs, Voodoo, or anything illicit—like say, human bones—you wouldn't want to be on social media, creating a trail for others to follow."

Donovan nodded. He should take what he had. He'd found an address, a face, a name—so much more than he'd started the day with. He should be satisfied. But he wasn't. He needed to know everything. Finding his brother created an uneasy sense that the answers he wanted were just beyond his reach.

"See if one of the Dauphine sisters has an account, or one of the brothers. Maybe Cabot. He seems the most likely." Eleri offered the option off-handedly, but it sent Donovan into a frenzy.

It took a short while to find, and most of the profile was not public, but Donovan managed to dig up a few photos with Bodi Heath's face in them. Donovan needed to trace back addresses for both Bodi and Amisha. He needed to follow Social Security numbers, to see if either of them had held jobs. He needed to broaden his search for his mother's death certificate, because if one turned up, that would upend everything again. He needed to go by her official government identifiers this time, not just the name.

So many things he needed to do. He also needed to work on the case that he was getting paid for—the one that he and Eleri would both be getting in trouble for, if anyone who cared found out what he was doing. He was turning to ask Eleri what he could do to help when her phone rang.

"Hey, GJ," she said as though this were a casual call and not the potential to get an announcement that someone else was dead or missing. ". . . Uh huh . . . Here." Eleri turned and spoke to Donovan. "Can you do this?"

He nodded. Whatever it was, he could and he should. Accepting the phone, he offered a kind hello. It came out better than he felt, and that was a win. "What can I do?"

The newly minted junior agent told him about the text messages she'd found and offered him the phone numbers and addresses. "Can you get me information on these people? Noah and I are going to see the woman at the top of the list. Maybe we can find out about Neriah from her. But if we can have more information about the others before we go in, that'll be helpful. Also, maybe Missy—our first stop—can connect us to some of the others. I'll send you the information."

"Excellent." Donovan pushed a smile onto his face, hoping it would change his tone for the better. Before he'd hung up, his screen had pinged with GJ's sent info.

Ignoring the twist in his gut and the nagging voice that told him his mother was still alive, he first followed Missy as best he could. "Missy" turned out to legally be "Melissa Maisel." A treasure trove of information on the twenty-five-year-old flooded his screen. Maisel hid nothing of her life, and Donovan combed through it looking for fast information.

Just the act of doing what he'd been trained to do finally began calming him. *Maybe he should set aside this crap with Bodi and his mother for a little while*, he thought. Maybe wait until he was able to look at it without his face feeling the pressure of wanting to push forward and growl his pain. Until his heart didn't feel the rage at being lied to, and his brain didn't pulse with the taunt that he'd been an idiot to believe his father all these years.

Quickly, he sent off several clear pictures of Missy so GJ and Noah could be sure they were speaking to the right person. If Neriah was in trouble and Missy was trying to cover for her, she might lie about who she was, what she knew, and more. At least an identifying photo could eliminate the first option.

He found what he could on most of the people on his list and sent it to GJ and Noah in neatly titled messages. Then, feeling at loose ends rather than being partially in charge of this investigation, as he was supposed to be, he turned to Eleri. "What do I do next?"

"Can you follow Miranda Industries? Find out everything publicly available on them, and anything privately that you can dig up?"

"On it." It felt good that Eleri didn't question his ability, though maybe she should have. Despite feeling calmer than he had before, he wasn't anywhere near Zen. This wasn't even close to his best work, and if he'd still been a medical examiner, he would have walked away from a body on the table rather than risk missing something.

An hour later, he was exhausted and hungry. Eleri would be proud.

It took time to trace each step to gather up the incorporation documents, input all his information in the FBI databases, and demand that the files be sent. Sometimes he had to go through city or state offices for the request. Sometimes paperwork would be filed and they had to look it up and send it to him. He was grateful that the letters "FBI" behind his name made people work faster. But it was still a time-consuming job.

He noticed then that Eleri had stopped tapping on her keyboard. She wasn't writing notes or. . . doing anything. She was staring up into the corner of the room. At first, Donovan wondered if she'd seen a spider. "El?"

She jolted as though pulled from a reverie and replied, "I don't know about you, but I need a break."

"Absolutely." At least he wasn't being sent away this time. "Before we head out though, this is *fun*." He was being sarcastic, and Eleri grinned as she wheeled her chair over next to him.

He pointed to the screen. "Miranda Industries is its own corporate entity. It has a variety of employees listed on its docket and payroll. I've been trying to follow up and see if these people actually exist. So far, I have no confirmation on any of them."

"*All* the employees might be fake?" She pulled her head back, clearly shocked at the possible scope of it.

Nodding, he kept going. This was a rabbit hole of epic proportions. "Miranda Industries itself receives funding from private and corporate donors. It actually receives most of its income through grants—and the grants come in about five separate names, but all trace back to a funding system that seems to run like a super PAC."

"Like what they do to hide political donations?" Eleri asked.

"I'm no expert, but I'd have to say yes." He took a breath and clicked to another tab that he'd pulled up just so he could show her the trail he'd been following. "So the PAC-thing operates as its own entity, and it doesn't have to disclose the names of its donors. However, one of the donors is Price-Gandry."

"What's Price-Gandry?" she bit.

"That's just it. It's not connected to any of the big pharmaceutical companies, though it's poised to look like a research company. When you look it up, it has a web page with drugs that Price-Gandry manufactures." He clicked through the pages, showing beautiful layouts of pills and vials with write-ups about the research and benefits. "It's a little overblown in the descriptions. According to how much this gushes, Price-Gandry should be wiping out all disease by December. But so far, I haven't found any of these drugs anywhere else."

"Wait. They have a whole website showing drugs they make that also don't actually exist?"

"Well. . . they're all supposedly in early research and FDA trial phases, but as of yet, nothing's coming up. Hold on." He opened a new tab and checked with the online PDR. The Physician's Desk Reference was one of the most useful tools in a medical practice, and Donovan flipped back to the previous page, inputting the color, shape, and code number.

"Well, fuck." He sat back. "That's an actual drug. But it traces to Merck." Merck was one of the biggest medical manufacturers in the country, and it was not associated with Price-Gandry at all. Donovan was beginning to believe *no one* was associated with Price-Gandry.

"Interesting. I've heard of Merck." Eleri leaned in closer to his screen.

"Exactly."

"What about their income reports?"

"The Price-Gandry tax returns are sketchy at best. Also they're connected to another company—Slater."

She looked at him for a moment and then said, "I'll bite. What's Slater?"

"It's a company for forty-five oil rigs in the Gulf."

CHAPTER 25

E leri leaned her head against the back of the small, uncomfortable couch in her junior suite. She was finally, blessedly alone. But she was uncomfortable.

She had no idea if all the furniture in Florida was simply uncomfortable, or if it was something inside of herself that was making it all seem so. Statistically, the second answer was most likely the correct one.

Sighing into the empty room and shifting her position, she picked up the remote and turned the TV on. The distraction lasted only as long as it took her to flip through the channels and realize that everything she recognized was complete crap. As for everything she didn't recognize. . . well, she didn't want to watch it.

She texted Avery, but even that felt stilted and a bit odd. Moments hit her randomly in which she wondered what she was doing with him. She did think maybe she actually loved him. On the other hand, she'd been dreaming of Grandmere and working spells from the Book of Shadows she'd found in the attic at FoxHaven. The old leather volume was hand-bound and ancient, handed down on the Hale side of her family.

Grandmere had been teaching her what was likely voodoo lore from the Remy side of the family.

So far, Eleri told Avery none of this. Several times, she'd considered starting the conversation. . . "So interestingly enough, the last name Hale—one of my family names—comes from the Salem witch trials. . ." and see what he thought about that.

If he passed that intro, she could let him know that Llewellyn was another of her family lines and was one of the most popular names in American witchcraft. If that, too, passed, she could have him to Google "Remy New Orleans" from her mother's side. And then, "Dauphine."

Somewhere along the way, she would lose him in more ways than one, she was sure. Though she'd composed the initial message and had opened her mouth more than once, she'd never gotten the conversation started.

Now she let her head fall against the back of the couch again, before she remembered how fucking uncomfortable it was and regretted her decision. This time, in a pique of irritation that she couldn't get settled, she pulled pillows off the bed and made herself a tiny fort in the corner of the sofa, and then pulled her knees up under her chin. It was time to do some serious thinking.

First, she was leading this case. It should have been her and Donovan leading together, but Donovan was in no state to handle that. She didn't resent his absence. It was what it was, but the case was still hers to carry.

GJ and Noah had spent the day running down Neriah Jones' friends. The friends had been first standoffish but then very helpful. Once they realized the FBI was trying to help find Neriah, several told everything they could think of. Eleri had no clue how GJ and Noah had managed to convince them the FBI had only Neriah's best interests at heart. So often, people got skittish around law enforcement officers, and having the FBI show up on your doorstep had to be nerve wracking.

But the two junior officers managed to get these friends to tell them every place they thought Neriah might go if she were in trouble. Of course, Neriah was at none of them.

They'd reported back that the friends had corroborated the missing dive tanks and BCDs. The fact that she'd taken the apparatus with her made it apparent that Neriah likely intended to dive, though whether she planned to dive alone, no one knew. GJ and Noah had exhausted every dive shop that showed up in her bank statements as well as every one her friends had provided as an option. As expected, Neriah had been to none of them since the previous Friday.

Sighing into the emptiness of the room, Eleri reminded herself this was Miami, and there were only about three-thousand more dive shops left to check. She did not have the manpower for this.

GJ and Noah had also smartly subpoenaed phone records from Neriah's friend list. The phone companies had given up the information quickly and without the friends' knowledge. Eleri wasn't sure if that was the right thing to do—one well-placed cousin at the phone company office might get wind of it, and the FBI would no longer be able to convince them of any friendliness.

Either way, it was too late; GJ and Noah had already done it. Eleri had told them she would have done it differently, and they'd appeared chastised—which was not what she wanted. She didn't think this decision would necessarily bite them in the ass; it merely had the potential to do so.

Still, the phone records turned up some useful information: none of the friends had gotten any texts or calls from burner phones. There was no evidence in the phone history that anyone had popped up and said, *Hey, it's N. And here's my new number.*

Neriah Jones had fully ghosted, and Eleri didn't know if it was because the young woman had reason to fear for her life, or if it was already too late and she was dead. Neriah was making herself very difficult to find.

Grabbing at her toes and tugging her knees up tighter, Eleri took a moment to be grateful that GJ and Noah were fully functional on their own. This case was becoming a shitshow.

Eleri had spent her day combing through Blake Langley's lab notebooks and data, and her brain was about to crack open and ooze out. It appeared that he'd finished his initial study before his grant money had run out. Then he'd used the remainder to extend the study into cocaine and heroin testing. But it was *why* he did that remained incredibly murky.

Eleri had been unable to tie Langley's work to Allison Caldeira's data. Oysters seemed to be the only connection, and maybe she was chasing an entirely separate case. But it *wasn't*. The combination of "oysters" and Miranda Industries coming forth with a ridiculous job offer just weeks before tragedy befell them was enough to tie the cases together. But Eleri wasn't finding the evidence she needed.

There were still non-nefarious explanations that were perfectly plausible, and Eleri knew it.

However, she'd found one new piece of evidence today that was more damning than anything else. Blake Langley's parents had filed a missing persons report, about a year after he left to work for Miranda Industries. In the report, they had explained to the police that their son had informed them he would not be in communication for several months upon leaving. He'd told them he would be out on the high seas, probably in international waters, with no connection. He would get back in touch as soon as they docked, which he expected to be in three months.

After six months of no word from their son, they'd followed every piece of information he'd left behind and some they'd deduced for themselves. This included contacting Miranda Industries directly. But none of their outreach had been returned. Voicemails, it seemed, went into empty holes in cyberspace. Texts disappeared into the ether, and handwritten letters bounced directly back to them. Eventually, they'd given up trying on their own and had gotten the police involved.

But given Blake's likelihood of being in international waters, and the fact that he'd gone away willingly—bags packed, job offer on the table—there had been very little the Montana police could do.

It shouldn't have taken Eleri so long to find that piece of information. But the fact was, Blake Langley's disappearance was secondary to Allison Caldeira's. It seemed everything they found about Allison led them to someone else—someone who's history had just as many problematic issues as her own disappearance.

Eleri felt the case was pulling her in thirteen different directions, and her head hurt. Standing abruptly from the couch, she looked around the room, suddenly hating all four of the walls equally. Her stomach growled and she'd had enough. Slipping on shoes and grabbing her purse, she headed downstairs to the restaurant. A big sign in the front proclaimed they had the best chocolate cake this side of the Mississippi. If it was even passable cake, she'd consider that a win.

In the restaurant, she looked around and noticed GJ Janson sitting at a table three rows back, by herself. She looked up at Eleri just as she forked a bite of the huge piece of chocolate cake that sat in front of her.

Though GJ looked a little resigned, she waved Eleri over, inviting her to sit down. "What brings you out at ten-thirty?"

"Cake, actually," Eleri smiled, but GJ didn't return it.

"I'd offer to share, but I have something to tell you," GJ said, "and I think you're going to need your own piece."

CHAPTER 26

"Well, that one didn't yield anything," Eleri said to Noah as they climbed back into the car. She let him drive, just as GJ had, because he knew his way around.

Together, they'd decided to take on the cramp-inducing legwork of checking the dive shops, one by one. Eleri fully expected it to take all day and turn up approximately nothing. But if it worked, it might be a gold mine, so they would visit as many as they could get to and see if Neriah Jones had been by.

So far, they'd managed to hit five, and all were bearing out Eleri's prediction.

They'd chosen these five shops because one, they were close together, so it was easy to hit them all up. And two, they were away from any of the dive shops Neriah was familiar with. She'd told her friends in her final text that wherever they thought she might go, she wasn't there.

"Where to next, boss?" Noah asked, slipping the car into gear and backing out of the parking space.

With what she hoped was a well-covered sigh, Eleri checked the addresses on the list she'd organized and said, "These three are nearby. And then there's two more right up here—" she pointed to the tiny map on her screen. "Let's hit up that cluster."

"There's another one on the way. I know the owners. They're brothers."

"Then let's hit it," she said. "We'll go by the others afterward." It didn't really matter. She had no hopes for the day, but this was a box that had to be checked. Leaning back and acting casual, she continued to surreptitiously observe Noah.

Last night, over out-sized slices of chocolate cake that neither of them had finished, GJ had confided in Eleri. "I think *something* is a little off with Noah Kimball."

GJ had been unable to articulate exactly what she was talking about, and it clearly frustrated her. Maybe that was why she was eating chocolate cake alone late at night. "There's just something about the things Noah accomplished. . . quickly. Maybe too quickly? I don't know." She'd rescinded her statement almost as fast as she'd tossed it out. "Maybe he's just really good at his job."

As she talked, she'd waved a forkful of cake around, making Eleri afraid it was going to go flying. At least the place wasn't busy at 10:30.

It was good to mix their small teams up, Eleri acknowledged, rather than admitting she wanted to watch Noah herself today. This morning, she'd contacted Donovan first and let him know she was changing the assignments. She'd told GJ last night that Donovan was having family issues and that he might need a bit of time to look up personal information.

GJ had looked at her with an expression that made it clear the junior agent understood Donovan *did not have family.* Therefore, what kind of family issues could he be suffering from?

Eleri had watched all the emotions play out over GJ's face before the words came out of her mouth. "Oh my God, is it Lucy?"

GJ always referred to Lucy Fisher as "Lucy," while the rest of them tended to still use the old "Walter Reed" nickname. Even so, Eleri didn't flinch. She only shook her head and refrained from saying that she didn't even know how much Lucy Fisher understood the situation. She had no idea how much Donovan had been telling her.

As agitated as he was, he might have been word vomiting to his girlfriend each night over the phone, but it was equally likely he'd told her nothing. Eleri, eating the cake bite by bite, was glad to get some sugar and fat into her system and let chewing cover for her lack of answer. At least the cake satisfied whatever craving had sprung up as she'd sat in her hotel room getting angry at the walls.

"Look," she told GJ. "He's likely to be distracted, and that's all I can say. He did say he was going to try and put it aside for today and focus on this case. So feel free to say, *Hey, Donovan, I need you to. . .* whatever. But you may very well be in charge."

"Ooh," GJ had replied, right around another bite of chocolate cake. "I get to be the boss of Donovan."

That phrase alone gave Eleri pause, but she didn't comment. GJ was nothing if not logical. So chances were, she simply thought the line was funny. She also would do a good job of keeping Donovan's work in order. So Eleri let it stand.

This morning, GJ and Donovan had taken off for the branch office and Eleri handed Noah the car keys, ready to spend the day watching him.

She couldn't say she was unhappy about getting GJ's eyes on the data again. GJ seemed to see the statistics without having to calculate them. Eleri figured they could use that now because, so far, she'd been unable to find any correlations. So far today, nothing had struck her as odd about Noah, but she did not discount GJ's intuition—not by a long shot.

"So," she said, into the empty air of the car. "Tell me, how did you wind up as an FBI agent?"

Noah immediately laughed in response. "Kind of preordained, I guess."

"Really?" Eleri almost wondered if his story was similar to hers. Life-changing events—in her case, it had been her sister's kidnapping—often made an impression and set young minds on life paths. But then Noah opened his mouth and proved her wrong.

"Salt Lake City, Utah, blonde, Mormon," he said, pointing to his head and circling his face. "What else was I going to do?" He added a half-shrug and Eleri began to understand.

"Oh, you're one of *those*." Lots of Mormons from Salt Lake City wound up in service to the FBI, many as agents. It had something to do with the need to serve a higher power and the kind of thinking that the FBI required—logical, precise, orderly —though Eleri had never quite been able to reconcile those qualities with what she understood of the Mormon religion. Mormons in Salt Lake City did so easily, to the point that many incoming Quantico classes featured upwards of twenty percent of these families.

"Yep," she said. "That does sound preordained. Does your religion mesh well with the Bureau's?"

"I wouldn't know. I've been excommunicated. For the gay." At least he said it with a grin on his face.

"I thought they had changed—"

He was already shaking his head. "I'm not going back. And the whole thing just bothered my family. Apparently, I'm just too obviously gay, and they can't have that. I was glad to get out of the house."

"Wow," Eleri replied. Though maybe it wasn't the best response, it was her initial reaction. Turning around, she began examining him a little more closely. "I have to admit, *I* don't see it."

"According to them, it's pretty obvious."

Eleri thought for a moment. "Were you kissing other men in

front of them? That might have done it. Otherwise? Not seeing it."

He laughed in response and let the topic drop as he turned the wheel. The route took them off the major road and aimed them once again toward the waterfront, where the dive shops tended to be located.

Eleri was a methodical scuba diver. She made plans ahead of time. She booked tours. Around here, the dive shops were almost always right on the beach, as though you might just show up to swim and suddenly decide to scuba. *Must be a Miami thing*, she thought.

"Here. This is the one I know." Noah pointed at the sign above the strip mall store, which was less than three blocks from the beach.

Inside, they listened to the door ding and looked around the shop as a man came out of the back, then lit up when he saw Noah. "Secret agent man! You ain't diving in that, are you?"

Noah laughed. He was clearly dressed as a fed today. "Nope. I'm actually here on secret-agent-man business."

Eleri could see the friendship went back a long way as he introduced her and they quickly got down to the business of flashing pictures of Neriah Jones. Once again, no one had seen her. But two dive shops later, as Eleri and Noah walked back out to the car, they looked at each other and said, "They were lying."

They had a lead.

CHAPTER 27

"What?" GJ asked, figuring this was the exact opposite of what Eleri had told her to do. She was supposed to be keeping Donovan on track.

GJ had been comparing oyster data between Blake Langley's and Allison Caldeira's records. Donovan had been looking into Allison's past history, for anything he could find: bank accounts, travel, credit card expenditures, reports, published papers, and more. He was simply trying to put together a history of the woman's life without any input from Hannah or anyone else who would likely be biased.

Everything had been going along great. Or so GJ had thought, until Donovan huffed out a breath and sounded angry. "Son of a bitch!"

When GJ had asked *What?* it turned out the answer had nothing to do with Allison, Hannah, or even Blake. Donovan had sat back in his chair slowly, his eyes glazed. She pressed him again and this time found out that what he'd found was his mother's death certificate.

"Why is that so stunning?" GJ was getting drawn into his research, rather than keeping him involved in hers. *Shit.* Still, she wasn't going to just say that. "I thought you knew she was gone. What's the new information?"

He was shaking his head, as though dispelling something that had gotten lodged there. "My mother died when I was seven." He said it evenly, as though recounting a case rather than his own experience.

It must have been horrible for him, but GJ wasn't going to say that.

"For me, that was the beginning of the shit show of life that was my father. He was never good, but he was worse without her." None of this was news to GJ, and Donovan had already explained to her about the package from his brother, but not much more. She nodded along and waited.

"What I found out yesterday was that she didn't die when I was seven—"

"*What?*" This time, GJ chucked the word at him like a fastball, before realizing her question was horribly inappropriate.

"Yeah, I found out she *didn't* die. So yesterday, I thought she was actually still alive. I'd been lied to all these years, though I don't know why I didn't question what my father said. He's a liar." Donovan was throwing his hands up in the air, agitated, just as Eleri had described. GJ had never seen him like this before.

He went on, not looking at her but continuing the story anyway. "So I just now found her death certificate."

"But I thought she wasn't actually dead?" Oh look, she did have other words and they weren't much better. "Or. . . they faked it when you were seven?"

"Yes, they faked it when I was seven, but this death certificate is from fifteen years ago. Apparently, she's actually dead now."

"Oh, *shit.*" GJ finally got it. "Fifteen years ago? That means she lived almost—what?—another ten or fifteen years after you thought she had died?"

As she watched the expression move across his features, she realized it was exactly the wrong thing to say, to point out just how long his mother had remained alive that he didn't know. Surely, Donovan would have calculated those numbers quickly on his own. But GJ knew she should have kept her fat mouth shut and not been the one to deliver the blow.

"Holy fuck," he whispered into the air, as stunned as when he'd started talking.

Well, GJ thought to herself, managing to keep her lips tight this time. *Eleri had told her that something was up with Donovan's family.*

She had not been prepared for this and, honestly, she would have expected Donovan to keep it all to himself. But the Donovan sitting with her today couldn't keep anything to himself. He was radiating his anger, hurt, and stunned confusion outward, sending vibrations that passed like slow-motion shockwaves through the room each time he realized something new.

This time when GJ spoke, she whispered. "What do you want to do?"

He took several forced short, deep breaths, and she began to feel afraid he wasn't even going to answer her.

"I'm going to go get a soda and a bag of chips and take a short walk."

She was smart enough to ask, "When will you be back?"

"Give me twenty minutes." He was already halfway out the door, so she called to his back.

"Set alarm on your phone!" The words bumped out between her lips as though she hoped she might create a scenario where he would, in fact, come back. She did not know how to call Eleri and confess that she'd lost the senior agent she was supposed to be watching.

Donovan didn't answer. He merely moved slowly out the door, not looking back, walking as though he didn't quite see where he was going. She thought about asking him to bring her a snack, as though giving him a task might give him a plan, a direction.

It took five minutes for the vibrations of his shock to leave the room enough for her to realize she was staring at the walls, accomplishing nothing. Taking her own deep breath and counting backwards from ten, she let go of her surprise and buckled back down to the work.

Thirty minutes later, when Donovan still hadn't returned, she was starting to get worried. But she'd learned FBI-specific time management for expected outcomes. She could handle this. She wouldn't fly off and call Eleri, only to have Donovan walk back in while she was on the phone losing her shit.

So GJ noted the time, made a plan, and went back to taking notes. The distraction of the clock had pulled her gaze away from the pages, and when she looked at them again, she noticed something. It wasn't about the oysters. It was the *barnacles*.

Flipping pages, she looked for more connections. If it hadn't been for the alarm she'd set for herself, she wouldn't have noticed when Donovan had been gone for forty minutes. But she messaged him and was grateful when, five minutes later, he sent a return message. "Twenty more minutes."

At least he was communicating. Turning back to her own work, GJ thought, *Yes, this is the link: barnacles.*

But then her own alarm went off for the second time that day. This one was a reminder to do a second check on a handful of email accounts associated with Neriah Jones and her friends. Neriah had three accounts, each of which needed to be logged into and checked for any correspondence. So far, all GJ had found was untouched emails, updates, and spam. She was hoping for something in which Neriah told her friends she was safe and not to worry.

Noah had supplied her with all of the passwords, though GJ still didn't quite know how he'd gotten them. Neriah's email yielded nothing. Neither of her parents' emails contained any news, though GJ was convinced Neriah's mother was dating at least one man outside her marriage. But when GJ logged into the email of Neriah's best friend—that of Missy Maisel—she hit pay dirt.

CHAPTER 28

E leri watched as Noah took a righthand turn out of the parking lot and merged the car seamlessly into Miami traffic. Within moments, they'd blended into the crowd and hopefully disappeared from view of the dive shop.

"We can park over here." He pointed to the lot two turns away from the one they'd just left. "I want to get far enough that they don't see us stopping."

Eleri agreed. Not being seen was of the essence. It had to appear right now to anyone watching that the two FBI agents had fully left the dive shop and were headed to their next destination. The liars inside needed to let their guard down.

If it became obvious the feds were coming back, the men would run. Flashing an FBI badge had both its up and down sides. As they looped around back the way they'd come, Eleri asked, "Do you know them?"

"Never been in that one before. I don't recall them having a good reputation, though."

That made Eleri wonder. In her experience, most dive shops were filled with knowledgeable, friendly employees who often worked there to support their own scuba habit. It wasn't cheap, and if someone wasn't born into the kind of money Eleri was, then working in a shop was a great way to dive for cheap or even free.

But coming from her own background, she couldn't say she'd had much experience with dive shops that didn't have a good reputation. She was trying to imagine what that might entail, but Noah was already pulling into the lot and parking in one of the back spots.

"Front door or back?" he asked her.

"I want the front. You're probably more familiar with what the back might be like around here. Plus, I'm going to play it super friendly. Like I'm an airhead and just forgot to ask something."

Nodding as he climbed out of the car, Noah absently touched each item he needed. She'd seen him do this several times before—gun, badge, belt, breast pocket—though she didn't know what was in the pocket.

She reached out with the earpieces she'd pulled from the glove box. Handing one to him, she stuck her own in and checked their communication, even though she was already ten feet away from the car. This needed to happen fast.

After waiting impatiently at the corner of the low, brick building until Noah said he was in position, she slowly strolled back into the shop, carefully watching all corners as she entered. Her casual, sweeping gaze was why she caught the subtle widening of the large clerk's eyes upon her return.

Clearly, he thought they'd pulled it off and the two FBI agents were gone.

"Hey!" She offered up the words with a sweet tone and a smile. "I forgot to ask something."

"Okay." But the clerk drew the word out and his tone belied his trepidation. He continued checking the pressure on the tank at his feet, as he'd been doing when she walked in. She knew it didn't take that long and he had to be hoping that having his hands busy would make him look less guilty. It didn't.

Eleri pulled up the picture of Neriah on the tablet she carried and showed it to him again. "You said you hadn't seen this woman?"

He nodded, merely agreeing with his earlier statement.

"So, just one more question," Eleri lightly tossed it out. "Why did you lie about it?"

He froze, clearly caught in the act. He was not used to bluffing his way out of interrogations with FBI agents. "I didn't lie. I've never seen her before in my life."

Eleri fought the desire to roll her eyes. *Never seen her before in my life* was common parlance for complete bullshit. How would anyone know that? Almost no one remembered every person they'd ever met, but Eleri didn't say that. Instead, she calmly and cheerfully let him know she wasn't taking any of his crap. "But you did see her. You saw her this week. Which day?"

"I didn't." So he was sticking with that bullshit.

"Cool story, bro." Behind him, through a small open doorway into the back of the shop, Eleri could see Noah had quietly rounded up someone else. The man behind the counter had no idea this was happening right behind him. For a moment, Eleri thought she might enjoy this.

"I didn't see her," he insisted. But the way his jaw twitched indicated he was frightened, rather than truly angry. He'd held her gaze while he reiterated the words, but as soon as they were out, his eyes darted all around the room, as though looking for an exit around the tiny FBI agent.

"No. Really," Eleri tilted her head. "Which day did you see her? Oh, did she *pay* you not to say anything?"

He was opening his mouth, but Eleri casually flipped one hand around as though discussing her wardrobe and railroaded her way right over him again. "Because you'd better know this. The people coming after her have more money and more force than anything you can stand up to. She's in trouble. So if you think you're protecting her, you're not. Tell me which day she was in here. Now."

By the time Eleri reached the end of her short speech, she'd laid her hands flat on the counter, leaned forward, and gotten into his face to the point where the man, who outweighed her by at least five stone, was backing up.

This time, he didn't say anything.

For a moment, she considered doing a trick that she had learned recently—and it was truly a trick. She had no other power behind it. But Noah stood behind the man at the counter and he would see her eyes. This was what she hated about working with non-NightShade agents. After being free to do everything she could and solve her cases using *all* her skills, she was now having to consider that turning her eyes black would freak out her suspect but would also burn all bridges with her new partner.

So she merely stared the round man down and said again, "Tell me what day she was here."

He sighed. "Thursday."

"What time?"

"Nine minutes before eleven."

"Well now, let's try that again. But don't lie to me again."

This time, his eyes widened instead of answering her. He spun around as though to bolt out the back but must have seen Noah right behind him with his coworker already in handcuffs. Instead, the man wound up making a full three-sixty. Surprising the hell out of Eleri, the big man jumped over the counter with shocking ease, ignoring the walk-through that was covered by a lift-up piece of countertop.

Landing on his feet, he bolted past her almost before she could process what he'd done. She was turning to bolt after him without even thinking. For a split second, she was grateful she'd worn these shoes. They looked nice, but they had excellent grips and stayed on her feet. Though it would be hot and sweaty, she was ready to run. And she was ready to tackle this big beef of a man and take him down. But she barely made it two steps before he tripped in the open space of the floor and went down, face-first, onto the tile.

Jumping on him—since he was already in the appropriate position—Eleri grabbed one hand and yanked it up behind his back. She didn't think about it, but naturally used the techniques she'd learned at the FBI Academy. She twisted his wrists and placed them back to back, creating a tension in his shoulders to keep him from fighting and make him easier to control.

"You're under arrest by order of the Federal Bureau of Investigation." The words were rote and, as she spoke, she looked around the room to see what he could have possibly tripped on.

There was nothing here.

CHAPTER 29

I *t figured*, Donovan thought. It was some kind of poetic perversion of the universe. Finally, as he'd gotten himself back together and walked into the room, GJ had hopped up from her chair and practically thrown herself at him.

"Look what I found, Donovan. You're not going to believe this."

Excited for break in the case, he moved around to the other side of the conference table and watched as she tapped on keys.

"I found it in Missy Maisel's 'drafts' folder." GJ looked up at him, but he understood. The folders were a great way to park email that the sender didn't want found, or maybe just wanted backed up somewhere. The message would be saved online, but because it never got sent, it didn't ping any systems. No one would receive it, or even find it, unless they got into this account and specifically looked through the messages.

"Good catch," he told her as the video popped up. It appeared to be an underwater shot of various fish. "What's on it?"

"I don't know yet. I only forwarded through it quickly one time once I got it loaded. There's an individual diver in the video. I think it might be Allison, but I don't know how to I.D. her in that dive gear."

"Let's check our records." He was already moving to see if he could pull anything up. When the research team had called it a day and filed the report that Allison had gone missing, they'd filled in the standard "what she was wearing when last seen" info. He hoped it was more than just "a wetsuit and dive tank."

GJ was talking again. "It's in Missy's email, so it could be video that Missy had from one of *her* dives. She was a diver, too, so this could be nothing."

"But why would you load a video to yourself and never send it?" Donovan stopped sorting through the missing person report for a moment and worked through the implications of that. It was possible that Neriah had logged into her friend's email and left it for her. "They might be using Missy's email to stay in contact. This way, Neriah's email doesn't ping us—or anyone else—that she logged in." *It also could be nothing*, he reminded himself. "You'll need to contact Missy and ask if she did this."

"Already on it," GJ said. She was enlarging the video, getting ready to let both of them watch through when their phones rang simultaneously.

It figured, Donovan thought. *Everything always breaks at once.* He assumed it was Westerfield, but when he picked up the phone, it was Eleri.

Eleri and Noah had two adult males in handcuffs and they needed GJ and Donovan to fetch one for transport to the Bureau branch office. Donovan hung up and looked to GJ. "They need us so the suspects can't chat on the way or trade info."

GJ was already hopping up, the video abandoned for now. Scrambling for speed, they quickly locked down the conference room, but left everything behind as they bolted out the door. It wasn't unusual to see agents running down the halls, and they passed right out of the building and into the lot.

GJ had slid smoothly into the driver's side seat, but then popped right back out, swearing a blue streak. "Oh, man, what the fuck made me think I should drive? Who the fuck bought black cars in Miami?"

Donovan would have laughed, but he was far too scrambled to process the humor. This day had tossed him like a rag doll. He'd barely gotten his brains back in his head after seeing his mother's death certificate. Even now, the thought flitted through his mind and he pushed it hard to the side. There was too much going on. He had a job to do here, and it didn't seem wise to stop and process the information about his mother yet.

Even if nothing was going on with the job, and if he was able to take a sick day—or five—to step aside and deal with what he'd found, he wouldn't. He was growing more convinced that he needed to let the information settle before he turned it over and looked underneath. He needed to ready himself for whatever crap he might find. He wasn't ready now.

So he slid into the car, his legs burning through the fabric of his slacks as he hit the seat. He tried not to let GJ know. Tossing her the keys, he said, "Get in."

"I know, I know." She was quickly sliding back into place, trying not to waste time or react to the burn of the seat. He blasted the air conditioning for her and GJ peeled the car out of the FBI lot like her ass was on fire. According to her swearing, it was.

By the time they reached the dive shop, Donovan had formed a handful of opinions. This section of town was not the richest part of Miami. Even so, the property values were probably sky high. The dive shop was in a strip mall with a huge plastic sign over the top that read "Smith Family Dive." He hadn't yet made up his mind about the shop yet. Either it was a cute, but not thriving, family business full of knowledgeable, friendly, helpful divers—or it was merely a bottom-of-the-barrel shop. *They might not even be related.*

Inside, dive tanks with the paint partially rubbed off lined the edges of the front room. Letters and number combinations marked the gases that were stored in them, and Donovan was surprised to see more than just O2. Equipment resembling what he'd seen in Neriah's apartment pictures hung from pegs on the wall. Black vests with tubes protruding hung on a hanger rack smashed thick, and on the other side of the room, various wet suits were available for rent. Everything appeared to be for sale.

The two men sat on the floor facing away from each other. Eleri looked up as they entered, but she seemed most grateful to see him. Though she had Noah Kimball here as backup, Eleri still looked like something was bothering her. But it wasn't the time or place to figure out what it was. Instead, he asked, "Which one do we get?"

Since Eleri had already communicated that their job was to drive the man back to the branch office, she merely pointed. Donovan leaned over and grabbed the man by his shoulders. "You'll be coming with me."

Awkwardly, the man rose to his feet. It was not an easy task for non-agile people without their hands to push off of the floor. Donovan offered what help he could, but that didn't extend to any kid-glove treatment.

Luckily, though the man wasn't happy to see either him or GJ and muttered his way through the whole process, he didn't fight them about getting into the back of the hot car. He was curt, but not belligerent as they clicked his cuffs to the car seat's security hook. This was not a cruiser. It was not designed for hauling prisoners. So they made do.

At the branch, they began processing him. It always took far longer than Donovan liked to go through security, getting their "guest" patted down and checked for weapons, or worse. He didn't see Eleri or Noah at all, but that was the point.

Purposefully, they walked the men in at separate times and put them into two separate rooms connected by a central observation area. The rooms were windowless, dreary, and designed to inspire despair. Only a tiny, wired piece of glass set into the door allowed any light in, and the mirror obviously let other FBI agents watch the interrogation.

The two men probably wouldn't know they were right next-door to each other.

Standing in the middle for a few moments to form a battle plan, the four agents looked through the two-way mirrors, watching as the suspects sat cuffed to the bar on the table and beginning to sweat.

"This one first," Eleri said, pointing to the man she'd found behind the counter. "I think he's the boss. Yes?"

Noah nodded his agreement, though Donovan withheld judgment—he hadn't been there. Something in Eleri's manner still seemed agitated. She'd made a motion to Donovan with only her eyes, and he'd picked it up to mean she would tell him later. He wasn't sure he could handle any more new information. But he would have to, so he merely nodded in response.

Walking out the door, Eleri motioned for Noah to follow her into the room while Donovan and GJ hung behind. He crossed his arms, still needing something to do with his hands.

Eleri and Noah sat abruptly across from the man and Donovan watched as his nerves ratcheted up just a little more.

"You do realize you're now in the custody of the Federal Bureau of Investigation?" Eleri offered it like a statement, but said it with a question mark. The man nodded in response.

She'd not yet asked his name or information or begun a recording. Donovan wondered what was going on. She asked one question next. "What did Neriah Jones do to convince you to lie about her presence in the dive shop?"

This time, when the man raised his eyes, he looked more like a cornered rabbit than a belligerent suspect. He looked down at the table, his lips pressed together.

He looked between Eleri and Noah to buy time, but eventually, he answered. "It wasn't her. I mean, she asked that I tell no one she'd been there, but I didn't care. I wouldn't have remembered her anyway. . . I didn't lie because of her. It was the people who came in after her."

CHAPTER 30

I t wasn't until the next morning that GJ was able to sit down with the video again. She'd even managed to wake up exhausted.

The interviews yesterday had gone on for hours. Eleri and Noah had walked back and forth between rooms asking endless streams of repetitive questions. Occasionally, they tag-teamed with GJ or Donavan, who were mostly observing. Not that it helped.

Both men ultimately gave the same story. The bigger guy— Bob—told the better version, because the smaller one—James— had been in the back of the store most of the time.

"She came in and she asked for some basic dive equipment."

"Like what?" Eleri had asked, as though she didn't care about the answer. GJ did. She'd also noticed that Eleri was careful not to feed Bob any information.

"She bought a mask, fins, and weights."

As GJ watched, Eleri's eyebrows narrowed. "That's an odd combination."

Bob only shrugged. "The way she talked, she sounded like

she knew what she was doing. So I gave it to her. I assumed she had her own BCD, stage, et cetera."

Eleri nodded along, though GJ wasn't quite up to speed on what all of the equipment names meant. Looking to Donovan for answers, she realized that both of the agents who knew anything about scuba were already in the interrogation room and unavailable for clarification.

"I wouldn't have remembered her at all," Bob said. The man leaned back, but his cuffs caught the bar they were chained to. GJ saw him try to cover the gaff and lean forward onto his elbows again. He acted annoyed at being here and also seemed to think it was his personal right to withhold information from the FBI. He obviously gave zero shits about Neriah Jones or her safety and—as GJ watched—she discovered he gave just as few about his co-worker. Now that he was talking, he seemed eager to tell his bullshit and get released back into the wild.

"But about thirty minutes after she leaves, two guys come in. They have her picture, and the say not to talk about her. . . to anyone. I'm assuming that includes the feds."

His eyes narrowed and GJ felt her chest tighten as she thought, *Man, if she found this A-hole dying on the side of the road, she would leave him there.*

"What did the men look like?" Eleri continued to press him with a calm that GJ could only hope to someday achieve.

"Like feds." He offered up his answer with the declarative period on the end. "Dark suits, sunglasses, guns."

Eleri and Noah looked at each other, and GJ could almost hear both of them thinking. *That's not feds.*

"What ID did they show you?" This time it was Noah who asked.

"None. They made their point. They told us we weren't to say anything about the woman. So what are you going to do to protect me and my shop? Now that I've broken my word? Because according to them, they're going to take out my family."

GJ noticed that he didn't ask about his coworker, but at least he seemed to give one small shit about his own family. It wasn't enough to redeem him, and as the hours dragged on, Eleri managed to get him to explain who his family members were. GJ and Donovan were quickly dispatched to pick up the woman and the teenage son, who gave them no small bit of trouble.

"I'm not leaving until my stories are over!" The wife looked far too young to use the term "stories," but it had come out of her mouth in puffs of menthol around the cigarette, and her ass hadn't moved from the recliner. The son acted like a teenager and offered nothing but negative monosyllabic grunts.

When they explained the threat, both protested that they needed to speak to Bob. But Bob was still in the interrogation, and GJ had reached her limit of bullshit for the day. "I am the FBI. You have two options. Option one, sign a form that you refused protective custody. If you do that, then *no one will come when you call for help*, because you are refusing that. Do you understand?"

She'd put her nose in the woman's face and noticed that Donovan let her roll with it. "Option two, your butts are in that car in five minutes, packed and ready to go—"

"I can't pack in five minutes."

It was all GJ could do to not smack her. "Well, you can only take what you can pack in five minutes. Because you had fifteen, but you pissed ten of them away being a bitch to FBI agents." She knew it should not have come out of her mouth. But Donovan stood beside her with a corresponding glare on his face and not even a twitch of his lips. At least it got the woman and her son in gear.

Eventually, they'd managed to get Bob's family into a safe house, put an agent on them, and get their own asses out of there before they had to interact with the mother or son again. Donovan bought GJ a burger on the way back, and she ate the whole thing, fries and all. He was expensing it of course, but the forms were a bit of a bitch. It was the thought that counted, she told herself.

It wasn't until hours later that the two men were also released. And then there was the issue of getting them to safe houses, and taking care of the business and getting it locked down for several days. When Bob threatened to sue for loss of revenue, GJ managed to hold back her rant.

Eventually, she went to bed, mentally exhausted. She woke up the same way. But this morning, at least, felt like her own time. GJ had gone back to the conference room, driving herself in and showing up before anyone else. She noticed Noah wasn't there yet. *She probably should have slept another hour.*

If she played her cards right, maybe she could find a way to take a nap. Lord knew, a tired agent wasn't a good agent. Still, asking for naps would only make her seem more like the youngest agent on the team, and she desperately wanted to avoid that.

Pulling the data, she went back to comparing numbers between Allison's barnacles and Blake Langley's oysters. No new information had turned up on Langley's whereabouts, even though they'd put out federal feelers in many different directions. She watched as the other agents filed in the door, one behind each other.

Eleri offered a half smile at seeing GJ already in and working. "You said you had information yesterday. Before we were interrupted."

Game on, GJ thought. "Look." Before they were even seated, she was turning the lab notebooks to face them, showing them what she'd pulled. "Now, I don't read barnacle data well, but I'm putting together what I can. Allison seemed to be looking at the chemicals, minerals, and any toxins she could find in the barnacles themselves. Because the creatures would apparently incorporate whatever was in the water as they grew."

GJ pushed Allison's lab notebook across the table next,

opened to the page she wanted. "Here. You can see that she drew some of the same conclusions that Blake Langley did from his cocaine and heroin study."

"He had conclusions? He barely got that one off the ground," Eleri commented as she looked through Allison's data. "Right?"

She was right. "He didn't have any formal conclusions. But if you take a look at the data, you can see spikes in the numbers. And when I compare it back to this first batch of data, I see it's different. I see that he actually found evidence of this in the oysters. Here's the kicker, though: I found some small notes on the side, extra pieces. It turns out he used four different sources of oysters. The first came from several trips around Weeki Wachee, where he gathered the oysters himself. Another source was commercial supplier from a company in the Gulf. He used a second commercial source from Mexico. And the last one—the group that prompted the second study—came from Nassau."

GJ watched as the information absorbed into Eleri's brain. "That's where Allison was last."

"Exactly," GJ confirmed, looking up at Noah and Donovan, who both appeared to be following right along. "It's also where Miranda Industries asked Allison to come and work. That was where they wanted her located. And it's where Miranda Industries lists their corporate address. They were located there even back when they asked Blake Langley to come work for them."

GJ paused for a moment, then looked up into the faces all giving her their rapt attention. "I did one more thing." She shuffled through the notes quickly as they watched her. Sometimes, she felt self-conscious when she was on the spot, but not with data. She knew what it was. She just wanted to find it. "I did some deep digging with Hannah. I called her up and asked her if she remembered Blake Langley's roommates from when he worked at Weeki Wachee."

"Wow," Eleri said.

"It gets better. Hannah has gotten no further job offers for Allison from Miranda Industries. She got one several days before Allison was murdered and no more have followed, indicating that Miranda Industries either coincidentally stopped their pushy offers the moment Allison died, or they knew she was dead."

GJ let that soak in a minute before she pushed forward. "I contacted Blake's old roommates for the same information. They shared a house for another three years. After he left, they got a new roommate, and they forwarded all of Blake's mail to his parents. They promise me they handwrote forwarding notices on everything that wasn't a coupon. Blake's parents confirm that they received the mail, and that they opened it."

She paused, then dove back in. "There were no more offers or contact from Miranda Industries after Blake left home, which indicated to them that he had arrived at his new job. Remember, his parents thought that he had gone to work, so they didn't even try to contact him for three months. But it's important to note that there was no job calling the house or writing letters asking why he hadn't shown up."

"So," Eleri said as she leaned over the table, though her gaze was far away. "The major conclusion here is that Miranda Industries has had their thumb on this the whole time."

"I think so." GJ took one more pause, because she wasn't done yet. "Wait until you see this video."

CHAPTER 31

Eleri was impressed. The day before had been trying at best, and the information gathered was slim. The two men had been almost as far from cooperative witnesses as they could be. Both seemed to be selfish asshats on top of that.

Eleri had to help them. It was her job. She had to set up safe houses and keep them safe. But the effort had been monumental, and for it to yield so little made it doubly frustrating. Mostly, by the end, they'd learned that one of the two threatening men was white, with brown hair cut short, and the other was possibly half African American, possibly half Latino, and probably was short, with dark, curly hair. That was it.

They tried to make use of a sketch artist but wound up wasting his time as well. Both men had sucked considerably at not only giving descriptions but at answering the questions the artist asked. In the end, they produced two drawings that were nearly identical—representing the two different men in the store—despite saying that the two men were at least somewhat different. The body shape, height, weight, and how they carried themselves had been just as much work to extract.

The shop guys either had the worst memories she'd ever seen, or they were holding back. In the end, she'd been about ready to smack one of them at least ten different times. She wished she could toss them back to the wolves.

GJ's information this morning was more than welcome. It was a lead. It was more evidence of what they had suspected, which was that Miranda industries was very involved in both disappearances. Now she leaned forward on the table, never having quite gotten into her seat. "So tell me about the video. Donovan said you found it in Missy Maisel's drafts folder?"

GJ nodded. "I called Missy to check on it. According to her, she has no clue what underwater video I'm talking about. She claims she did not park the draft there, which checks out. She was at work and not on email at the time the draft was made. It's time-stamped. I checked her phone; it pings repeatedly from her job during the time the email was loaded."

Eleri watched as GJ stopped and looked at them. Eleri almost made the mistake of thinking GJ was done. No. Her newest agent was thorough to a fault. Her science background meant she would stack data and evidence until she couldn't find any more. Eleri loved it.

GJ launched in. "Also—interestingly—Missy's email shows a login from South Miami while Missy was at work. There was no way she was at a coffee shop in South Miami at the time this came in. So this is definitely someone else using her account. She also confirmed that Neriah might know her email password. She doesn't remember giving it out specifically, but knows she's checked her email from Neriah's computer before."

"Holy shit. That's our best lead on Neriah Jones right now. Why didn't you say this before?" As soon as the accusatory question was out of her mouth, Eleri regretted saying it. Luckily, GJ took it in stride.

"I would have, but I only got the information back from

Tech about fifteen minutes before you walked in. And I knew you were already on your way."

Eleri scooped up her purse, checking for anything she didn't want to leave behind, and patted herself for her ID and sidearm. She was ready to head out the door. "We need to go to that coffee shop, now."

Donovan seemed to be moving with her, but Noah held back. GJ shook her head. "It's taken so long to find it and get into the email. This was sent two days ago from a place that's over thirty minutes away—probably longer right now in traffic. Rushing does nothing. I've already called the owners, but they aren't answering. When they open in another two hours, we can be down there and request any footage. But right now, the shop's locked up tight."

GJ waited a beat before adding her last bit of evidence for why she wasn't jumping up to bolt out the door herself. "Neriah was smart enough to use her friend's email. To not send it, but leave it as a draft where it doesn't ping, and to do that from a coffee shop none of her friends recognized. She's probably smart enough not to be sitting there sipping a latte when we show up. She's ghosted them, too. We'll be going to get the shop surveillance video and confirm that Neriah Jones was alive two days ago and that she's the sender of this email, but we won't find her there."

Well, Eleri thought, *she should never have questioned her junior agent on this one.* With a nod of acceptance, she set everything back on the table and headed around toward GJ. She pulled out the chair next to her and sat down. "You win. Show us the video."

"It's forty-five minutes long," GJ offered as introduction while she tapped a few keys and set the video to full screen. "This is obviously the biggest I can show it. But I think it's worth watching on a bigger screen when we comb through it more thoroughly. I'm just giving you a highlight reel right now. .

. It begins with this other diver in the distance. . . and I'm going to scroll through now to show you what I found."

Eleri watched as the video jumped from scene to scene while GJ continued talking it up. "We should also get an analyst on every frame when we get a chance. So here's the single diver in the distance. And you can see here—" she clicked forward about seven minutes, "—the diver holding the camera comes close. This is the closest the diver gets." She pointed to the 8:01 timestamp in the corner.

"And this is my best estimate from all the photos we've seen, but I believe that that's Allison Caldeira."

Eleri was stunned. It did look like Allison's face. She couldn't guarantee it, not with a regulator in the diver's mouth and the full face mask on. But it was a woman of the right size and shape, and the hair looked right. Given the warm waters, the diver was in a swimsuit with only a dive vest on top.

Eleri felt her breath suck in. Though she had been very good friends with Hannah and had known Allison while they both worked at the mermaid show, she hadn't seen them in years. Still, it was a blow. Every time she saw a video of Allison alive, it hit her harder than looking at pictures. "I think you're right. Maybe we can get Hannah to confirm."

Donovan jumped into the conversation then. "I was looking at the missing persons report to see what she was wearing that day. It said: blue, two-piece bathing suit. BCD dive vest. Mask, snorkel, oxygen tank—yellow, regulator, fins—entirely black but blue edge at the tip."

GJ looked up at him then, and Eleri watched as she scrolled forward and back through the video. "Blue suit, check. Yellow dive tank, too!"

"I don't know," Eleri said, looking up at Noah—the only other diver in their group. "Those are really common colors. Not enough to call this."

"Agreed." It was the only thing he'd said all morning, and it was heartbreaking. She'd wanted him to say something like, "Miami only uses green tanks." But it didn't happen.

GJ was still squinting at the screen. "It's really hard to tell. A blue line at the tip of the fins would be very distinctive."

Eleri nodded. "I've not seen that before. I'm not saying it's not common, but I haven't seen it." She, too, squinted at the video, almost banging her head against GJ's. "I can't tell. The water is very blue, and it's very hard to tell if there's a blue line. *Dammit.*"

She wanted to be able to identify Allison. She wanted to have *something,* but even the things that should have given them evidence to support that this was Allison weren't solid enough. *Dammit, Allison, why couldn't you have worn a yellow bikini with a lime-green wave design? Why didn't you keep wearing those purple dive fins you liked so much? Why did you have to be a sun-bleached blond in Florida?* Eleri still looked at the picture until her eyes almost crossed. There was nothing.

GJ waited until Eleri had had her fill of not being able to find what she needed to see. Then she scrolled a few more minutes through. "The camera looks like it's hanging down here. You can see where they move apart. And there's no sound, but I think the person with the camera is Neriah—I saw a hand a few minutes back, and it could be hers. And she was down with Allison on the last day."

"You think this is from the last day Allison dove?"

"I do. Watch. . . I think she intended to turn the camera off. You can see a few motions here." GJ scrolled back. "Then the camera falls away. We get footage of the ocean floor or empty water with the occasional fish passing through. . . See? Here's a fish tail up close. . ." She pointed to one short section. "I don't think it was what she intended to film. But look, there at the thirty-eight minute mark. It's clearly not centered. Obviously, it was casually caught by the camera that was left on, but the diver comes back into the frame."

Upside down and barely in the shot. Also at a distance, but Eleri thought it looked like the same diver. Gently, she swam toward the ocean floor. And Eleri could imagine that Allison was scraping some of the coral for samples, maybe looking for any kind of sea life she could take back as a specimen.

"Another diver approaches her," GJ narrated, just a moment before the other person appeared on the screen.

"Wait, who's that?" Eleri demanded. She should have been impartial, but it was too difficult, and she was about to stop trying. She was likely watching the murder of an old friend.

"I don't know." GJ didn't look up from the screen but paused the video for a moment. "But, as you can tell, it's a third diver. Clearly this person is at a distance from our cameraman, or camera woman, if the camera is held by Neriah Jones. From these images, we see this diver is bigger than Allison. Neriah was smaller. So that doesn't match any photographs or known information we have of Neriah. Also, I could be wrong, but I think this diver is male."

A third diver, Eleri thought. Hannah's story was that Neriah and Allison were the only two down at the time. If this was footage of Allison, then Neriah had not yet gone back to the boat and reported her missing. It was only after Neriah headed back to the surface and they'd calculated that Allison was definitely out of air that they'd begun looking. It was only after *that* time that another diver—Hannah—had gone down.

"That's not Hannah," Eleri blurted out. She wasn't one-hundred percent certain that the diver was Allison, or that the camera holder was Neriah, but she knew this much.

"No, it's not," GJ agreed. "As far as I can tell, this diver isn't anyone from the boat. The descriptions allow for complete rule-out."

"But they saw no other boats that day," Eleri protested. "Who could have been close enough to get to them?"

CHAPTER 32

"Again?" Donovan asked.

They were all crowding around GJ. She had to be uncomfortable with three other FBI agents clearly invading her personal space, but she didn't comment. No one really did. Donovan was still processing what he'd seen.

Though Noah kept his eyes trained on the screen, over the other agent's head, Donovan caught Eleri's gaze. Her return expression told him she had seen it, too.

"Maybe we play it back from the beginning," Eleri stated for him.

He couldn't disagree. They needed to watch *everything*. They needed to see if this other diver—the third person—appeared in frame at any time prior.

It was clear that the film caught the death of the diver they thought was Allison. Whether or not it was her, the diver began bleeding openly into the water after jerking around. The next thing the camera caught was three sharks attacking and leaving almost no trace of the diver on screen.

Because her body had been found several days later, Donovan surmised that maybe the sharks had pulled her off-screen. But the video was rolling on without him and he parked that question. The other diver appeared only as arms and legs at the edge of the picture, as if he had hung back to watch.

"Wait!" Donovan blurted before GJ hit the button again. "Talk me through this. Noah, Eleri? I don't know enough about diving. What am I watching? Because it looks as though the person filming, supposedly Neriah, has no idea that her fellow diver has been attacked by sharks and killed right behind her. Is that possible? Or is she responsible? Did she ignore this as it happened?"

He couldn't tell. He didn't swim in swimming pools any more than he had been forced to do as a child. That had occurred all of twice, and he'd never gone back in. He knew at the least that swimming pools were dramatically different from the ocean. "Is there no noise down there?"

He'd studied physics to get into med school. For just a moment, he was grateful that it was a required course. He calculated now that noise traveled faster and more clearly in liquids than in air. So how would it be possible that the diver with the camera had not heard the commotion?

Noah looked to Eleri as though to ask who should go first. When she nodded, he jumped in. "It's entirely possible." He pointed to the screen. "The camera isn't aimed. I don't know whether the camera-holding diver was looking at this scene or was looking away. But if the diver was. . . maybe. . . looking down at the ocean floor, collecting coral scrapings or trying to pick up or catch small fish specimens, this could happen behind them without their knowledge."

"There's no noise?" Donovan pressed. GJ lifted her head and watched the conversation taking place above her but didn't enter it.

"I'm sure there is noise, but when you're down there, you've got a mask on your face, pressure in your ears, and a regulator in your mouth. All your senses are distorted. And the regulator makes a. . ." he searched for words and gave up. "I don't know! *A compressed air noise* every time you take a breath. It hisses and wheezes and it's reasonably loud. That's most of what you hear under water—your own breathing."

Eleri chimed in. "Something going on thirty or more feet behind you could absolutely go by unnoticed."

Donovan tried to absorb the information. At least this other diver didn't watch their dive buddy get murdered and just ignore it. Or, they didn't know that. "So that means," he added, speaking as his brain worked when maybe he should wait, but he didn't, that Neriah might not have known she was filming this. "She would return to the boat, knowing that Allison was gone, and simply wait for her to surface somewhere else? Is that reasonable? She wouldn't search for her friend?"

This time it was Eleri who replied. "Yes, according to the original reports, she did search for Allison. But she didn't worry when she didn't find her. So yes, that report still holds water, even given this video."

"What about the blood?" Donovan asked. "Wouldn't she have seen it when she searched? Wouldn't at least the people on the boat see it? Does it not show up?"

It hit him then. Everything he knew about diving was from fiction—novels, TV, movies. "That's just in the movies. Right?" He admitted his own inadequacies when he found them.

"Yes," Eleri said. "Though I haven't ever witnessed anything like this underwater. Noah?"

"I saw a shark catch a tuna once. . . and it was petrifying," he said. "And the fish did bleed into the water. It wasn't human sized, but it was a big fish. Honestly, I'm not up on my ratio of fish blood to human blood in pints, but there was much less blood in the water than I would have expected."

GJ sat still, like Donovan, absorbing all the unexpected diving information. But Eleri pushed on. "It looks like this diver —probably Allison—was far enough below the surface that there's no way any kind of blood pool or anything would have been visible from up top."

"What about the camera person?" Donovan asked again. "Wouldn't she see it? Or *he?*" He had to acknowledge they really didn't know who had been holding the camera. "Wouldn't they turn around and see it?"

"No," Eleri shook her head at him. "The water currents carry blood away relatively quickly. So, if you didn't turn around pretty much *as it was happening*, you wouldn't know."

Donovan took a moment to put all those new pieces of information together. It wasn't like TV. Underwater, apparently, they *didn't* hear you scream, especially if they were in full scuba regulation dive gear. He threw out another question as it formed in his brain. "So if there were sharks in the area, wouldn't they come after a person who was bleeding? That's normal, right? So if they know the sharks are there, why aren't they taking better care of each other? Isn't this the whole point of dive buddies—to keep this from happening?"

He kept pushing forward, not understanding how one woman was murdered—that's what it was—while another just looked away and scraped coral or such. "I mean, she interacted with another diver who looks like he stabbed her?"

Donovan said it with a question mark. They hadn't even addressed that aspect of the video yet. "And she dies with several sharks attacking her, and the other diver possibly doesn't see it. Why isn't this something they have planned for?"

It was Eleri who sighed and tipped her head back and forth. She was thinking about her answer and Donovan liked that. She never devalued him for the things he didn't know. "Yes, there are clearly sharks in the water. But for the most part, they leave you alone."

Donovan felt his eyebrows climb. *Clearly, they didn't.* But he let her continue.

"I've seen videos where sharks have come up behind divers

and bumped them, but they don't bite. Even if they do bite, people often shake them off. So yes, this *can* happen." She waved a hand at the video. "And, obviously, it *did*. But it's really the exception rather than the rule."

"So this isn't her dive buddy's fault?" Donovan asked.

Again, Eleri tipped her head side to side, as though to say *yes-and-no* and this time Noah jumped in. "Neriah stated that she and Allison often got somewhat separated, but that they were very good at hooking back up, and that they would both simply surface if they didn't find each other underwater. You're right, it is a really bad practice, for exactly this reason. But while there are guidelines, there aren't really any laws stating you have to stay with your dive buddy. And, at least according to Neriah, this is what she and Allison usually did."

Eleri added, "It's the same thing Hannah said. They have grant money, but it only lasts so long. So, they have to get the work done in a certain amount of time. That often means splitting up to get samples. If they stayed together, they would need twice as many dive crews or twice as much time."

Donovan was getting it—standard practice, slightly cutting corners. It was usually fine until it didn't work out. Then it created a huge problem.

Eleri's next tip of the head indicated she had thought of something. "Donovan, you might have touched on Neriah Jones' disappearance with that idea. I hadn't thought of it before, but if she feels responsible for missing this, she might have run off to find the killer. It does look like she at least eventually found the video, so she might be playing sleuth."

Donovan was thinking that through. Citizen sleuths were a terrible idea. It never worked out like in cozy mystery books. People really died. He pushed that thought aside and tried to process Neriah's motive. He thought there was a disconnect between what Neriah might have done when she first fled versus what she might think now. "So you think it's plausible that Miranda Industries didn't get to her, threaten her in some way, and make her flee?"

"It's plausible," Eleri said. "But my personal guess is that it's both. I think she left because they threatened her. It all happened too fast, and the texts to her friends indicate she believes someone is after her. She's not just hunting, she's hiding. But at some point, she watched this whole video, and she might think she can solve Allison's murder."

Donovan was nodding along when GJ at last jumped back into the conversation. "We still need to watch this again. And none of us has addressed the issue about when she gets stabbed. . . or the fact that the other diver doesn't look like he's touching her when it happens."

CHAPTER 33

Everyone was hovering behind her, and GJ had to crane her neck to watch the conversation.

She was glad to know the information Donovan was digging into. She, too, had been wondering whether the diver with the camera had simply listened to a murder occur behind them and had done nothing. She pointed to the screen though and drew everyone's attention. "We have to address this issue."

They had only seen the video once, but she had watched it multiple times, particularly the portion near the end, where the diver died. Not willing to wait until the conversation came back around, GJ took control. "All right. Diver A is the diver we think is Allison. Diver B is the diver who comes into scene and appears to be responsible for her death. Diver C is our camera holder."

She hoped she was being clever and helpful—A for Allison, C for camera. Easy to remember, she hoped. They had a lot to sort out, especially if she'd seen what she thought she did. "So, Diver C and Diver A are how far apart, do you think?"

She was looking at Eleri and Noah this time.

"I know the water can distort the image," Eleri said, "though I'm not overly familiar with underwater photography."

Noah's hands went into the air, indicating it wasn't his specialty either. "Thirty or forty feet," he said. "Maybe more. We'll get an analyst on it."

GJ made a note and went on. She'd found the video. This was her show. "We're going to watch it again. And what I want right now is every bit of information we can glean on Diver B."

They'd already done everything they could with Diver A, she thought. They were relatively confident that was Allison. If the dive team was, as Hannah had indicated, Neriah, Hannah, Allison, and Jason—the fourth diver on the boat that day—then the camera person had to be Neriah.

Diver B was the wild card. Before anyone could object, GJ hit play and watched as their faces all pulled in closer to the screen. One by one, they pointed out things they saw and she took notes.

"Look, he grabs his knife here." Noah pointed and she noted the time stamp. "That may indicate that he's intending to stab her. Or that he sees the sharks are coming. Can we get in closer?"

GJ didn't reply but hit the appropriate buttons and enlarged that portion of the screen, making it slightly grainier. The water in the distance did nothing to help, but they continued to examine it the best they could.

"Now I can't guarantee it's a knife." Noah sounded irritated.

"But it sure looks like one," GJ replied.

"It's plausible." It was Donovan who popped in next. "He pulls the knife *after* he's moved away from her. How far apart are they there?"

"Eight to ten feet," Eleri estimated, and GJ wrote it down with a question mark. "So he approaches her, tangles with her, backs up, and *then* pulls out the knife." The words came out as a murmur, but GJ agreed.

Next, GJ walked them through the steps. She didn't say it, but she'd seen the same thing when she first watched it.

"Okay. Rewinding," she said and went back to where Diver B initially came onto the screen. "I want everyone to watch carefully. Is the knife out when they're tangling?"

The video played a few seconds and Donovan chimed in. "Look. She sees him. He's very close behind her and she turns to face him. But she seems to sense it or she sees something peripherally—"

"There's very little peripheral vision in that mask," Noah added. "But maybe. . ."

Donovan continued. "She turns. Diver B comes at her, but she pushes him away a little." His head craned closer to the screen and farther into GJ's personal space.

"I'm not even sure they touched physically. They may just be waving their hands." Eleri, too, was now leaning close enough that GJ could feel her breath. She didn't comment.

Going back to the start of Diver B's appearance, they watched the interaction three more times, drawing no better conclusions. When it finished, Eleri stood up straight, almost as though to stretch. "So, Diver A appears to be bleeding from stab wounds, and Allison's body has corresponding stab wounds."

It was Donovan who moved around the table and pulled up the autopsy report. He showed the photos to everyone at the table, pointing out the cuts that he had believed all along were knife wounds. They watched the video again, this time noting where Diver B touched Diver A.

"He doesn't touch her there." GJ could hear the frown and the confusion in Noah's voice. "He barely gets to her hands. It looks like their fins might have tangled, but he certainly didn't stab her in the shoulder. Not at that point."

GJ let the video keep going this time. The two divers moved away until Noah chimed in again. "She turns her back on him!

Whatever happened, she's satisfied enough to not continue watching him."

That struck GJ. She hadn't quite considered that possibility before. Whatever had occurred, Diver A—probably Allison—had decided it was *done*.

Turning the video on again, GJ watched her fellow agents' faces now, because this was the part that had struck her the most. On screen, Diver A twitched and reacted to something, though no one was in the water with her. Diver B was too far away. Then blood began trailing into the water from what must be wounds.

"Is it possible he stabbed her while they were entangled? And then he moved back?" Donovan pressed in even closer, as though being near could fix the graininess of the video quality and underwater blur. "Is it simply because she's finally still that we saw the blood?"

"I don't think so." Eleri stepped back, took a breath and said, "She's not still here. She's moving. I mean, you saw the pictures from the autopsy. You're the ME. Would those wounds bleed only a little? Would they start bleeding enough later? After she was stabbed?"

Donovan was shaking his head no, his assessment agreeing with GJ's own. Anthropology and biology had taught her about human form. Forensics had taught her blood. The stab happening at one moment and the bleeding happening noticeably later? She didn't think so either.

"She keeps moving about the same amount." Eleri made a quick motion with her hand for GJ to go back. Then, when GJ played the footage, she added, "Look, she's not acting like she was stabbed before. She turns her back on him. She goes back to her work. She's not checking herself for wounds. *Nothing.*"

There was a pause as they all watched the action play out one more time.

"And look." Eleri motioned GJ to forward the video. "She doesn't twitch until *here.*"

"Look at him, now—Diver B," Donovan mused, trying to make sense of it all. "So if we agree he pulled out a knife, then he's making stabbing motions. And she's suddenly acting stabbed and even beginning to bleed."

Yep, GJ thought, *here it came. . .*

"But he's a good three yards away," Donovan said with something akin to horror in his voice. "His knife *never touches* her."

CHAPTER 34

GJ absorbed the expressions on their faces as the three other agents finally saw what she had seen when she first watched the video. It was stunning, and they would need a minute to absorb it.

Leaning back, she hit the button and replayed the final segment.

"Shit," Noah said, drawing the word out. "You can see him making stabbing motions about three yards away from where she appears to be getting stabbed."

GJ merely nodded along. She wasn't sure if she'd been more anxious to see Eleri and Donovan's reactions or Noah's.

"Looks like psychokinesis." The Miami agent stood and crossed his arms with the proclamation.

All three heads swiveled to face him. Noah's eyes darted among the three faces. "I'm not saying that's what it is. I'm saying that's what it looks like."

They must have continued to stare at him, because he explained, "Psychokinesis is considered a psychic act. Moving objects at a distance without touching them."

"I know," Eleri said deadpan, but continued to look at him through slightly narrowed eyes.

GJ was working hard to keep her own expression neutral. It seemed she was often getting paired up with Noah, though whether that was because Donovan needed "personal time" for his "family issues" or because Eleri was trying to get rid of her, GJ didn't know.

"Well?" Noah asked the other three when they still hadn't commented on what they'd seen on the video. "What do you think it is?"

"I have no idea," Donovan replied, and he sold it as though he truly didn't. GJ was impressed.

She finally jumped into the conversation. "We've watched it seven times—this section of the video at least. Do you want to watch it again?"

It was Eleri who shrugged, rolled her eyes, and said, "I'm not sure what good it will do. Noah is right about what it looks like."

As GJ watched, Noah visibly relaxed. Apparently, that had been a big leap for him, throwing out "psychokinesis" as an option. GJ desperately wanted to turn to Eleri and Donovan and ask if they'd seen this before. But she knew they couldn't answer honestly—not with Noah Kimball standing by.

Eleri heaved a breath, pushed back from the table, and said, "I think the next thing we need to do is get our hands on the evidence and get that dive vest. Let's see if there's anything there indicating that she was stabbed."

When no one around the table objected, she added, "Previously, Donovan thought the autopsy pictures showed marks that looked like stab wounds. But we didn't follow through with that."

GJ nodded along as Eleri was talking. *She shouldn't be beating herself up,* she thought. But what she said was, "Of course, we didn't check. There hasn't been any time. While trying to figure out what happened to Allison, we discovered we've got one murder on our hands and two missing persons. The dive vest has been low priority."

"True," Eleri said with a pause, then stood, stretched, and eventually put her hands on her hips. Looking at the other three, Eleri doled out assignments. "Noah, I'd like you to head out to find the evidence. Find out if it's at the local PD or the ME's office, or if the local Marine Services has taken over this investigation. I truly have no idea where that vest is." She turned next to GJ.

Shit, GJ thought. She was getting an assignment, too. She would be sent on her way just like Noah Kimball was, but she looked up expectantly. She was going to be a team player if it killed her.

"Can you go back to Hannah and Allison's home? Contact Hannah first. See if she can hand over any other information. If she, *maybe*, has things that Allison was wearing or other things they had with them on the boat that day." With that decree, Eleri next announced, "Donovan and I are going to get this video to an analyst and then we're going to work a little harder to track down Blake Langley. Once the analysts weigh in, we can all think a little more about what we've seen on this video."

"Aye, Captain." Noah jumped up, grabbed his bag, and was out the door with GJ hot on his heels.

She followed him out of the building and hopped into the car. She trailed him a few blocks and then took a left where he took a right. As she was pulling up her information to get Hannah Raisman's address, her phone rang. *Eleri.*

"Hi." She almost added *I'm on my way*, as if to tell her teacher she was trying her hardest to do a good job.

"GJ, turn around and come back."

"What?"

"I sent you on a false flag mission. I needed to get Noah out of here. Just turn around and come right back. And seriously, I hope to God he doesn't come back for anything. Do not run into him."

"Yes, ma'am." GJ felt her heart lift. She had not been kicked out of the room along with Noah. She was getting invited back to play with the big kids. She didn't even mind going through security again.

As she practically crashed through the conference room door, she found Eleri and Donovan waiting for her.

"Thank God you're here," Eleri breathed out her relief. "We've been trying not to discuss this without you and it's really hard."

Sweet, GJ thought as Eleri looked at her.

"Did you agree with Noah about that dive video?"

"Absolutely. I noticed that the first time I went through. Diver B absolutely looks like he's stabbing. He's got a knife. He's making the motions." But she stopped and countered herself. "I'm not a video analyst. I don't have that kind of tech skill. I know what it looks like, but it's grainy and at a distance. And it's filmed by someone that I think had their camera upside down and dangling from their wrist—given the way the camera frame moves and sways."

"Yes, I thought the same thing." Eleri's lips twisted. "I hate to admit it, but I've made some similar videos." Then she backed that up with, "Not with murder in them, of course, but definitely where I left my camera on underwater and wasn't paying attention. Lots of video of my fins and occasionally my butt."

GJ laughed, but then Eleri turned serious again. "You've thought there was more to Noah for a while. Tell Donovan what you told me the other night."

Yes, GJ thought, *maybe she'd been right.*

CHAPTER 35

"GJ told me she thought something was up with Noah," Eleri said to Donovan, in an attempt to get all three of them onto the same page. They had a limited amount of time before Noah found the vest and brought it back.

She was a bit proud of herself. It was a legitimate assignment. Thinking about that, she turned to GJ and quickly told her, "Look, when Noah comes back, say you got a hold of Hannah, but you didn't turn up anything that we don't already have copies of."

GJ nodded, catching on that Eleri was trying to get them set up for when Noah came back with evidence and found that GJ was already here, empty-handed.

Donovan questioned GJ next. "What did you think was off with him?"

"When we were in Neriah Jones' apartment, he got her password very quickly. I love breaking code, but this was faster than anything I've seen. He wasn't looking through her information, checking her birth date, or pets' names. He just put his hands over the keyboard, as though he was hovering them there and thinking. So I want to say that part wasn't *too crazy,* but I didn't see his fingers move when the dots appeared on the screen that the password was getting typed. And then it was correct. He got it right somewhere between the first and third try."

Eleri sat back. She'd heard this before, but catching a password that quickly was pretty wild. "Was it maybe *monkey* or *dragon* or *password?*"

"Nope." GJ shook her head. "It's in the notes. It's a decent password. I don't know that I would have even guessed it from the information on hand. Even having seen what I've seen—and I imagine you've seen more. . ."

Eleri nodded but GJ kept talking. "It looked like he put his hands over the keys, and the keys *remembered* the password. I know that sounds dumb as shit—"

Eleri waved a hand and cut her off. *Dumb as shit* didn't exist in the world she occupied now. In fact, she was beginning to wonder if she could do that trick herself. *Things to try.* She added it to her ever-growing list.

Turning to Donovan, she added, "Once GJ talked to me about this, I thought about when we were at Weeki Wachee, in the office with Jessica LeBlanc. In the middle of her interview, she just. . . *startled* and looked over her shoulder. You remember? She said she thought somebody had tapped her?"

When Donovan nodded, she continued. "Noah was the only one who didn't seem to react to that."

"I noticed that too." GJ looked back and forth between them, but Donovan didn't reply. That didn't surprise Eleri. He'd been on his A-game lately, but not for this case.

"Then later," GJ said, leaning forward, "he commented that he didn't think Jessica startled easily."

"So do you think *he* did it?"

"I think it happened," GJ said cautiously. "I think he was in the room when it happened. And I think his reaction to it happening was abnormal."

Eleri almost laughed at GJ's clinical evasiveness.

It was Donovan who shrugged this time. "We've seen Westerfield do stuff like that."

"*What?*" GJ stretched the word as her jaw fell open, her head swiveling between Donovan than Eleri. "*Westerfield* can do it?"

"I've only seen little things," Eleri offered, but Donovan put in, "A bottle cap sliding across the table—"

"That's super obvious," GJ interrupted. "I mean, unless he could have had a magnet underneath—"

"It was a plastic cap. However," he replied, "he has that quarter he always walks across his fingers. . ."

Eleri watched GJ's eyes grow larger as she put the pieces together.

"Can I ask you a question?" Her voice was cautious, softer than normal. This was not the usual no-holds-barred GJ. "Is there anything else I should know about Westerfield?"

Eleri felt her breath hit her lungs. "There probably is. The problem is, Donovan and I don't know it either. He's got at least that mild psychokinetic ability. It may be stronger—I have no evidence for or against that. He seems to also have an ability to find us."

"I don't have any special skills," GJ said, her shoulders moving up and down, as though casually dismissing that she wasn't part of the group. But Eleri had her own take on that.

"I'm not so sure that you don't."

"*What?*"

Well, if nothing else, Eleri thought, *she'd managed to shock GJ three times inside of ten minutes*. That was a good record. GJ was hard to shake. "Your ability to find the patterns and things and to see the codes. . . That's unique."

"I'm not confident that's something beyond the normal. Just a skill like any other," was all GJ said as she sank back into her chair to let Eleri's words absorb.

"It's pretty impressive," Eleri smiled and watched the shift in her junior agent. Whatever Westerfield was or wasn't, he'd made a good choice in GJ. Eleri hadn't initially seen it, but he had.

"So what about Noah?" GJ asked, shifting the topic back. "What do we do?"

"I thought we had this case because I knew Allison and Hannah, but now I'm thinking we got this case because, as usual, Westerfield saw something in it."

"Is that a skill of his?" GJ asked.

"I'm beginning to think it is." Eleri had been growing more and more certain of this lately. "There have been a number of cases that Donovan and I had been on now that seemed perfectly human to begin with. Then, as we went along, we learned there was an element that—" *how should she put this?* "—only NightShade could truly assess."

GJ and Donovan were nodding along. It was GJ who asked, "So, do you think that's what this case is?"

"I'm starting to." Donovan was the first one who replied.

"But we've been saddled with Noah Kimball," GJ added. "I mean, whether or not I have any special skills, I am up to speed and I am in the Nightshade division. There's three of us. Then we've got this local agent who's supposedly showing us around, but we can't speak freely in front of him. How do we solve this if Noah is going to be more hindrance than help?"

Eleri had wondered the same thing from the start, but added "Maybe Westerfield is even better than we gave him credit for." Looking between Donovan and GJ, she made certain both were paying attention before she spoke. She had to get all of this out before Noah Kimball returned. "So here's the question: Why *did* Westerfield put us with Kimball?"

"Do you think he's the killer?" GJ blinked with a sudden revelation. "If he can move things without touching them, that puts him into a very narrow suspect pool. . . of which we currently only know one person. Noah."

Sucking in her own breath, Eleri felt it physically as the pieces clicked together. Noah was a diver. He lived in the area. He was here at the time of the murder. And he seemed to have the ability to do what was on the video. But what she said was a little different.

"Moving computer keys is not the same amount of skill as stabbing a human. Stabbing takes force." All three of them at the table knew that. "Still, it's plausible that he's the killer. He could have stabbed Allison and then gotten assigned to the case. But what's his tie to Miranda Industries? To Allison? Why would he do it?"

CHAPTER 36

"He's lived in Miami since the FBI placed him here." Donovan threw out the next piece of information he'd found on Noah Kimball. It wasn't very useful. "That was four years ago."

The three of them sat in the conference room with door closed tight—not locked, because it would be too suspicious. As quickly as they could, they were digging up every little piece of information they could find on Agent Noah Kimball.

Donovan was assigned to his FBI history.

GJ was tracking Miranda Industries and trying to find any links that might connect Noah to Allison Caldeira's murder.

Eleri was working on his personal past.

"His family's very involved in their church in Salt Lake." She tossed it into the middle of the room, as though they were growing a physical pile of evidence.

"Should I check his work log?" Donovan asked, catching Eleri and GJ's eyes for the first time. They'd each been hunched over their computers, their screens primed to flip to other information as though they hadn't been scraping the web and the FBI files for Noah's background. Their conversation was ready to change as soon as Donovan heard Noah enter the hallway.

He was keeping his ears perked and hoping he would hear the other agent from enough distance to give warning. But they were ready, in case he missed.

Eleri looked between the three of them. "Vote."

GJ put her thumb up. Donovan did the same, and Eleri did, too. It was an immature voting system, but it was fast and it worked. With a nod, Donovan jumped into the Miami Bureau system and pulled up Noah Kimball's time cards.

"Fuck, man. He's been working close to eighty-hour weeks since he got here four years ago. Only two weeks total of vacation. The last was more than a year ago." Noah was looking less and less like the killer, but Donovan wasn't ready to pull that plug yet. "If he killed Allison, he did it on the clock."

The problem with pulling the other agent's time reports was—while it gave them tons of information and would let them know where Noah likely was at the time of the murder—it also might ping somebody in the Miami branch office. If they learned that other agents were looking into their own agent. . . well, depending on how well Noah fit in, or how the SAC ran the place, they might let him know he'd been checked out. And by whom.

Too late now, Donovan thought. It was done. "Let me see if I can figure out where exactly they had him during the window for Allison's murder."

"There's no *window*," GJ reminded him. "It's just a handful of minutes. The video has timestamps." She turned back to her own screen, diligently scrubbing for her own information. But while Donovan and Eleri had been tossing out details they'd found, GJ had been quiet. Did that mean she hadn't found anything? Or had she hit a motherlode?

"Good point," he conceded as he dove back into the system.

"His social media is almost nonexistent, *currently*. Eleri

tossed her next tidbit out to the group. "But he has old profiles from college. He graduated high school in Salt Lake with honors and immediately left the homestead."

It was a few minutes later, as Donovan was rummaging his way through Noah's reports, that Eleri added, "He graduated UVA with honors again, this time in political science. Looks like he's got a law degree and partied a bit in college. . . Several boyfriends mentioned. Not at the same time. He's serial; nothing long- lasting. And no ugly public breakups."

Donovan was trying to take it all in while doing his own work and reading the reports in front of him. At least this was enough to keep him from thinking about his brother and his mom. He blinked away the building pressure that came each time the memory crept in unexpectedly.

He'd moved from confused to angry. His mother had been alive for years after she'd. . . died? Left him? Then again, he still didn't have the whole story, and he was trying to withhold judgment. With a harsh physical swallow that mimicked his mental need to tamp all of that down, he forced his focus back to the screen.

Eleri looked at her watch. "I hope Allison's dive vest is elusive and gives us more time. But I also hope he finds it. We need that vest."

Donovan didn't comment. His fingers flew over the keyboard as document after document popped up. "He was in Miami when Allison was killed." Points against Noah. "It looks like he was working with another local agent that day."

Both Eleri and GJ stilled as they watched him.

"So," Eleri offered slowly, "What if the other agent let him disappear for a little while?"

"Could he have done it? I mean, would it be physically possible?" GJ asked. "Allison was killed in the water, miles off the coast."

"I imagine it would be very hard," Eleri replied. "Even if he had everything ready, he would have to get to a dock."

"Was he even near one?" GJ looked back and forth.

"I don't know." Donovan didn't know his way around here. Their assignment with Noah Kimball had made sense—get a local who knew their way around. But if Noah was at fault, then. . . "It's Miami. Isn't everything near a dock?"

"Valid," GJ replied and Eleri continued. "He'd have to get to a dock and have a boat fully stocked and ready. Then he'd have to get out within range of where Hannah and Allison were—close enough to where their research vessel was, but far enough that they didn't spot him. He'd have to anchor, dive, find them, commit the act, leave, get back to his own boat, return, and probably dry off."

"So it would be a long absence," GJ clarified.

"Absolutely," Eleri said.

Donovan was grateful GJ had asked, because he hadn't been sure.

"Call?" Eleri asked, looking at him, before she clarified. "Do you want to call the other agent and see if it was possible that Noah left for that long? I don't want to clear him and then be wrong. GJ's right, the pool of possible suspects here just went way down with that video. Noah is on that short list."

"Do you think he can keep his mouth shut that we've interrogated him?" Donovan asked. He was already pulling out his phone, but he knew it was vital that Noah not be alerted to what he'd done. That was as important as the information.

"Tell him he has to stay quiet." Eleri was tapping her pen on the table. "All we need to know is: Was it possible that Noah could have left for a long enough period of time? If he couldn't, then we'll have our answer."

"Unless he can astral project," GJ offered, almost too casually.

Donovan felt it as both he and Eleri turned and glared at her.

As she watched them, her eyes went wide and her hands came up into the air, palms out, as if to ward them off. "I was just saying. I really don't think anybody can do that." Then she tacked onto the end of her question, "Can they?"

"I don't know." Donovan ground it out through his teeth. The last thing he needed was to have to learn about or deal with someone astrally projecting. "I'm going to go with *no*." But he said that mostly because he didn't want it to be possible. "So are we decided I'm calling Agent Dobrowski?"

"Vote," Eleri said and once again, they got three thumbs up. Donovan figured if they'd already pinged the Miami system, they might as well go all the way.

"I have to leave the room to call. I can't risk Kimball coming in while I'm on the line."

The other two nodded, and he was out the door and on the line with the Miami agent. Donovan clarified the date, and then pushed harder. "If you were on a stakeout, is it possible that he was out of your sight for more than two hours?"

That was the narrowest timeframe Eleri figured that the act could have transpired in.

"No way." Dobrowski was clear and firm in his answer. "He wasn't always in my sight, but we were on comms the whole time."

That, Donovan thought, was pretty telling. It would be hard to be on comms if Kimball was on the open water. Or under it. "Was there any period of time where you were out of communication? Say. . . for more than twenty minutes?"

"I don't think so."

"And he was in your sight most of the time?"

That, too, earned a very positive answer from Agent Dobrowski. He seemed to like—or at least respect—Kimball. But some of the coldest killers got away with it because they were so likeable. Donovan was about to ask his next question when he heard a familiar foot pattern down the hall.

He wouldn't be seen. He was tucked into another room across the way from where Eleri and GJ still worked. But he knew those footfalls, and that was definitely Noah Kimball coming back.

There was no way to warn GJ and Eleri.

CHAPTER 37

Eleri's head popped up at the sound of the bumping knock. She knew it wasn't Donovan, and something told her it was Noah.

She'd been afraid when Donovan left the room to call Noah's old partner that this would happen. Quickly, she tapped her keyboard even as she reached out and almost smacked GJ on the arm, startling her, hoping to tip her off to do the same. They needed to cover their searches on Noah's history before he came into the room and saw them.

The door was open before GJ could change her screen, but they had smartly faced away. All was not lost. Yet.

GJ looked up with a smile. "Hi, Noah. Looks like you had better luck than I did."

Beautiful, Eleri thought. Noah's hands were full. "Did you find the vest?"

Maybe they didn't have to fake a conversation about something else. Maybe GJ's comment had done enough.

"I found so much." He hefted the cardboard file box in his hands as though to gesture just what a haul he had. As he moved it, Eleri heard the rattle inside. Even as he did that, GJ subtly hit a button and changed her screen. Hopefully, everything would run smoothly and Noah wouldn't suspect they'd been digging into his past.

Eleri hadn't yet made up her mind. Donovan's information would most likely clinch it. Knowing that Noah was not capable of committing the crime because he hadn't been gone for long enough to do it worked pretty well in her world. She'd yet to find someone who could actually bend time. Then again, in her world, who knew? She pushed that horrid thought aside, deciding not to borrow trouble.

Noah set the box down and lifted off the lid. He reached inside and pulled out a large paper bag. Within moments, he had signed the log printed on the front of the bag and was snapping on gloves and wrenching the staple open. He gingerly held up the vest in question.

Eleri was snapping on her own gloves, and GJ quick behind her as she headed around the table. "Oh, man." She reached out, pushing a gloved finger into one of the slices.

"Looks like a knife cut," Noah conceded by way of agreeing.

"Did no one catch this before?" Eleri asked. The M.E.'s office, the police who investigated, and anyone who handled it should have looked the vest over. Standard black, it concealed the marks and damage rather well. Thus, the vest needed to be held up to the light and touched as they were doing now. But someone along the line should have already done this.

The other agent shrugged. "I don't know. I mean, they thought it was a shark attack. The body had very clear signs of shark bites. We now have video that there was, in fact, a shark attack."

GJ was nodding along, even as she continued to poke at the vest carefully, looking for more holes. She pointed when she found the next one.

"So," Eleri understood. "They must have decided they had their manner of death and they didn't look further. But I'm telling you—" she looked up at Noah. "Donovan took one look at those pictures and said *these look like knife wounds.* Is your ME usually this poor?"

Noah didn't defend them. "There are several of them. Miami Dade is huge, and you're probably already aware that we have a pretty horrific murder rate. Several of the MEs are very good. And several of them. . . well. . . they tend to go for the obvious. And unfortunately, I think Allison Caldeira's body wound up in one of those hands."

Eleri understood. It sucked, but she understood. This science was pretty solid, but there had been so many hands short-changing it, taking shortcuts, overstating the abilities of the science or missing things like the knife marks in Allison's dive vest. She understood why people got frustrated with forensics.

Just then, Donovan walked in the door that Noah had left open. "Hey, Noah." Perhaps he dove into the conversation as a way of preempting Noah from asking where he'd been. "You found the vest."

Still holding it in his hands, Noah turned and held it up to him. "Yes. With knife marks. There are other items in the box, too. Additional evidence from her case." Noah turned to put the vest back into the box and Donovan caught Eleri's eyes over Noah's bent head and shook his head back and forth.

It wasn't Noah. Eleri breathed out a sigh of relief. She felt her shoulders drop—they must have been up near her ears—and hoped Kimball hadn't noticed.

Noah was working on the table, laying out plastic to retain the integrity of the evidence. He picked the vest back out of the box and carefully set it out for them all to examine and then reached into the box. "Look at this. I didn't get her oxygen tank, but I do have pictures, and it remained in pretty good condition. So when she was stabbed—*assuming she was stabbed, I mean*— they didn't get the tank. I signed out all the other evidence except the tank." He waved his hand over the contents of the box.

Kimball continued with his presentation and Eleri was glad she could focus on it without having to worry that he was showing off evidence of his own crime. "So the tank wasn't damaged." He pulled the stage out of the box—the piece that screwed on top of the oxygen tank and held four tubes. Two were for the diver to breathe; one of the others hooked into the vest, and the last held a gauge.

"Look." He displayed the stage, holding out the tubes for inspection. "Nothing here is tampered with or damaged. Everything is intact."

Eleri understood what he was saying, even if perhaps GJ and Donovan didn't. It likely wouldn't make sense to anyone who wasn't a diver. "What it means is that Allison wasn't losing air. Which means she didn't have an immediate impetus to aim for the surface."

Noah nodded, but it was GJ who jumped in. "My guess is that she *couldn't* aim for the surface. From the video, it looked like there were sharks on her relatively quickly, once she was stabbed—as though whoever stabbed her knew they were there and would take advantage of the situation."

Eleri agreed. "That's concerning. I mean, I'm assuming he can't control the sharks. So it may indicate that he was down there for quite some time, maybe even following them for several days, waiting for a situation where a large shark was nearby. And if it were me—" She hated imagining how she would kill a diver; it was nothing she would have ever contemplated doing. "—I would have waited for great whites, or bull sharks, maybe hammerheads. There are plenty of other sharks down there, but they're often just not aggressive enough. Certainly not around three people underwater."

GJ was looking at the vest, hooking her fingers into the

shoulder and lifting it with a surprised look on her face. "It's really heavy."

"Underwater, that doesn't matter so much," Noah explained. "But actually, that's the vest's job. It holds air pouches that you can inflate from your tank, and it has weights. They counter each other to help you move up and down." He reached into the pocket in the vest and yanked out a velcroed-in weight pack, handing it to GJ to test.

"Oh." GJ drew the word out, telling Eleri that she'd realized something from holding the weight pack. "So that's why the body didn't float. It had weights."

Smart GJ, Eleri thought. She'd wondered about that herself but hadn't gotten that far in her reasoning. Bodies normally floated, but Allison's had taken days to wash up. "And look," Eleri pointed to the vest, tying it all together. "The stab wounds go through the float pouches."

Looking to the non-divers, she went on. "Normally, one of the things you can do is you just press this button." She held up the tube and button in question. "That will inflate the vest quickly and buoy you to the surface. Surfacing rapidly might give you nitrogen toxicity, but that's safer than say, getting eaten by a great white shark." She held up the vest again. "A careful diver—on a normal dive—rises in small increments. But if I were bitten by a shark, I might very well just hit and hold the button, to float myself to the surface and get away, if I could."

"But not with the holes," GJ said. She was catching on. "She could hit the button all she wanted. It goes into the vest, but the vest was leaking, badly. The button would just make her leak oxygen right out of her tank."

Eleri nodded. "What a nightmare. Though honestly, once Allison was bitten by the first shark. . ." She didn't even know if the diver had seen the others, or if it was already too late. "Her BCD not working was probably the least of her worries."

They all examined the vest for a few more minutes before

Noah looked up and met their eyes. "Did you figure out yet how he stabbed her?"

Eleri shook her head. It was mostly a lie, but she couldn't tell Noah Kimball what they thought. She even thought about expanding her lie.

Instead, Noah surprised her. "If I tell you something, it has to go no further than this room."

"Anything in this room goes into the FBI files. So that makes it pretty confidential up front. Are you saying—"

Noah was already shaking his head. "Not into the files. No further than this room." He waited a beat, and then told them. "I think it *was* psychokineses. It exists. I know someone who can do it."

CHAPTER 38

"Is it you who can move things without touching them?" GJ asked before thinking. *Shit*, she thought. She'd really been working on staying quiet, and here she'd gone and blown it.

Eleri's head swiveled toward her, shock on her face, as though to make it clear that GJ had fucked up.

"Not me," Noah replied as though it were perfectly logical that GJ would ask that. He took a deep breath, looked in each of their eyes, and made them again swear not to leak the information.

"I promise," GJ said. "I won't tell anyone." As soon as the words were out, she regretted them, though this time her regret was for an entirely different reason. Hell, he should have made them *pinky swear*. They were FBI agents, for fuck's sake. He had to know that if what he told them indicated someone was at risk, none of them would be keeping this secret of his.

"My brother Beckett can do it," Noah said.

That was not the answer GJ had been expecting. Well, at least he hadn't gone for the old, *I have this friend* thing. It was Eleri who stayed calm and asked for elucidation.

"What exactly do you mean? Your brother can stab somebody underwater?"

"No!" Noah's immediate rebuttal was harsh, but he brought his tone down quickly. "He wouldn't. I'm sure that you can check his records and find out exactly where he was at the time of Allison Caldeira's murder. I know for a fact he was in Colorado working his own case."

"He's an officer or a marshal or an agent?" GJ blurted out. But at least this wasn't the kind of statement that would earn Eleri's ire.

"He's FBI. Like me. . . Or I'm like him. He's my older brother. He entered Quantico two years before me." He looked at Eleri and Donovan and shrugged. "Yes, we are one of *those* Mormon FBI families. But Beckett is strong enough to move something at a distance with the force it would take to stab a human being. So you don't know that—because we aren't going to tell anyone that he's capable of that. But I'm telling you all this because, when I look at this video, I see someone doing something that most people would say was impossible if they hadn't seen something similar with their own eyes."

"What exactly did Beckett do that's similar?" Eleri pressed for details. GJ understood. This whole thing was concerning. How many people could do this? It was a small pool. GJ still thought Noah might be covering for his own abilities, but nothing in his demeanor suggested even a small lie. Maybe he was just good at it. She watched closely.

"We would go hiking in the woods," he told them. "We would take a different trail, away from our parents, and he would practice lifting rocks. Over the years, he could lift bigger and bigger ones."

"How very Skywalker of him," GJ commented before she thought, wondering if he'd pulled the story right from Star Wars. She really had to get a grip on her runaway mouth right now, but this was a fascinating conversation. GJ was about to ask her next question when Eleri jumped in.

"What's missing from your story?"

"I don't understand," Noah replied, stiffening slightly.

There, GJ thought. That was the point where he gave away the truth. He'd not been lying before, but he was clearly uncomfortable now with Eleri's press for more information.

"More than what you told us happened during those walks into the woods," Eleri said simply. She pushed as though she already knew this for a fact. Maybe she did. GJ did not discount Special Agent Eames' abilities. But was Eleri picking up cues from the way Noah told the story, or did she simply know, of her own accord, that there was more?

Right then, a stab of jealousy hit GJ hard. There were so many things Eleri could do. Donovan was a medical marvel. Though he would tell anyone that there was absolutely nothing outside the range of normal science about him, he was still insanely fascinating, with skills beyond that of a normal human. GJ was merely smart. She'd been raised in an extremely scientific family and understood about control groups and baseline readings practically before she could walk. But in this group, she was underskilled—and now she was realizing that Noah Kimball was like *them*. Not like her.

So his brother might be able to lift rocks while walking in the woods, or maybe that was Noah himself. This could easily be a way of brushing aside scrutiny from himself. GJ no longer had any doubt that he had tapped Jessica LeBlanc on the shoulder out of thin air.

Noah Kimball responded to Eleri's push with a frown and the shake of his head, as though he didn't understand the request. But even GJ could see there was something *off* in his response.

Eleri pushed harder. "There was more going on than just

your brother lifting rocks during some hikes." She seemed to be watching Noah for any kind of micro expressions she might glean. "Did he twist squirrels' necks without touching them? Pull snakes or lizards out from under logs and break them in half?"

Noah's frown grew tighter and tighter. His head pulled back as Eleri spoke. "*No.*" He protested her statements even more forcefully. "That's why he practiced lifting the rocks. He didn't want to hurt anything. He's an FBI agent, like me. He's one of us, the good, blond-haired, blue-eyed Mormon boys who go into the FBI because we believe we can make the world a better place. So no, he never harmed *anything*. And I never saw any indication that he would ever do anything like that."

GJ didn't like the tension that was growing in the room, but she understood Eleri's need to ask. Sitting down, GJ peeled the gloves from her hands and started tapping on her keyboard. She agreed with Eleri that Noah was holding something back and she had some guesses that what happened in the woods wasn't about what this brother Beckett could do. But first, she checked something simple.

Touching the edge of her computer, she turned the laptop screen to face Eleri. "Beckett Campbell." She pointed to the picture. She would have looked up more to see if he was, in fact, a brother to Noah Kimball, but the agent's face was so much like the one in the room currently frowning at them that GJ had no doubt she'd found the right guy. "He does have an FBI agent brother named Beckett Kimball. And Beckett was in Colorado at the time of Allison Caldeira's murder."

Noah crossed his arms then, almost as if to say *See? I told you,* but Eleri wasn't done with him. "Are you like your brother?" Eleri pushed the point a little harder.

But Noah continued to shake his head. "No, I can't do that."

Where GJ would have opened her mouth and asked, What is it that you *can* do? Noah kept pushing. "You can't tell anyone what I told you. I'll deny it. It can't get out what Beckett can do.

It's too—" he shrugged, uncrossed his arms, and waved his hands around as though searching for words. "—strange. Unusual. I don't know, *out there.* He doesn't want to be studied like a bug in a laboratory."

Noah's eyes darted among their three faces as if checking for confirmation that they would hold up to their promise. "I only told you because I think it's pertinent to the case. Because I think if you dismiss what we saw on that film, and don't understand that it is something that some humans can actually do, then we'll spend a lot of time treading water here. While we try to figure out how this is possible, the murderer will get away. I believe this is the key to solving this case." He was pointing now at GJ's computer, as though the video were pulled up, and not the screen showing the information on his brother. That screen still covered the multiple tabs GJ had opened when she had been searching information about Noah himself.

But then GJ figured out the perfect button to push. With a nod to Eleri as if to say *Let me, please,* she waited a moment and then took over.

"Noah, if you don't want us to tell anyone what your brother can do. . . then you need to tell us what *you* can do."

CHAPTER 39

Donovan watched as Noah made his decision. GJ was basically blackmailing him. While Donovan didn't like the idea of blackmail, he had a very hard time disagreeing with GJ's tactic.

Noah was holding out on them. There was something in his stance, in the way his eyes darted. It was clear that they had all believed the brother was fictional at first, and only GJ's picture from the FBI database changed their minds. Donovan still wasn't even sure that Beckett might not be a mere normal mortal and Noah was using him as a cover for his own skills.

Donovan crossed his arms, adding his sheer bulk to the pressure of GJ's statement. He watched as Noah quickly glanced at each of the others.

Softer now, GJ pushed again. "I saw you. I saw you with your fingers over Neriah Jones' laptop keyboard. I saw you crack her password faster than anyone should have. . . . I noticed that you didn't actually touch the keys."

As the words came out of her mouth, they seemed to absorb into Noah. His expression slowly changed as he realized that he'd been caught.

"You also tapped Jessica LeBlanc on the shoulder," Donovan said, adding more than just his visible bulk to GJ's tactic. It was a few more bricks on the growing pile that Noah had to adjust to hold. His expression changed again, showing that he'd made a decision.

"My brother and I were close. We have a big family. Big Bibles all over the place. Neither of us fit in. Me—obviously—because I'm gay. So when that one came out, they prayed and prayed and prayed for me. But shockingly, it doesn't pray away." He rolled his eyes.

"I'm sorry." The words came softly from GJ, and Donovan appreciated her efforts.

Noah's head tipped a little bit in acknowledgement. "There were times with Beckett though, that they thought he had the devil in him. They tried exorcisms on him."

"Oh, hell," Eleri sighed as Noah told his story. Was he deliberately tugging at their sympathies? Donovan couldn't tell.

Eleri's expression was becoming more sympathetic. Donovan had to think on that. Though Noah wouldn't know it, Eleri had had the opposite upbringing. If anything, her Grandmere had been trying to get more devil *into* her. Her mother had denied everything. And, well, he couldn't imagine what the Kimball brothers had gone through. "Is it just the two of you? The only outcasts in the family?"

Noah nodded. "So, we were close—both outcasts, both misunderstood. Beckett eventually learned to hide it much better. He pretended the exorcisms had *taken* and he no longer had this problem."

Pulling out a chair, Noah plopped down into it, as though getting ready for a long interrogation. He leaned forward, elbows on the table, hands clasped almost as if in prayer, but he didn't drop his gaze. Donovan wished he had Eleri's skills of getting into someone else's head.

Since he didn't, he did what he could. Flaring his nostrils and twitching his ears, he did his best to smell and hear the things beyond what Noah was telling them. Fear came off the man, but it was nervousness, not rage. It matched his demand that the other agents not tell anyone what his brother could do.

Next to him, GJ was tapping on her keys again, though clearly still listening. Eleri was staring the man down, running this interrogation. So Donovan kept his focus on the other agent.

"Beckett practiced lifting rocks. I could do smaller things. I can move wind." He said the last part with a motion of his shoulders as though it were nothing. "I can flip the leaves on a tree, bump a chair, tap Jessica LeBlanc on the shoulder. But I don't have Beckett's skill level."

Eleri crossed her arms now, almost glaring at him. "There's more. There's something you're not telling us."

Noah seemed resigned. The look that moved across Noah Kimball's face said that he realized Eleri wouldn't give up until he gave her more. "I can. . . communicate. . . with animals. I mean, I don't know what they're *thinking*. It's not at all like talking to a person, but I can kind of tell if they're sick. Or rabid. And I can. . ."

He kept pausing, Donovan noticed, as though the words were hard to get out. It seemed he'd never actually told anyone this before. That made sense. If he and his brother were close, then he and Beckett would know these things about each other and not have to speak them out loud.

Noah also seemed to be trying to read his audience but, so far, the three of them hadn't burst into laughter nor nodded acknowledgment. They were a rough crowd. Donovan fought the urge to feel sorry for the younger agent.

"You're Doolittle?" GJ asked, still focused on her keyboard.

"No," Noah replied. He looked to Eleri. "It wasn't Beckett who would pull snakes out from under logs. It was me. I can pick them up, the poisonous ones, and they won't bite me.

Butterflies land on my fingers when I go outside. Kind of like fucking Snow White."

This elicited a sharp barking laugh that Donovan couldn't hold back.

"Thanks." The wry comment from Noah told him he understood Donovan's reaction. But he turned back to Eleri. "I didn't twist them and break them. I love animals. I have two cats, and I would have more, but I understand dogs' anxiety when their owners leave. I feel how anxious they get when things are happening beyond the walls. I'm in an apartment and often gone, so I can't have one. But I can sneak into homes where dogs live. I can do it with my gun drawn, and the dogs don't bark. And diving? I don't worry about the sharks. I can keep them away—"

"Or," Donovan interjected suddenly, "you could turn them toward another diver."

"*Jesus.*" Noah popped up from the chair, hands flat on the table. "I would never! I wasn't there. Surely you dug up all that dirt while I was out fetching the dive vest?"

Well, Donovan thought, *the good Mormon school boy wasn't as naive as he looked.* He nodded in acknowledgement. Noah deserved at least that much.

But Kimball wasn't done. He smacked his hands lightly on the table. "Do you want to go outside? Do you want to see that I can get a bird to land on your finger?"

Well, hells bells, Donovan thought. The last thing he wanted was a bird on his skin. A bird would probably sense what he was and not like him. Noah would be surprised to learn that his skills didn't extend to making birds get near Donovan. Probably not cats, either.

Just as the thought crossed his mind, it seemed to cross Noah's, too. Pointing at him, Noah waved his finger up and down. "And what's with *you*? Why does it feel like there's an animal near you all the time?"

Fuck. Donovan bit his tongue to not say it out loud, and he hoped to hell that his expression didn't reveal Noah Kimball's direct hit. This conversation had taken a turn he did not like.

But it was then that Eleri heaved out a deep sigh and muttered a string of her own swear words. She looked first to Donovan, then GJ. GJ turned her computer around and pointed at what she'd been tapping in her keys to find.

"Beckett Kimball has an excellent rate of arresting people without touching or bruising them or firing his weapon. Apparently, the other agents like to send him in for difficult arrests, because he always manages to take down the perp gently."

"Well, that's in line with what Noah said." Donovan offered that into the air, though Eleri's expression didn't change.

She looked from Donovan to GJ and back to Donovan again, before she practically spit out her words. "Westerfield didn't send us here to find Noah because he's the killer. He sent us here to *recruit* him."

CHAPTER 40

E leri watched for Noah's reaction. She'd first asked him for a place where they could go and discuss the group members' abilities freely. Noah had initially suggested his apartment.

"That won't work." Eleri shut that down fast. "You're FBI. What if there's some kind of surveillance on you?"

"Are you serious?" His face contorted with the ridiculousness of her suggestion. "Why would anyone surveil me?"

"You just told us what you're able to do. To suggest that no one else knows this would indicate that you've managed to keep it under wraps all these years." He was being a bit naive, she thought, but she didn't want to be too harsh. Still. "I'll admit, GJ here has some phenomenal powers of observation, but she smoked you out in under three days, Noah."

Maybe she shouldn't have added his name to the last of that. It did sound a little like a hand slap. Yet she watched as the younger agent's eyes went round. For all his smarts and all his ability, it had clearly not occurred to him that someone might have figured out what he could do.

Eleri decided to pile it on a little thicker. There was a point to be made here. "Noah—beyond what GJ noticed in just a few days—please remember that our division of the FBI was sent down here to investigate a case that initially had no paranormal element. Yet our SAC requested you as our additional agent, to serve as our local eyes and ears. So now I have to ask if you think that was purely coincidental. Because I don't."

Noah shook his head slightly, agreeing with her assessment. The information sank in and she continued talking in an effort to give him a few more seconds to adjust. "Again, I'll admit that my SAC, Agent Derek Westerfield, has some phenomenal skills in this arena. But he found you before any of us even arrived in Miami. So, yes, I think it's highly possible that someone is surveilling you at your apartment."

"Is it your people?" Noah asked, staring her smartly in the eyes.

"I don't think so, but I can't promise you it's not. And I am sorry about that. It's not any agents that I know."

Noah nodded slowly but stayed in the game. "My brother and his wife lived here before they transferred to Colorado. They still have a condo here that they rent out. Let me see if it's open."

"Your brother's married?" She made small talk while Noah checked about the condo. "What does she do?"

"She's an agent as well."

"Is she now?"

That made his head snap up. "Don't get that look in your eyes," he warned her. "You don't know what my brother can do. And I'm not giving you any information about my sister-in-law."

Eleri nodded and held back the words, *Actually, you just did. Holy crap.* She now was convinced this was why Westerfield had kept her on the case, even though she had known the murder victim personally for well over a decade. Her SAC was attempting to scoop up possibly as many as three more agents into his NightShade division! It would have been nice if she'd been warned. But she was beginning to think Westerfield had a bigger agenda, and the only people he shared his plan with were above her pay grade.

"It's open," Noah said.

The condo was only a short drive away. They took two cars, and GJ volunteered to ride with Noah. Eleri didn't know if that was so he could ask questions of one of NightShade's newer recruits or so they could apprehend him if he tried to bolt. Either way, Eleri was grateful.

Once they were inside the unit, she and the other agents settled in for a little demonstration. She watched Noah's eyes as Donovan emerged from the bedroom on four feet rather than two. It was fun to watch GJ, as well. Even though GJ had encountered him in this form before, she remained scientifically fascinated by Eleri's partner.

Noah looked from the wolf to Eleri to GJ and said, "That's a nice trick."

Eleri was shaking her head, but it was GJ who jumped in. "If you can talk to the animals, talk to him. That's Donovan. You're the one who said that there was always an animal around him."

Both women watched as Noah's eyes turned back to Donovan. His expression changed a number of times before he finally settled on closing his mouth where it had fallen open.

Donovan's head tipped, but he didn't whine or growl. Then he turned and padded slowly back into the bedroom. Eleri regretted she didn't have a space for him to run. But what were they going to do in Miami?

Noah turned back to her. "That was beyond insane. So what exactly is it that *you* do?"

It wasn't a question she was fully prepared to answer. Eleri still found there was much she didn't know about her own skills. But she had harassed Noah and made him give up his own information, and turnabout was fair play. She was opening her mouth when GJ beat her to it.

"Eleri has ancestors in the Hale family, as well as the Llewellyn family, and the Remy family of New Orleans." GJ said it with a smile, as though she were revealing a great secret.

Noah merely shook his head, not understanding. At least his confusion made sense. Mormon families likely didn't know their American witchcraft history.

GJ went on to explain. "One of her many-greats grandmothers is Sarah Hale. Sarah Hale was tried at the Salem witchcraft trials and then disappeared. Eleri is the descendant of the witches who got away."

Eleri watched as one of Noah's eyebrows rose slightly. But GJ just kept steamrolling along. "The Remy family is one of the big New Orleans Voodoo families, originally out of Haiti. There's also the Dauphine family, and the two are highly interlinked."

This time Noah frowned. "What about the LaVeaus?"

"All show." Eleri waved a hand at him as though to dismiss the famous torture-and-crime family associated with New Orleans Voodoo. "Here."

She held the same hand she'd waved out to him now. The gesture offered to hold his hand and she watched as he gingerly set his own and hers.

A moment later, with flashes of images she still couldn't control, Eleri looked at him. "Your sister-in-law understands your brother better than you give her credit for. She's also very good at finding missing children. Isn't she?"

But Noah had already yanked his hand back from hers, his whole form jerking with her words. "That wasn't yours to know."

"I know. I know a great many things that aren't *mine to know*. You can rest assured I won't share it—not even with my SAC.

All I can believe is that Westerfield sent us here to recruit *you*. I'll leave it up to you about your brother and sister-in-law."

"What if I don't *want* to get recruited?"

Eleri shrugged. "That's a conversation between you and my SAC."

Donovan emerged from the bedroom then, fully clothed except for his socks and shoes dangling from his fingers. Sitting on the couch, he began sliding them on once again, inserting himself into the conversation. "Now that we've all played show and tell, I think we need to get back to the case. I think we need to get the boat and get on the water."

Eleri felt her whole body pull back at the idea. Donovan was suggesting they get *on the water*. Looking at him through narrowed eyes, she tried to assess his sincerity, or his motive.

"Trust me, I can't think of any other way to do it, or I would suggest that," he told her as he tied his shoe and placed his feet flat onto the floor as though holding onto the land. "I think we need to get Hannah, and then retrace their trip."

"They were attacked by pirates and their boat blew up," GJ countered.

"Right, that's part of why we need to go. That happened in Nassau. I wish we could have the original boat—*The Naiad*—but Allison disappeared off the replacement well after the piracy incident."

"We need to look into that more. Everything is possibly relevant." GJ looked at them and Eleri agreed. There were too many threads here and they'd seen Allison's notes about the attack on the original research vessel, the *Naiad*. It was more than possible that the piracy wasn't a coincidence.

Noah was nodding along.

"They lost some of the specimens when that happened," he said. "Maybe we can find them. Maybe we can find the same people. If Allison was a threat, why not Hannah? Are we good to take her along? She'd almost be bait. Do you think she'll be up for this?"

Eleri felt the weight of his gaze but couldn't say what her friend might be willing to do. Hannah had seemed both angry and scared. Eleri had no idea which would be dominant now. "Maybe. I don't know."

"I wish we could find Neriah Jones, but I get the feeling she's going to evade us for at least a while longer. If we can get a satellite connection, we can continue to monitor her email— and Missy Maisel's. We can leave her a message and let her know who we are and hope we don't spook her. If there's some way we can make ourselves look like Hannah's new dive crew," Donovan suggested to the group, "then maybe we can draw out the killer."

CHAPTER 41

E leri helped Noah loosen the boat from the dock. She couldn't recall if she'd ever done this kind of thing in the dead of night before, but it seemed her life was full of firsts.

"Are you sure you don't want me to come?" Noah asked. "Seems to me it'd be safer if someone else was on board."

"I don't know if *you* want to come," she countered. She'd only invited him out to guard the dock because GJ was still poring through the data. She'd taken much of it back to her hotel room and apparently was working well into the hours of the night, sleeping less than any of them. And because the idea of leaving Donovan on a rocking dock, for possibly several hours, was more than she was willing to put him through. It would be enough that he would be on the boat for days pretending to be Hannah's new dive crew.

So Eleri had gone out on the limb and invited Noah to watch over her late-night excursion. If Westerfield had sent them to meet Noah Kimball for the specific purpose of drawing him into NightShade, well then, she would initiate him. Tipping her head, Eleri said, "Look, Kimball, you're going to be on a boat with me in the middle of the water. I have several jobs to do with this boat and none of them may be like anything you've seen before. You can't flip out on me. You can't go overboard and make me have to swim after you. I'm a strong swimmer, but—"

"You're a mermaid." He added it with a smile, breaking a little of the tension. "So no, I would never try to out-swim you. And I'm still an agent. I've seen all kinds of weird shit, including a woman getting stabbed to death in the water near here. If this guy can do what the video makes it look like he can, then you might not be safe out there by yourself. Especially if you're casting some kind of spell." He pointed to the bags she'd brought on board. "You might not be paying attention. So yes, I can deal with it."

He paused a moment and added, "And if I can't, it's probably better that we all know it now rather than when we're fifty miles off the coast of Nassau."

He made a valid point, and in return, Eleri made a motion for him to jump aboard as the boat pulled away from the dock. He'd helped her load the bags she'd bought at one of the local witchcraft shops. A first glance around the small store had revealed that the place was mostly full of shit. But they did carry the pieces she needed.

She'd thought a shopping trip would be an easy way to break him in. Instead, she'd entered the store and the overly enthusiastic, pony-tailed employee had pushed hard to sell Eleri books on her own family history. Of course, the girl hadn't known. Honestly, Eleri wasn't completely sure she knew what to do now. But she'd cast a few spells here and there with Grandmere in her home, and she planned to duplicate that.

Eleri could have called her cousin Frederic to ask for advice, but she wasn't sure how he would feel about her using their great-grandmother's spells for FBI cases. So she'd chosen her supplies by feel.

Now, Noah drove them out across the dark water, the blackness of it almost sinister in the night. Beneath the surface, there were corals and currents and killers. It was probably better that she wasn't out here all alone.

With Noah steering the boat, she was able to head into the back and lay out her materials as best she could, given the rocking deck. She pulled out candles, white and fat, and placed them in the middle. She grabbed salt, a standard bag from the grocery store, and snipped the corner open, pouring an even circle around her. With a piece of blue chalk, she drew a symbol on the deck—the sigil Grandmere had given her in a dream.

Eleri stood up then, her clothing flapping around her in the breeze manufactured by Noah's speed. She was dressed in what looked like a rich woman's oceangoing clothes—white linen pants, button-down shirt, and a handkerchief tying her hair back. But what an onlooker might not realize was that she was wearing only cotton, and only white. That was what mattered to the spell.

Caught up in her own work, Eleri was almost surprised when Noah said, "I think we're here."

She had instructed him to drive them out where he could see no one and had seen no other boats for some time. *Here it was,* a spot alone where whatever happened with her spell wouldn't be seen by onlookers. *Here* was as close as they could get to where Allison was murdered, without alerting anyone.

She looked around, seeing no lights other than the moon bouncing off the waves, and declared the spot good. It was the best they could do.

"Do you want to go below deck?" She gave Noah a steady look. Getting on the boat and watching the proceedings were two different things.

"Honestly, I really don't."

But she tipped her head toward the door leading below deck, not quite ready to do any of this in front of him. Though she was fascinated at the science of it and had begged Donovan to change form in front of her, he had always refused. Now she was beginning to understand. It wasn't embarrassing. It was *personal.*

"I'm going." Noah held his hands up in surrender. He headed down the sharp flight of stairs into the hallway below.

The boat was bigger than necessary for day dives, because Hannah and her crew often took it into the Caribbean and back to the Gulf. They needed to sleep aboard. They needed a bathroom. They needed places to store their specimens and supplies. They needed air tanks for the entire journey, as they were diving consistently along the way.

Now Eleri paced the length of the ship, two bags of salt under her arm. She carefully poured a line just under the railing, trying to create a continuous ring that encompassed the entire boat. When that was done, she went back to her smaller circle, toeing the line of salt open and then pouring it closed behind her with the fistful she'd carried in.

Kneeling, her knees touched the edge of the sigil she'd sketched. One by one, she called the four corners, candles lighting as she listed their names. She chanted the spell Grandmere had fed her while she slept and repeated it until the winds pulled upward around her and the water sloshed against the side of the boat. Her brain went fuzzy and the world grew dimmer, but she kept the force behind her words. They had to stay safe on this boat.

It might have been an hour later that Noah stood over her, shaking her by the shoulder as her brain fog slowly cleared. "Are you okay?"

"Yes." Clearly, he hadn't expected this. She hadn't expected it, either. The spells often threw her for a loop.

"Holy fuck," he muttered, yanking his hand back and jerking his entire body away from her as if she scared him.

"What?" she asked.

"Your eyes. . ." He was looking her up and down as though checking for demon fingernails or a forked tongue.

"Ah. Are they black?"

He moved closer, squinting at her in the dark. "Maybe not. Maybe I saw it wrong. It must have been the light."

Eleri only nodded and didn't tell him he had seen correctly. "Why did you come up?"

"The whole boat lit up like St. Elmo's Fire. I think we got struck by some random lightning—" The last word cut off abruptly. "Holy shit. That was you."

She nodded and pushed to her feet. "Well, the good news is that the boat is now protected."

"So if somebody tries to put a bomb on it again. . . it won't blow up? Or it *will* blow up, but the boat will be fine?"

She motioned to him to head to the front and drive them home. She still wasn't quite steady on her feet. But as she took the seat next to him, he started the engine and let the boat gain momentum before he turned it to face a shore she could no longer see. Her limbs felt weak and heavy as she tried to explain.

"It doesn't really work like that. Sometimes, if you get enough power, you can send a shockwave or light a fire. But mostly, if it's done well, witchcraft works by making things *never* happen. Whoever tries to get a bomb on the boat will discover that they have a very hard time doing so."

"So it just thwarts them?" The wheel turned easily under his hands, making her confident that she would have another seasoned diver on board.

"Pretty much," she added as, slowly, she regained strength in her limbs and her brain cleared. But as she breathed easier, she stood and made her way to the back of the boat and looked out over the back railing, across the dark-and-light pattern of moon and water.

Was there a shadow back there?

She wasn't confident that her eyes saw it, but now she was sure: They were being followed.

CHAPTER 42

"Hannah," Donovan said, pushing his way into the conversation as gently as he could. His hand touching the other woman's forearm was, he hoped, comforting. "We can't take Jason with us. We would like to, but there are plenty of good excuses for him to stay behind. Like losing Allison was just too much. Or he's not ready to be on the water. Or maybe he can't travel at the last minute. So, you picked up a new crew."

In that moment, he wished he had Christina Pines' ability to push people into thinking what she wanted them to. They had come to get Hannah to first agree to the trip, and then agree to take on a new crew—mainly *them*. Eleri had already struck out, and Donovan could feel that he was about to, too.

Hannah shook her head. She wasn't buying any of Donovan's arguments. "Jason needs the job. He's my right hand. Allison *and* Neriah are both gone. I have to have someone I trust on board. Honestly, I think the whole thing looks suspicious if I take on a completely new crew."

She made a compelling argument. But Donovan and Eleri were unable to give their most important response: What if something had to happen that revealed what they really were?

There would be nowhere to escape, and no way to hide it from Hannah... or Jason.

NightShade was the FBI's best-kept secret. If they ruined that? Well, Westerfield would have their heads.

"I'm not going out without Jason."

Where Donovan had thought he would have the upper hand because he wasn't Hannah's friend, he now found he had nothing. Leaning back, he conceded that advantage to Eleri, though it didn't give her much of an edge.

They left ten minutes later.

"First off," he said, irritated as they climbed into the hot car. He was certain he would not miss this while they were on the ocean. "What the hell just happened in there?"

"We surrendered." Eleri shrugged as if to say *What could they do?*

"I got that. But *why?*"

"Because Hannah was *right*. And the harder we fought her, the more it became clear we had something to hide. We're just going to have to hide things from Hannah. If we're hiding it from her, we can hide it from Jason, too. We can't go out without Hannah."

Donovan was beginning to think he'd had a really stupid idea in making Hanna retrace her steps. But Eleri was still making her case. "Hannah knows the scenario. She knows where they stopped to get specimens. If anything happened to Hannah, even if she just got a stomach bug, we'd be dead in the water."

Donovan swallowed hard, disliking Eleri's choice of words as much as he disliked the new plan. But he conceded, there were no better options. Eleri wasn't wrong.

They had three days before the six of them hit the water. Hannah, Jason, GJ, Noah, and Eleri and Donovan. Everyone but Donovan and GJ would be diving in teams. At least, that was the plan—attempting to figure out where Allison had gone, and what she had seen. As there were no threats against Hannah or Jason, they needed to figure out what Allison and maybe Neriah had seen when they were underwater.

GJ was already compiling coordinates, using information from Allison and Hannah's old lab notebooks to find points to stop. She was adding information from where Blake Langley had obtained his original oyster clutches—the ones that had tipped him off to the problem and kick-started his second round of testing.

GJ had held up the notebook to them. "The fact that Blake's oysters came from a place almost in line with Hannah and Allison's trip is really concerning to me. That's why I think we need to check."

Their trip would take them to the oil rigs Hannah and Allison had stopped at. Using the coordinates, they found the one stop that seemed to have no man-made structure associated with it. Out in the middle of the ocean, this seemed to have simply been a point where they stopped. Yet somehow, Allison had gathered barnacles.

So far, Donovan hadn't been able to trace any known shipping container, research vessel, or other boat that had been in the area during the time Allison and Hannah had passed by. So it was difficult to say what Allison might have taken her samples from, since her notes were vague on that part.

Eleri had been contacting authorities in Nassau, attempting to find out if any headway had been made on the piracy case in which Allison and Hannah's initial research vessel had blown up. Noah was gathering dive equipment and backup gear, figuring out what would fit in the space on the boat. The whole while, Donovan's stomach turned.

He was the one who'd recommended getting on the boat. He'd possibly done it so that no one had to recommend it to him. He knew going out into the ocean was inevitable, given the case, but he wasn't looking forward to it.

Eleri promised him that being on the boat was very much like being on land—as long as he didn't go diving. There was absolutely no worry that he would go diving. He was not only *not* scuba-certified, but he wasn't even a solid swimmer. He was determined to be the nerd in the life vest, twenty-four-seven.

Telling himself that at least he wasn't the only non-diver was a little soothing, though he was already convinced that GJ would be able to handle the water with far more grace than he would. Still, he knew he had to go. This was the job.

There was one small, comforting factor in leaving the land. Leaving the land meant leaving his *brother.* It meant leaving the sordid history of his mother behind.

Wade had called the day before. He'd made it into Donovan's house to check for intruders. Not only did he not scent that anyone else had been in the house, but the scarf was still in the drawer.

Donovan had needed more than just a moment to absorb that. He'd gone to the box still on the hotel room table and pulled the very same scarf out. Holding it in his hands, he sent Wade a picture. Immediately, Wade sent back a picture of the scarf at Donovan's. The shot showed exactly where he had found it, which was exactly where Donovan had left it.

That meant that the scarf in Donovan's hands was *not* stolen from his drawer. The picture of his mother wearing the scarf must have been a picture of a duplicate. Donovan had sniffed it again. And again and again. Still, Amisha Bannerjee had worn *this* scarf. This one that he had in Florida with him—she had worn it plenty.

He thanked Wade. It wasn't a small favor. But it had given him a big answer.

No one had broken into his home. At least Donovan hadn't missed that.

He had been setting a timer each night. One hour was all the time he allowed himself to dig into his brother and mother's history. But even in the three hours that those nights afforded, he had found far more than he wanted to know.

His mother had given birth to Bodhi Banerjee. As best Donovan could remember—or stitch together from the dates in his own past—that birth had occurred a mere five months after she'd left Donovan and his father.

And that's exactly what she had done. She had given him the scarf and *left him behind with his father.* She'd been pregnant at the time, though seven-year-old Donovan had had no clue.

He found himself running at a constant simmer under the surface. Though at first, he'd managed to hold it back—telling himself not to be angry at her until he knew more—now he knew more.

The information he'd dug up revealed that she'd gone on to get work and an apartment, by saying she was single and had only the one young child. She'd said she was widowed. She'd used her limited English and gotten herself a job in a factory. She had raised Bodhi Bannerjee on her own. Donovan still didn't know if the factory work had done her in, or if she'd simply had a hard life, traveling all over Calcutta selling rags and phuchkas for loose change before finding her life tossed into a far worse situation with Aiden Heath.

As he searched his own memory, Donovan found nothing indicating his mother didn't love him. *But she hadn't died.* He didn't know if she had faked her own death and done a good enough job for Aiden to believe it—or if she'd managed to get away and he'd simply let her leave. That didn't seem likely.

Maybe that part didn't matter, because the hard part was that she had left Donovan behind. She'd had Bodhi and she'd given her younger son fifteen years of her life, more than twice as long as Donovan had gotten with her.

Rubbing salt into the fresh cut of Donovan's new knowledge, Bodhi had turned out to be a complete piece of shit. Though the *brother* angle was fascinating, Donovan realized what he was looking for was not his brother, but a connection to his mother. He'd found it. And it was disconnected.

He couldn't help the bitterness that roiled in him.

Getting on the boat the next morning felt like leaving it all behind—leaving the memory of his mother, leaving the trail he'd followed to find her behind him on the shore. He was leaving his brother, too, because his brother was built like him. And while Donovan might have enough friends and be brave enough to get on the water, he knew Bodi Heath would not be.

CHAPTER 43

"Eleri was wrong." GJ's head turned as Donovan continued. "The tricks don't work."

He was sitting on the deck of the boat, huddled miserably with his back pressed into the corner. His face was still a little green, despite Eleri's clear instructions to eat crackers, hold his breath occasionally, and stand with his legs apart, letting his feet rock with the boat while keeping his torso steady. None of it had worked for Donovan. Even anti-nausea medication hadn't quite solved his problems.

"You look better than you did," GJ offered with half a smile. But not good—he didn't look *good* yet.

His arms wrapped around his waist, almost as though he were clutching his life vest like a teddy bear. He merely tipped his head at her in acknowledgment and then leaned back against the railing again. So GJ let him be.

Hannah's research boat was older—a second hand vessel she'd bought because of it was big and affordable. Her money clearly had gone into the research, but at least her life vests were top-of-the-line: slim, Velcro-front pieces in bright colors. They were not full of huge chunks of foam, like the life vests that GJ was familiar with. No, these inflated either manually or as a person hit the water.

So Donovan wasn't quite as dorky as he'd threatened to be when he first stepped onto the boat. *And that's a good thing*, GJ thought, looking down at her own vest. They were all wearing them; Hannah had insisted.

The only excuse Hannah allowed was if you were on a dive or asleep below deck.

This new crew was sleeping in shifts on the small boat, only partly because of the vessel's size. The *Calypso* had three almost-queen-sized beds, so they all could have snuggled in if they'd wanted. Hannah and Jason had volunteered to share a bed for a rotation, which meant Eleri and GJ had another and Donovan and Noah also shared a space. But they couldn't sleep at the same time—it wasn't safe.

Though it struck GJ as paranoid behavior, they arranged to have at least half the crew awake at any given time. It was certainly more than a research vessel needed, but this wasn't a research outing.

GJ had been on boats before—ski boats, slim racing boats, a few cruises with her family, and even the occasional yacht that one of her grandfather's friends owned. However, this was her first time out on a research vessel, as well as her first time living aboard and not seeing land for several days. It was unnerving how wide the ocean was and how small the boat. She wasn't quite sure she was prepared. But it seemed that "not quite prepared" described her entire experience with NightShade.

"Are you okay?" This time the words came at her from Jason as he covered the distance with three long strides to join her at the railing. Standing next to her, he peered out over the waves.

"I'm fine."

"You're gripping the railing pretty hard for someone who's fine."

Looking down, GJ found that her knuckles were, in fact, white. "Fair."

Her eyes flicked back up, taking him in, all black skin, hair shaved close to his head, worried brown eyes. She suspected he had a killer smile, but she hadn't seen it yet. "I feel as if I'm the one who sent Eleri and Noah down on this dive."

Jason nodded. It was her recommendation that had them voting to dive here. Logically, it made no sense to sail directly over the murder scene and not check it out. But GJ couldn't do it herself; she'd had to send others, and that didn't sit well with her. "I don't like anyone being in a scene where someone was murdered. Not without full backup."

"You argued pretty hard for it."

"I argued for logic," she returned, still not liking it.

The agents had shared some of their information with Jason, carefully picking and choosing what he needed to know to be helpful, so they wouldn't have to stop at certain moments and explain why they were doing something. Or, God forbid, explain their actions if the pirates came back.

"I'm worried, too," he offered by way of consolation, "but they're not just research divers, they're FBI agents. They should be okay."

GJ shrugged. Her friends were underwater with regulators in their mouths. They couldn't hear very well. Their scuba masks blocked their peripheral vision. It wasn't the safest of things to do, even in the best of circumstances. Hell, even experienced divers Neriah and Allison had gone down, gotten separated, and one of them had gotten murdered without the other knowing. GJ said none of this. The words that came out of her mouth were, "They should be."

"I miss them," Jason said as he looked out over the ocean. "I miss Allison, and I'll probably miss her forever. She was one of the best teachers I've ever had." He was leaning on the railing beside GJ now. His knuckles were not white, but his breath was labored and his muscles tense. "And now I'm worried about Neriah."

"I put an email in the draft folder for her." GJ hoped the information would help ease his worry. "I used the information you gave me."

She'd stored the draft with the subject line: *Just toss it to me, it will be fine.*

According to Jason, this was how they often joked about the delicate specimens that they were always handling. If Neriah saw it—big *if*—she would at least know that Jason approved in some way. GJ could only hope it was enough to signal *friend*, not *foe*. They needed Neriah back. They needed to not lose anyone else in this clusterfuck.

Missy Maisel had been locked out of her own email since the FBI had taken over the account. They'd been watching hourly in case Neriah Jones parked anything else or even checked in. Some poor analyst had been assigned the job of sorting the daily detritus of Missy's email and forwarding it to a new account. But it had to be done. Video from the coffee shop had confirmed that it was Neriah who'd logged into Missy's account and parked the video from a hard source she'd brought with her.

So GJ had parked her draft right next to the one with the video, titled it with Jason's joke, and hoped it would be enough to convince Neriah to talk to them. Looking down, she saw that her fingers still gripped the railing too tightly. It would probably be that way until both the other agents' heads cleared the surface of the water. There were killers down there—both human and fish.

Now all she could do was cross her fingers and hope that Neriah was able to find the email and understand she was safe responding. Forcing a deep breath, she told herself the best thing she could do was remain calm while the divers were down.

Just then, Eleri's head popped above the waves, her curls—redder than usual from the water—compressed beneath the thick bands of the scuba mask. A moment later, Noah's blond hair surfaced as he came up beside her. With the warm waters, they were all bare limbs and loose hair, Noah's sticking out in all directions.

GJ had never been so happy.

Then, Eleri held up a mesh bag clutched tightly in her fist. As a frown pulled across her features, GJ wondered: *What did Eleri find worth bringing to the surface?*

CHAPTER 44

Eleri finally stood on the deck, fighting the urge to lean over and put her hands on her knees. She'd forgotten how strenuous diving was, and she was not quite in the right shape.

Hannah—who was clearly in the right shape—turned to Eleri. "If this is the knife, why is it okay for me to touch it?"

Hannah had insisted on holding the weapon, even though it was likely the instrument that had murdered her wife. She turned it over, looking at the blade with all the bottled anger one could show an inanimate object. "Aren't I ruining evidence?"

"No."

But as Eleri opened her mouth to speak, GJ jumped in. Sucking in another deep breath, Eleri was grateful she didn't have to use more of her precious oxygen.

"After this long underwater, likely all evidence would have disappeared."

"So you have no idea. . ." Hannah posed, still turning the knife as if it were fascinating, rather than quite standard-looking. "I mean, this could be any knife that was down there. Boats go through here all the time." She lifted her other hand

and marked a line from horizon to horizon as if it were a trail in the forest and not a wide open sea. "This is the kind of knife anyone could find on board."

Eleri nodded, forced to agree with Hannah's reasoning. Though the knife's silhouette matched what they'd seen in the video, it was rather generic. There would be no tracing this knife to find the killer. But this was the knife. She knew, because she'd gone searching for the knife that killed Allison.

The team on the *Calypso* had originally chosen this spot specifically because it was shallow compared to the rest of the gulf and excellent for gathering research specimens. It hadn't taken long for Eleri and Noah to get to the ocean floor and, once there, she'd taken a deep breath and counted on Noah to watch her back while she searched.

Of course, their communication had been severely limited, but she'd whispered her plans to him before they dove. It was a gamble, trusting him with the knowledge about her abilities, but she had to assume this was what Westerfield wanted of them. If she confided in Noah and he didn't work out... she didn't think about what would happen to agents who knew about NightShade but didn't join.

She'd hovered mid-water, cleared her mind, and waited for anything to tell her which direction to look. The knowledge had hit her with shocking speed, almost as though the water itself— ever-changing and moving with the currents—still held the memory of Allison's murder.

Now she was at least able to count this first stop as a success, though she wouldn't tell Hannah how she knew the knife was the murder weapon. Not only had she known where to find the it, but she'd understood the ocean floor had shifted enough that she'd had to go to the exact spot and then shove her hand down into the sand to reach it.

It was not something she would usually do. The general rule of diving was: if you dig in the sand, you might get your fingers bitten off. But she'd done it anyway—maybe to give Noah faith in her abilities, or maybe because she'd come that far and she wasn't going to let some sand stop her.

Even with her diving gloves on, so she wasn't actually touching the knife, the images had hit her hard. Just grabbing it had sent flashes of visions into her, rocking her senses as though she'd been there to witness the murder.

It was a man who had killed Allison. Eleri would have told Noah right then, except she had a mouthful of regulator and limited sign-language fluency. Noah had wanted to take another turn around the ocean floor, and she'd shoved the blade down into the mesh bag, relieved that she didn't have to hold it and bear the images it sent reeling through her system.

Searching for the same kind of specimens Allison would find, they examined anything unusual they found. But they weren't marine biologists, and Eleri didn't know if they'd recognize a problem if they saw it. She kept her eyes out for sharks, too. Though Allison had been stabbed, she'd also been bitten. . . right here.

When the gauges told them it was time to come up, the relief hit her harder than she'd expected. Though this dive had been shallow relative to others, it was still deep enough to require stops on the way up. The slow ascent had felt relentlessly long and she checked her dive watch like a child stuck in timeout.

Unable to tell Hannah most of what she'd learned or how, she aimed Hannah's attention elsewhere.

"Here." Eleri took the knife back and handed it to Donovan, who at least was on his feet, even though he rocked a little bit as he came forward. He held out a paper evidence bag, labeled and ready to go. Normally, they would have stored anything found in the water in a sealed paint can, to preserve any evidence that might still be clinging to it. But Eleri knew this knife had been down there too long. "I found these."

She held the bag up to Hannah while Donovan took the

offending instrument away. Hannah stayed clinical about the work as she sorted through the small pieces of coral Eleri had felt shitty about breaking off.

"This all looks normal. Well, *new normal.* A decade ago, the coral was a different color and thicker. You would have loved it." Though Hannah's eyes didn't lift from the sorting table where Jason joined her, at least she smiled. Holding up a shell, she educated them. "These would have been larger and brighter. The water was clear, too, before. It's grown murkier in the last two years."

Hannah had always fought to protect the oceans. It seemed now, as Eleri listened, that Hannah had war on her hands— including casualties.

"Do you want to go back down?" Hannah asked her, seeming to already be calculating wait times between dives, but Eleri shook her head.

"Just like the knife, any evidence we found wouldn't have anything we could trace. DNA, blood, even fingerprints would have washed away by now. It's why criminals are always throwing their guns in the river. And salt water is even harder on evidence. We have some samples, so you can do any tests you want. My hope is, eventually, when we get back on land, you'll find out more. Maybe we'll even find out what Allison saw or figured out that got her murdered." Eleri hated saying that, but it was what they were here for.

"So, are we done at this site? Hannah?" Jason asked the group, his tension evident in his tone.

It occurred to Eleri for the first time, as she looked between her old friend and her very new one, that they had been horrifically tense here. *Jesus, how had she missed that before now?* She'd been too focused on solving the case.

Standing up perfectly straight, Eleri inhaled deeply for the first time since coming out of the water. "Yes, let's head on."

Within moments, Hannah took the wheel and aimed the

boat eastward. Slowly, they began to move out of the sacred, horrible space.

Eleri made it to the back of the boat, pulling her sunglasses on yet still needing to shield her eyes with her hand so she could see far into the distance. Donovan joined her, looking only marginally steadier than he had before she'd gone under.

"Why do I get the feeling you know more than you're saying?" He spoke softly, letting the wind steal the sound as soon as she heard it.

Eleri's whispered reply was even softer, as Donovan could hear just about everything. "I can't see it with my eyes, but I know we're being followed."

CHAPTER 45

Donovan finally managed to get the rolling in his stomach tamped down to the level of low-grade nausea. He lay on the oddly-shaped bed and tried to ignore how the churning in his stomach matched the pitch and yaw of the boat. Everyone else seemed to have adequately found their sea legs, including GJ.

Though everyone else on board enjoyed it, Donovan preferred not to stand at the railing and watch the vastness of the waves or smell the waft of salt and algae. It only made his stomach worse.

Unfortunately, the boat wasn't large enough that there was anywhere he could go where he couldn't see the ocean. Even below deck, where he'd been hiding out, the rooms were peppered with a series of small, high windows, and being tall cursed him to see the view outside.

Eleri's presence at the top of the stairs drew his attention. "We're here."

Here meant they'd reached the strange coordinates in Allison's lab notebook.

With a deep breath that pulled in too much salt and

sunscreen, he stood and immediately felt the motion beneath his feet and in his stomach, but he made himself duck his head and climb the narrow stairs. As he arrived on deck into the tiny circle of people, he saw that this was a full-out meeting. The six of them filled the back dock to capacity, even though some of them were supposed to be on sleep shift. Like him.

"Why are we stopping here?" Hannah seemed confused. *As she should be.* Donovan offered a wan half smile.

Eleri shrugged in reply. "We should have said something sooner. We just got so busy with the rest of it."

A lie, Donovan knew, and a well-timed one. They hadn't wanted to give Hannah or Jason a heads-up that they would be stopping here. GJ had Allison's notebook page—photocopied and protected in a plastic sleeve—ready to show them. "In Allison's notes, you stopped here on a previous trip."

"Oh." Another confused frown from Hannah, but she didn't deny it. And she didn't give off any pheromones of fear. Not that Donovan could detect without a good inhale—which he wasn't willing to do right now. Hannah took the page that GJ held out and examined it. She spent a few moments trying to make sense of it.

Deciding he'd best be part of the meeting, Donovan added in, "Do you remember stopping here?"

Hannah looked up from the page and then gazed carefully at the ocean that circled the boat. She looked at it as though it were landscape—even though *this* ocean looked exactly the same as the ocean had ten, twenty, or forty miles back—as if she could identify this spot by sight. "I don't remember it." She looked down at the paper again before handing the notes off to Jason. "Do you remember? Were you on this dive?"

GJ started to nod that he was—he was listed in the lab notes —but Donovan reached his hand out and stalled her. Maybe if they didn't give Hannah and Jason all the details, they would get more information as the two reconstructed their memories. If

Allison had been involved in anything illicit, this might bring out useful information.

Donovan waited patiently. The churn of his stomach was something he could ignore for a bit.

Hannah turned and pulled out her heavy, bound logs from their sealed plastic containers. In a few moments, she'd checked previous dates and courses. Then she looked up. "This dive would have happened aboard the old boat—the *Naiad*—given the date. I don't have any logs of any dives on *this* boat in the same position. The ship logs on the old boat were destroyed with it."

All of that makes sense, Donovan thought, glad that Hannah and Jason didn't seem to be the culprits here. But they always had to check. Forging his way back into the conversation, he said, "Allison and Jason made the dive here. Neriah was on board, according to Allison's notes." He turned to Jason, "Do you remember doing this dive?"

The young man shook his head. "I don't remember diving anywhere completely open. We always dove where there was a rig or something."

"Was there a rig here at the time?" Donovan asked. It seemed like a stupid question. Oil rigs shouldn't be mobile like that, but surely they went up at some point in time and eventually came down. He had to admit he'd learned a lot asking stupid questions in the past, so he tossed this inquiry to the young diver.

Before either Jason or Hannah even really had time to think it through, GJ jumped back into the conversation. She handed out other pieces of paper, photocopies of Allison's data encased in plastic sleeves. "These were the other stops that you made right around this area. Does any of this ring a bell?"

As Donovan watched, Jason's brows pulled together and he looked up at Hannah. "The yacht!" he said. "Remember? Allison wanted to dive beneath the yacht. They were just drifting, but they were fully powered. So we didn't stop to ask if they needed help. So, yes, I do remember this."

"Why did she want to dive near the yacht?" Eleri pressed.

"I don't know. Or I don't remember." Jason handed back the papers. It was difficult for Donovan to assess whether he was lying. His senses didn't like the open ocean, and gleaning extra information around the overwhelming scent of the tide was difficult.

Even Eleri offered a slight twitch of her eyebrow, indicating to Donovan—and hopefully no one else—that she was growing frustrated with the conversation. "You dove with her? What did you do or find on the dive?"

"If I remember right, nothing much. Saw a bunch of fish. Took some pictures." Jason shrugged in response to the question. Though the answers were vague, his body language was clear in the late-morning light.

Donovan pushed a little harder. "What about Allison?"

"I don't remember." But then he pointed to the plastic-protected page. "Obviously, she managed to pull up a few barnacles."

"Were you separated?" Eleri played interrogator, but a light version. The three of them threw questions at him as though they were merely curious, but keeping them coming non-stop.

"I think so. It was a while ago, honestly. And we do these dives all the time. Often several a day when we dive."

"I understand." Eleri softened her overall response with a relaxed change of stance and a commiserating smile. Donovan was relatively sure that she did, in fact, understand that Jason might not remember every detail of every dive. But then she tried again. "Where would Allison have gotten barnacles? Wouldn't they have had to have come off the bottom of the boat?"

Both Jason and Hannah nodded.

"Why would she dive under another boat?"

This time, the question was met with a dual shrug, and Donovan felt an idea forming in his brain. "Wait. Barnacles grow on the underside of boats. But don't they usually grow on *old* boats? Do they grow on fiberglass?"

It was Hannah who jumped in, full of knowledge. "They can. There are new paints that claim to be slick enough that the barnacles can't get a foothold. And most of the people who own luxury yachts pay to have them scraped clean and even repainted, sometimes as often as each time they come into dock. So no, I don't *expect* to find barnacles on luxury yachts, but they can certainly grow there."

Hannah sounded more confident now. "I think, if I remember correctly, that's what happened. Allison's notes say she came back with barnacles, but I don't remember seeing them. So it's the only thing that makes sense." She paused and looked out at the ocean again, the same way Donovan would look up and down a city street or a park trail to spot landmarks and get his bearing. Then she gave him pause. "Unless there's some kind of underwater structure here. . ."

It was Eleri who looked to Hannah then. "Shall we dive it? To see if we can figure out what Allison saw?"

"Not if the boat's not here." Hannah's skepticism was clear. "But we can dive it anyway."

The uneasy feeling in Donovan's stomach was possibly *not* due to the waves now. As he watched, the two women—already in their swimsuits, with their hair pulled back—easily slid into the black dive vests with all the hoses before getting ready to roll backward into the water.

He did something he hadn't done yet. It had been too hard, but he hoped maybe he was feeling well enough. Finding his way to the railing, he looked out over the waves and slowly, carefully opened his sinuses.

Shit.

He almost ran to the back of the boat, his stomach the only

thing stopping him from bolting. Luckily, he made it in time to catch Eleri just before she tipped off the edge.

He leaned over and carefully whispered in her ear. "El, I don't know what it is, but the ocean smells different here. Something has been coming through here repeatedly."

CHAPTER 46

With one hand holding her mask on her face and her regulator in her mouth, Eleri rolled backward, the surface of the water smacking her as she hit.

The ocean folded up and around her as she plunged below the surface and slowly popped back up. She was in flux between gravity and buoyancy. Rolling onto her back and making sure not to hit her head against the top of the tank, she offered up her best backstroke to get farther away from the boat. Beside her, Hannah's head surfaced, and the two moved several yards away before cutting below the surface.

Though there were still sounds coming through from above, everything was now muted. The sound of her regulator—the oxygen flowing through the tubes and mouthpiece—was the overwhelming source of noise in her ears. Eleri imagined she could hear the slosh of water around her, the waves at the surface almost battering her. The constant pushing and pulling would dissipate the lower she went.

Ahead of her, Hannah moved like a fish; Eleri was not quite as agile. She stopped every few feet, grabbed her nose, puffed her cheeks, and tried to clear her ears. With a slick motion of her hands and fins, Hannah rotated to look up at her, then stopped and waited.

It always took her a few moments to adjust. It wasn't *panic*—that was too extreme a word for what Eleri felt. But maybe it was a little bit of anxiety each time she entered the water. It didn't help that Donovan's words were spinning through her brain with no other real sounds to fight them.

The water here smelled different.

He didn't know what it was, and neither did she, but Eleri had no doubt that it was something. Was it linked to Allison's findings? It might not be. But her gut said it was.

Slowing her breathing, she counted her inhales and exhales, trying to let the weights pull her deeper and exerting a little less effort in swimming downward. She realized she was competent enough to be on this dive, but not skilled enough to do it well or easily.

She'd thought about sending Noah down with Hannah, as he was more experienced, but she wanted to see for herself how Hannah reacted. She was watching the other woman when Hannah again rolled over and looked up at Eleri.

Pointing with two fingers toward her eyes, then out and around, Eleri offered an outsized shrug for her question. *Did Hannah see anything?*

No. Hannah shook her head in return. There was only blue water. There weren't even fish. They had likely all scattered when she and Hannah hit the water. Unlike the last dive, this was not a shallow spot, and the bottom was unreachable, unless she'd had a different mix of gases in her tank and a dive certification she didn't hold.

The light filtered easily through the water, though as they descended, it got darker. Still, her eyes adjusted. Eventually, off on her right, a large fish swam by. It might be a tuna, or a sea bass. She truly had no idea. Then it was gone and they were alone again.

She and Hannah swam in a huge circle as best as Eleri could tell. She was depending on Hannah's underwater senses, as there were no landmarks, not even a sandy bottom to mark their passage against, and no way for her to truly tell where they were going.

Why had Allison decided to dive here? It must have been the boat.

A quick check of her gauges indicated to Eleri that they'd not been down long. With an ungraceful roll, she turned to face Hannah. A motion toward the surface and another shrug asked if it was time to go up.

Was there anything else down here to find?

Hannah seemed to think so. With a shake of her head, she motioned Eleri to follow her. They swam for a few more minutes before running into a school of small, sharp, silvery fish. The whole school turned abruptly away from them and disappeared as quickly as they had come. A large piece of seaweed floated by and Eleri moved out of its way, not wanting to get tangled.

Eventually, even Hannah gave up, and they headed for the surface. Eleri passed one lone, small jellyfish squeezing its way across her narrow field of vision. But when they reached plain air, the boat was gone.

CHAPTER 47

GJ's heart tripped and stuttered.

"Donovan." She grabbed him by the arm and shook. "Donovan!"

He hadn't been awake. She and Jason had been left in charge of the boat while Donovan and Noah slept a shift.

Now, he was instantly alert, feet on the floor, and GJ was already leaving. Darting into the next room, she pushed at Noah's sleeping form. They all slept in their clothes for exactly this purpose. GJ understood it; she just hadn't expected they'd have to enact their emergency system. She flew to the top of the steps, finding as she cleared the deck that Jason already had the motor on and the boat turning.

It wouldn't be enough. The water was wide and flat, with only the curvature of the earth to hide them.

The only thing they could do was get far enough away and aim the boat in the opposite direction. They couldn't disappear, so the remaining option was to appear to be no threat.

"What is it?" Donovan cleared the top of the small staircase barely a heartbeat before Noah did.

"Boat." GJ choked out the one word. In case someone on that

boat had spotted the research vessel and was watching her, the way she'd been watching them, she refrained from waving her arm around and pointing.

She almost tossed Donovan the binoculars she'd been using. She had another pair ready for Noah and, with a subtle flick of the wrist, positioned them behind the deck chairs to cover their motions before aiming them both in the correct direction.

She knew what they would see: a sleek, probably red, probably cigarette-style boat speeding their way. Perhaps it was silly to be this paranoid. After all, they had divers down, but GJ had already pulled the flag.

Allison had dived here, and there was every possibility that something bad had happened in this location. GJ did not want to signal anyone that they were on the same path as Allison had been before.

She didn't even want the research vessel to still be here when the racing boat arrived. Hannah and Allison had already had one boat boarded by pirates and blown up. What if the invaders hadn't simply been after money?

GJ had seen the pictures of the *Naiad*. It was clearly a research boat. Anyone looking for money would have gone somewhere else. With racing thoughts, she put all the pieces together.

Hannah and Allison had been targeted. They'd been allowed to live. They'd been left in the water to find their way to a shore that was miles away, but they'd not been shot and left to bleed for the sharks. The boat, however, had been bombed. The pirates probably had no interest in the research—but someone who hired them had been. That research had been thoroughly destroyed.

GJ had no plans for a repeat performance. She told herself now that the location was entirely different. That pirates didn't race around in cigarette-style speed boats—without enough room for a crew. But she still kept watch as Jason sped them away as fast as he could manage.

They'd abandoned their original position and had now achieved enough distance to appear innocuous. It was dangerous to leave while the divers were underwater, but it was also dangerous to be here. If Eleri and Hannah surfaced in the middle of the boat being boarded or bombed, things would be far worse than if they found they'd been left to fend for themselves for a few hours. At least, that's what GJ hoped.

Right now, she was repeating a mantra under her breath.

Stay hidden. Stay just below the surface if you can. We will come back. Stay hidden. We'll come back. Stay hidden. We'll come back.

It was possible the other boat had spotted them already. With her hand on Jason's arm, she told him to slow the *Calypso*. "We can't look like we're running away. How do we make ourselves look 'casual'?"

Jason answered by nodding and easing up on the throttle slightly. "We can't get too far away."

Though he didn't say it, they both understood why.

"Fishing poles!" GJ tried not to dart away, in case they were being watched more carefully than it appeared. They'd brought the poles along to catch samples but, right now, it would hopefully make them look like a fishing crew or a random household out on the water rather than researchers on an investigation.

If Allison and Hannah had previously encountered someone else in this location, then looking like a research vessel could become a problem very quickly. GJ found herself being grateful that this was a new boat with a different name, so at least they wouldn't be instantly recognizable. Though she wasn't overly religious, she crossed herself as she pulled out one of the fishing poles. Although she had no bait, she threw the hook over the side and held onto the rod. "Donovan! Is there a way you can watch them without letting them see you?"

"I think so." With a brief nod, he headed toward the front of the small boat—the side now furthest from the approaching boat. It was, in fact, red. And cigarette-style. And moving fast. Anyone watching would them would hopefully become obvious as the smaller boat approached.

GJ crossed her fingers. She might lack Eleri's command of the elements, but she could still perform schoolyard wishes.

The small boat was sleek and fast, and she prayed that it crossed their path before Hannah and Eleri surfaced. She watched as Donovan ducked low and surreptitiously trained his binoculars toward the small boat. Then, as Jason joined her at the side, tossing another fishing pole into the water, she prayed again that the people on the boat didn't look past the surface. But then Donovan's head swiveled, looking past her.

"Guys," he said, "don't move your heads, but there's another boat coming from the north."

GJ flicked her eyes and saw a movement on the horizon that she could only assume was the boat Donovan spoke of. One boat in this particular area on the open ocean was an anomaly. But two?

This was no coincidence.

The small, sleek racing boats were aimed directly at each other. GJ felt her heart rate kick up even higher.

CHAPTER 48

E leri bobbed with the waves for a few moments as she slowly turned in a circle. Looking for the *Calypso* yielded nothing, but she tried not to worry.

Beside her, Hannah did the same and, by the worry that pleated her brows, came to the same conclusion. They were alone out in the water. But why?

Hitting the button on her vest let a woosh of air into it from her tank. The unit tightened against her chest, but buoyed her higher in the water. The waves had been smacking her around —a good reason to keep her regulator in, but now she needed to take it out. Getting her head higher up made it less likely she'd swallow sea water.

Pulling the mouthpiece out and holding onto it, she turned to her dive buddy. "Did we move too far? Or did *they* move?"

Several yards away, Hannah bobbed and then suddenly disappeared. Holding her breath, Eleri counted for three beats, hoping it was a wave and that Hannah was just sitting in the trough as the peak split the distance between them. The breath gushed out of her lungs as—a moment later—Hannah's head appeared in her vision again, none the worse for wear.

"We're in the same place. Well. . ." Hannah lifted her wrist, checking the high-end dive watch she always wore. It recorded her depth, dive time, and even her GPS location. "Actually, we're in *almost* the exact location where we went down."

Hannah was moving toward her now, and Eleri offered her own strong strokes to bring them together. She knew she shouldn't be burning her energy when she couldn't see the boat, but the fact that it was missing made her want to tether herself to Hannah while they made their decisions. But Hannah was hard to hold onto, once again turning fully around and searching the blue horizon that stretched in all directions.

No matter how she strained, or tried to pop up higher in the water, the *Calypso* was nowhere to be found. Of all the times that she'd gone on a dive, Eleri had never come up alone. Not before now. Her heart was beating far too fast, though she lied to herself that it was from the strain of the dive.

It was only on her third rotation—when she'd basically given up on just spotting the research vessel—that she heard it. Turning to Hannah, she saw the other woman pulling on the cord that would release her emergency signal: a three foot, inflatable tube that could be seen from a distance. "Shit! Hannah, *deflate*. Get *down*."

But the air was fast, the tube unfurling even as Hannah looked at her oddly. She probably couldn't hear the boat coming as the sound of the air wooshing from her tank and into the plastic tube was filling her ears. With a quick thought—that signal could *not* go up!—Eleri reached for her dive knife and lunged forward out of the water.

With a five inch tear now marking the side, the signal device deflated and settled on the surface of the water. Though Hannah was looking at her as though she'd gone mad, Eleri was already pushing the button on her own vest, releasing the air and feeling the water slosh past her head as she sank slightly. Shoving the regulator back in her mouth, she tugged at Hannah, who seemed to have not caught on that there was a boat approaching quickly. Too quickly.

If nothing else, they needed to get low enough so the engine's blades wouldn't be a problem. Had the crew of the *Calypso* seen this other boat and hightailed it out of the area? That seemed entirely possible, and it would mean that their team wasn't that far away. But right now, Eleri and Hannah sat so low in the water that their vision was blocked by the choppy waves.

Finally understanding, Hannah shoved her own regulator back in her mouth and, in a smooth, practiced move, disappeared under the waves. Eleri's own instinct was to flip upside down, mermaid style, but flipping her fins in the air here would only signal her presence. She'd just destroyed Hannah's beacon in an effort stop them from being seen.

If the *Calypso* had seen it necessary to abandon them, then she and Hannah needed to get underwater fast. Eleri grabbed at the floating corpse of the signal tube and dragged it under with her. She was grateful this had not been a long dive and she was not—at least, not *yet*—worried about their remaining oxygen. Apparently, she wasn't sinking fast enough for Hannah, who grabbed onto her ankle and tugged her slowly deeper into the ocean.

Even so, it was necessary for Eleri to grab her nose, shake her head, and work her jaw in an attempt to make her ears equalize. She sank for the second time. She knew this was not smart, immediately going down again. But they would not go so far this time—just low enough to stay out of sight of the approaching speedboat.

When they were far enough under, Eleri looked up and watched. Barely able to see a mark in the distance, she could still tell it was the underside of the boat, and it was fast approaching. She could hear it now. Turning, it startled her to find Hannah panicking.

Hannah hadn't even seen the video of Allison's murder, but it appeared something here triggered Hannah. Grabbing her friend's hand, Eleri tugged and began the slow work of swimming her away. Despite Hannah's panic, moving was smart. If they could put some distance between themselves and the boat, they could come up to the surface, use their snorkels, and save their oxygen. Moving farther also made it less likely they'd be spotted.

Even as she thought that, the noise of the engine cut, the boat coming to a stop right behind them. The lack of sound almost brought Eleri to her own panic. What if the boaters *had* spotted them? What would that mean? Were they just friendlies out for the day on a cigarette boat? Did they stop because they saw divers and no dive boat around?

Though that story made sense, Eleri knew it wasn't true.

Right then, in the silence, she noticed another noise, one she'd missed given the overwhelming sound of the first boat. But now it was clear, as the sound traveled faster, if not sharper, under the water. She turned her head the other way. Even as Hannah continued to tug at her hand, pulling her farther away from the scene, Eleri spotted the second boat on the horizon. This one was coming from the opposite direction.

Then it, too, stopped.

The distance between the two small boats remained rather broad. Eleri had no idea what was going on. She didn't know if she and Hannah were swimming *towards* or *away* from the *Calypso*. She didn't know how long they could be stuck here with the boat stopped, or whether these smaller boats had seen them.

Surely, the divers couldn't be spotted now, the women were too far underwater, the surface too choppy to peer through. Even if someone managed to get eyes under their boat, the two women were too far away, with the seaweed and algae and distance obscuring them.

They should be safe, Eleri thought as a way to console herself. Stopping underwater and managing to float without much movement, besides that put upon them by the current, Eleri motioned again toward the surface.

Hannah refused. Her panic was would run her out of oxygen faster than most anything else. And—in a situation like this— they needed more O2, not less. They had to conserve what they had left. Which meant *one*, not sucking it down in a panic-induced fit and, *two*, getting to the surface to breath the free air there.

With a nod, clear and soft and yet full of authority, Eleri pointed again to the surface. She began swimming upward, tugging at Hannah. Though Hannah resisted slightly, she didn't fight hard, for which Eleri was grateful. Underwater, Hannah would have definitely overpowered her. When they broke the surface, Eleri put her finger to her lips, pulled out her regulator, and put in her snorkel, staying just below the surface. Quietly, they breathed air from above the waves and waited for the boats to pass.

They waited.

And waited.

And waited.

Until the sky began to turn dark.

CHAPTER 49

Donovan stood with the railing clenched tight in his fists, as though he was holding both the boat and this day together. No one on the boat was asleep yet. Everyone stood watch, though the sky had grown dark and they still hadn't found Eleri and Hannah.

He was beginning to panic. Next to him, Jason had moved well past the initial stages. The abject fear rolled off of him in pheromone waves that almost knocked Donovan over.

At first, Donovan had wondered about Jason's snap, and his near inability to function in a situation when they needed all hands on deck—literally. Surely things had gone wrong on the boat before. Despite only knowing Hannah for a short while, Donovan's impression was that she would never hire a crew member or researcher who couldn't keep his shit together. In fact, Donovan would have bet money that exactly *this* had happened before. But that was when he figured out Jason's problem.

This *had* happened before. And the last time it did, Jason's boss—his friend, mentor, and dive buddy—had never come back up. She'd been murdered. Now he was staring down another loss. With Neriah MIA, Jason was about to become the last of the original four-man crew, and he was not dealing well with it.

"We'll find them." Donovan gently touched the other man on the shoulder and tried to offer his best reassurance. He wanted to believe that, somehow, he had tapped into Eleri's innate sense and that he would know if things were wrong.

His gut told him they were okay—or *okay enough*, and *for now* —but not because he would know about Hannah, not at all. He had come around to the full faith that if something had happened to Eleri, he would be feeling it now. He'd heard her voice in his head when she was threatened before; Surely she would reach out to him now if she needed him. So why hadn't she? Why didn't he hear her? Why didn't he know which way to go?

"Excuse me." The words were curt, and GJ didn't wait for him to step back from the railing. She just pushed her way through.

The younger agent was walking full circles around the deck, her feet almost clomping in her fear. The repetitive sound was enough to drive him crazy, though he understood the necessity of her action. They had waited for the two cigarette boats to leave. Both had stopped in proximity to each other, but had not had any kind of real contact, as far as he could tell. Maybe they yelled to each other, but even his sensitive ears had heard nothing aside from a few splashes that could easily have been big fish or passing sea mammals.

The boats had turned and then headed back the way they had each come. An odd dance with no interaction.

"That wasn't normal," Jason protested for the umpteenth time, as GJ scooted past him, her high-lumen flashlight aimed out over the open water, scanning for any sign of Eleri and Hannah.

He had been told they had a yellow inflatable they could wave around and catch the gaze of anyone looking for them. Why hadn't they done that? He had to believe she was okay for now. But the growing darkness was like a key, cranking his chest tighter with each shade change.

Noah had volunteered to dive, to see if he could find them underwater, but the other three quickly talked him out of it. If the women were underwater, they should see the boat—unless they were very deep, which they shouldn't be now. The water was too vast, too murky, and too dangerous to send anyone else down. It wasn't yet time for a hail Mary.

They should have surfaced by now, Donovan reasoned. They would have run out of oxygen long ago if they had stayed under. Donovan's only conclusion could be that they weren't looking anywhere near the correct place. His lack of sense of direction on the open water was disorienting. The churn of his stomach was probably no longer due to the waves beneath his feet, and was now caused by fear. Or was he just picking up Jason's panic? No, much of the feeling was his own.

GJ pushed past him again with the flashlight, working diligently to make sure that she didn't miss anything hiding between the waves, anything in the distance, or anything that blended in. She passed in front of the men at the rail, once again making them step back. Like some kind of nervous glitch, she said, "Excuse me, excuse me," and then turned around and went the other direction, as though searching counterclockwise might make it more likely that she would spot Eleri and Hannah.

"Excuse me." She pushed past again.

But this time, Donovan's hand shot out as he grabbed her arm. "Shut up."

"What?"

"Shut up."

Beside her, Jason and Noah turned to him with the same ugly frowns on their faces that GJ was giving him.

"Don't move." He ordered all three of them. The slap of the water against the boat and the rasp of the waves as they hit each other on the open water obscured the sound he was listening for. But when, at last, everyone on the boat was quiet, he heard it again. *Donovan.*

"*Eleri!*" he shouted out, no longer concerned about the presence of another boat. It might still be out there. They might just not be able to see it. But it didn't matter now, as they had already more than given their position away with GJ shining her flashlight all over the water.

"Donovan." It was faint, but it was there. "Bow. Two o'clock."

The words had come on the wind from a distance. No one else had heard them. That was clear from the way GJ was tugging against his hand, as though she needed to break free and resume her circular pacing. Instead, he tightened his grip, dragging her to the other end of the boat. "It's Eleri. She's off the bow, two o'clock."

GJ had been shaking her head to ask what he was doing, but he saw the change in her features. "Oh!" Instantly, the tension where she was yanking against him relaxed. "Where are they?"

"Over here?" He dragged her more forcefully than he should have. Grabbing her hand, he directed the flashlight. GJ didn't protest. She waved it once, twice, sweeping the surface of the water. This time, he saw movement.

Turning back to Jason, he made a circle with one finger in the air. "Go!"

As he looked back at the water, a lone yellow inflatable unfurled. They hadn't had the signal up before now, and Donovan didn't know why. But he trusted that, if Eleri stayed out in the dark water without signaling the boat, she had a reason.

He just didn't know what it was.

Ten minutes later, they were hauling the equipment and the women into the boat. Both were exhausted and shivering, though they'd been floating for the most part, treading water where they could. They'd been jostled by the waves. They hadn't eaten. Their oxygen tanks were near zero.

As he checked them over, GJ disappeared, her feet stomping down the stairs, the noise ringing in his head. GJ was often incredibly smart, and usually far too logical. He wasn't going to argue and tell her that she needed to stay. It was an effort for him to trust that those around him were doing their best. He'd worked alone for so long that any teamwork took conscious effort on his part.

But GJ made his gamble pay off. Sure enough, as the women sank into chairs, GJ reappeared, a cold ginger ale in hand for each of them. "I started soup. I'll bring it up in a minute. I'll be right back with crackers."

Of course, GJ didn't hug anyone. She assessed and she fixed.

Hannah turned to Eleri, an apology tumbling from dry lips. "I'm sorry I panicked. I was thinking of Allison."

"Of course, you were." Eleri reached out and took hold of her friend's hand. "We're fine, and we knew we would be." She looked up at Noah and Donovan. "We didn't stay down that long. The boats were weird, though. You were right to leave. We're all back together and it's okay now, but I think there's a reason Allison stopped here."

"Did you see something during your dive?" Noah asked, finally willing to treat the women as divers rather than rescues.

Eleri shook her head. "No. I think it was about the boats. We'll have to discuss it later, but the behavior was far too odd."

The two women ate with everyone watching. Next, they were handed down the stairs for showers and sleep. Eleri motioned to Hannah to go first, and Donovan took advantage of a moment with no one else around.

"Eleri? The smell that I told you about? It was the boats. I didn't recognize it before, but it was boat fuel. Something specific, just like the ones that showed up at the dive site."

"Oh," Eleri said. "Then this is worse than I thought."

CHAPTER 50

"I was terrified," Eleri confessed as she lay on the bed, staring at the ceiling, attempting to get some sleep. It wasn't working, despite the fact that she was exhausted, mentally and physically.

The surface of the water was not an easy place for a diver. Underneath, the ocean was serene. There were currents a diver could float along, and breathing was easy. But at the surface, the waves bashed everything, and the weight of the tank pulled and fought anything you tried to do. It often took more effort to breathe through the regulator than to fight off the waves that were constantly trying to splash into open mouths and lungs.

"I was petrified, too." Donovan had come in to lie down on the bed beside her and was now staring at the ceiling with her. Though her activity hadn't changed, the company improved her situation a lot. "I was petrified about sharks," he admitted.

Eleri almost grinned. "I wasn't. We weren't bleeding. I mean, I know they're in the area, but the chances of them being in range to where we were floating and close to the surface was pretty low. The chances of them thinking that I was something they would want to eat was even lower. I wasn't in a black wetsuit, so I didn't look like a seal."

"Even with what happened to Allison?" That question was posed in a softer, gentler tone, a question that no one else likely would have asked her.

"Even with Allison. That was a murder, not a shark attack."

"Well," there was a small chuckle behind the word, "you are far braver than I am."

"I'm a diver," she countered. She was trained in what to do if she ever got separated from her boat. She hadn't done it all, but she always dove knowing this was a possibility. "And I've been learning from GJ. I'm trying to believe what the numbers tell me. The statistics say the sharks won't eat me."

Donovan laughed. If GJ looked something up in a paper and discovered that it was not as she had previously believed, she changed her entire worldview in a snap. "Besides," Eleri sighed, "I was trying to cast spells on us the whole time we were out there."

"What do you cast in the middle of the ocean?"

"Protection spells," she said. "To keep the sharks away. Hide us from the cigarette boats."

"You can cast spells on sharks?"

She laughed again and it felt good, despite the heavy, used-up sensation that permeated her muscles. "I have no idea, but I cast the spells and I didn't get bit. You decide."

"Sounds like statistics to me." There was a grin in his voice, and she could tell he was as relieved as she was that they were together again. When she'd been out there, she hadn't worried as much about her mother or father. They hated that she was an agent. If she died on a case, they would likely believe she'd brought it on herself. In a small way, they wouldn't be wrong. But she'd thought about Donovan and Wade. She'd worried about GJ coming up through the ranks without her. She thought about losing her family, but it was Donovan who was that family now.

His words interrupted her deep thoughts. "Is that why you didn't have your signal balloon up?"

Eleri nodded silently, and then added, "Also, when Hannah tried to put hers up, I stabbed it because I saw the cigarette boats coming. So we only had mine to use later." Beside her, she could feel the bed moving slightly as he nodded along. "What *was* that? Do you think they were meeting? They didn't even get close."

"I don't know."

"They didn't talk to each other. Hannah and I were working at staying under the water most of the time, so our visibility was pretty limited. And we were trying to get further away. As far as I could tell, they didn't do anything. I didn't hear them shouting to each other. Maybe they called on a phone or something?"

"Plausible," he agreed for a moment, but then countered the idea. "But if you could call on a phone, why drive out into the middle of the ocean? Why go where reception is spotty? If they can get a signal, then they can be tapped or traced. So there's no reason to come to the middle of nowhere to make a call."

Lifting her sore arms up, she gingerly placed her hands behind her head, finally beginning to feel secure. The shower hadn't done it. The bed hadn't done it. But the conversation was comforting.

Even if she still had no idea what was happening on this case, her partner was next to her. She was safe in bed, no longer jostled about in the ocean, wondering if they would be found. No longer hungry and getting colder as the night grew darker. They'd seen a big mass go by but luckily, that had actually calmed Hannah down. She'd readily identified the fish and chatted about its migration path, how it was slightly out of season to be here and odd that it was here alone.

She'd entertained Eleri with commentary on how they'd seen more of the fish coming by solo, particularly coming through this corridor, probably following a channel. Had she not been stranded in the ocean, Eleri would have laughed. But she let Hannah keep talking, as it seemed to have a beneficial effect. Now she realized she was doing the same thing with Donovan, and it was definitely working. Her heart rate was dropping. Her breath was evening out.

"If what you smelled was fuel from the smaller boats, do you think you smelled it from the *Calypso* first?"

"No," he said quickly. "It's different enough. It's not this boat. I would have noticed that."

She almost smacked her head. Of course, he wouldn't have commented on the smell their own boat was making. His skills were better than that. "You smelled it before you saw the boats."

Beside her, he lifted his hands behind his head, mimicking her stance, his elbows far wider than hers. Still, the two of them looked at the ceiling, thinking their way through the day and the trip. "The smell has to mean there's a trail of boat fuel here. Particularly *this* kind of boat fuel. So the boats are coming through quite a bit. In fact, we were here because Allison saw another boat in almost this exact location and she probably thought it looked suspicious then, too." Eleri pondered the implications, and then turned her head to look at Donovan's profile. "Do you have an idea yet?"

He shrugged, somehow managing the move without removing his hands from behind his head. "It's got to be a drug corridor."

Eleri sucked a deep breath through her nose. "I was beginning to think the same thing. It's bad, Donovan. Very bad. We're headed to Nassau. We're already out in international waters. We have evidence from ten-plus years ago of a researcher finding trace evidence of cocaine and heroin in his sea life and then disappearing. And now Allison—finding the same information—gets murdered."

Donovan readily picked up her train of thought. "The drug angle explains the lengths they went to to blow up the first research vessel, the *Naiad*. It explains Allison's murder, and Blake's disappearance."

"It means we're all in far more danger than we gave the situation credit for. And as FBI agents, we have almost no power here." Eleri didn't like the way that idea sat on her chest.

Donovan didn't respond. Probably, he agreed. Her breathing was evening out, and she was thinking she might finally get some sleep. She'd been granted this shift while Donovan and Noah stayed awake. GJ was still on deck.

Eleri's thoughts began to scramble. She began seriously pondering soup and thinking about Emmaline, her sister, and how long it had been since she had seen her. Just as she was drifting off, a shout came from the deck.

CHAPTER 51

G J felt like an idiot, but her heart was pounding.

She was following the best protocol possible, given the fact that she was on a floating piece of fiberglass in the middle of a wide ocean. Though she was on a boat with others, they—as a group—were all alone. Only they weren't all alone anymore.

Her FBI-issued glock was now in her loose grip, pointed at the deck of the boat, but ready should she need it. Behind her, Noah walked toward her, and she motioned him to crouch down.

Everyone else was below deck, having declared the day a success with Eleri and Hannah back on board. The two of them remaining on deck had shut down most of the light and retained watch. GJ had left just enough going on so they wouldn't appear suspicious if anyone saw them. But now Donovan's whispered warning had come back to her. *I think we're being followed.*

Coming up beside her but staying low, Noah nudged her shoulder. "What's going on? You've been hanging out at the back of the boat all day, and now you're hiding?"

"I've been back here because one my fellow agents had a hunch that we were being followed."

Noah had almost argued with her. There was no evidence. He was on boats all the time. Wouldn't he know?

But she'd kept looking, because if there was one thing she'd learned in the NightShade division, it was to trust her fellow agents' hunches. Now she was glad that she had—because they were, in fact, being followed. She pointed into the blackness. "Someone is back there."

The other boat was much smaller than theirs. As best she could tell in the dark night, it was a gas-powered inflatable, the kind people took on one-day whale-watching trips. Not the kind you used to travel between land masses.

Noah duck-walked the last few steps to where she was and peeked, as she did, between the edge of the boat and the railing.

"Don't shoot," she told him, seeing that he had followed her lead and pulled his own firearm. "Not unless you have to. If we don't hit the person, we'll pop the boat."

"Just one person?"

"As best as I can tell. It's dark as fuck out here." The new moon had made it hell finding Allison and Hannah. Now it was playing with them again. All in one night. It figured. What they saw was only what random light caught and illuminated. "I *think* it's just one."

"Well, that's not safe." Noah continued to peer out into the inky darkness, which was broken only by short slashes of light from the tips of waves, or something on the dark boat in the distance. "Being alone in an inflatable this far off shore."

"I don't think *smart* is the major goal of anyone following us. And, according to Donovan, something has been behind us for several days." The trip they were making from Miami to Nassau could have been completed quite rapidly. But they'd first headed around into the Gulf, then come back past the tip of Florida. They'd been stopping periodically along the way to conduct dives and tests at all the points Allison had marked in her lab books.

It seemed to GJ that they'd been on the water for a long time. Though never horrendously far from the coast, they were certainly out in the open. GJ hadn't seen land for. . . days, at least. However, their meandering course meant this tail wasn't a coincidence.

The small boat hovered just at the edge of what GJ could be confident she was seeing. Had she not caught a firm glimpse of it before, she would have wondered if it was even there at all.

"Any idea who it could be?" Noah asked softly from beside her. Though whether he was worried about his voice somehow traveling beyond the slosh of the waves to a boat she could barely see or if he thought he might wake the sleeping crew members below, she couldn't tell.

"No clue. But they haven't shot at us."

"They didn't help us find Hannah and Eleri either."

GJ had to concede that point.

For thirty minutes, they watched as the other boat did nothing but hover behind them, disappearing long enough to make them wonder if maybe it was finally gone. There were no sounds of an engine, nor even any splashes of someone paddling frantically. Each time GJ thought it was gone, she would catch another glimpse, see the outline by the dim light from the stars.

The night sky amazed her. She'd seen it like this a few times before, out on digs. But so often, they had lights on at night, the security for her grandfather's work obscuring the sky. She lived in a populated enough area that she didn't see the stars as often as she would have liked.

Now she began to understand how and why the sailors had used the stars for navigation. Pulling her gaze from the marvel above her, GJ refocused on the threat behind her and asked

Noah, "Can you nudge the boat toward us? Maybe turn on the light over there, so we can see what's going on."

"No." His grin was white in the dark night. "I can't do any of that. I don't know how to push anything that far away."

She was nodding along, thinking. "You can *create wind*—I was going to use another phrase but it sounded like farting—" she said with a sigh, keeping her eyes on the small craft behind them. "Can you make a wind that would blow that craft in our direction?"

He was laughing again, but then he grew more serious. "Maybe. I've never tried it on the open water. You should understand, that would be a lot of work. And all he would have to do is put on the engine and reverse it."

"Okay, no wind," GJ conceded. "Can you communicate with him?"

"What?"

"Well, you said you can talk to animals, and people are animals." Her eyes flicked to the side to catch his expression.

"No. It doesn't work like that."

It had been worth a shot. GJ shrugged and looked at her watch again. They grew silent and stared at the small boat, which was staying just beyond where they could discern anything that might be helpful. GJ still wasn't even sure there was only one person on board.

She was checking her watch frequently, so she knew that it was thirty-four minutes later when Noah broke the silence. "One of us should go get Jason."

"What?"

"Nothing is happening. We're sitting here, and we're either going to wind up shooting somebody or feeling like fools. We need someone who knows these waters, and Hannah needs to sleep."

"Alright." GJ was already moving, crawling along the deck,

not wanting to stand up and be visible over the edge of the rail or let whoever was following them know what she was doing.

She'd slipped her gun back into its holster. She'd been trying to take good care of it, cleaning and oiling it almost daily, though it was difficult to get away from the dirty looks Hannah gave her. The woman did not like having firearms on her ship, she said, and having four out of the six people onboard carrying was clearly giving her issues.

Still, they were all being careful, and GJ was not going to crawl along the deck with her gun in hand now, tapping on the flooring with each step. That was a recipe for disaster—and for more of Hannah's ire.

Turning, she backed her way down the steps and softly knocked on the room where Jason was sleeping. She *hoped* it was his room. Though they were sleeping in shifts again, the shifts themselves had been wrecked to hell, the room pattern scrambled. Hoping to God she wasn't mistakenly waking Hannah or Eleri, GJ turned the knob, thinking she'd be better off to first see who was in the bed and maybe close the door if she'd gotten it wrong.

Jason, wide awake, rolled his head to look at her. At least he didn't seem angry that she'd walked right in. "What do you need?"

"I need you. We have a small inflatable following us—"

Jason was on his feet and pushing past her in the small hallway almost before she could react. Reaching out, she snagged the back of his shirt. "When you go up, *don't* stand up. Don't show yourself on deck. Noah's keeping watch at the stern. Go to him and let him point it out."

With a nod, Jason at least slowed a little, and this time followed her as they reached the deck and headed toward Noah's position. The three of them knelt in one spot, watching the same direction as before. Now three pairs of eyes peeked through the gap just below the railing. They now had more eyes than were necessary here, and less than GJ wanted on the rest of the water.

"I'm going to take a turn around the boat."

Noah told her, "Check all directions. Make sure this is the only one out here casing us."

Shit, GJ thought. She wasn't the only one thinking it. If they were surrounded, this was trouble. But as she moved to work her way around the boat's perimeter, Jason stood up suddenly. She grabbed on him and tugged him down, but it didn't stop his hands as they waved frantically over his head. He was clearly signaling the ship behind them.

Suddenly, he lit up as a flash of light clearly trained on him. GJ tugged harder as it blinked on and off three times in succession. Someone was going to shoot him. Or they were using him to aim a rocket launcher.

"*What is it?*" GJ hissed the words, but Jason had already broken free of her hold again and climbed onto the railing. Then he was gone, splashing into the waves before she could finish the question.

CHAPTER 52

"Special Agent Eleri Eames." She held her hand out, shaking the young woman's hand.

Neriah Jones was dry, having been hauled up from the raft onto the *Calypso* along with her two duffle bags and dive equipment. Though Jason had been handed up as well, he'd gone head first into the ocean to collect his friend. So now he was huddled on the deck, still dripping wet but with a blanket wrapped around his shoulders.

Actually, Eleri thought, Neriah was only mostly dry because Jason kept hugging her. "You got the messages?"

"Yes." She smiled. "That's how I found you."

Eleri couldn't help but be pleased. GJ had been using their satellite hookup to park coded emails for Neriah into Missy Maisel's draft folder. They'd all pitched in, crafting careful combinations of clues that, honestly, anyone could have figured out if they tried. But they also added information that Jason supplied, things that only he and Neriah or maybe someone who'd been on board the *Calypso* would understand.

Though Eleri was glad to see Neriah safe and sound, the whole thing was making her nervous. From the way Donovan stood back and how his eyes darted in all directions, it was clear that he felt the same. Though it was obvious that Hannah and Jason were nothing but excited to see Neriah again—and that the others trusted her completely—Eleri didn't. Neriah had disappeared. What if Miranda Industries had gotten to her? What if Neriah now had a different agenda?

Eleri's second problem was that the lights on the boat, though dim, lit them up like a stage in the middle of the ocean. All six—now seven—of them were standing on deck. Slowly, so as not to alert anyone watching, she motioned everyone to sit low. If anyone was watching, at least they weren't getting a performance anymore.

Next, as casually as she could, Eleri put her hand on Neriah's shoulder. "Is there anything I can get you? Do you need food? A drink?"

Though she was listening for a verbal answer, there was more behind the gesture.

"I'm fine."

There was something in her expression that indicated she understood why Eleri's hand had lingered longer than necessary. Still, Eleri was reading what she could. Pulling her hand away, she wished she'd been able to see more, but she had caught only glimpses of Neriah's memories from dives—images of fish swimming by, the slosh of waves, peace in the blue-green water. Anything else she might have sensed was overwhelmed by a deep sense of relief and concern.

But what was Neriah concerned about? By meeting up with the *Calypso*, she was back with her people, and she was safe and alive. So where was the worry coming from? Eleri could think of legitimate reasons, but she didn't know if they were Neriah's reasons. There were still too many questions.

Though the others wanted to have themselves a reunion, Eleri dove in to the important parts. "Why did you leave?"

Neriah's expression quickly changed. "I got an offer from

Miranda Industries. And Hannah—" the young woman gestured with her palm, "—told me about Allison's offer and that she didn't like the company. I threw it out. It came the day before we found Allison."

As Eleri watched, tears formed at the edges of the woman's large, brown eyes. Her grief seemed real, and she let her continue to talk.

"When I got the second offer, I got worried. I still didn't respond. But two days later, I got a threatening note under the windshield wiper on my car. That freaked me out, and the next day. . ." she paused, as though thinking about what to say. Eleri was grateful when everyone gave Neriah the space she needed for a pause. "I realized I was being followed. So I cleared out and disappeared. I left my computer behind—so they couldn't use it to follow me. I took only cash, bought new clothes, a new purse —in case they had put something in there."

Not a bad job, Eleri thought. Turning to Jason, she asked. "Did anyone follow you?"

He only looked sheepish, his wide mouth curling down at the edge. "It didn't occur to me anyone would follow me. I never checked. I mean, I didn't see anyone. But if it's not a fish or a hot woman, I'm often not paying attention."

Eleri would have laughed, but he looked so upset. That matched with what she'd seen of Jason over the past several days. After all, he had just gone headfirst into the ocean at night just because he recognized Neriah.

Looking back at Neriah, Eleri played another card. "You went to Dive Brothers to get equipment. Where did you dive?"

The young woman didn't seem startled that they'd managed to trace her, but she took a moment to answer. "I took the equipment and drove to Boca. There, I rented the inflatable, and I did a few dives offshore by myself."

"That sounds dangerous, diving alone," Eleri commented, waiting to hear Neriah's take on it. She didn't disappoint.

"Miranda Industries is dangerous. Fleeing my apartment with only cash is dangerous. I'm an incredibly experienced diver." Something flickered in her eyes. Unless Neriah had parked the video without watching it, she understood what had happened to Allison. That meant she understood what could happen to her if she was found underwater by someone who wished her harm.

"What did you find?" Eleri asked, trying to be cautious. She didn't want to push too hard, but she needed to find out what Neriah knew.

There was something in the woman's eyes that said she understood more than she was saying. Now, with the six of them sitting on the deck in a small circle as though they were going to start singing Kumbayah, Eleri realized she'd turned the conversation in entirely the opposite direction.

Neriah's eyes darted toward Hannah again. "I went to see Gelman and Patel. I thought they might have some information."

Eleri didn't know who Gelman and Patel were, but Hannah clearly did. This time, she was the one who prompted Neriah to continue.

"They're missing—both of them. Their assistant is still there, running the lab, but he's gone paranoid as hell. Both Gelman and Patel have been gone for at least five days."

She looked around the room and her next words told Eleri why she'd been nervous before. Neriah had committed a *bona fide* crime.

"I stole some of their research."

Once it became clear that the information was more important than arresting her, she nodded toward where they'd left her things on the deck. "It's in the second duffel."

CHAPTER 53

D onovan didn't like what he was sensing. Neriah smelled of ocean and fish, which wasn't unexpected, but it was almost overpowering his senses. His dislike of this particular smell didn't help. He also disliked what Neriah was telling them.

Despite her nod toward the duffel bag, no one had opened it yet. Her words were concerning, and all six of them listened with pounding hearts. He could hear it.

"Gelman and Patel's office was tossed. And they aren't just gone, they're *missing*."

Donovan could see and smell Eleri's growing fear as she pushed Neriah to tell the rest of the story. "What exactly happened? Were they out on a dive together?"

"That's just it. . ." Neriah said, letting her words trail off. She sat on the deck in the middle of the six-person crew of the *Calypso*, looking at each of them. "I can't say, exactly. I heard from their lab assistant, and *he* can't say exactly. But he did say they disappeared separately." Looking at the group for clues, Neriah waited a moment and then told more.

"They think Gelman was at home. His house was broken into, his computer stolen. And Gelman is gone. According to online posts and texts he sent that night, he did make it home. The neighbors heard something in the late evening, but no one reported it. Not until later.

Then he didn't show up the next day. A neighbor first reported that his trash bin stayed on the street for too long. When the homeowner's association checked, they found the house was disturbed and called the police. But of course, that's the story that Gelman's assistant told me."

Donovan's thoughts careened. Neriah's last words were telling: She didn't fully trust Gelman and Patel's assistant. Not anymore—if she ever had. Glancing back and forth to the other three agents, Donovan offered, "I'll look it up. I can access the official police report, if not the true story of what had happened." He knew that doing so might ping whoever was after Gelman and Patel. . . and maybe the same people who'd been after Neriah. But more oceanic researchers were missing, and that was too much to ignore. Looking back at Neriah, Donovan prodded her along. "And Patel?"

"She just disappeared." Neriah's sigh let out a pain in her heart. Whoever Gelman and Patel were, she was hurt that they were gone. "It was several days later that Lars, the assistant, filed the missing person's report on Patel. She had shown up at the office the first day Gelman missed, but not the next day. The police looked into it and traced her activity. There's footage of her at an ATM. She's looking over her shoulder. And that's the last anyone has seen her.

"Lars filed that report right away, thinking it was far too coincidental that Patel went missing within twenty-four hours of Gelman not showing up for work. That was before they knew Gelman's place had been broken into."

"I've got it." Noah held up the tablet he had with him. Donovan had not brought his up when he'd been roused to check out the inflatable that was trailing them. But the population on this boat was over half FBI agents, and everyone had the same records access that Donovan had. It was good that it was Noah's system that had pinged the police report. It was less likely to alert someone if a Miami agent checked. "The police report says the ATM withdrawal video was a positive ID on Patel. So they dropped it. She was alive and getting money. They don't say anything about her looking over her shoulder or anything suspicious. . ."

"That's what Lars told me." Neriah shrugged, but then her tone turned to hope. "Do you think she might have left voluntarily?"

Donovan didn't think so. Looking over your shoulder at the ATM could mean she was paranoid—if she was looking in multiple directions. If she consistently looked the same direction, that would most likely mean there was someone there, directing or threatening her. He didn't know how to ask, since Neriah's information was already second- if not third-hand.

It was Eleri who gingerly fielded that question. "We found footage of you at the bank, and you're here and still okay. So we can keep our fingers crossed that Patel did the same thing."

Neriah's slow nod indicated she didn't believe it and was merely allowing herself to be placated.

"So what's in the duffel bag?" Donovan moved the topic again. "If the office was destroyed, what was still there worth stealing? Wouldn't whoever searched it have taken all the important documents—whatever they'd come for?"

Neriah took a deep breath. "I wanted to work with Gelman and Patel during the summers. I'm starting an advanced degree in the fall. Hannah and Allison are—were—" she stumbled a little, "helping me get ready. I talked to them and I had already started doing little collections, reading their papers before they peer reviewed. I'd been in the lab more than once. That's why I went there to check on things!"

Shit. Donovan thought. These weren't just researchers she

knew, this was another personal blow. For a moment he wondered if Neriah had been the center of everything all along. . . not Allison.

"The office was a complete mess. Missing documents, broken glass. But I had worked there, so I know where everything is. I knew what I was looking for. I know I'm just an assistant here, but I pay attention, and I'm working hard to learn. So I grabbed everything that was still there that looked important." She turned to Hannah then, fear in her eyes. "I hope I got the right things."

Hannah looked up at her diver, though she had already unzipped the duffel, and was rifling through it. She held up and then set aside wadded-up papers, a lab notebook torn in half with pages falling out of the stitching, and a blob of papers wrapped around a hard object. Peeling the paper away, she held up a beaker Neriah had seen fit to save. "What's this?"

"I don't know. But there were several in the lab with that same crystalline residue in them. Most were broken. But, given what you and Allison have been pulling up, I thought we might be able to test it and see what they were working with."

"Good thinking," Donovan told her, wanting to say something positive. Though Neriah had held up remarkably well, now that she was somewhere safe, he could see her starting to break down. It was a common reaction to rescue. Though the agents needed information, he didn't want to add to her trauma.

For a moment, he reminisced about his days as a medical examiner when he wasn't responsible for anyone's feelings. Everyone he worked with was already dead. But now? With all the interrogation and hostage negotiation and psychological training they'd gotten at Quantico, he realized he'd always been wrong. He communicated with coworkers. He sometimes talked to families of the deceased. He testified in court. And he had not done it well.

Turning to the crew, he wanted to tell them they had to get to Nassau, and fast. But he was afraid no one would believe his urgency. It was painfully obvious to everyone how much he hated the open water. He said it anyway as six faces all turned to look at him. "Neriah is here now. And we know they—whoever *they* are—were after her. The new problem is that we just gathered everyone they want into one tiny location that we can't escape from."

Luckily, they'd all agreed with him and set a new course with no more stops. Whatever they might gather from replicating Allison's dives was not as important as getting this group somewhere safer.

They were heading directly into Nassau, though it, too, was probably not the safest place, given Miranda Industries had their home base at the edge of the town. But the crew had to go there anyway, and at least on an island, they could run from danger better than they could on a research boat.

And on an island, he wouldn't have to swim away from someone chasing him. . . if it came to that. Though Donovan hated the water, he hated what had been done to Allison Caldeira more. Now, with Hannah, Jason, and Neriah all in one spot, he could see how things might go very wrong.

They were only a few hours away from the island and now they scattered like bugs in an attempt to gather everything they'd need to get off the boat. It was Noah who stopped them.

"We need to do this like everything else: in shifts. We changed our course, but not our need for a guard. In fact, that need is higher now. Who's on first shift?"

GJ and Noah ended up taking watch, letting Hannah, Jason and Neriah get to work on the lab, which they had to clear out, in addition to their own things. It wasn't a small undertaking. There were samples to double-check, making sure the sea water they were stored in didn't slosh or leak. There were lab results to organize and pack into waterproof boxes. There were aquariums that they debated cleaning out—so that anyone who came on board couldn't test the residue the same way they would test Gelman and Patel's beaker.

The list of things Hannah was not willing to leave on the boat when they docked was large. "It's bigger this time," she offered apologetically. "I might have left them last time, but. . ." *Not anymore.* She didn't have to say the last part.

Donovan and Eleri were sent to pack their own things as quickly as they could. As soon as they were done, they would take over for GJ and Noah on deck. But once the door was closed behind them, Eleri, who was rapidly pulling things from the spaces she'd stashed them and shoving them back into her small suitcase, turned to Donovan. "Is the smell gone?"

"Yes. It was only in that one spot. Which is what made me think it was a drug corridor and that the small boats are there all the time."

"Good," she said. Then her hands stilled completely, while she looked him in the eyes. "Because we're still being followed."

CHAPTER 54

As the boat bumped against the dock for the first time, Donovan felt a weight lift from his shoulders. *Dry land.* He wasn't sure he'd ever been so grateful to be stuck on a relatively small island as he was right now.

He really wasn't much for traveling, not before joining the FBI. He'd had enough of being dragged around. Nothing had ever felt so good as buying his own home and knowing he could stay there as long as he liked. So he'd never come to the Bahamas before. Islands didn't appeal to him, and he still fought the concerns that came with being an FBI agent, but one no longer on American soil. They had no authority here. They were nothing but tourists.

Still, he was grateful that, in a few moments, they would all be off the tiny research vessel. They would no longer be corralled in one place. In fact, they were purposefully splitting up. He still hadn't seen anything to confirm Eleri's comment that they were still being followed, but Donovan didn't doubt her.

The boat continued to rock slightly with the waves, but the dock was a steadying force. Donovan would have leapt from the deck right onto the wooden planks had he been able to. There were still so many things to get off of the boat. So many things to protect.

First and foremost was the duffel bag Neriah had fought to bring to them. They had been towing her small inflatable behind the *Calypso*. It slowed them down a little bit, but they hadn't wanted to leave it.

Though Donovan had argued they should ditch the little boat and make it look like an accident, Eleri and Hannah had argued to keep it. In his mind, it might stop whomever was following them, if it looked as though Neriah had either decided to go for a dive by herself or had fallen overboard and never come back up.

"We need the raft," Hannah had claimed. "It makes us harder to kill. Having an entirely separate flotation device that—despite its small size—all seven of us can fit onto is something we desperately need right now. It gives us an escape route if we are attacked. And with our own stored inflatable, we have two modes of escape."

In the end, Donovan's argument had lost. He was fully in favor of having a speedy exit, though he hoped he would never have to set foot on the tiny craft.

On the dock, workers passed by him, ignoring his presence as they carried boxes and drove small forklifts with pallets full of goods coming into the city.

The *Calypso* had sailed past the large dock where the cruise ships stayed, instead coming around into this tiny port that Hannah knew of. It fed them into Nassau about five blocks away from the other dock, dramatically reducing the tourist traffic. Grabbing his own bag, Donovan stepped into the stream of moving workers and was carried along a few yards before he managed to turn around.

Despite this not being the bright and shiny cruise ship dock, it was still tremendously busy, and he was assaulted by sounds and smells coming from the boats and people and even all the way across the open beach in front of him. Turning, he saw Eleri still standing on the boat, bags in her hand, stuck behind a trio as Hannah, Jason, and Neriah gingerly stepped off onto the dock. They were embraced in what appeared to be a very touching moment.

As he looked at them, Hannah caught his eye. "This is the last land we were on with Allison. We were actually on this same dock, in the same slip, the last time we were here."

Shit, Donovan thought. He hadn't seen Hannah grieve her wife. Not yet. Maybe she'd worked through some of it before she contacted the FBI. Maybe she had a renewed purpose with Eleri and the other agents on the case. It always felt good to find justice for a lost loved one. . . or so he had believed until he'd found the paperwork on his mother. But right now, he wouldn't get in the way of the three of them having a moment they clearly needed.

A small, quick group hug passed, the only thing allowable in the traffic of workers. Hannah looked up at him and caught his eye again. "I'm furious about Allison. Livid. They took her from me. I'm mad that she suffered. And I'm mad that I don't get to have her for the rest of my life. But right now, I'm focused on finding them. Those fucking assholes aren't going to get anyone else."

He nodded at her. The FBI—like police officers—were trained to never promise they would solve a case. But right now, he felt like telling Hannah he would make sure it happened.

Once they moved off the dock and waded through customs, they regrouped in a little square across the street. A fountain held court in the center, and the sound of the water would help drown out their conversation for anyone listening in.

They each had a specific task to get them and their bags of evidence out of the open as quickly as possible. Donovan and Eleri handed out communication systems, while Noah booked hotel rooms. Hannah let him do it, since Noah didn't know the ones she and Allison usually went to. The agents didn't want to follow the research crew's normal path. Hannah and Jason procured two separate rental vans from different agencies, and within thirty minutes, the group was loading all the bags they had hauled off of the boat.

One of them contained the flask with the dried crystal substance on the bottom. Though he and Eleri were both anxious to get results from it, they knew they would have to wait for Hannah, who actually had the equipment to run the tests. The other option was to find a lab here on Nassau that could do the work, but that was risky, too.

It was all risky. Someone was after them, and for the last twenty-four hours, they'd all been in a single, thirty-foot by ten-foot space.

Donovan inhaled the warm air. The moisture hit his nose, along with a myriad of new scents. Despite not having been at the cruise ship dock, they must be close to touristy locations. He smelled what must be the local street food, but also rum cakes and a distillery nearby. Behind the fountain, the street marched up and away, a curious mix of modern pavement bracketed by older buildings.

Divided into the vans, the two groups split off from each other, carefully heading in different directions. Hannah and Noah turned left. Their van had most of the lab equipment, ready for Hannah to test what she could. The other van held Donovan, Eleri, GJ, Jason, and Neriah. Their first stop was to drop GJ and Jason at a hotel where Noah had made a reservation for the two of them.

In each case, they would stay in one room or suite. Eleri had not been willing to split them up more than that—not with Miranda Industries hot on their tails.

Jason and Hannah each now had their own armed agent for protection. Eleri and Donovan had taken Neriah, as she was the one that Miranda Industries had made the biggest gamble for already.

"Do I really need guards?" she asked while leaning forward from the middle row. She'd belted herself exactly into the center of the van, as Eleri had instructed. "I mean, I managed to evade them well enough on my own for a while."

"No, you didn't." Eleri tossed the comment back over her shoulder as she took the turns like a native. "*We* found you. And we sent you information. We also knew you were back there behind us."

"I thought you didn't know it was me."

"No, we didn't," Donovan admitted, wondering if they were playing into a lighter version of good cop/bad cop. "But we knew someone was following us. And if we decided to turn around, we would have gotten you."

"Then why didn't Miranda get me?"

That question had Donovan turning around in his seat. He looked her in the eyes. "I get the feeling they could have grabbed you if they wanted. They killed Allison and almost made it look like a marine attack, an accident. They got two other researchers—sorry, if you count Blake, they got three—and they made those look good enough that the police are only investigating one of them. So if they didn't get you, it wasn't because they *couldn't*. So the million dollar question is: What did they get out of letting you live?"

Neriah was nodding along as she followed his ugly logic, her expression changing rapidly from confident to afraid. "Well, if I was them, and I let me live, it would be because I was going to lead them to you."

"Exactly," Donovan said as the van bumped forward sharply, snapping the side of his face into the headrest as the car behind them plowed directly into their rear bumper.

CHAPTER 55

E leri could tell her head would hurt later. She was starting to feel the throb from the intensity with which she'd smacked the headrest in the large van. She'd then been snapped forward, thrown into the yank of the seatbelt, and slammed backward again.

"I'm trying to decide what—" she was hollering to Donovan when they got smacked again.

She didn't feel pain. Not yet.

"Get down, Neriah!" She yelled it, unable to turn and give the instruction cleanly or carefully. By being in the middle of the van, Neriah was the most protected. That had been the plan. However, the middle seat had no headrests and Neriah was in danger of getting serious whiplash, especially if they took another hit. The last thing they needed was somebody disabled by an accident.

As her eyes scanned the streets for available escape routes, Eleri realized they were going to have a fight on their hands. She watched the other cars and saw that the traffic was wholly unconcerned with the collision that happened in their midst and the two fleeing cars. She was not in the US anymore. "Donovan, where can I go?"

Punching the gas pedal, she sped up. The traffic on the street was heavy enough that she was in danger of hurting someone else to keep her small crew from being hit again. Eleri didn't like that option.

Speeding in short bursts, she wove through cars and gave bikes the widest berth she could, though it wasn't enough to make her comfortable. There was nothing safe in this, and no one else was paying any attention.

The black SUV behind them was a cliché, but a very dangerous one.

Donovan had pulled up a map service and, in her peripheral vision, she could see him scrolling through the city streets, looking for the best option. Though she knew he was doing his best, and that running them into a blind alley didn't help anyone, she wished he'd hurry the hell up.

Her hands clenched the steering wheel as she crested a hill, hoping she'd get some kind of sign to take a turn—any turn—so she could get away before the SUV came up behind them and spotted them again. But she had to stay on this street and give Donovan a chance to find them a workable path.

Just as she clenched the wheel to keep from just taking one of the side streets, he hollered at her. "Left. Here!"

They were almost past the turn where he was pointing. But she cranked the wheel and probably took the van up on two tires as it squealed around the slightly-sharper-than-ninety-degree turn.

Honks followed her as she threaded her way down the alley, not ready to believe she'd lost the SUV.

No. It hadn't been that easy. She watched as the large, black vehicle filled her rear view mirror and she took a moment to notice the insanely tinted windows. It could be a self-driving car for all she knew, and it was too close to get more valuable information.

"Neriah, turn your head slightly, hold on, and get me their license plate as soon as you can see it!"

"Yes, ma'am!"

She hadn't been ready to be "ma'am"ed, but she'd take it.

The vehicle was getting close enough to make a third hit. *Shit.* "Next turn?"

Donovan didn't disappoint. "Take the third right." He talked her through. "Not this. Not this. *Here.*" He was trying not to point too obviously for the turns, just in case anyone in the back could see him. Eleri certainly wasn't using her turn signals.

They were now on back streets, threading their way between pretty pink- and cream-colored houses. This was what she had wanted. Here, the cars were parked too closely.

"Turn here." Donovan gave her the next turn onto an even tighter street.

Yes. The van truly didn't fit, but she would make it work. Eleri was thinking that very thing as she knocked the mirror off of one of the cars parked along the side. It was the only way to get through, and she hated to destroy property, but she did it anyway.

As big as the van was, the SUV was wider, probably intended to be intimidating. It was impractical as a chase car, and Eleri was taking advantage of their poor choice. The SUV did not fit between the cars. They might have been willing to smash the parked cars to get through, but there was a high probability they would get stuck.

Eleri watched in her rear view mirror as they stopped, threw the SUV into reverse, and squealed backward.

There! She'd managed to effectively lose her tail. Still, they weren't done; that was just the first step. "Next turn, Donovan?"

"Straight through the intersection." His eyes were darting to the side roads and back to the map, but never to her. She was doing her job, and he his. Hopefully, Neriah had gotten that plate number.

"Straight?" she confirmed, because it was easier said than done. Cross traffic was heavy enough that she was afraid the black SUV would get around the side streets and pull across in front of them. They could effectively block her, forcing her to reverse out of their predicament. Not a pleasant thought. Even if she got across, if these guys—whoever they were—caught sight of them darting across the street, the chase would be back on.

While she watched for a break in the traffic, she was planning an escape route for every contingency. As soon as a space was big enough that she wouldn't get honked at, she took it. She couldn't afford the attention of bleating horns now that the SUV no longer had her in sight. She was suddenly grateful for every hour she'd endured of tactical driving.

Her mother hadn't driven a car in years. She just had one of the staff drive her wherever she wanted to go. She'd never even encouraged her daughter to learn to drive at all. *If her mother could see her now, she'd swoon and pass out.* For a girl who grew up in Louisiana's Lower Ninth Ward, her mother had gone remarkably tender. Eleri had certainly not inherited that quality.

She smashed the gas pedal and dodged her way through two different directions of traffic, holding her breath the whole time. Once in the alley, she didn't exhale. She just followed Donovan's instructions.

"Second left, two blocks. . ." He waited until she'd taken the turn. "Right, then an immediate left. *Here!*"

She pulled into a parking lot where she had no permit. The street she'd just ducked off was a smaller alleyway that hadn't even borne a street sign. The city clearly did not expect the tourists to make it back here.

"Get out," she commanded as she caught the eye of a lone man sitting on an upturned bin in the corner. He stood up to walk over to them, but she looked away. She had more important things to worry about than a parking permit. The van was too obvious; they had to abandon it.

"Grab everything." Already out the door, she was at the back of the vehicle, struggling to wrench open the doors, which had crumpled slightly when they were hit. She tugged them wide and handed the luggage out to Donovan.

"We're going on foot?" Neriah asked. Her tone was confused, but she took the bag Eleri shoved at her.

"Only until we can drop the bags."

Donovan didn't question anything, but it seemed Neriah questioned everything. "We can't leave the bags."

Eleri had already grabbed two and was hightailing it around the corner, knowing Donovan would shut the van doors behind her and likely offer cash to the man who was inquiring about the van. It didn't matter if he recognized them or the van. It only mattered that it was off the street and would be hard to find.

She turned to Neriah. "We can leave the bags, and we will if we have to. We won't leave the people. Got me?" When she received a sharp nod and a straightened spine in response, she continued. "My plan is to ditch the bags and pick them up later. In my best case, we don't lose any of this."

"Okay!"

There, she thought, *this was the young woman who'd survived almost two weeks on her own being chased by this same shadowy corporation.*

Eleri was peeking around corners and darting onward, now knowing Neriah would stay close behind, even if it was because she really had no other choice. Eleri hit the end of the first alleyway and tipped her head beyond the edge of the building.

Sure enough, there was a large, black SUV coming down the

main street toward her. Snapping her head sharply, she ducked backward into the alley and nearly smacked into Neriah.

Donovan was right behind her, a bag in each hand, his head tipped slightly as if he could sniff out the SUV's route. He was telling Neriah, ". . . If you want to stay safe, you follow Eleri."

Bless him, she thought. Though she figured Neriah had already gotten that message, it was good to hear it again. No other command or questions would be entertained until they were out of danger.

Keeping an eye on the black SUV as it slowed down, Eleri noticed the driver seemed to be making a decision which way to turn. She watched as the big car hooked a left on the next major street. With a nod, Eleri led her small crew up the sidewalk, away from where the SUV had gone.

Walking up the main streets with their luggage in hand was almost as obvious as being in the large white van. But that was her only choice besides abandoning the bags, and she wasn't ready to make that sacrifice. If they dropped the bags here in the open, they would be lost. As she'd told Neriah, she was trying to preserve them.

The three of them trudged up the hill in the heat and humidity, trying to look as normal as possible. Eleri was grateful that Neriah managed to look like a local in her cut-off jeans shorts and loose t-shirt. She helped normalize the two agents, who didn't look quite like feds, but didn't blend as well as Neriah did.

"Here," Eleri called as she spotted a street-side stand and decided it was worth a stop. Grabbing two hats, she placed one on her own head and one on Neriah's. Donovan was paying for them even before she finished choosing and they were back on the sidewalk again, still trudging up the hill.

The street was relatively steep, and the bags in her hands were not light, but she didn't stop. In fact, she picked up the pace and expected Neriah and Donovan to keep up. At last, Eleri saw what she was looking for.

CHAPTER 56

H alf an hour later, Eleri was sipping a deeply colored rum at a bar in an open-air tap room. They'd managed to slip into the second half of a local distillery tour. There appeared to be a handful of businesses making Bahamian rum on the island, and Eleri was more than happy to hide in the crowd.

"I'm not really a fan of rum," Neriah whispered. The fleeing part was over, and so was her steel spine, maybe.

"Drink it anyway," Eleri told her in a hushed tone. She offered a smile to the other woman and clicked the tiny paper cups together as though celebrating.

They'd asked no questions on the tour, followed along with the crowd, and oohed and ahhhed in all the appropriate places. They'd stayed in the middle of the group as they wound in and out of the farmhouse, the original family plantation home, and the fermenting rooms. At one point, the tour guide had pointed out deep wells in the ground, covered with wooden flaps on top. Then he'd lifted one and let them all feel the alcohol wafting off.

Despite the high alcohol content, this was the safest place, she decided. They could have stayed on the street, but where would they have left the bags? They could have tried to head for the hotel. Honestly, she hadn't seen anyone in the crowd who looked suspicious, but she wasn't letting her guard down. While the cluster of strangers was safe for them, it wouldn't be safe for the strangers if the agents were spotted.

Her big fear had been that the SUV found them so damn quickly. Since it had, it probably wasn't luck. They'd either watched the crew debark from the *Calypso* and walk through customs, or else there were several cars waiting at various points around the city. The one that hit them would have simply been the first one to find them.

Her eyes looked to Donovan and he offered a small nod. At least that was okay. He'd been texting back and forth to Hannah and GJ while they were on the tour. Eleri and Neriah had played the interested travelers, figuring it was better if only one of them was acting like an asshole. That was more normal than the three of them coming in late, and none of them paying any attention. So she and Neriah had participated to the best of their abilities, though Eleri was counting herself the better actress here.

As the tour finished up, they meandered back down the driveway, lingering and buying a rum-filled lemonade to make their slowness seem appropriate. Donovan headed down to the street and hailed a cab while the two women ducked into the woods and pulled the bags out to the curb hoping nobody would notice. Eleri caught herself wishing any observers had purchased one of the frozen rum drinks and was sloshed enough to not realize what was happening.

Shitshitshit. She was thinking like an FBI agent, and that wasn't wrong. But she also needed to start remembering what Grandmere had taught her. She should also be thinking like a witch.

After sending Neriah to the gravel-lined road to watch their things, Eleri straightened before grabbing the two remaining bags. Lifting her hands up to the blue sky peeking through tall trees, she called on Loa Eshu to protect them.

Above her, the clouds blew away for a moment and the sun found her. Coincidence? She didn't know. She could only hope she was strong enough to enact Grandmere's protections.

As she emerged with the last two bags, she found Donovan and Neriah beside the cabbie, dropping their luggage into the trunk. Donovan tipped his head as though he'd seen her, but she couldn't answer now. He turned to the driver and asked, "What's the best local hotel? Someplace fun. Nice."

"Oh, I know a place." He was already climbing behind the wheel.

"Is it out of the main part of the city?" Donovan asked, handing over a bill to encourage the cabbie.

For someone with a questionable desire to be sociable, Donovan was greasing wheels and asking all the right questions like a pro. Thirty minutes later, Eleri was standing inside a second-floor suite, soaking up the air conditioning that had been cranked long before the room was rented. The building was like a motel, with an open walkway outside the entry door. But the walkway had arches and pillars and tile on the footpath. The vending machines had been tucked out of the way, and the building was recently painted.

Inside was just as nice, though Eleri wouldn't have complained. Gauzy white curtains framed the windows. She would have pulled the shades, but that would have called more attention to this room, and they couldn't afford that. So instead, she and Donovan and Neriah hung toward the back of the space.

"Do you want anything?" she asked Neriah. Eleri had raided the vending machines while Donovan rented them the suite. She'd grabbed a variety of sodas and a handful of snacks—certainly more than the three of them needed right now, but they had no idea how long they'd be stuck in the room.

Neriah, obviously still exhausted from their flight and possibly feeling out of control, shook her head. Eleri let her refuse. It might be the only thing she could make her own decision on until the case was closed. It wasn't Eleri's job to make her happy, just to keep her alive.

Popping the top on her own soda, Eleri guzzled it. She'd gotten over her compunctions about eating or taking a break in the middle of a stressful case years ago. Hopefully the fizz and the sugar would counteract the rum she'd been drinking.

Though she wasn't confident of it, she felt relatively safe now—"relatively" being the strongest word. She had a spell cast that seemed to be holding. No one was jamming the back of her car, but she was also not confident it wouldn't happen again. She liked this suite in that it ran the entire width of the building, with large windows on the front and smaller ones on the back. She and Donovan were ready to jump out of those windows, dragging Neriah with them, if someone came banging on the door.

Taking her first slow, deep breath, she turned to Donovan. "I don't like this."

He was just reaching into the fridge, grabbing his own soda as she spoke the words. Being Donovan, when he turned around, he also had a bag of chips in his hand. He was opening the crinkly foil, the noise almost setting off her alarms as he deadpanned, "No shit, Sherlock."

"What if it was just an accident?" Neriah posed to the pair, her hands wringing together.

But it wasn't, Eleri thought, although her answer was kinder and offered an explanation. "It wasn't an accident because they hit us more than once. They found us, Neriah, and they found us fast."

"But who are they?"

"That's the problem. I don't know."

With that, the other woman let her line of questioning drop.

Eleri was grateful when she stood and went to the small fridge to finally grab herself a drink. But as she plopped down on the couch under the front window, Eleri had to remind her to move.

Clearly, Neriah had lost the edge that had kept her alive. She probably thought everything was okay once she climbed aboard the *Calypso*. The problem was, not only was it not okay, but her arrival had made it worse. Neriah was trying to relax now, not ratchet up a notch, but Eleri and Donovan needed her to stay alert.

Donovan looked up from his phone then. "Noah and Hannah managed to get to their hotel room safely." He'd been texting everyone while they were on the tour. "So did GJ and Jason."

Eleri dialed her own phone, about to dick up the day for everyone else, too. "Hannah, have you seen anything suspicious now that you're in?"

"No, I haven't seen anyone. . . but I don't know what I'm looking for."

There was a pause, and then Noah's voice came on, suggesting she'd held up the phone for both of them to hear. "I haven't spotted anyone."

Eleri noticed he didn't say they weren't being followed, only that he didn't see it. With a sigh, she threw her next instruction at them. "I'm suggesting that you pack up. Make sure you aren't followed, and head to another location."

"Shit." Noah understood, but no one liked this game.

She understood, but knew their irritation could get any of them killed. So, when his next words came across with conviction, she was happier. "I'm on it."

Hanging up, she next made the same phone call to GJ and Jason.

But GJ had a different response. "We're already out and about."

It made sense, Eleri thought. GJ and Jason were Team One. They were supposed to be the first ones out on the street, investigating. "We're checking out Miranda Industries' street address. We're about five minutes away," GJ said. But then she followed up that statement. "To be honest, it doesn't look good."

CHAPTER 57

This had been a mistake, GJ thought. She grabbed at the hem of Jason's shirt and tugged him down into the bushes beside her. He royally sucked at hiding.

It was true, he was much larger than she was, so hiding was a more difficult job—but he wasn't even trying. "Stay low!" she hissed. "We can't be seen."

She didn't add that *Clearly, she wasn't the problem here.*

It hit her then: She was an actual agent—acting like one, trained like one, and getting annoyed at Jason's rube-like behavior. But giving herself a pat on the back didn't last long.

"Look at the—"

"Shush," she told him, stifling yet another question. His mouth audibly clicked shut as though he'd just forgotten not to talk, although she'd told him the same thing no more than three minutes ago.

They were following her plan, but GJ was now questioning the sanity of the arrangement. It was growing more and more difficult to spy on Miranda Industries and babysit a two-hundred-pound man at the same time. Jason was clearly an excellent diver and marine researcher, but he would have made a shitty agent.

"Can we go—"

She cut him off again before he even finished the question. That time, less than a minute had expired between breaches of protocol.

She didn't care what he wanted to know. He couldn't be asking it. Her instructions had been very clear: Stay quiet, and ask your damn questions later.

Lifting a small camera, just big enough to have a screen she could frame images on, she snapped off pictures of the large building behind the fence. The camera could have been even smaller. . . but she would have had no clue if she was getting the image she wanted or not. This was the compromise. It needed to be small enough to hide if necessary, but big enough so she could see that she'd gotten a clear shot of the fence, one of the front of the building, one of the sign on the gate, and so on. Even if she couldn't see any of the details in what she'd snapped yet.

The chain link fence that surrounded Miranda Industries' Nassau location was mostly hidden behind vines peppered with pretty purple flowers. GJ was grateful the tiny camera could be pushed through the wire and leaves to get pictures of what she couldn't see.

The company had done a good job of obscuring what could be discerned from the street. The fence was ten feet tall, or maybe twelve. She was eyeballing it. There we no gaps in the foliage, either. Miranda had been serious about obstructing the view. Where the vines had fallen away, shrubbery had been planted. In one spot, where it appeared a plant had died off, a large metal sheet had been leaned against the fence from the other side. Though it appeared casual, she knew it was anything but.

The fencing continued on three sides, running down into

the ocean and making sure that anyone who got in had to pass the guards at the gate—or come up through the water. GJ didn't dive, but she was starting to wonder how a water breach might happen...

Before they'd planted themselves here, she and Jason had rented brightly-colored, touristy bikes. They'd pedaled around town and gotten ice cream. They'd crossed the bridge onto the smaller key just off Nassau, Paradise Island, and then headed through a heavily wooded area bracketed by high-end beach resorts. The trail spit them out on a stretch of sand known as Smuggler's Beach. GJ appreciated the complete lack of irony.

The pair had biked down the street, passing between highrise hotel complexes and at the end, when the street ran out, they stashed the bikes and continued on foot. They'd walked along as though headed somewhere beyond the Miranda Industries complex. Their casual stroll had been a first pass to case the place before they carefully doubled back.

The beach was a crappy place to try to sneak up on anything. That was probably why Miranda Industries had chosen the location.

They'd spent a good amount of time waiting between the dunes and then trying to stay low enough not to get caught on any surveillance. GJ wasn't sure she'd achieved it, but so far, no one had bothered them.

She turned the tiny camera another direction and snapped off more pictures, hoping to catch an image her eyes couldn't see. "Keep an eye out, but stay low," she whispered.

She'd tapped Jason on the arm, getting his attention, hoping this assignment was one he could do. The small camera was separate from her phone, because the phone was the first thing anyone would confiscate or check if they caught her. The camera was small enough to be hidden so she could smuggle the images out.

GJ had smartly snapped a few pictures with the cell before

pulling out the real camera. Her hope was that, if someone harassed them or checked her phone, they would see a few innocuous pictures and believe that was the end of it. Her ability for subterfuge had increased exponentially in the past six months.

"What am I looking for?" Jason, of course, was asking another question.

"Shhhh." She kept her own voice low, trying to hide her growing irritation. "Anyone who might spot us. Ow!"

Something had stung her. Cranking her head around, she tried to examine the back of her arm. A red welt was forming, though she wasn't sure it was from a bite or a sting. With a deep breath and a drive to ignore the throbbing sensation, she turned back to the fence.

"Fuck!" This time something got her between the shoulder blades.

Not a bug. Though her arm was bare, the middle of her back was not. This had stung her through her shirt. But before she could comment beyond her initial outburst, Jason was talking again.

A white pickup truck was pulling up the drive. Their location, on top of a large dune, hidden in an indentation from the wind and the grasses that clung to the top, allowed them to see down into the truck. GJ desperately wanted a view beyond the gates when they opened and she strained her neck, hoping to see anything.

"That truck is—"

GJ made a cutting motion at her throat, stopping him once again. It didn't matter what he knew or what he saw. He couldn't talk. And somehow, he hadn't quite figured that out yet. *At least maybe he'll be able to run fast when he got them caught.*

Turning the camera, she shot more pictures of the truck and of how the gates still obscured everything, even when they were open. Once she got enough pictures, she moved them to another location and did it again. She made a motion to him. It was time to get out.

Another of the harsh stings hit her then, grazing her neck and surely leaving a welt. "Ah!" GJ reached up to cradle the new wound, only then registering what her eyes had seen. Something had come at her at high speed. It was not a crawling, flying, supersized Caribbean insect, but a projectile. "Jason!"

She spat his name out in a whisper, but they'd been crawling along and, as he turned to see what she wanted he, too, got caught, taking the hit on his arm. "Crap!" He smacked at it as though to kill the non-existent bug and she understood.

"Get down!"

Someone was after them. She heard the ping of something hard contacting the wire in the fence behind her. Then she watched as a rock fell near her hand.

Snatching it up, she felt it sit warm and small in her palm, just a piece of gravel. But where was it coming from?

She ducked suddenly, a reaction she wasn't consciously aware of. Reaching up, she tugged Jason down again as she heard several pings, more gravel hitting the fence behind her.

"What?" Jason asked and she marveled at his lack of self-preservation. In the water, he was supposedly brilliant. She wasn't seeing it on dry land.

"We have to get out of here. They've seen us." The problem was, she wanted to see them, too.

Holding still for a moment, GJ assessed the situation. The rocks were coming from outside the Miranda Industries compound. She and Jason were high up on a dune, and the trees and parkland they'd come in through were the only thing across the wide gravel street. She peeked over the top of the sand, letting her gaze filter through the thick grass obscuring her or so she'd thought. There was no one in the street.

So anyone chucking rocks at her would have to be across the street, hidden in the trees. High up, too. GJ didn't have Wade's brain for physics, but she understood that small things didn't go far and not at high speed—not unless they were shot out of a gun.

Or, she thought, unless there was some other force at play.

She'd either found someone with skills like Allison's killer, or she'd found *him*.

Another rock zinged past her head, and she ducked again, now trying to assess a safe way out of their little hiding spot. This guy knew exactly where they were. How long did they have before the Miranda Industries gates opened up and someone came out and hauled them inside? They would close the gates and. . . well, she had no idea what multitude of sins hid behind the green vines and pretty purple flowers.

"Jason, we have to go."

But as the last word passed her lips and Jason turned to look at her, a red cut appeared suddenly at the side of his temple and he dropped like a stone.

CHAPTER 58

J ason flopped like a flour sack as she nudged him. GJ immediately checked his head, relief rolling off her as she found he had no broken bones. Though the cut was bleeding, it wasn't bad. It appeared to be a perfect shot, right to the temple.

But another *ping* came above her head, followed by a *thud* as the pebble dropped beside her. Grabbing Jason firmly, she shook him until his eyes opened. "What?"

Huffing a small sigh at him, GJ admonished, "Don't look at me like that. You took a rock to the side of the head and went down. We have to get out of here."

His hand reached up, touching the wound, brown fingertips smearing with red blood. Luckily, he did no more than frown at it. He couldn't pass out again—her first thought had been that she wasn't strong enough to carry him. And leaving someone behind was not an acceptable FBI agent move. Leaving a civilian behind? No way.

They weren't supposed to bring civilians on assignment anyway, and GJ was developing a new respect for the rules. Quantico had been full of them. She'd had no trouble following the ones she understood, and she understood the ones about civilians a lot better right now.

She pointed back the way they'd come. It might not be safe. The guy aiming at them might have seen them come in. But the other direction would take them closer to the gate and the guards. Though their weapons were concealed well, GJ had spotted them, so getting closer to that section of the fence was not on her to-do list. She and Jason would have to make due with retracing their steps. "Army crawl. That way."

He did as he was told, and for that, she was grateful. Rocks continued to come at them; GJ even took another one to the arm, the sting not slowing her down. As she hooked her elbows into the sand and pulled herself along, she took stock. The rocks were small, which either meant he didn't have enough force at this distance to fling bigger rocks, or he wasn't trying to kill them.

Is this Allison's killer? If so, he'd easily dispatched Allison and even made it look like an accident.

Accident?

Her brain scrambled. What accidental death was he trying to create with them here? If they hit the water, they might get pulled out by a riptide. GJ almost discounted that idea. Unless he could control an ocean tide—unlikely if he couldn't throw larger rocks—the chance of survival was too high. She looked for other traps and couldn't find any.

Shit.

That left the option was that he wasn't trying to kill them at all. Miranda Industries was playing her, the same way they'd played Neriah. They were going to follow her back to the others.

By the time she and Jason made it to crossing the gravel street, the rocks had long since stopped flying, but GJ refused to be lulled into a false sense of security. She ducked and wove her way across, then pushed through the trees, hypervigilant about her surroundings.

When they arrived back at their bikes, she spent far too long examining them for trip wires, explosives, tracking devices, and more. When she could find nothing wrong, she finally told Jason, "Go. Let's ride out of here. See if we can stay on the trail and off the roads."

He nodded, understanding the severity of the situation—or at least, that was her take on his silence. They took the long way around, giving in to GJ's fears. She could not lead anyone from Miranda Industries, especially Allison's assassin, back to the hotel. She would have run out the clock, but it seemed the safer option not to. At least she'd turned off any cell service to her phone. They couldn't have cloned it, because they couldn't see it.

When she and Jason finally hit a stopping point, they sat at a table at a sidewalk cafe and she turned her service back on. She was risking exposure, but it would be worse to risk her fellow agents mounting a search for her and Jason if they didn't check in. Hitting a few buttons, she took a deep breath, glad to finally stop for a moment, even if she couldn't let her guard down. "Eleri, we got pictures, but we got found out."

"Are you okay?"

"Yes, but I'm not certain we aren't being followed." She sighed and explained. "I think you need to move everyone. I'm sorry."

They would have to casually wait here for a long time, trusting the others to pack up the things they'd left behind and get them to a new location. She and Jason waited it out by eating at the café, a boon as GJ was ravenous after her heart-pounding exit from the beach. She bought a hat and got Jason a new t-shirt, giving him another color and hopefully scrambling anyone who knew what they were looking for. She could only trust it was enough.

Two hours later, she was hauling the bike up the stairs of a new building. This one looked like GJ's idea of a Southern home. Not a plantation, but the sprawling house with wide porches set with ceiling fans. Thick wood railings lined the outdoor seating area, and dormer windows stood sentry on the roof. Only here they eschewed the final touch of the deep south with more lacquer and less white paint.

Inside the suite, all five of the others waited for them. Hannah and Noah had been the designated sleepers for this shift, though they didn't look rested. Eleri greeted them at the door with, "What did you get?"

Sitting at the table—she sank like a brick into the chair, because she was now thoroughly tired—GJ plugged in the tiny camera, eager to see the pictures. Behind her, Eleri was trying to give the original crew of the *Calypso* something to do that didn't involve FBI business. But, though the three of them sat on the other side of the room, there wasn't much to keep them out of private FBI business.

They were all in this, Eleri realized. It was hard enough discussing the necessary things as agents without even delving into any of NightShade's business with three casual onlookers standing by.

The four agents crowded around the screen, analyzing the building layout.

"They're right on the shoreline," Eleri commented. "You'd think that wouldn't be good at high tide. Or if there was any kind of surge."

"It looks like they may be elevated a little bit. Can we get satellite images?" Donovan asked even as he was reaching for another device, probably already logging in to pull up whatever images he could.

GJ looked to the other three faces. She didn't want to tell them. "Here's the bad news. I can't be positive, but I think we encountered our guy."

"Our guy?" Noah looked up at her, brows pulled tight.

She hadn't wanted to say it, but there was no way around it. As GJ opened her mouth, Jason—from the other side of the room—filled it in. "The one who killed Allison."

"Somebody was throwing rocks at us. Overall it was pretty mild." That brought a scoff from Jason, but she continued. "But we couldn't see who. They must have been in the trees, across a wide road. Unless it was someone with a rock gun he could aim, the gravel should not have sailed that far at that speed."

"Well, crap. He's here," Eleri commented, agreeing that this was the same person who'd murdered Allison.

Hannah's voice chimed in from across the room. "But that means we can get him. Right?"

The agents looked to each other. Nobody wanted to make that kind of a promise.

"The satellite images are good." Donovan quickly changed the subject. "They show Miranda has a high volume of boat traffic at this location. I guess they're delivering whatever they've got here. The question is, what is it?"

This time, Jason stood up and walked over to stand behind GJ. *So much for keeping the other three out of the conversation.* "They aren't boating it out. They're *diving* it out."

"What?" GJ asked. She'd been there, too, but she hadn't seen that.

"You wouldn't let me talk." Jason's tone held a bit of accusation.

"No," she replied. *Not that anyone could have stopped him.* "We were found out quickly enough as it was."

He didn't apologize, but he didn't push his point anymore, either. "It's a dive operation."

"How could you tell?" She was still looking up at him rather than at the pictures.

"The trucks that came through the gate had a series of straps in beds. Those straps hold dive tanks. So they're not only bringing in tanks for whatever they're doing at the compound, they're bringing in enough tanks to line the walls of pickup trucks. That's an operation, not just a few casual dives." He motioned to GJ to scroll back a few pictures. "The guys we saw coming in? Those are divers."

"How can you tell?" Donovan asked.

This time, it was Hannah who answered from her seat against the wall. "I don't know what to tell you, but we divers recognize each other. It's probably that we're generally lean. We're fit. We have saltwater hair. We've got good lung capacity, and we can walk around with forty pounds of equipment on our back and fins on our feet. There's a certain look."

GJ glanced to Eleri, then to Noah. They were the divers of the group, and she didn't see anything on them that said "diver" —but they were only occasional divers. They didn't dive for their livelihood or run an operation the way these guys did. The three agents shrugged to each other and let it stand.

"So, we have tanks and divers going in—" GJ said, just to keep the forward momentum, but Jason interrupted her again.

"More than that." He motioned her to stop on a particular picture. "These buildings—here—that you were looking at. The steps go up the front." He turned next to Eleri. "And you were right about the water coming up to them. The steps go up so high in the front because the base floor is at the top of those steps, about a floor and a half above the ground level here." He pointed to each spot.

"These tanks—" he said, pointing next to twin, silo-like features on the front of the building.

They're tanks, GJ thought. It hadn't occurred to her.

"They're for sea water. They've got piping that goes out the back of the building. That's why the building is so close to shore. They're sucking seawater directly into the tanks to hold it for use inside. Then, once you're in the building, if you go downstairs. . . you can't see it from this picture." He pointed as though motioning around to the back side. "There are boats under there. The water does come up under the building, and that's the point. You walk down the stairs into a floating dock and launch directly into the water."

Donovan held up another picture on the tablet. He'd found an overhead shot of the building. "Unless you're out on the water, you can't see the backside of the building. Which means they are loading these boats in almost complete privacy."

He flipped through a few shots, and Eleri stopped him on one. There was a boat in the picture a decent distance from the Miranda dock, aimed outward into the ocean. "You can't be sure, but it looks like it's leaving the compound. And it looks like the cigarette boat we saw."

CHAPTER 59

Donovan stood in the woods, stripping naked. Mosquitos came up to check him out, but sniffed at him and then left him alone. He was as much an anomaly to them as he was to everything else.

Peeling his shirt off and stepping out of his shoes, he thought about how monumentally stupid this was. But he still folded the clothing and shoved it into his bag before tying the bag to a branch. Normally, he did this to keep his supplies away from other animals that might run off with them. Although here, he'd only seen iguanas and the occasional pig—nothing that was going to steal his clothing while he was out.

He wanted to call out to Noah and ask if anyone was coming by, but he knew Noah would tell him. Despite Noah's newness to the whole situation, Donovan had to trust that it was better to stay quiet. He was already trusting Noah with all his ID and a backup set of clothing. He hoped it was the right move.

There had to be laws about public nudity on this island, but he didn't know them, and he could only hope they were much more lax than those in the US. If anyone caught him, he had no authority whatsoever. Flashing his FBI badge would likely only get him laughed at.

Still, he stood there, fully nude as he began the process of changing. It felt good. He rolled his shoulders, twisted his neck to one side and the other, wiggled his jaw. And slowly, piece by piece—almost like being double-jointed or slipping a shoulder out of a socket—he rolled into his new form.

Even as he did so, the smells of the forest bloomed and came fully alive. The pine and sea grass snuck up into his sinuses. The mangroves nearby were no longer just trees he saw, but beings he smelled and heard. The sand and the sea changed as his face opened up. He could now differentiate the scent of the algae here from that where they were staying, just several miles away.

In the distance, the waves crashed rhythmically, but now he heard each one. He heard the undertow pulling them back out and he heard the water as it was slapped against rocks in the far distance. In the hotels down the street, as well as inside the Miranda compound, his ears could distinguish all the little ups and downs of the business. Things being lifted, set, the beeping of motorized equipment. Footsteps. And, of course, the boats chugging to life.

He padded out on four paws, hoping he looked more like a big, friendly dog than an ancient myth. He had no idea what the local superstitions were, but he had decided to brave them.

Noah took point, acting the human. He led them out of the woods, through the back pool and lounge areas of one of the hotels and across the street. They hit the beach and followed the water line around the tip of a small rock jetty toward their destination. The sand squished beneath Donovan's paws, offering a slight squeak of saturation each time he stepped. Noah's shoes offered a rubbery sliding noise, but Donovan was grateful his partner's breathing was slow, if heavy. Noah wasn't oblivious to the danger of the situation, but he had himself under control.

The birds squealed as they dove for whatever tiny fish they were finding, each shriek followed by a splash. The waves sloshed and slapped. If he hadn't been going out for reconn, the day would be beautiful. Donovan took a deep breath and he smelled it.

Heroin.

Cocaine.

Dogs could easily sniff it out, and so could he. His ability to detect drugs this far from the Miranda Industries location either meant some was here on the beach, or they were dealing in incredibly large quantities. He stuck his nose to the sand and checked. No. It was here, but only in trace amounts. That wasn't what he was smelling.

Earlier, they had looked up Nassau's laws regarding drug-running. But with so much tourist and non-local traffic through the islands, it seemed the rules were enforced haphazardly, if at all.

Miranda apparently wasn't feeling any pinch from the authorities. Whether that was because the company was staying under the radar or because they had some kind of handshake deal with the locals, Donovan didn't yet know.

He hit the point where it was time to head off on his own. Turning, he looked back to Noah and offered two short barks. That was the signal for Noah to stay put. His blond partner looked perfectly at home sliding his backpack off and setting it on the sand. He even declared, "This looks like a good spot."

Donovan nodded along. This was the game they had decided to play: Noah, the beach-going book reader, and Donovan, his dog who ran off and explored. He didn't wait as Noah set out his towel and settled in, he just listened to the noises getting fainter in the distance as he trotted along the sand. Soon, he was weaving in and out of the dunes, several of which still carried the scent of fear from where GJ and Jason had hidden earlier that day.

Overlying that, though, he smelled blood—human blood—and that was concerning. It didn't belong to either GJ or Jason. Though they both had wounds, neither had bled enough to leave this strong a scent. So he wondered, was it from an injury that was small but more recent? Or was it something big and maybe more distant?

The day was pushing on, and he didn't have time the check out the blood. Instead, the fence got his attention. Sniffing at the vines, he pushed them out of the way for a good look inside, counting on the fact that everyone would discount a dog.

Walking down toward his right and into the ocean and swimming around the edge of the fence was not an option for him. Although he could probably swim—most dogs swam, but not his kind—he wouldn't want to get bracketed in like that. So he followed the fence around to the left, absorbing all the smells as he went.

There were a large number of people inside the building. They talked at low levels, joking as things like heavy bags smacked against each other. It sounded as though they were hauling sacks of flour. But Donovan suspected it wasn't flour they were moving.

Trotting right up to the gate, thinking he would go for his biggest move yet, he poked around. Maybe they'd let a dog inside. He was, after all, just a friendly puppy. *Right.*

He hated playing house pet. But right now, he was far more curious about what was inside than he was irritated at being treated like an overly friendly, dumb object. Hanging out, he watched as several vehicles passed by, including one large truck and a few personal cars. On the third one, he made his move.

When the gate opened, he trotted in after the car, doing his best Golden Retriever impression. At first glance, it was clear this was a full-scale operation. There were fabric canopies strung between the trees. They probably weren't so much to keep the workers shaded as they were there to stop satellite and drone images from catching the activity.

But once under the awnings and inside the fence, they weren't hiding much of anything. All the people were moving freely. He couldn't pad around and gawk all afternoon, so he went up to one of the guards, nudging at his hand.

The hand smelled of rifle oil, and Donovan spotted the weapon set into a cradle just inside the gate. This way, the guards could step outside with only a handgun holstered at their waist, but with far more firepower easily in reach.

Looking up, he whined at the one he was almost forcing to pet his head, hoping the sound came across as though maybe he were hungry or lost.

"Hey boy, aren't you pretty?" The guard crouched a little and actually scratched between his ears now.

Donovan nudged up against his legs, using the gesture to pass farther into the compound. He spotted a row of rifles, set into notches and ready to go.

Shit, he thought, there was more fire power at hand than what the guards could pick up. They were ready for more than just defense. Even as he thought that, he heard the sound he wanted: the gate closing behind him.

"Who do you belong to?"

Test Number Two. The guard handled the collar Donovan had reluctantly worn. He didn't find a tag, but he didn't seem to find the hidden camera, either. Donovan almost licked his face, but he was afraid he might get a swath of coke—or worse—from the man's skin. Powder was free-floating in the air, and everyone had to be at least a little high. So far, Donovan wasn't feeling any hit.

He meandered away then, moving agilely between the workers, accepting pats on the head and scratches under the chin as he took in the operation, hoping the camera he wore caught it all.

It was interesting that Miranda was running two kinds of drugs simultaneously. That was unusual. They were also operating with the packages out in the open—not the way it would be done in the US. And while they weren't obviously bricks of cocaine, given his sense of smell, it was clear to him what was happening. Between the ocean and the drugs, the scents were strong, and that may be why he missed it.

If he were wearing his human face, he would have been frowning as he picked up the one other scent, one that he knew far too well, but it was already too late.

One of the workers crouched down in front of him. He didn't reach out to pat Donovan on the head, and he didn't smile. Instead, he said, "I know what you are."

Then he pulled back his lips, pushed his face forward, and bared his fangs.

CHAPTER 60

Eleri moved downward through the water, clearing her ears and checking her gauges until she finally hit a depth where she was comfortable. She'd learned from her first dive instructor that when everything was right, she would float up just a little with every breath in and sink the same amount with every breath out. At the right point, she could hang weightless in the middle of the water.

The waves were feisty today, the wind tossing around the little boat they'd rented. They dare not touch the *Calypso*. If it was being watched, someone would be able to follow them. If it was being tracked, that would be even easier. So they'd rented a cigarette boat, like the ones they'd seen out on the water. The goal was to look as much as possible like the ones coming out of the Miranda Industry docks .

Eleri was putting the pieces together and she was hoping that, after this dive, even more pieces would fall into place. Next to her, Jason and Hannah pulled alongside her in the vast, blue space. Each of them had small, specially designed whiteboards dangling from their wrists so they could communicate underwater. Eleri had warned them to erase the board as soon as they used it. Normally, dive instructors would leave their writing on the board, in case someone else needed a similar instruction. But she knew that, if they were captured, the writing could help indict them.

With her head to the side, her vision tunneled by the mask, and her regulator making its regular Darth Vader-like noises, she watched as Hannah and Jason motioned to get going. Though they usually loved to dive, it seemed to be finally occurring to them just how serious this was.

Eleri would have preferred to have Noah on this dive, but neither of the other agents was qualified. All the rules about bringing civilians into FBI cases had now been thrown completely out the window. They weren't even on US soil anymore. She could probably get extradited if she was arrested. But this time, she was afraid she wouldn't get arrested. She would get killed... or they would.

As she pushed along with her fins, keeping up with the pros in front of her, she thought about Avery. Eleri had been talking to him most nights, but she'd ghosted about a week ago. He was used to her disappearances, and he likely chalked it up to the case. She couldn't risk having Miranda Industries find out about him and use Avery to get to her. But now, as she moved underwater, she made a decision. As soon as she was safe, she would call him.

In front of her, Hannah turned back from her position in the lead and gave them the prearranged signal. Eleri was no longer in charge of this dive. FBI agent or not, she simply wasn't skilled enough. It took a few moments for the three of them to get their equipment lined up, but when Hannah motioned again, Eleri turned on the small, handheld motor she carried. It had been specifically designed to pull divers through the water, and suddenly she was zipping along, the water rushing past her almost as if she were caught in a riptide.

This was also the first time she'd done a twin-tank dive.

Wearing two oxygen tanks at once was both a redundancy design and a plan to extend the duration of their time underwater. They'd had to enter the water quite some distance from the Miranda Industries shoreline in hopes of not being spotted. They'd left GJ and Neriah on the boat, too. So they had to be safely out of view.

The plan was to come as close to the building as possible while staying underwater. Hopefully, they wouldn't get spotted and could get more information than would be possible on the land. But Eleri had her fingers crossed that Donovan was having good luck getting into the compound. She almost checked her watch to calculate what he would be doing now, but she couldn't pull her hand from the fan motor. She had to concentrate just to keep up with the other two.

It took a good thirty minutes to cover the distance to the shoreline, and Eleri was more than grateful the little motor had done the work for her. She passed all kinds of fish, including a few relatively large sharks, schools of tiny silver creatures, and even a few jellyfish. Sightseeing would have been wonderful— but this was no pleasure dive. There was a murder to solve, and the assassin was nearby. Concentrating on the task at hand, she worked to calm her suddenly speeding heart rate.

Hannah finally gave the signal to turn off the motors. It would have been easier to leave them and pick them up later. But with the current, there was no way to be sure the machines would stay where they were deposited. Eleri would have to carry hers along, so she attached it to the hook on the back of her dive vest, hoping it wouldn't bump her on the leg. But that was not her biggest problem now.

So much slower now without the motors, they crept forward, inching closer to the surface. The longer that they didn't see any activity underwater, the more they dared to get near the light above them.

Hannah's hand flashed out to the side in a sudden *stop* signal.

Eleri cupped her hands and pushed her fins in front of her, ending all her forward motion. The three of them looked up as the line of a slim boat passed overhead. They waited carefully, breathing slowly, Eleri working to not suck down any more oxygen than she needed. A subtle change in breathing rate could dramatically reduce her underwater time. They were also trying to mask their bubbles by brushing them in various directions, to avoid alerting the people overhead that there were divers below.

Cautiously treading water, they hung back, doing exactly what they had intended. They were hoping to only observe. If no one ever knew they were here, that was for the best. But none of the workers seemed inclined to hang over the side of the boats or the dock to check the water below for divers.

Though the sea was crystalline blue-green here, Eleri hoped they wouldn't be visible among the seaweed clusters and the shadows. When no one spotted them, they hung out in the one location, eyes trained to the surface as they waited. It wasn't long before another boat passed by, this time heading into dock. Eleri memorized its features as well as the time. And she continued to wait and watch.

At Hannah's signal, they slowly headed out into the distance, hoping to come up on the surface. Eleri had a tiny camera that might catch pictures of the activity on shore. The lens was designed for detail at a distance, but she wasn't sure it would work with the motion of the waves and interference of splashing water. She wanted to try, though.

With the trees and the fabric coverings and the way the mostly hidden dock was designed, this was likely the only way they could get any proof of the activity inside. Eleri wondered if she would catch any of the shots of Donovan roaming the compound and making "friends," and she almost smiled around the regulator in her mouth.

Bobbing at the surface, they worked to keep their heads low and stay far enough apart so they wouldn't look like three anomalies on the surface all together. The effort of maintaining her position was taxing, and Eleri reached only one hand up to capture the pictures. Breathing was harsher in the waves, but she didn't pull out her regulator or try to use her snorkel.

Only a few moments later, she motioned to Hannah that she'd gotten what she needed, or at least the most that she could. They ducked back under the surface. A quick conference involving showing each other the gauges they carried revealed that all three had plenty of oxygen left. Hannah motioned that they would stay here fifteen more minutes.

Putting themselves directly in the path of the dock again, they saw another boat heading out to sea, though there was no telling if it was heading toward Miami or just jaunting around the island. Looking at her watch, Eleri calculated the time between the two, hoping to figure out what the traffic level was. But then a large fish came up between them, dragging her attention away.

She would have smiled, but as her gaze swept down the length of the fish, she caught sight of a shadow behind it.

Another diver.

A lone man was slowly heading toward them.

Trying to mask her movements and hide the fact that she'd spotted him, she worked to slow her now-pounding heart. She had to be taking in more oxygen—she could hear the heavier sounds as she sucked it through the regulator.

This, she believed, was the man who had killed Allison. Surreptitiously, she tried to catch a glimpse of him. She also tried to signal Hannah and Jason that they were not alone, but wanted to do it without alarming them. She wanted to see his face, find any identifying characteristics.

All the trouble of being out of the US carried some freedom, too. She didn't have to arrest him—she couldn't. What would she do to an assassin without the standard construct of her job? She didn't know.

He carried a bag with him, and when she spotted it, Eleri changed her mind. She didn't need to see his face; if he'd killed Allison, they should just get away.

In a normal situation, she would have pulled her weapon and moved to arrest him. But she couldn't pull a gun underwater. She didn't even have a speargun to threaten him with. However, though Hannah and Jason didn't know it, she did have some weapons at her disposal.

But as she was trying to get her companions' attention, she saw the diver empty the bag into the water. Chum floated around him, chunks of raw fish that slowly gathered into a singular knot. The blood that had swirled around them as he pushed the meat from the bag now gathered in tight as Eleri watched in horror.

His control of it was stunning. And it was going to get them killed.

As she watched, the chum moved quickly toward them.

Only then did the others catch on.

Hannah was gesturing for Eleri to explain her frantic gestures, but Eleri was now pointing toward the man and the bloody chunks of raw fish coming their way far too quickly.

Bait, she was scribbling on her board and holding it up to show Hannah.

The three of them turned and began swimming as fast as they could, but he was faster. He only had to keep up; he didn't want to be near them as he somehow mentally propelled the chum through the water.

Eleri saw the shadows of big fish moving closer. Despite the fact that the other diver was keeping the bait in a tight formation, the smell must have gotten loose. Though she was swimming frantically, she couldn't escape. The chum caught up to them and began to spread throughout the water, turning everything around her red.

CHAPTER 61

"What?" GJ asked, sticking her finger in her ear and pushing the phone closer to her head. She turned away from Neriah and faced a different section of wide open water, as though any of that might help. "What did you say?"

"He's been captured. Donovan is in a holding cell inside the Miranda Industries compound. No—" Noah replied. "I think it might be more like a dog crate. The camera is still filming. There are bars of some kind all around him, and he's relatively low to the ground. He's sweeping his head from side to side. He's purposefully sending me some very interesting footage."

"Shit," GJ said, thinking through the options.

"Grab the others and come back here," Noah told her. "We've got a rescue mission to start."

"I can't." And that was the big problem. Eleri, Hannah, and Jason were supposed to be above the surface of the water at least thirty minutes ago. "Is there nowhere you can find a breach to get into the compound?"

Even as she said it, though, she thought perhaps Noah would wind up getting caught, too. Then they would have to rescue not one large dog, but one dog and one man. The man was definitely more of a threat in the compound.

"I can get in," Noah volleyed back quickly, giving GJ a much-needed smack of relief. But then he added, "The problem isn't rescuing him. It's that they know *what he is*, GJ."

"I'm sorry, *what?*" Surely, she had heard wrong. Waves were making white caps and smacking against the side of the boat—each motion a noise fighting for her attention. Neriah was at least was being quiet, but the seagulls were not. The constant wind wasn't helping, either.

"I'm relatively confident that they know what Donovan is, and that at least a couple of them knew pretty much from the moment he walked in." Noah sighed, and that sound came through loud and clear. "I don't have audio. But the way they looked at him, I got the impression that at least one of them, if not several, knew exactly what he was."

Freezing where she stood, GJ felt her heart plummet. That was absolutely no good. "Send me the video. . . Can you do that?"

He was watching a live stream from the camera attached to Donovan's collar; she knew that much. They all knew each other's plans, but everything had to be rethought now. Her team was technically missing, though she didn't want to call it that yet. His was captured. And it was looking like they were all royally screwed.

She heard Noah moving about on his end of the call. "I don't know. It's a stream. I'll have to see if I can forward all or part of it. Let me check."

"Try it," GJ almost demanded before thinking that even Noah Kimball had a higher rank in the Bureau than she did. Still, she let it stand. "I need to know what's on that video. Call me back in ten minutes if you don't have anything."

She could almost hear him tapping on his tablet, even as he

watched what Donovan saw from where he was trapped in the compound.

"Let me see what I can do from here," she said, trying to hold out an olive branch she didn't have. "If I can get my three divers up, maybe we can come to you." She hung up the phone and swore a blue streak.

She wished she could say that it had been all the noise, or that she hadn't heard him correctly. But that wasn't the case. She had three divers down for thirty minutes too long.

They were on a dual tank dive, so they had oxygen—that wasn't the worry. But why hadn't they returned to the boat? She'd been okay when they were ten minutes late, and even twenty minutes late. Surely, they were just getting extra information. They might have found something and needed to check it out.

But they'd agreed not to be thirty minutes late. She and Neriah had hit the trigger to start a manhunt, and GJ felt cold in her bones, despite the Bahamian sun beating down on her.

Swearing more times than she could count, GJ watched as Neriah moved slowly across the boat and looked at her. GJ asked, "Do we see any signs of them?"

Neriah didn't answer, only turned and grasped the railing in front of her at the very bow of the boat as she quietly searched the water. "No. I don't see anything."

"All right. We're heading in, then." She had to follow the plan, even if no one else did. Even if no one else could.

With a nod, Neriah headed to the captain's chair. Though they'd been floating, the rented cigarette boat now gave a slow push, starting them toward the coast as GJ hung onto the rail.

This was not going to be good. They were risking getting seen, if not captured, themselves. Whatever was going on at Miranda Industries—most likely drug running—the corporation didn't want anyone to know. She could only hope that their boat blended in with the industry's fleet enough that they didn't get noticed right away. Crossing her fingers for whatever juju she could muster, GJ also hoped that their divers would see them and head for the surface.

As they sped forward, she shouted above the wind. "Can they see us if we pass right over where they are?"

Neriah shook her head. "Only if they look up at exactly the right time. Since the water isn't that deep here, they might see us as a shadow overhead and really take a look. But we can't see them."

GJ sighed. "So we're just going in to check that nothing obvious is wrong."

Neriah nodded. "Most likely, we'll come back out and they'll be waiting for us."

GJ tried to take her cue from Neriah. The younger woman didn't appear afraid. Maybe, the smarter thing to do was to wait. But they were already moving, and they had to do follow the plan.

Twenty minutes later, there had been no sign of the three divers, despite how close they'd come to the Miranda Industries compound. Neriah smartly pulled them in toward shore—an attempt to look like tourists merely tooling along, not as though they were aiming to insert themselves into the dock under the building.

GJ parked herself at the bow, searching both the shoreline and below the surface, but found nothing she recognized. As their tiny cigarette boat moved in, she could see they were almost passing the gate. If they passed the gate, they would have a direct view into the Miranda industries compound. However, the workers inside also would have a view of them.

GJ held her breath. Then she looked down. Waving her hands to catch her driver's attention, she yelled, "Neriah, stop the boat!"

As soon as they slowed and the noise from the engine cut,

she motioned again. "Look down. What's that on the rocks? It's barnacles, right?"

Neriah nodded, standing at the railing beside her now. "What about them?"

"Look where they are."

But Neriah only shrugged. "I don't understand what's so important about this spot."

"There's no current." GJ was getting excited. "Those aren't old, dead barnacles, are they?"

"No, I think they're live. I'd have to dive and get a close look to be sure, but the water's clear and I'm not seeing empty holes." Neriah seemed to catch on then.

Barnacles needed a current, which is why they attached on the bottom of boats. There was always a flow of water. They didn't need the current all the time, but they needed it enough to stay alive. GJ had been reading up since Allison had seemed interested enough to take samples.

There was a clear path of barnacles here. "That's an odd color too. It's indicative of pollution."

Neriah was nodding along, seeming to follow GJ's reasoning.

"But is there pollution here?" GJ scanned everything, almost having forgotten about the divers. "This water looks gorgeous."

"Clear doesn't mean not polluted," Neriah added.

"And the fact that they are here means there's a current here, in this spot. It's coming out of the Miranda compound, and it's happening often enough to keep them alive."

CHAPTER 62

Donovan sat quietly in what was essentially a dog crate. He'd turned around so he was looking out, but his view was narrowed now to one corner of the compound.

He'd been caged and tucked out of the way to wait.

"What do we do now?" One of the men leaning on a nearby wall motioned toward him with the flick of a cigarette. The scent of cigarette smoke always threw him backwards into memories of his father. Now, it turned his stomach for another reason.

"We wait for the boss."

The reply was said by the man whose face had changed, the one Donovan had smelled, but only too late. He wasn't the only one, either. There were at least four wolves here in the Miranda Industries compound.

At one point, he'd hoped to one day feel at home amongst his own kind. Yet here he was and, honestly, he was petrified. They were waiting for *the boss*, whoever that was, but it couldn't be good.

Though it would be much more comfortable to lie down, he stayed sitting, pushing his head up against the top of the too-small dog crate. Hoping to get a better view with the collar camera that he wore, he tipped his head slightly one way and then another. These wolves had found him quite easily, but they hadn't found his tech yet. Even if they found it later, he still would have sent a live video feed to Noah this whole time. As he looked around the compound, something nagged the back of his brain.

Blue shoe laces. All the wolves here wore blue shoes laces. Closing his eyes, he thought back. . . had he seen this before? Had he seen a few in New Orleans? Donovan opened his eyes. The laces were a code—a gang sign—and he was late to the party.

The one wolf he'd found in Curie, Nebraska, had no such signal. That made sense. The man in Curie was a scientist, not Lobomau. There was no need to have any Lobomau in a small town with a think tank. It simply wasn't what attracted them.

Miranda Industries did.

It was sinking in now, what Donovan and Eleri had failed to recognize before: the Lobomau were not just a few random gangs in a handful of cities. They were an extensive and tiered organization—more like MS-13 or al Qaeda than the Del Surs that ran a portion of Los Angeles.

He'd made a massive mistake in coming in here. He wasn't sure now if the bigger threat was Miranda Industries or the Lobomau. As he again swept his head side to side, trying to capture images, a worker came over and squatted down in front of him. Green eyes examined the man in the cage, even as Donovan caught the scent of *wolf*. The man's eyes narrowed. He opened his jaw, pulled his lips back and bared his teeth.

Working hard at keeping a neutral expression, Donovan sat quietly, slowly moving his head side to side, as if he were bored. He continued doing so, barely acknowledging the man in front of him.

"What do you know?" The man pushed the words forward

like a threat, as though Donovan might change right here in this crate and answer him in plain English. That wasn't going to happen.

Donovan merely blinked at him.

"We can make you talk."

But nothing about his smell said he was any kind of real threat. There was no whiff of anger, no waft of rage. Not even the kinds of pheromones one gave off if they were in the middle of a mental break. If someone was going to torture him, it wouldn't be this guy.

So Donovan did nothing. No nod, no change, and certainly no growl in response.

"Have it your way." Irritated with Donovan's lack of cowering, he stood up and smacked the top of the cage hard enough to rattle it.

He was so tightly wedged in that Donovan felt the hit in every bone, but he didn't react. If anyone asked, he would say he learned that skill at Quantico. But the fact was, he'd learned it years before. His father was always explosive and, at a very young age, Donovan had learned that no reaction was the best reaction.

He could keep a straight face through just about anything. But fifteen minutes later, the effort of that became exponentially more difficult.

First, he noticed the low murmured voices increasing slowly. The speech became peppered with more demands than before, more shouts. Donovan next realized the activity level around him had ramped up a notch. At last he caught the words, "He's here."

Donovan didn't know who exactly was here, but he was willing to guess it was the boss. And that was monumentally bad timing because, though he couldn't see him, Donovan could scent Agent Noah Kimball.

The other agent had snuck inside the compound.

CHAPTER 63

E leri fought against the push of the current. It rushed at her, swirling her around, pulling her in several directions at once. Flipping and turning her, it caused her to lose even her basic orientation to up and down—a deadly prospect for SCUBA divers.

Clearly, this was not an ocean current, but one made by the man following them. His actions showed that he didn't intend for any of her crew to get out alive.

Hannah and Jason—when Eleri managed to catch sight of them—were also getting tugged and turned. Her shoulder bumped something that turned out to be Jason at one point, the two of them out of control as the water tossed them like rag dolls.

As the man moved the water, he operated everything from a safe distance, pushing them together and swirling them through the red of the chum. The chum, too, moved in a controlled dance, coming back in closer each time it started to get too far away.

In the distance, she could see the sharks approaching. Her vision was the only sense she really had now, and her brain was only gathering snatches of information as the water turned and flipped her. Her sense of touch was limited to what she bumped into, and her hearing was masked by the heavy sounds of her own breathing through her respirator. She realized then that she would likely run out of air before the man could kill her.

Then again, maybe not. But she couldn't even get herself oriented, let alone calm her breathing or reach to her side to check her gauges.

A hand clamped her arm where Jason had gotten himself together enough to hold on to her. She was grateful that he anchored them together, removing one of her million concerns. Her emotions were swirling as much as the water as the sharks, flicking their tails, moved in quickly.

Closer and closer they moved, until she watched a mouth open near her, the rows of sharp teeth snatching up a huge chunk of what must have once been a tuna.

Jason held on to her, but maybe it was a mistake. They were facing each other, rather than away, and Eleri jabbed her gloved finger in the water, pointing over his shoulder at the quickly approaching shark. Circling her wrist quickly, she broke his hold on her arm and turned him just in time to see it.

He barely had the speed to move his hand. Humans didn't have the dexterity in the water that sharks did. The sharks were at home—sleek and fast. The humans were sluggish and—right now—disoriented. They weren't going to last long at this rate, but it wouldn't stop them from fighting.

Again, she breathed in and slowly counted to five, hoping to spot Hannah. But though she found her third diver, Hannah was only a blur; she was too far away to be seen clearly through the swirls of chum and the moving water.

Grabbing Jason's hand, Eleri began the hard task of swimming toward Hannah. Luckily, Hannah spotted them and managed to aim for their direction, but a swift attack came from the right. A shark targeted on Hannah and began swimming swiftly toward her as Eleri watched.

With her free hand, Eleri reached out, palm toward Hannah, and willed the shark away. But it kept coming. She wanted to recite her prayer to Aida Weddo, but the mouthpiece prevented it. Now that she had a focus—her friend, her assignment for this case—Eleri aimed everything she had at keeping Hannah safe. Though she couldn't say the words out loud, she let the spell chant heavily through her brain.

It didn't work.

She felt *nothing* as she watched the large shark continue directly toward Hannah, who only turned her head at the last minute. Luckily, the woman was a smart and competent diver. It seemed she saw the threat just in time to arch herself up. But it wasn't far enough, and the shark still hit her flank with the front of its nose, knocking her off path and sending her spinning again.

In the distance, Eleri saw the man, still there, still working. His hands moved just before Hannah spun harder. *It wasn't the shark that hit her, it was him!* Eleri thought.

Fuck. There was no way Hannah would be able to get oriented again, not if he kept rolling her. Judging by the shadows in the distance of her peripheral vision, there were more sharks coming. These were not friendly nurse sharks, not spotted with leopard prints, not sporting long whiskers to let them feel the bottom.

No, these were great whites and bulls. And Eleri was petrified.

She was fighting through every breath to maintain her composure. They might be underwater, and these two might be the divers, but *she* was the FBI agent. *She* was supposed to be in charge. *She* was supposed to save *their* lives. She was also the one in the NightShade division. She was the one who was supposed to be able to fight an attack like this. . . and she was failing miserably.

Three. She sucked in a breath as she counted herself down one more time.

Two. She blew it out.

One. She sucked oxygen in through her regulator. Her hand reached out to grab Hannah's, only to have the other diver bumped away at the last moment before they could touch.

Reluctant to let go of Jason, even though he was twisting and the force was trying to break their grip as the water swirled around them, she held on. Chum swirled around her, obscuring her vision and making her heart race. Something bumped hard at her tank—too hard—knocking her into Jason. Eleri wasn't sure if it was the man or a shark. She didn't look. She wasn't bitten, and she had to count that as a win.

Kicking as hard as she could and trusting the fins to propel her, she again fought to reach Hannah. Her free hand stretched forward, and she recited her prayer in her head again.

She was stretching out—*Aida Weddo protect us*—only to catch a flash of movement on her right as a shark jerked around and came for her extended arm.

Sleek and deadly, its mouth opened and, at the last minute, Eleri yanked her hand back. She did it with just enough time to reverse and throw a punch at the shark.

It was her only defense. She should have spells, but they weren't working. She didn't even know how much good punching the shark did. The only good she could count was that, *right now*, her hand remained intact.

Hannah had oriented herself and Eleri felt her chest expand in relief. Thank God the other woman was a strong swimmer and a talented diver, because Eleri was clearly not able to close the distance herself. Maybe it wasn't smart to be in a cluster, but it seemed that they were in more danger apart.

Hannah reached out, but even though no sharks were near

her at the moment, she again was bumped away. Eleri tried again to cast on her friend, to make the water bring her closer, or at least stop the currents the man created. In the distance, Eleri saw him operating the whole machinery.

Just as she was once again about to grasp Hannah's fingers, her other arm yanked as Jason was pulled away from her.

Turning, terrified, and sucking in even more of her oxygen, she watched as a large shark latched onto Jason's tank and tugged him away. Refusing to let go, Eleri grabbed his arm with both hands tight and kicked in the other direction.

Quickly, she saw this was futile. The shark would win. She could not outswim a monster and she could not overpower it.

There was no way for her to fight the shark from where she held onto a clearly terrified Jason. The bite was on the tank on his back, and the shark had a hold behind him. Unless Jason was double jointed in both his hips and his shoulders, he couldn't reach backward to fight.

Hand over hand, Eleri walked herself down his arm until she was close enough. Unfortunately, the fins made any kick to the shark's body pointless. Kicking with her toe lost all measure of force because of the fins. Kicking with her heel was just as bad—the fin was designed to slow motion in that direction to give her forward propulsion. She had to use her hands.

Quickly checking through her options, she considered sticking her thumb in the shark's eye and instead opted for another punch. Bringing her fist down hard on its nose, she made the creature let go of the tank. Punching it again, she landed the blow this time not on its nose or eye but into the gills as it quickly turned away. It felt like a bad dream of fighting with no force, but this was real.

In a quick check, she turned Jason, looked for punctures in his tank and found that, though it had been dented, no bubbles were leaking. She yanked him one way and aimed a clenched fist at the new shark that was bulleting toward them only to find another was coming from the other side.

And that was when she lost it.

She was trained to stay calm, but nothing she was trying to do worked. None of the spells she was trying to cast had had any effect. Whoever this man was, he had powers underwater that she could not duplicate or even fight.

Her emotions exploded, running wild. Her calm—or what little she'd managed to hold on to it—fled entirely.

Around her respirator, even though it broke all the rules of diving, her mouth opened as she let out a primal scream. Bubbles swarmed from her lungs as the mouthpiece that carried her oxygen floated away. But as she watched, the shockwave spread out around her, hitting the sharks and making them turn.

They flinched as though the sound hurt.

And—without any oxygen to breathe in—Eleri screamed again, letting out the very last of what was in her lungs. She watched as a second shockwave radiated out around her. It hit Jason, but she held on to him, maintaining her grip despite the wave that wanted to carry him away.

The force hit Hannah, but since it also hit the sharks, it stopped the imminent attack. Hannah took a moment to reorient herself for probably the thousandth time and began swimming against the massive outward current toward Eleri and Jason.

Though one of Eleri's hands hung onto the other diver, her free hand reached out. Luckily, this training was natural. She swung her arm in a wide circle, trapping the hose and dragging it with her until the respirator at the bottom was pulled through to her hand. She struggled to stick it back into her mouth before her body fought to take in a breath to replace all that she had lost.

She sucked down oxygen, the sound filling her head with a roar as air passed through the hose.

She had done *something*.

Fuck staying calm. That had done her no good.

Taking Jason's hand and turning it over in her own, she shoved him toward Hannah, pointing for them to swim off into the distance. Then she turned on the man.

Now, she could see him. The water had cleared with her scream, and he hung almost motionless, turned toward her. He must be staring at her, for he was no longer aiming his hands their direction.

The currents were no longer an issue. The sharks were no longer coming. And as Eleri watched, the chum began to float away.

She could reclaim her regulator if it floated out of her mouth again, so she sucked in a breath, shoved her hands in front of her and screamed once more. The regulator flew from her mouth, pushed by the sound and the bubbles, but she didn't care.

She just watched as the force hit the man and he tumbled over backward.

CHAPTER 64

A s GJ looked over the railing at the barnacles, the boat suddenly rocked hard, almost sending her sprawling.

The sound—a hard slap against the hull—told her a wave had hit. Something big.

Frowning, she turned at the same time Neriah did, and they ran the three steps to the other side of the small boat. Together they gripped the railing and watched as a series of ripples radiated out from a point on the water maybe fifty feet away. Each one rocked the boat again, though they were clearly aftershocks of the first.

"What was that?" GJ asked.

"Underwater explosion, maybe," Neriah posited, her hands coming up as if to shrug but quickly reaching back to grasp the railing as the boat rocked back and forth.

Despite their words, neither looked away from the water.

GJ was still trying to figure out what had happened when she saw the start of a second explosion. A bubble of water formed in a central location, rising past the surface and breaking into an outward, racing ring.

Tapping Neriah's arm, GJ yelled, "We have to start the boat.

We have to go there." She pointed even as she braced her feet and gripped her other hand tighter against the approaching wave.

"We're not going *toward* an explosion!" Neriah countered, still gripping the rail and planting her feet a little wider on the deck.

"Yes, we are."

Perhaps it was the assassin. Then again, maybe it was Eleri! It was possible, and GJ could hope. Maybe it was merely some C-4 and a good blasting cap. But whatever it was, it was strange, and GJ had learned that when strange things happened, she had to investigate.

"Go!" she told Neriah, who still had not moved.

"I don't want to go into that."

"We have to. What if our friends are down there?"

Neriah was still shaking her head. The rocking of the boat had lessened slightly and she held one hand up in front of her as though to ward off something bad.

GJ pushed again. "That could be Hannah and Jason and Eleri. We have to help them."

Neriah shook her head and blinked, and GJ couldn't help the strange shiver that passed through her. There was something odd about that blink. But she shoved it aside.

There were more important things right now. "If that's our crew, we have to go."

"If it's them, they're *dead*," Neriah said, her final word a heavy-handed pronouncement that GJ had not expected.

"How do you know?"

Neriah shrugged again, shook her head back and forth, and tried to soften her tone. "No one could survive that underwater."

"Sure they could," GJ replied, not knowing whether her statement was accurate. She had absolutely no experience with underwater demolitions, explosions, or even earthquakes—

nothing that would create the kind of wave they had just experienced. But she had experience in NightShade, even if only a little. She knew her divers might survive that shockwave.

She also suspected the wave was Eleri.

If it wasn't Eleri, it was likely the assassin. Either way, they couldn't just sit and watch. "Now, Neriah! Start the boat and go."

This time, Neriah planted her feet, put her hands on her hips, and shook her head in a defiant *No*. "*They're already dead.*"

The three short words sent chills down GJ's spine. Neriah spoke it as though she knew it. "What are you saying?"

"I'm saying they can't survive that." The diver waved her hand toward the spot where the force had originated.

"We still have to check," GJ protested. But Neriah still shook her head. "Then give me the keys."

Something in the woman's resistance bothered GJ to her core and she pushed back with firmer statements. "*I'm* the FBI agent. *I'm* in charge here. We have to check on them."

This time, Neriah smiled—a cold, evil grin. "They're dead."

Blinking and trying to shake away the cognitive dissonance of the diver's smile, GJ asked again, "What are you saying, Neriah?"

"He got them."

That's what it was.

GJ stumbled backwards as another wave hit the side of the boat, smacking into it and rocking it violently. The realization of what she missed struck her then, too.

The video of Allison's death left in Missy Maisel's email had not been a warning.

It had been *proof*.

Missy was working with Miranda Industries. And so was Neriah.

GJ tried to be as cold as Neriah, changing her thoughts before she had time to process them. She had to get the keys.

She had to get Neriah handcuffed and arrested. She had to get the boat to where Eleri, Jason, and Hannah were almost definitely underwater. Neriah's words meant that the assassin was here, and she believed that the shockwave was them dying.

Pulling her gun in a smooth motion that would have been foreign to her a year ago, GJ braced her feet on the deck and lunged forward, barking her orders. "Put your hands up. You're under arrest by the Federal Bureau of Investigations."

Neriah only laughed. "You're in Nassau, honey."

GJ had no jurisdiction and they both knew it.

Despite the barrel of the gun aimed directly at her, Neriah waved a hand and waved away the demand.

"Fine," GJ countered, her voice strong despite her nerves and the adrenaline in her system. She held her position. "You're going to do what I tell you, because I'm holding a gun on you."

"You won't shoot me. You can't drive the boat," Neriah taunted her.

"I can and I will." The boat was not her problem. The keys were not her problem. Neriah was.

Neriah hadn't wanted to come searching when the divers were late. She had wanted to wait them out, because she knew the assassin was with them. She was willing to steer the boat into the view of the workers in the Miranda Industries dock. If the two of them had been captured, the criminals would have just let Neriah go.

GJ saw it all clearly now.

And she saw that Neriah didn't seem to care that there was a gun on her. "Put your hands in the air," GJ demanded. "I *will* shoot you."

"You couldn't hit me if you tried." The sing-songy tone almost made GJ snap.

Pulling her aim slightly to the left, GJ made sure not to hit the water where her friends were, in case they were swimming to the surface. Despite the fact that the bullet had no power underwater, she couldn't risk aiming in that general direction.

So she aimed to the other side, but stayed close to Neriah's head. She pulled the trigger. The slide on the gun rocked back as the noise hit her ears and the recoil wound up her arms.

Neriah's face changed as the bullet whizzed by her head—as she became aware that GJ would, in fact, shoot her. But her reaction was not what GJ expected.

The diver leaned forward, not back, and her mouth opened in a scream. Only this time, her mouth was full of rows of jagged teeth. Her eyes had gone cat-like as two sets of eyelids blinked rapidly and then held open, staying wide. The high pitch of the scream almost drove GJ backward.

Dark skin changed color to a rangy green.

Confusion swept over GJ as she realized she had no framework for what she was seeing.

What was Neriah?

Her hands thrown back, her face jutting forward, Neriah continued to scream. The noise of it sounded so sharp that GJ almost believed she could hear the individual waves in the sound. She was reaching up to cover her ears and stop her skull from splitting.

Then, as abruptly as it started, it stopped.

She must have shut her eyes against the onslaught, because they popped open just in time to see Neriah lunging toward her. GJ raised her hands, initially as an instinctual move of protection, but quickly she adjusted to a heel-force punch of her hands.

But she was too late. The gun was still in her hands, and Neriah had gotten too close to make it useful. Unless GJ could angle it safely under the creature's chin and blast her head off, it was less a helpful tool, and more a disaster waiting to happen.

Using the broadside of the weapon, her hand no longer in a firing grip, she leveraged the weight for a harder hit into

Neriah's shoulder. But with nothing but her hand for force on the other side, the woman. . . *creature*. . . whatever she was, spun from the punch.

As Neriah twisted, she screamed again, the high pitch hitting GJ with each wave of the sound separately. The pain of it radiated through her skull. Then she felt it—red hot pain as needle-sharp teeth sank into her shoulder.

With her own scream in response, GJ shoved again at the other woman, sending her stumbling backward until she hit the railing square in the middle of her back. With a heavy hiss and a sudden turn, Neriah leapt over the side of the boat.

GJ froze until the splash of water released her from the hold of disbelief. Too stunned to think better of her actions, GJ ran toward where Neriah had disappeared. Slamming into the railing, she watched as the form swam quickly away underwater.

Her knuckles turned white with tension. Just as GJ thought she'd lost Neriah, the swimmer breached in the distance, flipping a tail as she reentered the water and disappeared.

Her tail looked just like the one they'd caught a glimpse of in the video of Alison's death.

CHAPTER 65

E leri tumbled, fin over head over fin, from a blast that
originated somewhere under the water. She'd barely had
a moment to register that it was coming, and all she'd been able
to do was brace herself for the hit.

There was nothing to hold on to thirty feet below the
surface. No one to grab for stability, as Hannah and Jason had
already tumbled away from her during earlier sound bursts. . .
the ones *she'd* caused. So she stiffened against the onslaught and
took the brunt of it.

It seemed she flipped and twisted in sharp and vicious eddy
currents forever before the water finally let her right herself.
But then, aimed head-up/feet-down at last, she kicked her fins
and cupped her hands, moving them side to side, as she tried
desperately to turn a full three-sixty while the water resisted
every effort she made.

She had to find Hannah and Jason. She had to find the
assassin. Not seeing him coming would be deadly.

Eleri spotted Hannah first. Long and lean, she was laid out
with her head down, hands slack at her sides and legs pumping.
The researcher rocketed through the water with a clear

purpose, heading toward Eleri's left. Cupping her hands and kicking her own feet, Eleri fought the water and turned again. Hannah was after something. *But what?*

If it was the assassin, Hannah was out of her league.

Eleri spotted a dark shift in the water in the distance and it took a moment to realize it was Jason. He was laying still with his face up, arms and legs out. He appeared to float, unmoving, in the water.

An alarm raised in Eleri's brain, but there was nothing she could do for him. Hannah was heading toward him. If he was unconscious or in need of emergency care, Hannah was the best person to take care of it. Eleri had a different job.

Turning back, she frantically shifted her head, trying to see through the limited visibility of her mask. Her head twisted side to side, her lungs pumped, and her adrenaline spiked again.

She was sucking down oxygen faster than was safe. She couldn't feel it, but she could *hear* it each time she inhaled. When she turned twice all the way around and realized she couldn't find their mysterious assailant or even a shadow of where he might have been, she gave up. There was nothing she could do about him now.

With an attempt to breathe easier, she began making her way over to Hannah and Jason. Jason was moving now. Hannah had either roused him or told him it was okay to stop playing dead. Eleri wanted to believe the threat was gone, but her lungs heaved in again as she couldn't quite muster a sense of calm.

He might be anywhere.

The sun filtered softly down through the water, but couldn't penetrate far. Fish swam by again, making her think maybe he really was gone. The water was beautiful, but deadly. With his talents, who knew what this assassin could do? He'd already killed Allison, and probably also the scientists Neriah talked about. He'd tried to take out Neriah. And now he'd come after the three of them. She couldn't quite make herself believe that this round was over.

Eleri continued turning one way and then another, still searching the ocean for a threat she could not see, until Hannah tapped her on the shoulder. Jerking back around, Eleri looked to her friend to see Hannah was holding up her own gauge for them all to see the oxygen level.

Hannah's oxygen pressure was low enough to suggest they had to ascend immediately. Their buffer was at an end. Eleri didn't even want to look at her own gauge. Hannah was a trained diver—she would not have been gulping air the way Eleri had been. But Hannah pointed to Eleri's vest, indicating she needed to check her own numbers. Too slowly, Eleri reached for it, pulled it up, and saw that she'd been correct.

Flipping the gauge for Hannah to see, she tried again to calm herself. Her FBI training should have been kicking in. Trying every technique she'd been taught, Eleri slowly began to bring her breathing under control. Still, Hannah nodded at the number and pointed upward. They would have to ascend here in full view of the Miranda Industries dock.

If everything went perfectly, they might be able to swim on the surface back toward where GJ and Neriah waited for them.

But swimming on the ocean surface was difficult in the best of conditions, Eleri knew. Swimming on the surface with a BCD vest and a tank strapped to your back was beyond exhausting. And they'd all three just been through a massive adrenaline burst. They would be bottoming out from that at any moment. None of them would have the energy to swim out of view of the dock, let alone back to where they were supposed to surface.

Eleri fought an additional battle. She had no idea how much or what specific energy the spells took from her, but she knew that they did. She was beginning to feel it. Even though she wasn't mentally certain that the assassin was gone, her body was beginning to let go of the hyper-aware state she'd been in.

She nodded to Hannah, agreeing before she pointed to her left, offering another option. Maybe they could stay underwater until they could get out of direct view of the dock before they rose.

But Hannah shook her head. She pointed up at an angle with a shrug, as though that was the best they could do. Reaching around, Eleri clipped her gauge back to the side of her vest and, in doing so, bumped the fan motor still attached at her back. Frantically unclipping it even as Hannah started to ascend, Eleri motioned that they could use the motors. They could travel just a little distance without expending much of their own effort.

Hannah gave a brief nod of agreement and Eleri sighed in relief. She could have demanded it, but half her training had been to know when she should be in charge and when to listen to an expert. Hannah knew about the dangers of Miranda Industries as well as Eleri did. Maybe better. And she certainly knew diving. Eleri would follow her lead on this one.

Just as Eleri held the fan out in front of her and began to flip the switch to turn it on, movement hit the light above her. A shadow passed overhead, big enough to be a boat. Then a rope slowly uncoiled itself, down into the water in front of her.

G J stayed hunched low over the steering wheel, trying to run the small boat the way she figured a race car should be run. She had to get them the hell out of here. Motioning behind her for Eleri, Jason, and Hannah to stay low, she could only hope the conspicuous divers were out of view.

"Neriah?" Eleri asked, her hands and her wet hair as she looked up at GJ.

GJ shook her head and scanned the water. That was a story for another time.

Her shoulder ached from the challenge of pulling the three divers up and over the side of the boat in their exhausted states. It was hard to believe that she was in the best shape out of the tiny group.

Once Neriah had disappeared into the waves, GJ steered the boat toward where she remembered the blast surfacing on the water. Dropping the rope, she'd hoped like hell that whoever she pulled up was one of her own people. There was every possibility she had merely extended an invite to the assassin. Maybe the one she knew about. Maybe even another one.

Even when the first head had broken the surface, it wasn't until the hand lifted the mask up and out of the way that GJ could see Hannah's face. Her body had almost collapsed with relief, but the work hadn't been over. She'd had to haul three very heavy divers into the tiny cigarette boat.

She looked back at Eleri now and found her tucked into one corner of the small, open space, knees up almost under her chin. But when GJ turned, she must have revealed what she'd been trying to hide.

"You're bleeding," Hannah told her, as though GJ didn't already know that.

"Yes." She turned the wheel, debating whether to hug the shore or aim out into the open water. She had enough gas for the latter option, but she didn't have enough of her partners safe to try it.

Staying close to the land, GJ wished that she could make a large arc out in the open water, to skirt the edge of any space visible to or protected by Miranda Industries, and then get quickly to the other side of the compound. Noah was supposedly there waiting for Donovan.

But GJ didn't know for sure what was happening with Donovan. He hadn't responded for well over thirty minutes. It was entirely possible now that Noah had gone into the compound and that they'd both been caught.

Looking back over her shoulder, GJ finally decided the little boat was clear of the immediate view of Miranda Industries. They weren't being followed, at least not that she could tell. It would have to do for now.

It wasn't a guarantee that she was safe, just because she couldn't see anyone. Right now, it was entirely plausible that Neriah—that *creature*, whatever she was—was directly below the boat. If so, she might be waiting for them to stop so she could pop up and make her debut as her true self.

Tensing, GJ cut the engine, letting the boat slide forward on its own momentum as she scanned the waves carefully, looking for curly hair and a tail. She truly had no idea what she might see, or if she would even recognize the creature if she saw it again.

Sliding low into the seat, keeping her gaze just high enough to peer around, GJ watched for a break in the surface. Before she could assess anything, Eleri scrambled forward, a first-aid kit in hand. GJ wasn't quite sure which tiny compartment her senior agent might have pulled it from or how she had known it was there, but she suddenly had supplies. That was Eleri.

"Show me." The command was clear as Eleri now stood over her.

Tugging her downward and out of the line of sight of. . . *anything* that might spot them, she turned and presented her shoulder. She was glad that Eleri caught on to staying low without having been told. She also figured out that GJ didn't want to make a big fuss out of the injury. But she didn't know yet that GJ couldn't explain it to half of the boat's inhabitants.

Eleri took one look at the blood-soaked white fabric covering the wound and narrowed her gaze, adding a parental demand to her tone. "Move your shirt down."

Something in GJ's eyes must have warned her. GJ complied but swiveled the seat as she unbuttoned the top and gingerly tugged at the very short sleeve. Peeling it away from where it had been bitten through left threads caught in the deep gashes Neriah had left behind.

Eleri's eyes widened at the sight. She whispered in an attempt to keep the others from hearing. "What did this?"

"Neriah," GJ whispered softly back, and she watched as Eleri's eyes somehow managed to grow even bigger.

"What did. . . how?" The other agent couldn't even get the whole sentence out. And GJ couldn't answer it.

She shrugged. "Selkie?"

Several emotions crossed Eleri's face even as her hands moved now, opening gauze and aiming a small squirt bottle at the wound. It must have been rubbing alcohol for the way that it stung. GJ clenched her teeth and let out a hiss.

"Are you okay?" Hannah called from the other side of the boat.

"She needs stitches," Eleri replied, holding back most of the vital information. "I can't tell what bit her, but it wasn't good."

"Where's Neriah?" Jason asked now, inquiring after his friend.

It seemed the three were getting a little of their energy back. *Good.* They were going to need it.

Keeping her shoulder aimed out of their vision, GJ tried to shield them from the series of sharp, deep, jagged cuts from a bite that was definitely not human. She pinned Jason with a direct gaze. "What do you know about your friend?"

He didn't respond for a moment, suddenly confused at the line of questioning. He'd only seemed to wonder why she wasn't on the boat, and now GJ was questioning him. "What do you mean *what do I know about my friend? Do you mean Neriah?*"

GJ decided to go directly for it. "Did you know she was working with Miranda Industries?"

The sudden shock on Jason's face told her he hadn't known. She believed it. The man was an excellent diver and researcher, but he was a bit of a flake, and he certainly couldn't have kept a secret like that if he had known. He was also clearly not the fastest to draw these conclusions.

Hannah, too, jerked at the accusation GJ levied. GJ edited the tale slightly and told them what happened. They needed to know in case Neriah confronted either of them. "Neriah went overboard after telling me that you were all dead. We'd come here to find you, even though Neriah had argued against it. I thought she was arguing for safety or thought that you would all return where we'd stopped, but that wasn't the case."

A.J. SCUDIERE

She took a breath, gauged how the story was going down, and then continued. "I insisted that we come here when we saw the blast in the water."

Eleri shook her head as though she didn't understand. Her quick warning expression to GJ said to go along with what she was saying. "It must have been some kind of C4 he planted beforehand."

GJ nodded, wondering if Hannah and Jason could possibly buy such a cheap line of reasoning, but they didn't seem to fight it. GJ continued, "Right. Neriah told me that you were all dead. That the assassin had gotten you. Then she smiled about it."

She watched again as Jason and Hannah jerked in response to her accusation.

GJ threw more bait into the conversation. "I suspect if we look through Gelman and Patel's laboratory, we'll discover that it was Neriah who broke in and tossed the lab. I don't know if she was involved with their disappearances, but I don't know that she wasn't, either. She was missing during that time, and then she showed up with some of their lab work in hand."

"Oh shit." Hannah burst out, her head in her hands now. She'd been sitting almost docilely, worn out beyond even removing her vest. Now she suddenly stripped out of everything but her bathing suit and stood up in the boat. "She may have brought us bad intel then. Or even planted something on the *Calypso*. What do we need to do?"

"Well," GJ said, flexing her arm where Eleri had just taped down a bandage. That would have to do for now. She'd already set a timer on her wound, just as Donovan had taught her, because she couldn't go to the ER right now. She had six hours from the bite to get stitches, but there were too many things to do before taking care of a simple thing like a hospital visit. "We have other problems besides Neriah."

Hannah frowned. Eleri did, too. Then GJ dropped a bomb bigger than any of the ones they faced underwater. "Donovan

350

has been captured. He's stuck inside the Miranda Industries compound." She pointed back toward the shore and watched as all three reacted.

But Eleri's reaction was the worst of all, because Eleri knew what shape he was stuck in.

CHAPTER 67

"It's right there." Eleri pointed to the location the signal had directed her to. Even as she looked to GJ, her heart fell.

The tracking devices they'd activated on all their tablets, mobile phones, and computers had paid off. They easily located the tablet Noah had been using to follow Donovan's progress inside the compound. However, it was clear now that it had been folded into a towel and tucked out of the way between a handful of reeds in a divot between dunes.

Noah wasn't here.

Their fears that he wasn't responding because he'd gone after Donovan were now confirmed. Had someone from Miranda Industries come and kidnapped him off of the beach, it would have happened in view of the nearby hotel, and there should have been evidence of a struggle in the sand. The tablet would not have been neatly hidden away.

GJ only nodded at her. Unfortunately, this was exactly what they had expected.

"I don't like this," she told GJ carefully, holding the phone up as though she were framing a photo of the sea. "This is bad."

They'd left Jason and Hannah alone in a hotel room, even

knowing that Neriah was on the loose now. Their only recourse for the researchers' safety was the hope that Neriah was at her most dangerous in the water. She and GJ had come to track down Donovan and Noah. And GJ was injured.

At least they could now talk openly about what they were dealing with. It had been hard enough to cover up what had happened underwater. How would she do the same on dry land? It was part of why she'd chosen to leave them behind, but there were no good answers.

"How do we go in?" GJ asked, not questioning that they *would* go in.

Eleri sighed. "I want to say *underwater.*"

When GJ frowned in response, she added, "Snorkels and masks only. We can stay under long enough to skirt the gate." She pointed out to the ocean as though she saw dolphins, hoping that anybody who was watching them would think they were just walking the beach.

With a nudge to GJ's good shoulder, they walked back toward the hotels, keeping up the ruse that they were tourist beachcombers. All the while, they talked in a way that appeared casual. But though their tones were easygoing, their words were a plan to rescue their partners.

Thirty minutes later—without having come up with a better idea—Eleri and GJ were in the water and close to the gate jutting out into the roiling waves. They'd swum half the distance between where they entered the sea near the hotels and where they could pass into the open ocean side of Miranda Industries.

Sucking air through the snorkel was taxing her, but Eleri did it anyway. She might just die after this. No, she definitely would.

But when GJ signaled her, she gave back a thumbs up. If GJ was willing to get into the water with an open wound, Eleri could find some damn energy to keep swimming. At least GJ wasn't openly bleeding anymore. She'd allowed Eleri to cast a small spell on her injured shoulder once they'd gotten Hannah and Jason back to the hotel. It had worked, much to Eleri's delight. So little had worked in the last few months.

Staying below the surface was exhausting, but she kicked anyway. Slowly, they got closer to their destination, despite the fact that they were near enough to the shore that the waves kept tugging at them and hindering every stroke. Once they passed the gate, it was easier because they turned and headed with the direction of the tide.

Though Eleri wanted to hold on to the gate and use it to pull herself in underwater, she didn't. Perhaps it was motion sensitive. Perhaps her grabbing it underwater would rattle it above ground. Either option was bad, so she kept her hands to herself.

As the water shallowed out with each surge that pushed them up into the compound, Eleri began getting ready. She and GJ removed their fins, their masks, and the snorkels and held them in their hands as they crawled up the sand, still fighting the waves that both propelled them toward and pulled them away from their goal.

Keeping her head just above the water, Eleri saw workers loading things into a boat. When one turned their direction, she ducked back under. After a few moments, and a few more cautious checks of what was going on in the compound, the boat sped off. Workers piled boxes on palettes. They unloaded trucks. They checked lists on clipboards and talked on small walkie-talkies. But she could not see Donovan or Noah.

After the boat left, the dock went quiet for a while. Motioning to GJ, Eleri whispered. "Let's use the dock for cover. Hopefully, they won't see us."

Almost like synchronized swimmers, they took in deep breaths and popped under the water again, coming up under the walkway where the boats parked. It was GJ who pointed out that the cross ties supporting the dock from underneath would provide good places to store their masks and fins.

Neither removed the sleek packs strapped to their waists. In her pack, in waterproof bags, Eleri carried her gun and Donovan's as well as shorts and a T shirt for him. Though GJ carried her own badge and gun and Noah's, there weren't any dry clothes for GJ or herself. They would simply have to do this wet. There was no way to dry off, even if they had spare clothing.

Motioning what communication they could, the two women stayed low, taking advantage of what appeared to be a lull in the activity. Quickly, the sand beneath their feet turned to boardwalk. The entire area had been covered in wood planking to make it easier to roll handcarts around and drive small forklifts back and forth.

Eleri crouched down behind a bush, hoping it covered herself and GJ adequately. Only then did she understand that the lull was not due to any need for a break, but to what she had been most afraid of.

All the scurrying workers had cleared out, opening a space in the center. Noah, handcuffed and shoved around, was being brought into the center of the courtyard. He let them control him as though he wasn't a trained agent and didn't have to take it. Maybe they didn't know. Behind him, one of the workers dragged a cage on wheels, bumping it along the rough wood planks with no care. In the crate sat a large, black wolf.

Donovan.

He couldn't whine or bark or anything—not if Noah was right and the people here knew what he was. Not if some of the people here were like him.

Slowly, Eleri unzipped her pack by feel and pulled out both guns. Donovan's sat heavy in her hand, but that didn't stop her. She motioned to GJ to do the same.

It wasn't much of a plan, but she had one.

Just as she was about to pop up, the gate opened. This was her chance—if they could run through, free Donovan, and pop Noah's hand ties, they might get out the open gate...

Before she could even think her way through her desired scenario, a truck rolled in. The large pickup stopped in the middle of the compound, the gate already rolling closed behind. That was not going to be her escape route, she realized, her heart sinking. It had been too easy to be real.

The door to the truck opened on the passenger side and the local police chief stepped down onto the wooden planks. With no commentary from anyone in the compound, he walked over to stand in front of Noah and Donovan.

CHAPTER 68

Donovan smelled them before he saw them. Though they were buried under the strong and changing scent of the sea, he still recognized Eleri and GJ.

The scent was coming from off to his right, but it didn't matter. He couldn't afford to even glance over at them. One of the good soldiers was walking right toward him. His hand slapped onto the top of the crate and he tugged.

Though Donovan hadn't realized it before, the crappy little dog crate sat on wheels. He was now getting dragged along, his skull cracking against the wire top with every trip of the wheels over the gaps in the wood planks.

It was go-time. There was every possibility that someone was going to draw a gun and shoot him right here in this little cell. They knew what he was. They weren't going to let him out. They would not just slip a chain over his head and walk him off the property. There were other wolves working here, and they would know better than to handle him like an ordinary stray.

The wolves who worked here wore uniforms like the rest. They might not be out and loud about what they were, but Miranda Industries seemed to understand what kind of men worked for them. It appeared the compound was using its *special* citizens to their fullest abilities. In fact, the more Donovan thought about it—and he'd had nothing but time to think as he sat in this crappy little cage—the more he believed that perhaps Miranda Industries was not just an employer of the Lobomau but maybe owned by one.

Another bump cracked his skull against the wire above him, his feet leaving the floor for just a moment. Though he tried to brace himself, it didn't stop him from getting bashed like pinball. It only kept him from becoming airborne. In front of him, Noah, whose hands were zip tied behind his back, was pushed along to the center of the compound. He stumbled a little along the planks but managed to keep his feet, despite the rough treatment.

He and Noah had no guns, no knives. They had only Noah's hands and Donovan's teeth. Everyone else had the same "weapons." Surely the soldiers were trained in hand-to-hand combat, and plenty of them had fangs. He could smell them all.

But maybe—just maybe—he had Eleri and GJ, even though that left them still horribly outnumbered. Maybe it gave them enough of an advantage. Maybe he could use whatever special skills Eleri and Noah possessed. He hoped so, because he was no different than the rest of the wolves in here, and he was outnumbered.

A truck had pulled inside the gate and a man stepped out— only he wasn't a normal man. He was dressed in the local police chief uniform and he was yet another wolf. With dark skin and large brown eyes, his face held what should have been a happy smile, but it was full of ruthless demands even before he said anything. "Open the crate."

Some of the soldiers scrambled to make it happen. Donovan could only hope it was their mistake, and that he could get an advantage. Pausing a moment, he then stepped quickly beyond the confines of the crate, deciding it was better to be bold than to give them a moment to lock him back in. If they wanted him back inside, they would have to use force.

The police chief wore a gun strapped to a holster at his waist and Donovan fought the surge of fear that his life might end right here, right now. He'd been mind-warped and stalked and even blown up since taking this job, but stewing in thoughts of his impending death right now was definitely worse.

He had no idea what the local laws were, but he suspected shooting a man wasn't allowable, and shooting a dog probably was.

Eleri and GJ were coming closer. So Donovan whined a little, trying to offer up a slight distraction, though he hated the noise himself. He set his butt on the ground in case he had to stand and change quickly. If he did it, the change would leave him naked and less protected than when he was in canine form.

"What is your name?" The police chief demanded as he looked Donovan in the eyes.

A mere twist of his head was all Donovan offered in return. He was hoping to hold onto the "friendly dog" ruse as long as he could.

A foot jutted swiftly toward him, as though to kick him in the side. But Donovan lunged backward at the last moment, avoiding contact.

"Tell me your name, and stand up like a man."

That was when Donovan decided he would not. If they wanted him human, he would not give it to them. Besides, Eleri and GJ were even closer now. He tried to stay still, tried not to let his heart soar with the possibility of hope.

Noah held his own gaze steadily forward the whole time, his countenance unflinching, not even acknowledging Donovan. However, while Donovan watched—and he might have been observed by some other workers as well—Noah slightly twisted his hands back and forth, as though he could break free of the zip tie cuffs. Certainly, if he did, fifteen of the good soldiers would be on him within moments.

But the Chief then looked to his left and drawled, "Ladies, please join us."

Fuck. Donovan had forgotten something crucial. If he could smell Eleri and GJ approaching, then so could every other wolf in the compound.

All heads, and guns, turned to where Eleri and GJ carefully emerged from the shadows.

CHAPTER 69

G J froze. But Eleri sucked in a breath and sauntered forward. It was all GJ could do to force her feet to move, and to not look as petrified as she felt.

"Hello, gentlemen," Eleri called, a smile on her face, one hand behind her back, a gun held firmly there.

But these were wolves, GJ thought. Wouldn't they smell the guns? The oil had to be a strong enough scent to pick up. Maybe, GJ hoped, there were enough guns around that they wouldn't recognize the scent of a few more.

Eleri had carefully tucked the spare into the back of her wet shorts. The pack covered it, but not very well. Maybe she was hoping that the soldiers would take the gun out of her hand and not know she had a second weapon. GJ did the same.

"It's a lovely day today," Eleri intoned, as though she were walking to a southern afternoon garden party. But GJ noticed that as she spoke, her hand was slipping into the zipper of the small pack. It took a moment to catch on. Then GJ did the same.

No one stopped their forward movement, as obviously the soldiers weren't afraid of them. They even kept the tips of their rifles pointed to the ground. It was Eleri who flipped open her badge, and GJ followed along a half-beat behind, finally seeing where the senior agent was going.

"The weather is just beautiful here at Miranda Industries. You've got your own dock to do business out of, and it would be a shame if that became a problem," Eleri said softly but firmly. "As you can see from my badge—" she held it out, aiming it in an arc so everyone could see. "—I'm an agent with the United States Federal Bureau of Investigation."

"You have no jurisdiction here, Chica," the police chief laughed the words out.

"Oh, I know," Eleri replied, almost as if she, too, were enjoying a good laugh. But she still held the badge up. "I have no real jurisdiction. But if you shoot a federal agent, you will have the whole of the United States investigative branch on your ass inside of five minutes." She motioned back toward GJ, who put on her best agent face. "As you've seen, my partner here is also a federal agent."

This time, the chief nodded to Eleri and GJ. Though he clearly didn't offer any deference to the badge, he at least seemed to be considering what Eleri had said.

Brilliant, GJ was thinking. Then she stepped forward, continuing Eleri's plan and hoping that her own speech would give the other agent time to actually *do* something. "This man—" she said, pointing to Noah, "—is Special Agent Noah Kimball. You've already detained a US special agent against his will. And there, in front of you. . ."

"Oh, sure," laughed the chief when GJ trailed off. "I suppose you're going to tell me *he* is a federal agent, too." He gestured to Donovan but didn't stop laughing.

"Of course he is," GJ replied, still calm on the outside. This, at least, managed to confuse a good number of them. They looked at one another, clearly understanding what Donovan was but not able to reconcile the pieces.

The chief clasped his hands and rocked back on his heels. "Surely the bureau doesn't hire *dogs*."

"No," GJ replied, watching in her peripheral vision as Eleri slowly put herself into a better position. Though her own blood tried to leap out of her body with every pulse of her heart, GJ fought to keep her exterior sweet, calm, and in control. "But the bureau does employ people with certain. . . *special*. . . skills." She emphasized the pause between each word, watching as the crowd seemed to catch on. "You already know what special skills agent Donovan Heath possesses, but you don't know about the rest of us."

She bluffed her ass off with that. *Noah and Eleri* had special skills. She was just an idiot who'd gotten herself bitten.

"How do I know you have any *special skills?*" The chief held his hands wide, as though inviting a kindly demonstration. He got one.

A whip of the wind brought a palm frond fast against his face in a hard smack. GJ almost laughed. *Go Noah!* Or maybe that was Eleri?

She tipped her head. "Would you like another demonstration?"

The chief frowned, though he appeared irritated at having been smacked. Gone was the fake, jovial tone. "That was *nothing*." But he almost didn't finish the words as a gust of sharp wind punched him in the chest, knocking him slightly backward off his feet.

"Want to try again?" GJ asked, talking through more time for Noah to get his damn wrists out of those ties and for Eleri to get in place, and for Donovan to do. . . apparently nothing. She fought a sigh but kept her gaze on the chief.

"In fact, let me ask you who your assassin was supposed to kill? Because I'm pretty sure it was Agent Eames here." GJ gestured with her hand. *Shit. She'd drawn attention to Eleri. Wrong tactic!* "Yet she's here, and your assassin is not."

She pulled all the attention back to herself, and for the first time, she saw his exterior crack. Surely this man had believed his special assassin could not be bested. Yet here stood Eleri. GJ rubbed a little salt in the wound. "The other two are safe as well. Not so much for your hired man."

Rambling on, she left no time for them to think. "You're going to set our agents free, and we're going to walk out of here."

"I don't think so," the chief replied, the words rough and angry.

Well, two could play at that game. GJ spoke with the most force she could utter, adding a guttural grind to her vocal cords as though she could push a spell forward with just the tone of her voice. But that wasn't her. That was Eleri. Still, she said it. "I do."

Something happened.

The chief's eyes flinched to Eleri as the senior agent repeated GJ's words in a voice GJ didn't recognize. She *knew* Eleri could do all kinds of things, but she had never actually *seen* it. She wanted to turn and look, but all their lives depended on her calm confidence. This had to appear like an everyday occurrence for her.

Behind her, the words came from a depth GJ could not visualize. *"You will let our agents go."*

GJ watched as the chief's eyes widened and he took a small step backward. Beside her now, Eleri took one forward, and the chief backed up again.

Only at that moment, a splash snapped everyone's attention to the dock. A large, fish-like creature had leapt up onto the surface. Slowly, it lifted its head, curls intact. The face was wide, scaly, and changing as it twisted back into human form, legs drawing up underneath it.

GJ spoke softly toward Eleri, hoping she could hear and no one else could. "That's Neriah."

To her credit, Eleri didn't flinch. But Neriah jolted herself off the dock and ran toward them, screaming. Eleri didn't hesitate. Aiming her gun, she fired two rounds. GJ saw Neriah jolt from the impact.

CHAPTER 70

Eleri watched in horror as Neriah Jones stumbled backwards, her hands clapping her sternum where Eleri's bullets had struck. She had jerked as the bullets entered, but she seemed to manage to stay on her feet, though Neriah's form changed as she moved.

Her greenish tint disappeared. The gaping mouth of teeth pulled back, disappearing behind soft, human lips, and the too-round black eyes blinked, once, twice, and became a soft, wounded brown.

But Eleri wasn't fooled. She could almost smell the sea water reclaiming its own as Neriah tripped backward off the end of the dock and landed with a splash.

Whatever had come up onto the dock had not been human, even if it had been Neriah. Still, Eleri hadn't done anything until the creature had lunged for GJ. Her friend had already been bitten once. Though Eleri might have questioned GJ's description of Neriah, she'd never questioned the bite itself or that it was Neriah who'd delivered it. Now, she didn't doubt any of it.

The roaring in her head—the echo of bullets fired—finally

began to recede and she turned back to the scene at the center of the compound. The horror of shooting another living creature tried to wash over her, but she pushed that sensation as far down inside as she could. There was no time for it.

Breaking through the rushing sounds in her head, the guttural noise of Donovan growling and lunging grabbed her attention and forced her to jump into the new fight. He had already gone for the police chief's throat.

The chief had clearly known what Donovan was. Eleri quickly put the pieces together, surmising that his familiarity with both what Donovan was and the compound behind the fence meant that he understood some of the workers here were wolves, too.

But, unless all the police were wolves, it would be difficult to prosecute Donovan for his death. Difficult to convince anyone that the animal-like bite marks on the chief's body were made by the dark-haired agent from America. She was just putting this logic together, thinking that she couldn't be surprised again, when the Chief's face slowly began to change.

Eleri felt her stomach roll and she stilled as she had to change her entire game plan. The chief was one of *them*. Around the fight, in a ring, some of the workers were laying down weapons, their faces jutting out, fangs bared as they reached toward the ground. They would lunge when all four feet hit the sand. She knew it.

Donovan wouldn't stand a chance against them all...

A flash of movement to her right caught her attention and she swung her gun at the threat. Jerking the weapon back, she realized her mistake. Her breath sucked in and she wanted to apologize for aiming first and looking second. It was Noah who had gotten his hands free.

Barely glancing at her, he fisted his hands and shoved them down at his sides. Eyes closed, he stood only feet from Donovan as the wind began swirling around them.

The center of the courtyard belonged to him. Noah, Donovan, and the chief were caught in the eye of the cyclone. Outside of it, the winds were bearable. . . until she tried to cross into the middle. Then it whipped at her hair, the dark red of the wet strands stinging her across the face. Her clothing tugged at her as the winds grabbed at it, and her feet stumbled as she encountered the full force of Noah's power.

On the other side of the gale, soldiers and wolves alike were knocked off their feet. If the wind didn't get them, flying sand and loose palm fronds and small twigs did.

In the very center of this supernatural storm, oblivious to the erratic weather around him, Donovan held down the police chief. The man clawed at the ground in an attempt to get up, his nails curling and jutting into the wood as his hands attempted the change. Though Donovan stood over him, jaws clamped to the man's throat, the chief's legs drew up as though shifting to wolf form. His head tipped back, his face showing fangs and angry eyes against an onslaught that overpowered him.

No one was coming to help him. They couldn't. The force of the air was too strong for anyone to get through. Except maybe for Eleri.

She could feel power singing through her system. *Finally!* This was what she'd been searching for. All the times she had tried to cast and it hadn't worked, she'd been missing *this*: the white hot rush of blood zinging to every cell.

Donovan had once told her that her eyes went black. Though she'd never seen it, she could *feel* it right now. Generations of witchcraft surged in her veins, and she knew she could walk through anything now: fire or water, or even this wind.

With a casual motion, she tossed her gun to GJ—a stupid move if there ever was one. The barrel was still warm from the shots she'd fired. But with the flick of her wrist, she gave it a gentle arc in the air, so that even though GJ grabbed it with her non-dominant hand, she still caught it easily in the appropriate grip.

Knowing that GJ would catch it, Eleri turned away, her anger like a drug. Power flowed like knowledge that she was invincible. With both empty hands in front of her now shaped like claws, her blood coursed, as though all the force of the ocean surged within her. She opened a space through Noah's wall of wind.

Stepping into the center, where the chief still managed to stay partially transformed into a wolf, she let the curtain fall shut behind her. Eleri stood over the fight, listening to the growls, grunts, and deep-throated barks.

She held her hand out as though she were physically holding the chief down.

"I've got him," she whispered to Donovan, though probably the chief could hear, too. The other wolves might not be able to hear her because of the cyclone.

GJ had jumped through the gap behind her, and the four agents were now together, which felt like a good thing, a safer thing. But they were also in the middle of the compound—the hardest place to escape from.

Donovan stepped back, still growling low in his throat. The threat of another attack was enough to keep the injured chief down, though he offered his own return hiss. One step after another, Donovan slowly backed off from the man in uniform.

But he didn't stand on two legs or even pull his face back into his human position. It didn't make sense for him to change.

Still more than five feet away, Eleri leaned toward the chief, her hand out, the force of her will holding him to the ground, though he had started to thrash. *Fuck him*, she thought. He'd caged her partner. He was lucky she wasn't crushing him.

Gashes from Donovan's teeth were now evident on his shoulders and very close to his throat. Apparently, Donovan had not been going for the kill, but Eleri was about to. These people had killed Allison.

Something struck her—the way the chief had reacted when GJ commented that Eleri was still here, and so was Hannah. The true shock was that his assassin had failed. Donovan might have smelled his surprise, but Eleri *felt* it, almost as though it had happened inside her.

She squeezed harder with her fist, her mouth forming into a primal scream with her anger. Watching as his face turned red, half transformed, unable to go any further, she felt the man's pain at her handiwork—and she *reveled* in it. His lips pulled back against long teeth, eyes wide and glittering as he drooled from the tightness in his throat.

"Open the gate," she commanded.

He only choked out a few sounds, barely managing to wave a hand at the others beyond the edge of the wind. But they didn't hear. Sand, leaves, and tiny twigs created a wall in the air around them. The chief slapped at the floor as though he could get their attention, but he couldn't.

Eleri thought it through. The gate was not what she really wanted. If they went out the gate, they would be on the road. That meant they would be flanked by the woods on one side. The compound would be behind them, with its fence and vines shielding her team from seeing what was coming after them.

No. They would have to go out through the water.

"GJ." Eleri turned, hearing the grit in her voice as though it weren't her own. She pointed to where they had come up by the dock and watched as GJ caught her meaning and nodded.

"Noah," she said next, but Donovan already sensed her plan. She could tell; she could feel everything around her: the tension in Noah as he held the wind, the clicking analytics of GJ's brain running through every possible permutation of outcomes as she aimed a gun in each hand, as though she could shoot gangster-style and take all of the soldiers out herself. GJ was already backing away toward the water.

And Eleri could feel Donovan. She wasn't just putting him in a pool. She was throwing him into the ocean. She felt his panic as though it were her own, but she saw no other option. As her heart stuttered, the chief sucked in a breath, and she punched her fist into the air in front of her. She sent him back to the floor, his head slamming down.

"Come on, Donovan," she said softly and watched as the police chief's body loosened, his head lolling to the side, his eyes rolling back, out cold.

Slowly, the four retreated into the water. The winds swirled around them, opening a path. As they hit the edge of the sea, the air picked up droplets of salt water, further creating a wall.

Eleri watched as the soldiers fought forward. For all that they'd been held back, they weren't frightened. They rushed to the chief, picking him up and moving him to a safer location. Others were advancing toward them, rifle tips aimed.

As Eleri's little band of four hit the water, Noah's control of the wind failed.

Behind her, GJ disappeared into the sea with a splash. Noah was hot on her heels. Ever the consummate diver, he was gone in a heartbeat. Eleri was left with Donovan balking, staring at the waves.

He growled at her before he made one gigantic leap into a wave coming at him. The sheer guts it had taken him reverberated through Eleri's system as she felt the sea push down on him and try to steal his breath. He struggled to get below the waves as she stood, holding what ground she could until there was nothing more she could do.

Her own push against the soldiers failed. There was only so much she could do against so many. They rushed her, and she heard the noise of rifles firing as though it was happening to someone else. But she felt the impact as she turned, and the bullets hit her back.

The rush of her power faded as she sank below the water, fading with the sharp pain where she'd been struck. But she pushed off the sandy bottom and prayed she would get away.

CHAPTER 71

" Come on!"

Donovan heard Noah's voice, though he couldn't see the other agent. Noah's hand held firm to a fistful of Donovan's fur, but though they were only an arm-length apart, the waves artfully separated them.

Donovan sputtered and coughed. Ocean water burst out of his mouth, coming up from his lungs as his body tried to expel it.

At last, the beach became shallow enough that he could stand, but the waves were constantly trying to push him down and tug him back under. Beside him, Noah reached out, grabbing for his hand, but Donovan shook his head. That escape was the strangest thing he'd ever fucking done. He didn't swim. He didn't know how to breathe underwater. But Noah had grabbed him by the scruff and tugged him along, forcing him into the safety under the waves even as Donovan fought him.

He couldn't breathe; the water had clogged his nose and the pressure and disorientation of the currents took away every sense he had, every resource he was used to relying on. Nothing was left. The saltwater burned his sensitive eyes and the inside

373

of his nose. He'd held his breath as best he could, but canines weren't built for that kind of water travel.

Still, Noah had tugged him along, keeping him under until they passed around the edge of the fence and out of a straight shot from the compound. Mentally, Donovan understood that Noah was trying to get them to safety—but emotionally, it had been an all-out panic attack, and he had fought back. Hard.

Eventually Noah let him get his head above water, but they'd still been far from the hotel where they needed to be, where they would most likely be safe coming ashore. So they'd swum on, Noah dragging him like dead weight as Donovan gulped water and tried like hell to keep his shit together.

When Noah had finally let go of him, Donovan had changed form, right there in the ocean. He rolled his shoulders and popped the bones in his face as the waves pushed back and forth. He'd thought it couldn't feel any worse than it already did, being underwater and panicking. But the water had rushed in as his face changed shape and he'd coughed and sputtered and become convinced he would drown.

Now, as they stood separately in the shallow waves, Noah's T-shirt stuck to his torso, held on by water and air pressure. Donovan could see claw marks and blood. He would apologize but, despite having his human face back, he still couldn't speak. He coughed again.

"Come on," Noah urged again, waving Donovan up toward the sand. But Donovan splashed in the water, shaking his head.

"*Eleri!*" Donovan finally managed to gurgle around the saltwater still invading his throat.

GJ was already on the beach, running up onto the sand. But Noah had heard him. He abandoned Donovan to the onslaught of the waves as he dove headfirst back underwater to look for their fourth agent. Their missing leader.

Donovan would have gone, too, but he knew he would be a liability. Still, he ran further out into the ocean, hoping to tell what he knew. Sound traveled better underwater, and his sensitive ears had picked it up, as usual. The others didn't know that Eleri had been shot.

GJ had searched the sand, then splashed back to where Donovan still stood in chest-deep water. Shorter than his standing height by a good margin, she'd simply waded back in. She had no fear of the water that terrified him.

"She's not here." GJ's voice was frantic and Donovan wanted to answer, but he could only shake his head. She, too, dove into the water with no reservations, leaving him on his own in the sand and the waves.

He would open his nose and try to catch Eleri's scent, but he didn't think it would work if she was underwater. He couldn't smell her, he couldn't see her, and he couldn't hear her. It hit him then that she'd never not come before. She'd always appeared when he needed her to. But this time, all traces of her were erased by the sea.

Now, he stood in the waves, unable to come out, buck naked, but more importantly, unable to find his partner. That felt worse.

"She's not here," he called out to GJ, despite the fact that his throat scratched with sea water his lungs were still trying to expel. He hollered the words despite the fact that GJ couldn't hear him and he couldn't yell.

In the distance, he saw GJ's head pop up above the water. "Noah?" she called into the air, but Noah didn't reply.

With a great gulp of air, Donovan fought over the burn in his lungs. "Over there!" he yelled, as Noah emerged, a small dot riding the waves. They had not reclaimed their snorkeling gear, and they were searching freestyle in the water.

Scanning the ocean for any sign of Eleri, Donovan saw curls. He stood, stunned, as they popped up above the surface. Neriah's head came up, and beside her—too close to be safe— Eleri's.

Neriah had a hold of her. Using some kind of inhuman strength, she rose out of the water enough for them to all see that her arm was around Eleri's neck and Eleri was unconscious.

Then Neriah laughed, a high-pitched screech of a sound that hurt his eardrums, before she and Eleri disappeared under the waves.

CHAPTER 72

G J was done with this shit.

Neriah had bitten her, and now she had stolen Eleri. Neriah had trailed the *Calypso* on the open water, probably checking in and letting Miranda Industries know where they were at every moment. She'd probably killed the other two scientists and raided their labs. If Neriah's story was solid at all, Gelman and Patel had mistakenly trusted her.

The photos in her apartment. . . GJ thought back to when she and Noah had poked around. Those photos showed Neriah on yachts, large-scale research vessels, and boats she couldn't afford. She probably wouldn't have friends who could afford them, either. Not if she was really in research.

And the tanks? The diving equipment? GJ hadn't known at the time, but after being on the boat, and after seeing what was around Miranda Industries. . . Neriah's equipment was far too expensive for her "poor student" status.

GJ had missed it all.

Neriah had helped kill Allison, and now there was nothing to stop her from killing Eleri. After all, Eleri had shot her at least twice.

"Noah!" GJ called out before she drove underwater again as she spotted a shape underwater racing toward the two women. She prayed it was him. As she broke the surface again, taking another deep breath, she spotted his head nearby and took her first relieved breath. But she knew they weren't out of the woods yet. Not even close.

Reaching out, she grabbed him, shaking his arm, to get his attention. "Noah, *the animals!*" She had no special powers. Despite her bluff in the compound, she had only her brains. "What can you do?"

She wanted to ask politely, but there was no time for polite. She demanded an answer and then spoke over him. "There are fish! There are sharks here! *Do something.*"

She shook him so hard, he had to push her off. "Give me a minute."

"We don't have a minute!"

GJ dove back under the water and kicked as hard as she could. But she was chasing a sea creature, and she didn't even have snorkel and fins. Her disadvantage was as monstrous as Neriah's goals.

Luckily, Neriah wanted to taunt them, so she let GJ get close.

Holding Eleri's head up, she let GJ see her friend was still unconscious.

There would be no help coming from Eleri and her spells. There would be no help coming from Donovan. He was barely breathing, and he functioned only on land. There was nowhere he had any ground to stand on. The only weapons they had were GJ's brains and Noah's unknown skills.

At any moment, Neriah might turn and zip away. She could easily steal Eleri, disappearing with her into the depths of the ocean, where GJ and Noah could not follow. Not without fins, not without tanks. Not without a miracle.

Brains, GJ thought. She had brains. And that was all, so she had better start using them.

Stopping maybe three or four yards away, GJ treaded water as Neriah held up her friend. A wicked green hue tinted her skin, and a sharp grin crossed the wide, sharp teeth.

Eleri had once described this as GJ's superpower. Now she hoped it could save her friend. "Neriah, how did you hide this from Hannah and Allison so long?"

Another grin. Maybe it was hard to talk with those ugly teeth in her mouth.

"How did you hide it from *Jason*? He thinks he's your best friend. That's pretty impressive. . . Or does he *know*?" GJ pushed, trying to draw the creature into a conversation. To keep her from disappearing with Eleri.

"He doesn't know anything!" The voice came on a hiss, a whine, high-pitched enough to hurt GJ's ears.

Fighting her natural reaction, she didn't flinch. "You managed to hide this from your best friend. For how long?" She tried to sound incredulous. It was a stupid game, and surely Neriah was too smart to play along.

"Two and a half years." The voice strung out the S of "years" in a long, snake-like hiss. Her eyes were wide, large, black. She was not a selkie. Selkies were like seals—GJ had looked it up— but she didn't know what Neriah *was*.

"You filmed Allison's death, didn't you?" GJ asked. "It was pretty clever, parking that video in Missy Maisel's email. Did you expect us to find it?"

Her arms moved back and forth as GJ held her space in the ocean, fighting to keep the waves from building the distance between them. If anything, she wanted to get closer. Perhaps Neriah would notice. Perhaps if she could shorten the distance between them, she could make a lunge and grab for Eleri.

"Do you want to come and get your friend? Come closer, little agent."

Ah, so that was the game. That was why Neriah wasn't running off with Eleri. She must think she could get them both.

Maybe she could. But GJ inched closer. "Was that the plan? For us to find it?"

"You weren't supposed to. But I suppose now you think you're clever."

GJ tipped her head. "Not as clever as you. Did us finding the video trigger them sending you after us?" she asked, needing to stall, because *damn*, Noah should have made something happen by now. How long before Neriah lured her in close enough to capture her, too? How long before she caught on that GJ was toying with her? "You followed us on purpose? Were we supposed to see you?"

Then it happened.

Thank you to all the gods that Eleri worshipped! GJ thought, because Neriah's head tipped back and she screamed, releasing Eleri.

Thank the gods for Noah, GJ thought next. Though she had no idea what creature he might have coerced into biting Neriah, he'd done it.

The sleek, scaled body jerked to one side and then the other, while Eleri slid out of her grasp and slipped beneath the waves.

It must be a shark, and a big one. GJ was diving forward, though she swam into red water. Eleri had saved her life more than once. If this was how she ended, it would be a worthy death. Still, she wasn't willing to die easily.

The blood was likely Neriah's—*hopefully*. She'd probably been bleeding all along from the bullet wounds. GJ herself had seen the blood before Neriah splashed off the dock, but those wounds obviously hadn't killed her. Maybe she had been gut shot.

Maybe this wasn't Noah's doing at all, but Neriah had been trailing blood the whole time as she stole Eleri away. Maybe GJ was swimming head-first into a *bona fide* shark attack.

But now, whatever had grabbed Neriah yanked her hard, eliciting a scream that could clear the water. Eleri was floating loose, but she was still much too close to the sharks. With the lunge that she'd been preparing for, GJ pushed underwater and came up beneath her friend's lax body.

She couldn't tell if Eleri was bleeding. She hoped her senior agent wasn't, but that didn't change that there was blood in the water and all around them. She watched as a fin broke the surface, heading straight toward them. With as much skill and strength as she could muster, GJ kicked away, pulling Eleri's heavy body along and watching as the fin veered toward Neriah.

Though Neriah seemed to have screamed the predators away, they were heading back.

And GJ thanked the gods again.

It was a hard swim. Adrenaline had replaced her blood. Everything pounded. A shark bumped against her and she would have pissed her pants if she had any fear left. But it didn't bite and it didn't try to yank at Eleri. Her ears ached from Neriah's screams, but at least that hurt was good.

It took far too long to reach Noah, but he met up with her in an open space away from the sharks and the fighting sea creature. GJ had hoped the sharks would kill Neriah. Now she was grateful they were at least keeping the beast occupied.

"Wrong way," he told her. "Shore's this direction."

Fuck. She'd wasted precious effort. But he, at least, was a qualified diver and a strong, trained swimmer. Apparently, GJ had been doing it all wrong.

"I've got her," he said, reaching for Eleri, but GJ found it hard to let go. Behind them, thrashing at the surface, a shark had torn Neriah to pieces, and GJ noticed that the shrieking had gurgled and then stopped.

With a sigh of sheer, dead exhaustion, at last she handed Eleri over. A sloppy passing in the middle of the bossy waves, the transfer occupied her hands enough to keep her from raising her hand and saluting Neriah with one finger.

She was out of energy and about to stop and sink, but she swam toward the shore on sheer determination, trusting Noah to keep the sharks away from them. He'd already looped his arm under Eleri's and tucked her head up against his shoulder, keeping her face up and out of the waves.

GJ had not done that. Without a burden, she should have been able to swim, but it was all she could do to stay beside him. She counted strokes for something to keep her going, telling herself if she just moved her legs, she would eventually make it.

And she did. The sand bumped against her feet as she tried to stand when she reached Donovan. His large hands came out, one grabbing her and the other adding his strength to help pull Eleri to shore.

"Oh Jesus," she whispered as she realized Donovan was naked. "Hold on," she said, then rolled her head and asked Noah, "Is she breathing?"

"Yes," he replied, somehow having managed to check her while swimming her back from the middle of the ocean.

GJ unzipped and reached into Eleri's pack, pulling out the one remaining bag—the clothes. She held them out to Donovan, lacking the energy required to toss it to him. "These are for you."

Then she found a third or fourth wind and pushed her feet under her so she could help lift Eleri up onto the beach. But as she grabbed Eleri's arm, her senior agent's head lolled to the side and GJ saw her lips were blue, her eyes open and unseeing.

Noah had lied.

CHAPTER 73

D onovan shoved Noah and GJ out of the way. He'd been useless until now, but this was his forte.

He'd slipped into the trunks Eleri had brought along for him and run toward them, his thoughts ping-ponging. He'd met her in Westerfield's office, having no clue who this "Eleri Eames" might be. He only knew that she'd be his new senior partner. He'd been fresh enough out of Quantico to still have the bruises.

Now she'd saved his life more times than he could count and she'd saved his secret even more often. For a moment, he flashed through what would happen if she died here on this beach.

He shut it down.

"I know CPR." Noah was elbowing his way into the space over Eleri's limp form.

"I'm an MD," Donovan countered, never more glad to have those letters at the end of his name than right this moment. It might mean he could do something.

Turning her head to the side, he only barely registered that Noah had stepped back and run off as Donovan swept Eleri's mouth, looking for anything that might have gotten lodged in her throat.

He worked to forget that this "patient" was plausibly the best friend he'd ever had, or ever would have. Tilting her head back, he checked her airway as best he could with no tools or instruments. Then, as GJ scrambled to assist in a situation where she couldn't, he searched for Eleri's pulse and found none.

It terrified him.

Managing to overlay his hands and lace his fingers together in the correct form out of rote memory, he found her sternum. He placed his hands and began compressions.

One. Two. Three. He refused to sing along, even just in his head.

He'd been taught, in a recent update course, to sing the BeeGees' Staying Alive, or even Queen's Another One Bites the Dust. Neither hit the right note for the severe gravity of his situation, so he merely counted off the rhythm.

Beside him, GJ muttered, "Come on Eleri, come on," as she knelt by Eleri's head and held it straight when it tried to loll to the side.

"Tip it back," Donovan commanded. "Open her airway."

As GJ did, they both stopped for a moment and waited to see if she might breathe on her own. He checked her vitals again.

Jesus, he was the one who couldn't swim. This should have been him. What did Neriah do to her?

Eleri had been shot. *Fuck*, he'd forgotten, only concerned that she needed CPR. Now he realized that, if her lung was punctured, then all his chest compressions were for naught.

Noah, already back from his run to the dunes, was returning with his possessions. Even as he ran, he pulled his tablet from the towel.

Looking up, Donovan thanked a God he'd long ago released from any responsibility for his life. Noah's abandoned tech was still where he'd left it. Everything else had gotten wet.

But Noah was talking into the mic already. "I need an ambulance." He looked around frantically, seeming to search for an address, but GJ and Donovan didn't have it. Donovan was wondering if he had *anything* this situation called for. Maybe this was going to be his biggest failure.

"I need it fast. I have one female patient—" Noah was practically yelling into the device. "She's not breathing. Thirty-three years old, drowning." He demanded speed with all the assurance of a federal agent on home soil.

Focusing again on Eleri, Donovan rolled her up on one side to check her back. He barked out instructions to GJ. "She was shot. Help me out."

"What?" GJ asked, incredulous.

"When we left. We all got in the water. Eleri stayed and held them back. But eventually she couldn't do it. She turned to dive in and they shot her."

His hands were flying over Eleri's skin, lifting her shirt. . . a shirt with *no holes in it*. Had all the bullets missed her? Was she okay?

His brain raced. Maybe she'd merely sucked in too much water from Neriah dragging her through the ocean? Was Neriah able to hold her breath underwater long enough that she had drowned Eleri in the process?

His fingers worked frantically, checking every bit of her back, her legs, her arms. Then he found what he'd been afraid of.

Three separate, blooming bruises. Small, round, and precise. Even as he cataloged them, he saw that GJ was staring back at him. She didn't need words to ask if this was what she thought it was.

Holy shit. It was. Eleri had been hit.

Donovan didn't have time to contemplate her miraculous

survival from gunshots, because it didn't matter if she didn't start fucking breathing again.

Laying her on her back again, he counted down her ribs by feel and placed his hands in the correct spot, and then started counting again. *One. Two. Three. Four. Five—*

He felt it. The heave of her chest as her body tried to suck in air. Her ribs opened under his hands. "Yes!" he yelled, rapidly turning her on her side to let her vomit up ocean water.

Yes! he thought, watching as Eleri slowly rolled onto her stomach before gingerly crawling to her elbows and knees. Then up to her hands, coughing up water again and again. It was a hard position to be in. Her throat would burn from everything she'd swallowed. Her eyes would blur. But she was *alive.*

Noah was running toward them, his feet pushing through the sand again, as graceful as a Miami resident who surfed and dived regularly. He looked like he fit in with the scenery, though his face was panicked. "The ambulance is on its way."

Donovan was nodding. But it was Eleri who looked up and ground out the words, "Cancel it."

Over her back, Donovan and GJ locked eyes again as if to silently ask "Why?"

With heavy breaths, her muscles obviously working too hard, Eleri flopped over onto her back. Sand covered her skin from where she'd rolled in it as they'd tried to save her, but she didn't seem to care.

"Cancel it," she croaked. "If we go to the hospital, they'll find us. If they find us, they'll kill us."

CHAPTER 74

E leri sat gingerly propped against the headboard of one of the two queen-sized beds in the room. The pillows had been moved around to make her spot comfortable. The blanket had been yanked off and wrapped around her, as though she were a bit of fluff that might drift away if not stuffed into a corner and weighted down.

She wasn't sure she needed all the soft treatment. But Hannah had brought her tea with honey, and that had been wonderful. Still, she'd had to shut Hannah and Jason out so she could talk about NightShade business—about the things the agents were still hiding from the two remaining researchers.

So Eleri sat on the bed, in pajamas made for warm weather and a blanket made for cold, holding court as only one who had been pulled dead from the ocean several hours earlier could. Three agents sat around her in a small semi-circle, anxiously awaiting whatever she might tell them.

Talking hurt, but she had to do it. None of them knew sign language, and her telepathic skills were for crap. At least most of the time.

"We can't go after Miranda Industries," she told them quietly, watching various reactions across three different faces. They ranged from disbelief to blatant relief. "We can't take them down. They're large. They're multinational, and they're running drugs. None of this is under the purview of the Bureau. And we're not even on US soil. There's nothing we can do here."

"We can't alert the police," GJ pointed out. "They're rotten and specifically involved in this particular set-up."

"We need to call Westerfield," Eleri said in agreement. "He'll probably hand it off to the DEA or something. Maybe they'll confiscate the drugs when they come into Florida. But we can't do *anything* with this. We need to get out of Nassau."

Luckily, the other three agreed with that account. And her explanation seemed to sit well, even with Noah and GJ, who had seemed to think they might be able to shut down Miranda Industries on their own.

Eleri was afraid this was going to become a case of someone catching one of the low-level workers and trying to use a small fish as bait for a big fish. That was how most of the drug organization stings that she knew of worked, but she wouldn't be involved. She couldn't watch while the law enforcement officers strategized and the drug trade ran on, wheels turning, drugs funneling into the US while they waited for the kingpin to fall. There was a reason she wasn't in the DEA.

So, right now, there was nothing she could do about it.

It was Donovan who shook his head. He'd seemed relieved not to have to take down Miranda industries, but now he made a valid point. "Miranda Industries is full of *Lobo*mau. How will the DEA handle them?"

"I have no idea," Eleri admitted. "Chances are—if this network is as big as we think it is and if the *Lobo*mau are running it—then it's beyond our scope. It may be beyond theirs. No one has fully taken down any of the big gangs yet. This may be just as big. Add in what the *Lobo*mau can do, and it's a crap shoot if anyone will be able to shut Miranda Industries down.

Regardless, it's not a job for a team of four agents outside of their jurisdiction."

When no one replied, she added, "NightShade might work the *Lobo*mau angle, but it's not going to happen here in Nassau. Not right now." With one arm loosened from her blanket wrap, she gestured, pointing down at the comforter as if to emphasize. "But we do need to find that assassin. He killed Allison, and our job right now is the same as it was before. We have to take him out."

Donovan nodded. "We'll have to report back what we know of Miranda Industries. After that, it's probably up to Westerfield."

Eleri hated to admit that Westerfield made decisions she didn't like. In fact, she hadn't wanted to be on this case at all. Or she had, but only as a friend, as a consultant to Hannah. But *no*. Westerfield had flat-out insisted that she and Donovan work this one. So here she was, on foreign soil with *Lobo*mau *everywhere*.

The four of them mapped out a game plan for how to beat the assassin. First, they'd need to bait him out into the open. Despite many ideas that Eleri was ready to get started on, Donovan insisted they make no moves until tomorrow. "I don't want you taxing yourself."

"I feel fine," she protested, though it was a lie. Her throat scratched with every sound. Her eyes still felt like sandpaper each time she shut them, and her ribs hurt. She thought back to Curie and the last time her ribs had ached so much. Even that had not been this bad. Quietly, she conceded to Donovan's demands to wait.

"Noah, GJ," she said quietly. "Can you give Donovan and me a moment?"

Though the other two looked at her, curious as to why they were getting shuttled from the room, they politely nodded and made themselves scarce.

When the door clicked shut behind them, Donovan's expression changed to one of concern. "What is it, El?" Worry pulled at his features and knotted his brows together.

"I think I figured something out. My powers, my spells? I think I understand now why sometimes they work and sometimes they don't."

"That's good, isn't it?" he asked, his expression still concerned.

"I guess so. But it's all mixed up." Her fingers plucked at the blanket as though the answers might tease free like a thread.

"I don't understand. You were so strong in New Orleans. And then here, you. . . *stuttered*." He'd paused before saying the word, as though trying to find a polite way to say that she seemed to fail more often than succeed. But Eleri nodded. She would never disagree with the truth.

"I stuttered in Curie, too. That's the thing. In New Orleans, it wasn't *me*."

"Of course it was. I saw you."

"The power didn't come from *me*," she clarified. "I directed it, but it wasn't mine. Think about it. We were standing in the middle of Darcelle Dauphine's shop. There may not be a more powerful spot in all of New Orleans!" She threw her hands up in frustration. "The power was already there. All I did was direct it."

"But that wasn't the only time you used it." He still didn't understand.

"No, but we were with Grandmere. Grandmere led those spells, Grandmere supported me. Now that Grandmere is gone —now that we're not in New Orleans anymore—there's nothing out here for me to siphon. It's all *me*. . . and that's not much." She was waving her hands frantically now and she could see Donovan watching as she grew a little more panicked at the idea.

"But you did it," he murmured. "I just watched you. When we

were in the compound. What power could you have siphoned there? It's not a voodoo shop. Grandmere is gone. I saw you, and it was *all you*."

"Yes. That's what I figured out." She took in a breath. She'd been thinking about this.

She'd been stuck, ever since they left New Orleans. She'd been practicing, and she'd become fantastic at parlor tricks, at spells with wine and drops of blood and moonlight. But she hadn't gotten good at the big things she needed to combat the strange and powerful forces they came up against. Her skills were still no match for someone like the assassin.

She tried to explain as best she could. "Grandmere always talked about being *focused*. The books always talked about being *in control*. I always read that as being calm—like being in a meditative state. Honestly, it works. If I do that, I can light a candle. I can make a little wind swirl, although nothing like Noah."

She was waving her hands again. She noticed and consciously put them in her lap, lacing her fingers together in hopes that they wouldn't fly away on their own again. "But the big things—when I need to save us, when I need to protect myself—none of it comes to me that way."

She took a breath and tried again. "I was trying to put all my FBI skills to work—how we're trained to lower our heartbeat and slow our breathing, to focus on one thing. But that doesn't help me with my powers. They only work when I let go. When I'm mad or scared or... crazy."

Donovan was nodding along, as though what she said made perfect sense. And she could only hope that it did, that he wasn't just placating her.

"But that's good," he offered. "Now you know how to do it. You know how to turn it on."

"But that's the problem!" Eleri protested. "If I'm *on*, I'm out of control. I almost killed the police chief back there. You know I killed a child before." Her brain tried to flash back to a dark moment in a stairwell, but she shut it down before it could take hold. She watched as Donovan solemnly nodded, finally understanding. "I don't know if it's *okay* to let go. Because. . . listen to me, Donovan. I don't know what I *can* do. And I don't know what I *will* do."

CHAPTER 75

"Are we good?" Noah leaned over and asked Donovan. Donovan stuck one paw onto Noah's foot, then twisted in the small space. The yellow polyester jacket he was wearing read "Service Dog," and it was hot and irritating. But he sat in the van like a very large *good boy* beside Noah.

The other agent occasionally reached out and touched Donovan on the head—a predetermined gesture meant to reassure the people around them and add to the ruse. They didn't have him on a leash—thank God—and the *service dog* vest had let them get away with it. Noah's dark glasses and claim of poor vision had gotten them on the local bus together.

They'd been out touring today, being obvious, walking up the slanted streets and stopping in shops. They ate, sitting at the sidewalk cafe tables in full view of every possible *Lobo*mau or Miranda Industries employee who might be walking by.

Noah hand-fed Donovan table scraps. It was demeaning at best, but it beat the alternative. Donovan hadn't wanted Eleri out and walking around alone today. He certainly hadn't wanted *her* posing as the bait.

It hadn't even been twenty-four hours since she'd been *dead*, he reminded himself.

He would have had her recuperate for at least three days. But if they waited, their assassin might leave Nassau, and then what would they do? How would they find him?

At least right now, they were all basically corralled on the tiny island. Although this plan didn't seem to be working.

It had been three hours so far that he and Noah had walked on the streets in town, hitting up the tourist shops. As Donovan waited outside, Noah went in and sampled the chocolate or bought rum cake or a t-shirt. Each time he disappeared inside for just for a moment—enough to look normal, but not enough to get separated.

When that had failed—no *Lobo*mau had showed up within sniffing distance and they had no obvious tail following them—they'd hopped onto this tourist bus. Noah paid his fee and put Donovan in the cramped aisle beside him in the large van.

The white van wound its way up hill as the driver both steered the wheel and talked into a crackling PA system that was unnecessary in a single van. Cars lined the street, parked so close on either side that Donovan was shocked he couldn't hear the scraping noises as they went by. Lush trees with small, pink flowers hung over brick walls that were older than anything he'd seen in the US. The fauna created a rich, heady smell each time Donovan breathed in. It was much better than the smell of the tourists on the van—not one of which was their target.

At last, the van pulled into a roundabout. The driver announced their destination in a quick staccato. Clearly, it was a speech he'd given a thousand times before, and he cared only that he got credit for repeating it, not whether it was understood.

Looking down at Donovan, Noah nodded once, sharply. "Ready?"

He couldn't really nod in return; it would look wrong. So he tipped his head at Noah and, as the door opened, jumped down to the hot pavement.

They'd arrived at the Queen's Staircase, but both he and Noah walked away, though the bus driver was saying he would pick up everyone on the bus at the other side. Not Donovan and Noah. They weren't here for the sights or the ride around town. Their job was to be seen.

They climbed the nearby hill and stopped in the grass for a moment, standing under a tree as Donovan surveyed those around him. They were hoping to catch the eye of the assassin, and Donovan was keeping his nose up for wolves. Despite the disturbing abundance of *Lobo*mau on the island, he didn't detect a single one.

"Got anything?" Noah asked in what was becoming his usual, one-sided conversation. He was no Eleri, but he was a decent handler.

Donovan set his paw on the top of Noah's sneaker. Once for Yes. Twice for No. He tapped it again and Noah nodded. Looking out over a crowd that wasn't as dense as the cars around would lead him to believe, Donovan listened as Noah tried a last-ditch effort. If this didn't work, they'd have to try again later.

"Let's go on up the steps. Maybe someone will be here. Though I don't know why."

It was crowded, Donovan thought. If the *Lobo*mau were looking for places to hand off drugs, this might be it. If they were looking to avoid local entanglement where they ran their largest operation. . . well, this day would be a bust. He and Noah only needed one Miranda employee to find them and report in, but so far, it wasn't working.

As they entered the carved stone area known as The Queen's Staircase, the walls rose up on either side, gentling much of the cacophony nearby. Mossy and carved from the naturally occurring granite, the structure tugged at Donovan's attention.

He wished he was in human form, so he could reach up and trace the cracks, as many of the tourists did.

He'd traveled more in his first six months with the FBI than in most of the rest of his life. . . or he should say he'd traveled *well*. As a kid, he'd moved from one hovel to another broken-down apartment and from one washed-up town to another. Now he wished he was a tourist.

But that wasn't why he was here. He added this spot to his growing mental list of places he'd like to visit some day with no agenda, and he turned around the lower area at the bottom of the steps, taking in a full, three-sixty view.

A waterfall shot spray into the air, sending a clean, green scent through everything in the enclosed space. Between the mist and the rock, it almost felt cooler on the hot summer day, and he could see and sense the awe in the tourists as he looked at and sniffed each one. But no one here was the man he was looking for.

"Climb the steps?" Noah asked him. But Donovan rubbed against his fellow agent's leg three times before Noah got the hint and pulled off the disturbing yellow, almost plasticky vest. He folded it and stuck it in his back pocket. Maybe they wouldn't need it again.

Then, following small clusters of tourists, they blended into the crowd. Some groups climbed slowly, huddling around members who seemed to not be physically quite fit enough for the task but were mentally determined. Others ran the steps as though it were a fitness challenge rather than an engineering marvel. Noah and Donovan took the stairs at a soft jog.

The corridor—despite the infestation of people—radiated history through years of rock. In the middle was a flat area where climbers could rest. The two stopped for a vantage point, scanning both up and down the steps, examining every individual in the crowd.

They were just about to head up the second stage when

Donovan smelled it. Noah was starting to take the first steps, but Donovan bumped at him, his paw coming down on Noah's foot. Hard. Just once for Yes.

They were here.

As both of them paused now, he sniffed at the air, slowly turning one way and then another. He tried to act as though no one were watching him, as though he were just a large dog along for the day. But then he smelled another. . . and another. He reminded himself that they had agreed to this plan. They would find whoever was following them, catch their eye, and then lead them to where Eleri and GJ waited.

But, as Donovan sniffed the air again, he realized they'd screwed up. There were too many. They weren't supposed to attack here—not with all the tourists around. He and Noah had wanted to draw the attention of the assassin, but this wasn't him. This was the pack closing in; the scent of wolf became stronger as more and more *Lobo*mau appeared on the steps above him.

Looking down behind him, he spotted a cluster of three men coming up the stairs, managing to look like casual observers. Though they were in human form, Donovan saw that they were *Lobo*mau.

Four more were now partway down the long staircase, heading right toward them. He moved his paw to Noah's foot again and this time pressed down hard.

They were closing in fast, *too fast*.

The nudge to his shoulder tipped him off his feet for a moment, turning his wariness to sharp alert. But as he looked to find the culprit, he saw that no one was even close to him. The crowed had thinned out, leaving Noah and Donovan exposed and almost alone on the landing.

As he watched, Noah rocked backward as though hit and might have stumbled further back had Donovan not already been standing on his foot.

They had done it. They had found the assassin.

But Donovan couldn't see him and—never having met the man before—he couldn't smell him, either. Another nudge—this one harder—threatened to make him stumble.

He took a few steps backward, trying to balance and remain upright, until his foot slipped off the edge of the step and he struggled to keep from falling down the long staircase.

CHAPTER 76

G J rushed up the hill as fast as her legs could carry her. Fighting the heat and high humidity of the air, she pushed herself to her limit. She wasn't getting enough oxygen, but it didn't matter. She had to get there.

In her ear, Eleri yelled, "*Go go go!*" But she couldn't see her boss.

Eleri was coming from the other side, and GJ hoped Eleri's health was holding up. They shouldn't be taxing her this way, but all four had agreed there was no other option.

"I can't see anything. I don't know what they look like." GJ tried not to breathe the words heavily and to not look like she was talking to herself. Tourists pressed in on each side, spending the day checking out the sights or being lazy in the heat, while GJ was fighting for survival among them. So she was holding the phone to her ear, despite the fact that she had an earpiece, just so she didn't look crazy.

"They're there," Eleri repeated her worst fears.

"I know." GJ didn't doubt what Eleri knew.

The two of them had been waiting down an alleyway, away from the tourist locations. It should have allowed them to ambush the assassin as he trailed Donovan and Noah, who'd put themselves out as bait. But, of course, it hadn't happened that way.

She and Eleri had been standing around the corner, waiting for their fellow agents to say they'd caught sight of someone and were leading them back, when Eleri had frozen. As GJ had watched, her senior agent's chin lifted up as though something in the clouds might tell her an answer. Her hand had reached out, clutching at GJ hard enough to make GJ wish to break the hold. But Eleri only said, "We have to go now. They aren't coming here. They're in danger."

Though she'd said those words calmly, nothing had been calm since. They'd run out of the alley, unprepared to move their fight. Frantically, they'd managed to hail a cab. They were still too far away. . . only a few blocks, but too far to be useful when their partners were in danger.

It had been a stupid plan, GJ thought now. They'd been counting on an assassin and a handful of *Lobo*mau to make a reasonable decision—to not want a fight in a public place. Apparently, none of their opponents agreed with that idea.

Eleri asked their driver to let her out at one entrance of the Queens Staircase and insisted GJ ride around to the other side. GJ didn't ask questions, but when the car stopped, she jumped out and ran.

Now she was trying to reach the top entrance of the tourist attraction, because Noah and Donovan were inside.

"Noah? *Noah!*" she said, still holding the phone up as though she might cover her frantic attempts at communication.

In her ear, his voice came back, soft. "We're surrounded."

"I know." She breathed out the relief that they were okay, if only for now. "We're here. I'm at the top of the stairs."

"Bottom of the stairs," Eleri chimed in as GJ crested the hill, stepping onto the stone walkway and moving forward. At the last minute, she stopped and peered down the steps.

NIGHTSHADE FORENSIC FBI FILES: DEAD TIDE

It was crowded enough that it took her a moment to locate Noah and, by his side, Donovan. They were standing on the landing, plastered against the stone wall. Noah held onto a handful of Donovan's scruff, though it was unclear whether that was for his sake or for Donovan's.

"We were pushed," Noah said. GJ watched his mouth move almost imperceptibly as she heard the words in her earpiece. "He almost sent Donovan down the steps."

He's here.

It wasn't just the wolves.

GJ lifted her gaze then. She'd easily found Noah and Donovan in the crowd, but the assassin? She didn't know what he looked like. She had no description other than "male, fit, between twenty and fifty." That described almost a third of the people here.

Her eyes darted back and forth, scanning the field for anyone who might be her target. She'd seen the video of him wearing full diving gear, but she'd not encountered him. Eleri, Jason, and Hannah had fought him underwater, but even they couldn't recall solid identifying characteristics. Neither of the researchers had been able to produce a sketch.

So here she was, attempting to draw out and conquer an enemy none of them could identify.

"Eleri?" GJ asked into the open air, finally pushing the phone down into her back pocket. She needed to leave her hands free, just in case. She had her gun holstered at her waist and tucked under her shirt, but in this crowd, she shouldn't even reach for it. She couldn't just yell "FBI!" and show her badge here, although she decided she might do it anyway.

"I don't see him yet," Eleri replied, her voice laced with a note that indicated she was beginning to panic.

Eleri panicking? That almost made GJ lose her own shit. Why was Eleri so keyed up? If Eleri was afraid, GJ should be doubly so. She scanned every face again, hoping against reason to find *something*.

"*Noah?*" she barked, drawing attention from a passerby, but she didn't care.

His voice came across the line. "I felt him push me, but I can't identify him." From her vantage point at the top, she watched Noah, who stayed plastered to the wall, turning his head as he, too, tried to find the killer.

Crap, GJ swore in her own head, her eyes rapidly scanning the area. Now she was simply looking for anyone with suspicious behavior. But her brain filtered back to the video and mentally, she replayed it. She watched again as he killed Allison. Her memory fantastic for the details of things seen. In her mind, she saw him making the stabbing motions with the knife. She watched again as Allison—underwater and just a few yards away from him—began to bleed.

"He can't just do it!" she stuttered the words into the air in front of her, knowing the others would hear. "It's not just in his mind. He has to perform some kind of corresponding motion! Look for someone who makes a move at the right time if you take another hit."

She paused then, and when no one replied, she barked out, "Got it?"

"Looking!" came back to her in Eleri's voice. Noah's "Yes" was close behind, and GJ turned her gaze not to faces but to hands, to anyone in motion, anything timed correctly.

When the next motion she saw was Donovan stumbling slightly, her instinct was to watch him and be certain that Noah caught him. Instead, she forced her eyes to the top of the stone wall. A few tourists stood looking over the crowd, but this time, one stood separately, his hand having waved in time to Donovan's sudden bump.

"Got him!" Eleri said just before GJ managed to get the words out.

But then GJ was bumped from behind.

Thinking it was their assassin again, she looked up—but it wasn't him. Instead, it was a large brown wolf passing by. The one that nudged her out of the way was followed quickly by another, and then another.

There were already *Lobo*mau on the stairs in human form. They already flanked Donovan and Noah on either side. And now they came as wolves.

Holy shit.

Eleri's voice crackled through the earpiece. "They're going to do this in public."

"Then we have to, too," GJ replied. They couldn't just let the *Lobo*mau and the assassin kill Noah and Donovan or make an attempt at all four of them. The only option was to fight back. The assassin had already started it, trying to send Donovan down the steps.

GJ's heartrate kicked up a notch. She watched as the three wolves carefully picked their way down to the landing where Noah and Donovan seemed impossibly pinned. She was about to open her mouth to ask them what they needed but, at the bottom of the steps, a movement caught her eye.

Eleri stumbled backwards and slammed against the wall.

Then—as GJ watched—she disappeared entirely.

CHAPTER 77

E leri felt her head smack the wall, the sharp pain radiating outward and then down her spine. She'd been shoved, and it hadn't been one of the tourists.

She didn't reach up to feel the back of her head, but she did let out a swear word on a scream borne of anger.

The tourists hovering around her had not seen her hit the wall, but they were offended by her high-volume cursing and moved rapidly out of her way. Her eyes darted up to the top of the ledge and immediately focused on the man standing there, solemnly looking down at her.

In a split-second decision—one born of what she had already figured out—Eleri let go. Staying calm wouldn't help. Lowering her heart rate or her breathing didn't help. Reaching for her weapon or flashing her badge, and everything else she'd been taught, was useless against this threat. So this time, she didn't scream. She let every feeling build up inside her.

She knew this man was trying to kill her, and not for the first time. To make all of it worse, this time, he was also after Donovan, Noah, and GJ. Her entire team was at risk. Eleri was done using calm, measured reactions.

Holding in the scream that wanted to escape, she vibrated with the tension and felt herself hit a new level. Eleri stalked forward into a group of tourists who didn't get out of her way at all.

"Move," she told them. "Move. *Move!*" Her voice was heavier with each angry chant of the word. Many turned, looking confused, and only stepped away when she pushed them.

"*Move!*" she yelled, pushing her arms forward and shoving the tourists to the side. But the people she didn't touch didn't move.

The realization was stunning. They *couldn't see her.*

What the hell had she done?

People suddenly began jumping out of her way, as though they were startled to see the woman in their midst spoiling for a fight—hopefully not with any of them. It seemed that—for a moment—she had blinked back into their existence. The whole crowd had frowned into the angry, empty space, but then suddenly jumped back as if she had appeared out of nowhere.

Even as she thought it, a hard hit crashed into her left shoulder. It was enough to make her stumble roughly to the side. She couldn't right herself before knocking into several of the surrounding tourists, who once again quickly got out of her way. She was trouble, and now they saw it. But the trouble wasn't hers, it was *his.*

Fuck him, she thought, turning to where she could crane her neck and see him at the top of the wall. She clenched her fists and tried it again, letting her rage take the lead. Again, she vibrated faster and faster until she could tell she shifted.

This time, the people around her started to look frantic and ask each other, "Where did she go? What happened?"

She yelled again. "Move! Clear the staircase!" because she was going to topple this guy down the steps, just like he'd intended to do to Donovan. Raising her hands upwards toward him and wondering if he could see her, she chanted a string of nonsensical words that seemed to fall naturally off her tongue.

Eleri spoke through the entire rhythm once, twice. At the end of the third repetition, she let out a primal scream.

The crowd around her parted, finally doing what she'd ordered.

But she only caught that movement in the periphery of her vision. As she watched, the man at the top of the wall lifted off his feet and blew backwards as though he'd taken an explosion head on.

But Eleri wasn't done.

With a sweep of her arm, she bowled down the tourists who hadn't yet moved and then turned and yelled, "Clear the fucking staircase!"

With screams and frantic gestures, they stumbled over each other in their haste to get away. The ones that Eleri had swept to the ground were the slowest to move now, though some of the tourists stopped and helped each other. Slowly, the staircase began to empty, even as people yelled and motioned to others at the top, telling them to run.

Then Eleri was climbing the steps, the heady loam of wet rock, old lichen, and clear water filling her senses and fueling her anger. Heading toward Donovan, where he and Noah were still plastered against the wall in defense, she took each step in a rage. Her agents were surrounded by wolves closing in from both up the staircase and down. Three muscular men held the landing with them, staring Noah and Donovan down.

Eleri stalked forward, up the long stone steps, calling out to the *Lobo*mau who were pinning her friends down. "You will leave if you know what's good for you."

They glanced down the staircase but paid no attention. One continued to look, but his gaze went right past her.

Crap. They couldn't see her. Using the invisibility to her advantage, she began to run. She didn't feel the burn in her thighs. She didn't even feel the stone under her feet as she nearly flew up the steps.

The ones in human shape might be the most dangerous, she told herself. The wolves at least couldn't fire guns or wield knives. So she rocketed directly into the three standing men, knocking them down and watching as one cracked his head on the nearest stair.

He immediately went limp.

Eleri ignored him. She didn't care and she still had two more to contend with, so she swept her arm wide, knocking them back. Did she contact them physically? She didn't know, because she couldn't feel anything—no pain, no contact, nothing but the rage.

The men looked around frantically for their attacker, but still couldn't locate her.

Good. She swept her other arm out to hit them again, but this time, nothing happened. It was Eleri who felt a broad punch to her chest, as though someone had hit her internal organs directly. Flying backward, she smacked the wall next to where Donovan stood. Then, as gravity took over, she slid downward, the sole of her shoe slipping off the edge of the top step as she began tumbling down the steep staircase.

She must have become visible then, because Donovan turned sharply to look at her and barked once. Noah yelled out, *"Eleri!"* A question was somehow embedded into her name.

There was nothing they could do.

She was falling. For all the times the assassin had tried to send Donovan down the staircase and hadn't succeeded, he'd managed it with Eleri. The edges of the ancient steps hit her across the back and punched at her ribs. She felt the stone smacking into her upper arm, the pain of the hit making her afraid the bone was broken. Her legs and feet flew up and over her head and she tumbled downward, finding no purchase and twisting her neck sideways.

But at some point during the rolling tumble, she found her anger again, and she roared. Managing to plant her feet on the next step, she smacked her hands down firmly onto the stone, stopping her downward motion. Now on all fours and lifting her head like a rabid animal, she yelled out.

The assassin had flipped over the wall, parkour style, and hung off the edge. In a smooth motion, he let go and jumped down toward the landing, where Donovan and Noah stood as the wolves circled. It was an inhuman feat. Had he created a landing pad for himself? She didn't know, but he'd settled, landing easily upright, looking uninjured from a fall of several stories.

Leaving Noah and Donovan to the remaining assailants, he turned toward Eleri.

She couldn't hear the individual thoughts in his head, but he was easy enough to read. The assignment he'd been given today was to kill them all. He was after her first, but his plan—as soon as he finished her off—was to take out Donovan and Noah as well.

Eleri thought that GJ was at the top of the steps and clenched the idea firmly in her own grasp. She didn't know what other talents this man might have, but she would not tip him off. So she held tight to the understanding that there was a fourth agent on the steps as her head snapped up to meet his eyes.

Step by step, hand over hand, she began to haul herself back up the steps like a rabid animal, screaming at him as she went.

CHAPTER 78

D onovan growled low in his throat as he tried to face the attackers closing in from each side. The ones up the staircase had a decided advantage, but Donovan was not going to strike first. Strategically, it wasn't in his favor.

A man he didn't recognize—but he only recognized two of the wolves from the compound—had dropped easily to his feet, right in front of where Donovan and Noah stood on the landing of the Queen's Staircase. Though the man had waved his hand at them, as though to throw them backwards or hit them or something, whatever force he wielded hadn't reached them.

Standing tense but quiet beside him, Noah created another wind barrier. He'd initially pulled his gun to defend them, but he'd only held onto it for a moment before it was zipped out of his hand by a force neither of them saw. The weapon went clattering down the steps, lost among the pounding feet of a crowd of tourists suddenly retreating. Apparently, he'd also been trying to talk or communicate with the wolves but, like Donovan, they weren't actually animals. They easily shook off any control Noah might have exerted.

Unable to communicate with his fellow agent, it was

difficult to form an actual plan of attack. He'd watched as the assassin headed down the stairs, toward where Donovan had last seen Eleri. He considered running down to help her, but he didn't know where she was. She'd disappeared again. He couldn't tell if that was his own inability to keep track of her or if she'd actually winked out of existence. But he didn't have time to figure it out. He had wolves flanking him on every side.

Two of the *Lobo*mau who'd shown up in human form had managed to regain their feet from where Eleri had laid them out. The third lay dead, his head still propped awkwardly against the step, a puddle of blood forming beneath it.

Even without the one who was either dead or out cold, Donovan knew he and Noah were still at a huge disadvantage here—not only numerically, but strategically. Donovan knew how to fight a human. A human didn't see him coming. But aside from Noah, everyone here was like him. How could he fight someone who knew every advantage before he used it?

Ignoring their fallen friend, the two men stepped closer. Though Noah managed to maintain a small storm of twigs and leaves around them, the others pushed through, marching forward despite the small projectiles hitting with every step they took.

One of them flicked his right hand, and a knife suddenly came into view. And that was it. No more standoff. Noah dove forward, having the advantage of FBI training. Most attackers did not expect their victim to rush *toward* the knife, so that was exactly what Noah did. Ducking his shoulder and coming up under the arm holding the blade, he formed his hands into a V and shoved the knife over his head. With his other hand, he grabbed the *Lobo*mau's wrist and squeezed until he wrenched the knife free.

Donovan barely saw any of this, as the second man rushed at him. But the signal had already been given, and the wolves closed in from either side.

He didn't see it coming, but he felt the bite on his flank. Turning sharply at the pain, he clamped his own teeth on the neck of the other wolf. He saw the advantage he had here. The wolf that bit him had come up the stairs, and that meant Donovan could push him back down.

Shaking his head hard, he yanked the other dog off his feet. Getting a bite on the neck meant control, and Donovan used every bit of it. He ignored the pain in his back leg as the jaws bit down harder, and he shook and shook until the wolf let go and stumbled.

His back paw was only inches from the edge of the landing, and Donovan shoved him. Hard.

He had a brief moment to watch as the creature tumbled down several steps. But there wasn't time to see whether the fall was completed or if it had had the desired effect. Donovan already felt another wound in his side, a stabbing sensation. Another knife had entered the fight, though he couldn't tell from where. Donovan didn't have hands to come up under the knife the way Noah did.

Human predator, he thought as he felt the knife slide, white-hot, out of his side. Quickly, he calculated which vital organs it might have hit and whether the cut was deep enough to do real damage.

Not too serious. So he lunged.

With a snap of his heavy jaws, he bit down on the forearm of the hand that held the knife. Tugging the man along with him, he used his mass to propel them both forward.

Donovan yanked and shook his head, once again going for control. When he stood on his hind legs and punched all his weight forward into the other man—still holding the arm in his teeth—he managed to take his newest assailant down.

The knife stayed clasped firmly in the assailant's grip, which made Donovan push and pull more carefully, but he managed to get the man's arm wrapped almost around his own throat and held tight. Donovan kept his jaws clamped and stood over the man who was now face-up, lying on the stone floor of the landing.

But what could he do now?

Not quite ready to lunge and rip out a throat, he bit harder until he heard the bone snap. His sensitive ears picked up Noah's threats to the man he held. It seemed Noah was trying to offer up an arrest.

The rights embedded in the warning didn't exist here, and an arrest was not the right move. Donovan would have growled at him if he didn't hold an arm in his own mouth. If he'd been in human form, he would have yelled at Noah, "Stab him, for fuck's sake!" But none of that was an option.

Donovan bit harder into the arm, even as he was jostled from several sides at once. He would be going down any second now. There were too many of them.

He had only this one under control, and the biggest advantage the attackers had was that they didn't care about each other. They'd left the one bleeding from a head wound, lying on the steps and hadn't even moved him out of the way. No one had tried to help or even checked if he was still alive.

Donovan could rip this man's throat out with his teeth, and the others would keep coming. They wouldn't be angry because their colleague had been killed; they wouldn't even be upset. They would merely be neutral, still coming at him, following through on their assignment, which was to kill him.

He yanked at the arm he held while, in his mind, he saw flashbacks of his father. Even the slightest negative, or sometimes just a *perceived* wrong, could set Aiden Heath off. His face would twist, his hands and fingers curling into claws and paws. And he would do damage to everything and everyone around him, unconcerned with the effects.

Though Donovan had never seen his father kill anyone—not that he was able to remember—he was confident his father was responsible for more than one murder. He'd hoped to never become the same. Yet right now, he was ripping at a man's arm, gnashing his teeth and pulling, hoping to cause maximum damage.

He had to keep this assailant from getting back up, because another set of teeth sank into his flank. The hot pain was his third wound, but the fourth came in rapid succession, as more teeth tore into his shoulder.

So he ignored his own pain and yanked the arm, pulling it out of its socket, which was accompanied by a disturbingly satisfying scream from the man. Then Donovan had to back off. He had to turn and growl and gnash at his new attackers, burying his fangs into anything that would cause pain or damage.

Noah had finally given up on his arrest attempt and stabbed the man he was holding. Donovan felt the teeth release from his shoulder as Noah at last turned and plunged the knife in between the shoulder blades of the attacking wolf. He didn't know if Noah understood *what* their assailants were, or if he had somehow talked himself into the easier belief that this was merely a rogue pack of large dogs. Either way, he fought them, finally ready to maim if not kill.

One down, five to go.

Donovan turned sharply, burying his fangs into the throat of a *Lobo*mau that had found a good angle and lunged hard at him. There was no room for mercy. They were at *kill or be killed.*

Donovan was not ready to be killed. Not here. Not today.

He heard and felt the deep warning growl that came from his own throat as the other dog tried again to leap for him. Donovan countered, but suddenly pulled up short, having heard a bullet rip through the air.

CHAPTER 79

G J pulled the trigger, her heart pounding up into her throat. She had to hit the *Lobo*mau, and *not* Donovan.

Luckily, Donovan was nearly black. These dogs were gray, brown, white, and one almost blonde, a color distinction that might have saved her partner's life. But even though there was a color code, they were fighting in a pile: Donovan and Noah and more dogs than FBI agents.

For a moment, she consoled herself that, statistically, if she hit something, she was less likely to hit one of her own. But the numbers weren't enough. She'd never forgive herself if she killed Donovan or even Noah accidentally. So she stopped everything, slowed her breathing, and lined up the sights, just as Walter had taught her.

She remembered now that she'd been pissy at the time. Her Quantico partner had dragged her onto the shooting range, again and again, drilling her on weapons and shots even harder than the FBI trainers had. But right at this moment, GJ was grateful.

As she watched, one of the *Lobo*mau in wolf form twitched and fell onto his side. *Yes! A clean hit.*

Planting herself halfway down the steps, GJ hoped she could set her feet steady and aim. She needed to not get pulled into the fight, but still stay close enough to see exactly who her target was.

There was no time for congratulations on the one she'd taken out. Donovan had already turned and gone for the throat of another. Noah was now wielding the knife and had stabbed one between the shoulder blades. But it hadn't fallen. GJ took aim for it.

Crap! She had to wait as Noah repeatedly pushed his way into her target area. She couldn't do it. She couldn't risk injuring her fellow agent.

Even with her and her gun, they were outnumbered.

Unable to get a clean shot on her first target, she turned and aimed for one who had hung back more on the periphery. He hadn't thrust himself into the fight with quite as much gusto as the others, and she wished she could have let him live. But their survival was no longer an option.

Taking a breath, she held it and waited a heartbeat, then pulled the trigger and watched as the wolf fell. *Yes,* she thought again, and took two more steps down.

Noah continued to fight the one wolf, stabbing him repeatedly, though the creature fought back, refusing to go down. The knife itself was short and stubby, which made it easily concealed but not quite as useful as it might have been for the endeavor.

Quickly counting, GJ found five wolves left that weren't Donovan, and they were all tangled up in the fight. One was getting stabbed by Noah. One was attacking Noah on his shoulder, trying to take control of the hand that wielded the knife. But Noah quickly switched hands and worked to shrug the other off, all while making forceful swipes with the blade at the first. She couldn't aim for them from back here. The three others were all attacking Donovan simultaneously.

GJ had taken out the only one that wasn't part of the fray, and she couldn't get clear shots on the remaining fighters. She headed down closer, wishing that she, too, had a knife. But she didn't.

She had her fists and her feet, and she had the gun. Everything else was useless.

She stepped up close enough to one of the *Lobo*mau attacking Donovan to get his attention by kicking him. Waiting until he turned toward her, she stepped sharply to the side, to make sure her bullet didn't go through him and into Donovan or Noah, and she pulled the trigger. He didn't quite go down. It wasn't as clean a shot as the last one. So she pulled the trigger again and watched him fall.

Turning, she tried the move a second time. Kick a wolf, get his attention, pull the trigger. But this time when she kicked, the wolf didn't let go of Donovan. In fact, he didn't seem to even feel her hard punt to his ribs. As she moved around to aim in a better direction, she felt the stone floor suddenly shake beneath her feet.

Her head snapped up as all of them froze for just a moment.

This was a staircase that had been carved into embedded stone by an ancient army. Nothing should have been able to move it except an earthquake. Something told GJ that wasn't what had happened, though. She looked down the staircase to see Eleri suddenly blinking into existence.

GJ wanted to shake her head, to not believe what she'd just seen. Eleri had several odd talents, but blinking in and out of existence? There was no time to contemplate it as the wolf she'd kicked rounded on her. She kicked him again, unable to fully take her eyes from Eleri, who was shaking the earth beneath them.

The assassin was laid out on the stairs. Eleri straddled him, punching him repeatedly. It was the force of her hits shaking the rock and almost knocking GJ off her feet.

CHAPTER 80

E leri felt it—the pure joy of winning. Her fists plowed into
the beast's face again and again. She knew how to throw a
punch; she'd been trained by the best. This man, who'd been
trying to kill her and people she cared about, was now laid out
against the stairs.

He was paying with every hit. He paid for Allison. He paid
for the attacks on Hannah. And Jason. And herself.

Though he'd initially fought back and tried to push her off—
both physically and with whatever force he wielded—the
assassin had failed. Eleri was stronger. He had an assignment,
but she had rage. For a moment, she had felt the same reflected
back from him.

In the beginning, maybe he'd thought of her merely as a job.
Now that she had refused to be killed easily, now that she was
fighting back, he was mad, too. She could feel all of it. Suddenly,
it was no longer about completing the task; Eleri had turned his
work into survival.

And she was winning.

She had no knives, only her fists and her forces. But she'd
damaged most of his face to the point where it was now difficult

for him to breathe or think. She aimed for the rib cage, making it hard for him to gulp air, let alone inhale properly. Now that he was starting to go limp, she reached for his throat. She didn't even do it with her bare hands—that would be too crass.

Straddling his limp form, she pulled her cupped hands in front of her, making the squeezing motion almost a full foot away from his actual throat. It was satisfying to watch the bruises form on his neck as she clamped down on his airway, tighter and tighter.

It took longer to strangle someone than most people thought. On TV and in movies, the attacker pressed in for a few moments, the victim struggled briefly and then went limp. But in reality, it took much longer, sometimes five or six minutes. Fighting had brought on an adrenaline high that made it seem to drag on even longer.

She felt his movement, even though she wasn't touching him as he began to struggle underneath the onslaught. His conscious brain might have lied when he was getting punched. It might have told him that he could take the hits now and rally later. But now his oxygen was disappearing. This wasn't *damage*, it was *death*. And he was beginning to fight back.

With a roar, she let go of one hand, even knowing that he would suck in air as soon as she released him. Using her change in position and his attempt to rush her, Eleri slammed him backward again into the steps. She could almost hear his skull crack against the edge. Then she calmly resumed her grip on his throat.

Three. Two. . . she counted down until it was over.

She had almost won this damn fight. While she almost smiled to herself, she missed his move.

His hands pushed between hers, muscular arms shooting his fists upward, breaking her grasp in a classic escape move. Even though her hands weren't literally around his throat, the move worked. With her hands thrown wide and his ability to suck in air restored, he punched the heels of his hands at her shoulders —though whether he did this with his hands or his powers, she didn't quite know. Either way, she was tumbling backwards down the steps again.

With a scream and a motion to duck her head beneath her arms, she did the best she could to protect her body from the sharp stone edges. Although worn from centuries of feet from armies and tourists, the steps were still hard and painful, each hit radiating through her bones.

For a moment, she could see them all—the others who had died here, the ones she was about to join. But once again, Eleri felt something burst up from the center of herself. With a primal scream, she rolled over, knowing where and how to plant her feet to stop her downward roll. She pounded the side of her fist into the stone several steps above where her feet had landed and lifted her head. She was ready to lunge back into the job that had suddenly become a fight again.

As her eyes opened to everything around her, her brain registered details. Donovan had taken bites and had been stabbed more than once. Noah was injured as well. GJ was shooting at the wolves up on the landing. But Eleri. . . Eleri had the assassin to herself.

When she looked up at him, she saw he was only focused on her.

He was wearing shorts and a T shirt—much like her, apparently trying to blend in with the tourists, all of whom had fled the staircase. Now he swaggered down the steps as best he could, bruised and bloody. She smiled to herself. Surely more would bloom if he lived.

He wouldn't live.

Eleri would make sure of it.

He walked toward her more confidently and easily than he should have been able to, striding downward almost as though he had no other cares in the world.

How could he be so calm?

His sheer disregard for everything he had done, and everything he was still trying to do, only made Eleri angrier. Now she was struck for the first time with a reality she'd been pushing aside since the first news of this case had come.

Allison was *dead*. Her old friend would *never* return. Never swim again. Never send another picture or letter about where she and Hannah had popped up. Most recently, Allison had been doing good work. She'd seen a threat and faced it, unafraid —and she paid the ultimate price for it. Hannah, who had loved Allison unflinchingly for years, was now facing the remainder of her life without her partner.

To top it off, this asshole was trying to kill Donovan and GJ.

He was two steps away when she found her center. With a scream and a strength that she didn't know she possessed, she punched right through the center of his rib cage.

CHAPTER 81

G J's head snapped up. The scream had been Eleri's—or at least, that had been her initial impression. But she couldn't quite place where it came from.

Eleri had disappeared again.

Below her on the staircase, the assassin stood upright, looking like a battered tourist who had taken a wrong turn into gang territory. He swayed on his feet—left, right—and then when his head tipped forward, his whole body followed and he tumbled down the steps, far too limp to be alive.

Eleri did it! GJ thought, but still the fight in front of her raged on. She hardly had time to celebrate when Donovan was still getting bitten and Noah was being stabbed yet again. She tried to pick whoever was in the most danger, and she chose Donovan, not certain if she'd made a statistical choice or a biased one.

"Donovan!" she yelled and watched as his eyes darted toward her. Waving her gun until he caught on, she lowered and aimed again. Donovan grabbed his opponent by the throat and, dragging himself out of the way, gave her a clear shot.

Though she'd done everything right earlier, she knew she had failed to focus on much of what Walter had taught her. This time, GJ's deep breath was short and shallow as she pulled the trigger three times in rapid succession. As the *Lobo*mau who had been biting Donovan twitched and fell, another bit hard into his flank. Instead of turning to face the new attacker, Donovan pulled away, stretching them out, so he was clear of the other. GJ did it again. Sucked in breath, and... *blam blam, blam.*

The jaws on his thigh released as the eyes rolled and blood bloomed through the pale fur. GJ realized she had not only lost Walter's training, she'd lost all sense of compassion for the living creatures she was killing one by one.

Turning next to Noah, her brain sorted through too many things at once. Noah had a knife and he'd managed to stab someone with it. He'd stabbed a fully grown naked man who had somehow found another knife—maybe pulled it off of a dead comrade—and was busy trying to slash Noah to shreds. Noah had stayed true to his training, blocking and countering, fighting like he knew what he was doing. While that minimized his damage and kept him from getting killed, he was still taking hits and getting cut.

In a flash, things crystallized for GJ. She had always considered herself an advocate for justice and for history. As the granddaughter of a famous anthropologist and archeologist, she had dug up soldiers and victims alike. Now it occurred to her that she was creating them.

"Noah!" she yelled out. There was no more time here to contemplate her life choices.

He didn't look up. Donovan, now clear of his own attackers, had jumped into the fray. Chomping hard onto the man's ankle, he yanked the attacker backward, once again stretching him out and making him into a clean target. It took Noah three tries to pull himself out of the way of GJ's bullets, but when she fired, it was quick and clean.

There was only one assailant left when she heard the feet rushing past her. She was about to pull the trigger. But she couldn't—not when she had no idea what was coming, only that *something* was. Her eyes darted down the steps to where the assassin lay face down, his body at an angle, one arm loose, the other yanked up behind him in an inhuman position. *It wasn't him.*

But *something* bumped into her with what felt like an inadvertent body check. Somehow, she got the impression it was *Eleri*. But now whatever had nudged her was headed up the stairs at high speed.

"GJ!" Noah hollered out, not even noticing that something else was rushing toward him.

GJ had lost her focus. She was looking up the steps, not even trying to pay attention to the fight that she was needed to help clear. "GJ!" he yelled again.

This time, she spun toward him too fast and pulled the trigger.

Her heart stuttered as the shot hit far too close to Donovan. He flinched and jumped backward as quickly as possible, as though his reaction might be fast enough to escape her bullet.

Fuck! she thought as she finally lowered the gun.

In her brain, she counted off how many shots she'd fired. Yes, she was out of bullets.

The eighteen-round magazine wasn't standard issue, but nothing about Nassau was standard. Eleri had handed out the illegal magazines like candy, and now—without thinking, with muscle memory born from hours of practice—GJ quickly slammed in a new one.

She was ready to fire if anything on the landing below her so much as twitched.

No one spoke. The three remaining agents just stared at each other, breathing heavily and bleeding from far too many wounds as they checked the surrounding area for unseen threats. None came.

GJ was about to open her mouth when she heard the sirens.

CHAPTER 82

Donovan stood in the shower, his forehead pressed to the wall as though he might otherwise slide down into an exhausted and confused puddle.

With a deep breath in and fortitude he didn't know he still had, he turned off all the water and twisted awkwardly to examine his most prominent stab wound.

Noah and GJ, dirty and bloody, had entered the back door of the hotel with a wolf-shaped Donovan in tow. They'd walked him right up into the room. Maybe because they looked too much like refugees—or maybe because they looked like they were not to be dicked with—no one questioned them.

The suite boasted two full baths, and GJ had sent Donovan and Noah into the showers first. He'd called out for a first-aid kit, grateful that GJ had jumped up to grab it.

Now he cranked off the water and stood, still dripping, as he pulled a pre-threaded needle from a sterile pack and then twisted around, attempting to stitch the gaping wound on his thigh. *He should have given himself an injection of lidocaine to numb it,* he thought at the first jab of the needle's pain. But he'd believed he was already too numb from his injuries, and it would be a waste of medication. Now he felt every stab of the needle, every soft tug of thread through his skin as he pulled.

But he didn't stop.

He had two layers to stitch. Although the wound hadn't been mortal, it was still deep enough that this first round of stitches were beneath the surface. He used dissolving stitches from the first-aid kit, which was an ER version rather than a standard home kit. The bath tub was a damn awkward place to try to stitch up a deep gash on the side of your thigh. It took too long, and it hurt too much, but it was necessary.

This was the second time he'd used sutures in as many days. He reminded himself to check on GJ's shoulder when he got out. Next, he would have to take care of Noah—unless the other agent decided to hit up a real hospital.

When he snipped the last suture from the black chain that ran the few inches down his thigh, he turned to his lower rib cage. This gash wasn't as bad. His attacker had sliced rather than stabbed him here.

Drying the area quickly, he applied pressure and then laid steri-strips across it, pulling the edges together as he went. He found other cuts and bruises galore, but luckily, nothing else seemed to require full medical attention. They would just take time to heal.

He needed to get dressed. *He couldn't go out in public in a T shirt and shorts any time soon, unless he wanted to frighten people,* he thought, gazing at his reflection. But he knew he might have to. He still didn't know where Eleri was.

With one towel around his waist and another in his hand, rubbing at his head, he finally stepped out of the bathroom. GJ stood in the doorway, shaking her head at him. "She's not here."

"Do we wait? Or do we need to go find her?"

Eleri had gone missing from the Queen's Staircase. In the melee, Donovan had lost track of her. Noah had hardly seen her at all, and GJ was suggesting that an *invisible* Eleri had bumped past her and fled the scene after the assassin died. Donovan didn't know what to think about that.

He only knew she'd been nowhere to be found. She wasn't answering her phone or any other attempts to find her. He was worried she wasn't safe. But GJ shook her head again.

"She doesn't want to be found."

"What? How do you know?"

"Look." She held out a scrap of hotel stationery. The handwriting was definitely Eleri's—neat, prep-school cursive, although a little shaky, as if she had written it in a hurry.

I've gathered my things. I'll get myself back to the States. I need some time alone. E.

This was maybe the hardest impact Donovan had felt all day. Eleri had *fled*. Scanning the message quickly for a second time, he looked for a hidden code, for words or things only he would know the secret meaning of, but he found nothing new. Maybe GJ could find answers.

GJ's voice broke his thoughts. "There's no code. There's no sequence shift. There's no message created by every first word or every third word. It's just a note from Eleri. Her things are packed up and gone, too."

"What?" He should have had more interesting things to say, but he was too stunned to think of them.

"She got here before us, packed everything, and left the note. Apparently, she even said goodbye to Hannah and Jason."

Jesus, Donovan thought, he'd almost forgot about her friend and the research assistant. They were likely huddled together in the other room, having watched Noah walk by, dirty and damaged, as he headed into the shower.

Not sure what else to say or do, Donovan waved his hand back toward the open door behind him. "The shower is all yours."

GJ took him up on the offer.

Closing the door, he pulled on his human clothing again.

Everything felt wrong, from the fit of his shirt to the emptiness of the room. But there were still things that he needed to take care of.

He stitched up Noah's wounds. GJ emerged from the shower, clean and freshly dressed, even before Donovan finished. Noah had needed medical attention for three wounds, and it took a while. If Donovan thought he looked bad, Noah looked worse. Noah had fought with bare skin. Donovan had at least had the protection of thick fur. He hadn't thought about it before, but it clearly made a difference.

Letting Noah's shirt fall to cover the last of the bandages, he couldn't stop wondering where Eleri was and why she hadn't spoken to him. He found himself picking up his phone to text her, even though she had asked that they not bother her.

He got the message half typed and then erased it. He wanted to follow her wishes, but he also needed to talk to her. Undecided, he headed into the main room where Noah and GJ looked up at him. *Now they're expecting him to take over as head of the operation.*

CHAPTER 83

Twenty-four hours later, Donovan sat in yet another hotel room, grateful to be back on US soil.

They had escorted Hannah and Jason back to the *Calypso* and seen them off. Though Donovan volunteered the FBI's dime to fly the others back to Miami, Hannah and Jason had refused. They belonged on the water, they said.

They had asked repeatedly after Neriah, and he'd had to explain that she had died at the Miranda Industries compound. While they seemed shocked to hear that, they were clearly still reeling from the information that she had been working with the other side, and that the data she had given them was likely tainted. He hated telling them things that hurt them, but they needed to know.

"She was likely involved in the death of the researchers Gelman and Patel," he'd had to explain. "There's every possibility that she sabotaged the work she did for you in small ways, too. You'll have to carefully comb through any of the work Neriah did for you in the past and make sure that it stands on its own."

The two looked shell-shocked, devastated at the loss of their friend both in her death and her lies. They had wanted only to get back on their own boat. Their crew of four was now slashed in half. They'd started with a devastating loss and ended with a betrayal. He suspected they needed the familiarity of the small vessel and the sea to help put themselves back together.

Donovan, Noah, and GJ had watched them pull away from the dock with Hannah as captain. Jason had stood at the stern, waving to them as though it were a friendly goodbye and not the end of a hard and painful run.

Now in Miami, Donovan had a hotel room to himself. The threat that had made them band into one room was finally behind them. He hoped.

The doorway to the adjoining room opened and GJ walked in, with Noah right behind her. Noah at least had been able to return to his own home. Donovan and GJ were still operating out of pocket.

"Can we go home tomorrow?" GJ asked.

"I don't think so. We have paperwork to file. Hannah and Jason have been emailing me non-stop. Allison's work and the points they rechecked appear to be spots on the drug trail. The ocean life is filtering the cocaine and heroin and incorporating it into their muscles and shells. That's what Allison noticed."

"That's huge," GJ commented, though her enthusiasm didn't match the words. "We've known where the drugs enter the US ports, but with a clearer oceanic path, we can stop far more of it." She paused and seemed to have a deep moment. "Allison's work wasn't in vain."

"It never was." He thought her death was still pointless, but he didn't say it. People needed meaning, even if he'd long ago given up on trying to find it. He changed topics then, hoping to pull GJ out of her funk. "Westerfield said he intends for us to stay here for three more days to wrap everything up."

GJ rolled her eyes. He knew she was much older, but at that moment, she looked all of fifteen. He wondered how she was handling the number of times she'd pulled the trigger this week, but he hadn't yet worked up the nerve to ask her. Instead, he asked a question that was both easier and harder. "Anything from Eleri?"

GJ shook her head.

He'd held on to the note as proof that waiting to contact her was the right choice.

Behind her, Noah appeared sympathetic to the loss of their senior partner, but not sad. It seemed he'd managed to put all of the last week's episode behind him. Maybe he was just happy being back on his home turf. "I thought I'd come over and pick you guys up for breakfast, and then we'll head into the Bureau office where we can finish up whatever we need to."

Donovan nodded. He wasn't overly enthusiastic, but the work had to be done. As per Westerfield's wishes, Donovan inquired after Noah. It turned out that Eleri had been right.

"Westerfield added you to our team with the intent of recruiting you," he said. It wasn't his smoothest opening line, but it was all he had.

"I don't understand," Noah responded. "I'm FBI, you're FBI. Haven't we *already* been recruited?"

He wasn't wrong, and Donovan fought for a reasonable explanation. "We work for a highly specialized division." He paused, and then went on to explain what was unique about NightShade.

Leaning over the small side table, he used the little notepad to write down the direct number to Westerfield's office, which he held out to Noah. "You should contact him. Let him know if you're interested."

He was stunned when Noah took the note, wadded it into a ball, and casually made a two-point throw into the trash can. "I don't think so."

Both Donovan and GJ were silent. Neither of them had this reaction when they'd been offered this position. Yet, somehow,

Donovan thought maybe Noah had the best response. Maybe he was smart to turn this down. *Now*, while he still could.

"That was the craziest thing I've ever seen," he said to their astonished faces, as if he had to explain his response. He didn't. He'd just thrown them for a loop. "Nothing against what you two do. You're very good at it. But I've never had to employ any of my skills before—not like *that*. It's one thing to make it easier to arrest a perp in a dangerous situation. But half of *that*—" he waved his hand behind him, as though indicating all of what had passed on the open ocean and in Nassau. "*That* was because of whatever *special skills*—" he offered up air quotes, "—that this team brings to the table. I think I'm going to stay in Miami at my current position."

Donovan still didn't respond, though he had to actively hold his tongue to not try to talk Noah into it. Donovan felt a strange need to try to actively recruit the younger agent. It wasn't that he felt any allegiance to Westerfield, but he knew Noah would be an excellent addition to the team.

Each time Donovan failed at keeping his mouth shut and offered another reason for the Miami agent to join them, Noah politely refused.

Three days later, he and GJ hopped on separate planes, heading for their separate homes.

CHAPTER 84

Donovan climbed into the cab he'd hailed at the airport. Black and sleek and expensive, it was the only one willing to drive the distance to his home. Donovan had promised a healthy tip.

Now he laid his head back against the headrest, glad he didn't have to drive, and happier still that this case was over. He was ready to shut out the world for a while.

He didn't notice the buzzing of his phone until it quit and immediately started up again. Dreading who it might be, he tugged it from his pocket and flipped it over. It was that second buzz, the caller's unwillingness to let the phone send them to voicemail, that let Donovan know he would see Agent Westerfield's face on the screen. He did. And it took still another moment for him to shake out of his haze and answer the call.

Donovan tried to put his best professional voice forward. "Heath," he offered by way of greeting, not really achieving his goal.

"How did the recruitment effort work?"

Frankly, Donovan was surprised that his boss hadn't asked

433

before now. When he hadn't heard by the time he boarded the plane in Miami, he assumed that either Westerfield didn't care, or else he'd already assessed Agent Kimball's answer for himself.

Donovan had forgotten all about it, and he was not looking forward to dredging it up now. "He said no."

"What?"

Well crap. Westerfield hadn't known about Noah's answer already, and Donovan was in no mood to deal with it. He'd thought he was *done*. "He said this case brought him face-to-face with things he hadn't seen before, and he preferred not to delve into that world again."

That wasn't what Noah had said, but Donovan was not conveying the "Oh hell no, not in seven lifetimes" attitude that Noah's actual answer had politely invoked.

"Never mind that. We have something more concerning."

And there went any break Donovan had hoped to take advantage of. He wanted to see Lucy. He wanted to run in his woods. He wanted to take a week and watch bad TV and eat medium rare steaks each night. But as he pulled his focus back to the phone conversation, Westerfield's voice sharpened it even more. "Agent Christina Pines has gone dark."

"I know," Donovan replied, almost irritated at Westerfield's interruption over something he already knew. "Walter—Lucy Fisher—has been tailing her for a while."

"No." The sound was an abrupt cut-off, and the edge in it straightened Donovan's spine. "You're right that Fisher has been following her. But yesterday, she reported that she'd completely lost the trail. And today. . . well, I've lost Fisher, too."

CHAPTER 85

E leri ignored the phone.

She had successfully done the same for the past five days straight. She knew it was her mother, and no caller ID was necessary. She could *feel* it.

She had messaged the woman saying she was okay. But that hadn't stopped her mother from ringing her phone. Repeatedly.

Eleri had reached out to Donovan and GJ and Avery, saying the same thing, asking that they give her space. She'd received three short messages in return.

Each said basically the same thing: They were worried, but they were respecting her space. Her mother offered no such response and had called several times a day, despite the fact that Eleri refused to answer—or perhaps because of it.

Eleri had been sitting on the large, fluffy couch, looking out the floor-to-ceiling glass windows at the fields behind Bell Point Farm. She thought of the last time she was here, of how she'd sent Donovan out to run through the tall grass and the orchards. She thought of her mother back at Patton Hall—their grand home in Kentucky. Her thoughts wandered to the always freshly painted black and white horse barn. She wanted to ride the horses.

There were horses here, too, she reminded herself. If she could just get off her butt. If she could just make herself do *something*, she would go for a ride.

Maybe tomorrow.

This time, after the phone had stopped ringing—and the house had sat in deadly silence for she didn't know how long—Eleri switched the phone off. *No more pesky calls.*

She had just settled back into the couch and the deep, contemplative silence that came with it, when something pushed into her brain.

A house sat pleasantly at the end of a gravel drive. She recognized it—it was Donovan's front door. Further back, down the street, she saw a car coming up the winding country road.

It wasn't his car, but he was in it. Shiny and black, it looked like a high-end taxi. She could sense the driver in the front and Donovan's irritation radiating from the back seat.

Donovan was coming home.

But he was coming home to a surprise.

Sitting on his porch was a man who looked almost exactly like Donovan.

Eleri reached for her phone to warn him. But even as she touched it, she realized she was too late.

The car had already pulled into the driveway.

ABOUT THE AUTHOR

AJ holds an MS in Human Forensic Identification as well as another in Neuroscience/Human Physiology. AJ's works have garnered Audie nominations, options for tv and film, as well as over twenty Best Suspense/Best Fiction of the Year awards.

A.J.'s world is strange place where patterns jump out and catch the eye, little is missed, and most of it can be recalled with a deep breath. In this world, the smell of Florida takes three weeks to fully leave the senses and the air in Dallas is so thick that the planes "sink" to the runways rather than actually landing.

For A.J., reality is always a little bit off from the norm and something usually lurks right under the surface. As a storyteller, A.J. loves irony, the unexpected, and a puzzle where all the pieces fit and make sense. Originally a scientist and a teacher, the writer says research is always a key player in the stories. AJ's motto is "It could happen. It wouldn't. But it could."

A.J. has lived in Florida and Los Angeles among a handful of other places. Recent whims have brought the dark writer to Tennessee, where home is a deceptively normal-looking neighborhood just outside Nashville.

For more information:
www.ReadAJS.com
AJ@ReadAJS.com

Made in the USA
Las Vegas, NV
13 September 2022

55246691R00256